AND THEN SHE FELL

ALICIA ELLIOTT

ALLEN&UNWIN

First published in the United States in 2023 by Dutton, an imprint of Penguin Random House LLC.

Published in hardback and trade paperback in Great Britain in 2023 by Allen & Unwin, an imprint of Atlantic Books Ltd.

Copyright © Alicia Elliott, 2023

10 9 8 7 6 5 4 3 2 1

A CIP catalogue record for this book is available from the British Library.

Hardback ISBN: 978 1 83895 941 8
E-book ISBN: 978 1 83895 942 5

Printed in Great Britain

Interior art: Night sky © Khaneeros T./Shutterstock.com;
Feather © veronchick_84/Shutterstock.com

BOOK DESIGN BY KRISTIN DEL ROSARIO

Allen & Unwin
An imprint of Atlantic Books Ltd
Ormond House
26–27 Boswell Street
London
WC1N 3JZ

www.atlantic-books.co.uk

AND THEN

SHE FELL

*

Publicity enquiries:
Kirsty Doole – kirstydoole@atlantic-books.co.uk

Sales enquiries:
Natasha Drewett – natashadrewett@atlantic-books.co.uk

Alicia Elliott is a Mohawk writer and editor living in Brantford, Ontario. Her short fiction was selected for *Best American Short Stories 2018* and she won the 2018 RBC Taylor Emerging Writer Award. Her first book, *A Mind Spread Out On The Ground*, is a Canadian bestseller.

For Missy and Melita,

and

For all those
who have seen and heard what others can't.

As evidence of the Western world's fascina
the Iroquois, it is widely held that anthropol
academic field of study began with Lewis He
gan's *League of the Ho-De'-No-Sau-Nee, or*
published in 1851. While an overwhelming
of scholarship has been devoted to the H
saunee since that time . . . Haudenosaunee
have had very little opportunity to analyze
history, culture, and traditions.

—RICK MC

WE SHARE OUT M

TWO CENTURIES OF WRITING AND RES

AT SIX NATIONS OF THE GRAN

I'll be sitting in your mirror.
Now is the place where the crossroads meet.
Will you look into the future?

—KATE BUSH, "JIG O

Around the Riverbend, Mostly

A lice never seemed to hear the microwave beeping—not even when she was three feet away from it, feet propped on the kitchen table as she painted her toenails neon green. It didn't matter how loud or how insistent her ma was when she called her to dinner, either. She'd saunter into the kitchen whenever she felt like it, even if it meant her food was cold and congealed on her plate. At first, her aunt Rachel thought Alice's hearing was to blame; she did sit alarmingly close to the speakers at pow-wows, after all, and her music pounded through her headphones so loud even the people she passed could hear each note. But a free hearing test confirmed her problem was not and had never been her ears. She could hear the microwave perfectly. She could hear everything perfectly.

Quite simply, Alice deliberately chose to ignore what she didn't want to hear. Either the most teenage of all ailments, or the most human: for who *wants* to hear an incessant hammer banging down on one's carefully constructed version of "real life"? Who wants to admit there was a moment when they saw disaster coming but chose to do nothing, only for the impending wave to crest and crash, forcing their carefully constructed version of "real life" to give way and collapse entirely?

This is probably why, despite the trail of girls Mason Jamieson left behind him like bread crumbs in the forest of masculinity—girls with mascara rippling down their teenage cheeks, with heartbreak and hatred now trapped in their very marrow—Alice still desperately wanted to follow that trail straight to him. What choice did she have? She was months away from becoming a faceless freshman, and he was once the coolest boy at J. C. Hill Elementary. There was something very chic about the idea of holding hands through the halls and getting pulled against his chest while he smoked, even if she knew from other girls that he repeated the most boring stories and his cigarette ash got caught in their hair. It might not be fulfilling, but it'd be validating, the way male attention could be. That was good enough. Probably.

Before this year Alice had been mostly ignored. She'd watched each of her friends fall victim to the onslaught of puberty: entering grade six with sweatshirts and pudgy cheeks and emerging from the other side with breasts and blackheads and skintight leggings that shouted every dimple to the world. Alice's chest remained stubbornly flat, her hips defiantly narrow. When she walked down the street in a pair of shorts it was unremarkable. When her friends walked down the street in shorts it was an event. There were hoots and hollers from windows or porches, beeps from rusted-out rez cars, deep frowns from disapproving elders. There was something almost insidious about puberty—the way it slammed shut the door to childhood, never to be reopened, and shoved you face-first into this strange, dangerous place called womanhood.

But on the eve of her thirteenth birthday, puberty came for Alice, too. It molded her chest into tits, her butt into an ass, carved cheekbones out of her face. She tried to stifle her body with oversized shirts and poor posture, but it was no use. Those rebellious curves were still there, pushing out from the fabric, demanding their due. Both her ma and Aunt Rachel had tried to explain to Alice how her period connected her to our mother, the earth; our grandmother, the moon; how she was one in a line of women who could be traced all the way back to Sky Woman, the mother of our nations. They were trying to be nice, Alice knew, but it was too late. She saw the way men looked at her now. Women, too. As if she were land to claim, a rival to kill. She'd already resigned herself to the idea that her body was no longer hers: just flesh and bone on extended loan, bound to be collected by some man sooner or later. After that she would be his to own, his to decide what to do with, to sit on some pedestal or throw in some corner to cry.

That summer, Alice got a job selling 50/50 tickets at the speedway with her cousin Melita. She didn't need a résumé. The boss, Helen, looked her up and down and told her she started Friday.

"Just dress sexy," Helen said. Alice immediately summoned up the most beautiful woman she could think of: Jennifer-Lopez-as-Selena, in sequined jumpsuits and glitter bustiers, smiling with bright red lips.

"Um, I don't think I have anything—"

"Trust me, we'll make it work."

And they did. Apparently, anything could be made sexy when you were a thirteen-year-old girl. Helen would roll up Alice's shorts if they were too long, or strategically tie up her shirts to show off her flat stomach. She even kept an emergency stash of lip gloss at the concession stand so Alice could do touch-ups whenever dirt careened from the racetrack onto her sticky lips, temporarily ruining the underage bombshell fantasy with ugly, inconvenient reality. It smelled like cotton candy.

The customers, mostly older white men, would stare at her long tan limbs and smile at her like they knew something she didn't. It bothered Alice, but the other 50/50 girls seemed resigned to it. Even adapted to it. They knew how to divide into two selves: the one that smiled sweetly to the men's faces and laughed at their bad jokes, and the one that grimaced as soon as their backs were turned, collecting the interactions like baseball cards to trade with the other girls at the food stand. It became a game for them: the girls would share their encounters with these desperate old men, and at the end of the night whoever had the grossest story—the one that made the other girls groan and squirm with unease—was the girl who won.

Most of the time the stories were pretty tame. A wink here, a sudden unsolicited hand grab there. But one time a regular named Chuck followed Alice into the porta potty, rushing in before she could lock it, his body pushing hard against her backside. He was so close she could smell the damp of his deodorant, which barely covered the harsh stink of his old, sweating man body. She turned fast and looked up at him. His eyes were entirely black. He looked like he was possessed. Alice was too shocked to scream, to move. There was a long silence that stretched on, during which Alice could feel the walls of the porta potty vibrating with the race cars on the track. She closed her eyes, hoping that whatever came next would be quick.

Chuck laughed, the sharp honk of it forcing her watering eyes back open. "The look on your face!" he howled as he turned around and stumbled back to the stands.

Alice stayed in the porta potty until her breathing was normal again. She decided to hold her pee until she got home.

"What happened to you?" Melita asked her when she walked up, jittery. Alice told her.

"Ever gross! Oh my god, you gotta tell the girls. You'll totally win tonight."

"Should I tell Helen?"

"No point. As long as they're spending money, she don't care. Anyway, that's the job, innit? Look cute so dirty old men buy tickets from us?"

Melita was right. That was the job. But after the races, after the eyes and the hands and "sweeties" and "dolls," after Chuck and the porta potty, as she stared at the limp bills in her hand, she understood how little value they had. What's more, she sensed that her own value was tied up in the whole transaction, only instead of watching it grow week by week like the small stash of bills she hid from her ma in her sock drawer, she felt it slowly diminishing, as if it were being pressed hard against a sieve.

Still, money was money, and Creator knows her mom didn't have much to spare since her dad died in a car accident a couple years before. So Alice showed up promptly at seven every Friday night, shorts hiked up, lips smeared shiny and pink.

You'll never guess who's hanging around the food stand," Melita said one night.

Alice was under the bleachers, tearing apart the strips of 50/50 tickets she and Melita had sold. The repetitive motion calmed her, so she offered to do it for her cousin, who was, it must be said, pretty lazy, at least when it came to work. Gossiping, on the other hand, Melita took very seriously. Alice stopped ripping tickets and looked at her cousin. Melita's ears turned a red that rivaled her already blushed cheeks, the way they did when she knew something you didn't.

"I don't know. Nelly Furtado?"

"Don't be stupid, Alice. What would a queen like that be doing in a place like this?"

"Watching the races?"

Melita ignored that and smiled. "Mason Jamieson," she said, savoring the words as they rolled off her tongue, weighing the effect of every syllable.

Alice immediately felt light-headed. "No way. He'd never waste a Friday night here."

"Go look for yourself."

She peeked out from the bleachers and there he was, leaning against the food stand, smoking. Her breathing stopped as she croaked out two words: "Holy. Shit."

Alice stared. She obviously remembered him—who wouldn't?— puffing his chest on playgrounds and in parking lots, demanding and commanding eyes with every step of his nearly six-foot-tall frame. It'd been two years since he'd left J. C. Hill for Pauline Johnson Collegiate Vocational School. He was definitely taller now. His movements were smooth and confident, almost feline, as he lifted his cigarette to his lips. When she got older, she would realize how much of this was performance, how much was lifted from James Dean and early Marlon Brando movies, which, unbeknownst to all but his mother and sister, Mason studied fastidiously, even practicing the movements in front of the mirror, the way Alice herself practiced smiling in the perfect way to hide her snaggletooth. The self-consciousness that came with puberty pushed them both into odd shapes and awkward poses, but at thirteen, Alice didn't notice the effort it took other people to look effortless, just her own, and so she only hated herself for it. Alice also had no way of knowing at the time that Mason's stock had fallen considerably since he'd made the leap to high school, as happened with all Native kids once they stepped off the rez and into the mostly white high schools they were forced to attend in neighboring cities. Had she known all of this, it's hard to say whether she would have proceeded in quite the way she did.

"He just broke up with Nancy, so I bet he's looking for a new snag," Melita said, needling.

"I don't know . . . ," she started.

"Well, I do. What are the odds your crush would end up *here* right after a breakup? It's fate! You gotta go over there and ask him for a smoke. Now." She grabbed Alice's arm and dragged her toward the food stand. Alice tried to pry her fingers off, but it was no use. The Creator himself couldn't stop Melita once her mind was made up.

"But I don't smoke," Alice whispered. "Or snag."

Melita cackled. "You do now, honey." She pushed Alice toward Mason, who was, thankfully, staring down at his black Razr phone. Alice managed to catch herself on a big blue metal garbage can before running into him, making a terrific clang in the process. Mason looked up, saw Alice, then took another drag of his cigarette.

"Hey," he said.

"Hey," Alice said, her throat raspy and dry. "Got a smoke?"

"I'm down to my last one."

"Oh."

"But we Hauds are trading people, innit?"

Alice looked down at her shoes, her heart racing. "What do you want for it?"

"That depends. You busy tomorrow night?"

Everything was happening so fast. Alice couldn't think. Was she busy? Probably not. She was never busy. But she couldn't tell Mason that.

"I could make time." That sounded pretty cool. Like something the sort of girl Mason wanted to hang out with would say.

"Then this is yours." He pulled out a pack of Sago Menthols and handed her his last cigarette. His hands were so big they looked like they could crush her head between them. *Stop thinking and just be cool*, Alice told herself as she placed it between her lips and pursed them expectantly. Mason produced a lighter and flicked the head ablaze. Luckily, Alice remembered Melita once told her the secret to faking smoking: don't inhale.

"Put your number in here." Mason handed over his cell phone. He was saving her number under the name "hot racetrack girl." She debated typing her actual name in, but decided against it at the last minute. She didn't want to look pushy.

"See you tomorrow," he said as he took his phone and backed away, smiling at her. She watched him spin around and continue toward the bleachers. *God*, she thought. *Even the way he walks is sexy.*

Melita was beside her almost immediately.

"So? What happened?"

"We're gonna hang out tomorrow night."

"Are you KIDDING ME? You're hanging out with Mason Jamieson tomorrow night? The girls are never gonna believe this."

At that exact moment Alice remembered she'd agreed to babysit for her aunt Rachel.

"Fuck. I forgot. I'm babysitting Dana tomorrow."

"I swear to fucking god, Al, if you throw away the chance to lose your virginity to Mason Jamieson for a babysitting gig I will kill you myself."

"Do you really think we'll have sex?"

"Of course! Guys like Mason basically need sex to live."

Her friends had all lost their virginity by the time they graduated eighth grade—an event they felt compelled to share because tradition dictated they should, but which they described with little more than a shrug. It seemed to Alice that a woman's virginity was a man's trophy: they placed it on a shelf for all the other men to see, high-fiving one another as they celebrated how totally secure and super masculine they were. Women, on the other hand, threw their hymens to men like an old chicken bone to shut them up. There was nothing inherently valuable about virginity, or nothing she or her friends knew how to name. Having sex was just checking off another box, and at this point, Alice just wanted it over with. But the idea of losing her virginity at Aunt Rachel's house kind of weirded her out. What was she supposed to do with Dana? Send her outside?

"Can you babysit for me?"

"No way! I've got a date with Corey. Anyway, isn't Dana, like, five? Just put her to bed before he gets there."

"Will that work?"

Melita shrugged.

Aunt Rachel's house was small and cluttered and looked like a pow-wow vendor threw up on the walls. There were at least thirty dream catchers, twenty medicine wheels, and a dozen posters that read NATIVE PRIDE in a dozen different fonts. Seed beads of every color sat in plastic cups like hidden treasure around the house. Alice never knew when she'd step backward and knock a hundred tiny beads deep into the fibers of the carpet. It stressed her out.

But it was the one place where she felt like time hadn't passed, might never pass. Her aunty and her little cousin's love for her was eternal, unchanging. Her name even sounded different when they said it—precious, musical, like that one word was its own small ceremony. It sounded like that when Aunt Rachel was with Dana's dad, even though her arms were bruised and her lips were swollen; it sounded like that when Aunt Rachel was pregnant and lived at

Ganǫhkwásra, where she had to sign Alice and her ma in and out during visits, her eyes constantly trained on the door, as though Dana's dad would barrel through at any moment; it sounded like that now, even though Alice's period had started and wiry black hairs were sprouting everywhere faster than she could shave them. She needed that love without expectation. She needed it bad. Her ma had always referred to them as a "team"—which meant Alice was making dinner for herself by age nine, doing her and her ma's laundry by age ten, and babysitting for extra cash by age eleven. And after her dad died, her mother expected her to pull *more* than her own weight. It was like she wasn't allowed to be a kid at all anymore. Alice's free time was always being judged, and so Alice herself was being judged. Strangely, she could feel the strain of her mother's expectations even more strongly when she wasn't around. But Aunt Rachel never judged her, never would.

That night, Alice and Dana were watching *Pocahontas* for what felt like the fiftieth time that month. Alice used to watch it obsessively when she was a child, too, wide-eyed with disbelief that someone who looked even remotely like her was the star of a Disney film. She made her mom buy her a Pocahontas costume for Halloween when she was six, only instead of a Native girl on the package modeling the cheap imitation buckskin, there was a little blond white girl. Her *Pocahontas* obsession waned significantly after that.

Alice was busy trying to craft the perfect text to respond to Mason's rather lackluster "k" after she sent him her aunt's address. She settled on "c u soon," then immediately reported back to each of her friends to get their reactions. She barely noticed when Dana sat up and cocked her head to the side, her parroting of every word silenced as she stared in confusion at the screen.

"That's wrong," she said.

"What?" Alice asked, distracted.

"Pocahontas sang the wrong thing."

"You probably just heard it wrong."

"No," Dana said, her lower lip protruding. "She said it wrong. She's supposed to sing, 'Should I marry Kocoum?' This time it was something . . . weird."

Alice's eyes were glued to her phone screen. There were happy texts congratulating her; there were snide texts pointing out Alice was last at everything, from getting boobs to losing her virginity; there were conciliatory texts warning her it wouldn't hurt that bad, that even if it did, it probably wouldn't last long anyway. There were some very exaggerated—and somehow very sexual—emoticons.

"Alice. Alice. ALICE! You're not even listening."

"Yes, I am." She looked up to find her cousin standing in front of her, her tiny face scrunched in indignation. "Pocahontas sang the song wrong. What's the big deal? She probably just forgot." Alice liked making outrageous comments like that to her baby cousin. Even at her young age, Dana had surprisingly good bullshit radar, which made it even more funny when seemingly adult comments came out in her childish voice.

"Oh, for crying out loud. Now you're being ridiculous," Dana said in a perfect imitation of her mother, rolling her eyes and turning back to the screen. Alice stifled her laughter. She didn't realize Dana knew how to roll her eyes. She made a mental note to tell her aunt about this development later.

Even with that little outburst, it didn't take long until Dana was snoring, arching her small body across Alice's lap, her belly swollen with sugar and soda. It was eight p.m. and Mason was due to show up in an hour. Open bags of Cheetos and plates still thick with ketchup lined the floor like offerings to some prediabetic god. Alice didn't eat any of it, she was too worried. What if she had bad breath when Mason kissed her? He'd tell all his friends, who'd tell all their friends, and it'd mark her as gross and undatable. She couldn't risk it. She popped gum into her mouth instead and chewed with purpose.

She carried Dana to bed, cocooned her in her faded Mickey Mouse comforter, then gazed down at her, brushing a stray black hair from her face. She looked so serene, like she knew she was completely safe. Alice wondered when she last looked like that herself, if she'd ever look like that again.

She kissed her cousin on the forehead. "Don't grow up," she whispered as she pulled the door closed.

In the living room, Alice gingerly picked up bags of chips and chewed cookies, half worried she'd contract their calories like a virus and become bloated and ugly. Her stomach groaned with each whiff of salty grease or baked sweets. It felt empty, wrung out, a hunger past pain. She chewed her gum, checked her phone.

"Put your phone down. We need to talk."

Alice spun around, terrified.

No one was there. But from the sound of the voice, the speaker was close.

"Hello?" she called.

"You're about to make a big mistake."

The words were harsh, accusing; the voice familiar but strange. There was water on the TV screen, making the entire room glow blue. It was the part of the movie where John Smith first saw Pocahontas: a sexless silhouette in the fog, a target for his gun, another body to brag about to his shipmates once his trigger finger squeezed.

Slowly, Alice backed up toward the kitchen. She needed to get her hands on one of her aunt's knives. They were all so dull they could barely peel a potato, but at least they looked menacing.

"Is someone there?" Alice asked, her heart beating fast.

"Of course someone's here. I talked to you, didn't I?"

At that, Alice ran to the knife drawer, yanked it open, pulled out the biggest one, then nervously walked back in the direction of the voice in the living room.

"I—I've got a knife, but if you leave right now, I won't use it." She wasn't sure she'd be able to use it. She was a kid, not a killer. But if it came down to this weird person or her and Dana, she knew who she'd pick. Theoretically.

Just then, Pocahontas laughed and leaped toward her, stopping just short of the thirty-two-inch TV screen that held her in a hand-drawn prison. "And how, exactly, are you gonna use that big old thing on me?"

"What the fuuuuuuck!" Alice yelled as she ran back to the kitchen and dove under the table. Her breathing got short and fast, almost as quick as her heartbeat. "Whatthefuckwhatthefuckwhat-thefuck. This isn't real. This can't be real."

"Well, it is. Deal with it," Pocahontas called back.

Alice screamed, dropped the knife, and started rubbing furiously at the tears pooling in her eyes. She rubbed until they hurt. If she could feel pain, that meant this wasn't a dream. Right?

"Is he cute?" Pocahontas called, softer now, across the distance.

"What?" Alice asked as she poked her head out from the table, too startled by the question and the sudden change in tone to realize she was taking the bait. "Who?"

"The boy you're cleaning up for."

Shit. Mason. What if he got here and this . . . whatever this was . . . was still happening? Alice looked out at the microwave clock. 8:32 p.m. Twenty-eight minutes before Mason got here. Twenty-eight minutes for her to deal with whatever was happening and get her shit together. She took a deep breath and stood up on shaky legs, then approached the TV.

"He's okay, yeah."

Pocahontas watched her approach curiously, something nearing a grin playing at the corner of her lips. Her voice like poisoned honey.

"Oh, come on. He must be better than 'okay.' I saw this place a few minutes ago. Total disaster. You don't put in this kind of effort for a guy who's just 'okay.'"

"I mean, I wouldn't betray everyone I've ever loved for him, but I'd really strongly consider it." Alice was trying to play it cool, using her sarcasm like a mallet to flatten all other emotions. She found that once she accepted that the situation was happening, it became much less scary, almost normal, even. It didn't cross her mind that what she *should* be scared of was how quickly she adjusted to something so strange and terrifying. It wouldn't for some time.

"He's not named John, is he? I've known two Johns. Both of them ruined my life." Pocahontas delivered the words casually, dispassionately, as if she weren't talking about herself at all but some hypothetical self in some hypothetical universe.

"Oh, please. I've seen this movie a million times. John Smith doesn't ruin your life. You go your separate ways at the end, but he would have stayed if you asked him to. He loves you."

Pocahontas chuckled. "The only thing John Smith loves is killing savages. Didn't you watch the opening scene? He sings a whole song about it."

"Well, yeah, but that was before. He doesn't kill *you*."

Pocahontas smiled bitterly. "There's more than one way to kill a person."

"What's that supposed to mean?"

Pocahontas opened her mouth, then closed it quick. As Alice

watched, waiting for an explanation, she saw Pocahontas's face twist and grow into an otherworldly mask, her eyes crooked and sliding down her cheek like egg yolks. She squeezed her own eyes shut, shaking.

"Alice?"

How does she know my name? Alice wondered. She felt sick. All of this was wrong. Some sort of cruel game, maybe. Yes, her instincts told her, a game. And in this game she couldn't let Pocahontas know the effect she was having on her.

"Who the hell are you? I know you're not really Pocahontas," Alice said defiantly, popping her eyes back open. She tried to make her face blank.

The princess's laugh rang out in Dolby Digital surround sound—pitch-perfect, slightly manic. But then, as it went on one beat, two beats, three beats too long, it shifted. The sound became louder, shriller, and more supernatural, less a laugh and more a punishment.

"Shhhhhhhh!" begged Alice, worried the noise would wake Dana.

"That's true," she quietly replied in a calm though amused tone. "I'm definitely not Pocahontas." She straightened her spine, then lengthened her neck. "Matoaka. That was what everyone in my village called me. This was back before John Smith and his stupid little stories. Don't bother trying to pronounce it, by the way. Your clumsy English tongue will ruin the rhythm."

There *was* a certain music to the princess's real name, something that reminded Alice of oceans she'd never seen, waters she'd never swum. It was a peculiar feeling, one she instinctively knew no English word could replicate. But all things considered, she didn't want to play nice. She preferred to make the princess wince.

"Pocahontas is better."

"You *would* think that name's better." The princess rolled her eyes. "I remember you. Back from when you were that girl's age," she gestured in the general direction of Dana's room. "You watched this perverted version of my story all the time. Just loved it. Knew the words to all the songs. Even 'Savages.' I'll never understand why Native kids sing along to that one."

"I didn't know what the song meant back then," Alice said defensively. "I was a little kid."

"And I was a little kid when I met John Smith. All of ten years old. Did you know that?"

"No," Alice replied, startled. "Does that mean he's, like, a pedophile?"

"I don't know about *that*. He's a liar. I was never in love with him. I just played with the kids at his camp. But once I got famous in England he made up this dramatic story about me falling for him and saving his life. Really tired tragic romance stuff. Anyway, enough people believed it and now I'm stuck here"—she threw her arms wide—"painting with all the colors of the wind."

Alice paused, considering.

"You said two Johns ruined your life. Who's the second one?"

"John Rolfe. My second husband. I met him after the English kidnapped me."

"Wait, they kidnapped you?"

"Sure did. It was awful. When John Rolfe came along proclaiming his love, it was the best protection I could get at the time, so when he proposed I said yes. Then I got baptized and had to change my name to Rebecca. Rebecca Rolfe." She made a face. "Can you believe that alliteration? I prefer Pocahontas to that monstrosity. After that, my husband paraded me around England like a circus attraction for a few years. I gave birth to his brat and died of pneumonia in some ugly English town at twenty-one. The producers left all that out of the sequel, for obvious reasons."

Alice felt overwhelmed by the many contradictions to the story she thought she knew. How could so many people see such injustice and consciously rewrite it as triumph and romance? But she had to remember: Pocahontas was playing a game. Alice couldn't let any creeping empathy slide in. She had to cut herself off emotionally from this person and her claimed tragedies, no matter how horrific. So she scoffed at the screen, the terrifying way teenagers can when they want to show how little they care about anything outside themselves. "Okay, your life sucked. Am I supposed to feel bad for you now?"

Pocahontas shrugged. "I can't tell you how to feel. Enough about me. I want to know more about this guy coming over. He's totally going to ruin your life, you know."

"He won't ruin—"

"Oh, believe me, he will. He can't help it. He's your John."

"Mason isn't white, so he can't be my John."

"You think white guys are the only ones capable of ruining a Native girl's life?"

Alice felt her stomach contract in disappointment and embarrassment, but also in recognition. She was absolutely right. Mason's race didn't really matter in the long run. He could still be her John. The one who took her story and changed it to best fit his narrative, oblivious to any impacts it might have on her. In fact, judging by the state of his many ex-girlfriends and ex-snags, he'd already been the John in many of their young lives. Why would it be any different for her? She couldn't say that, though. She couldn't even really allow herself to think it. Not after all the expectations she'd set up. This boy coming over was the weak peg Alice had hung all her self-confidence on. Even the smallest jostle would send it tumbling to the floor, and where would she be then? The same stupid virgin wishing for a boyfriend she'd been since forever.

"You don't know what you're talking about."

"Why else do you think I'm here? I have a message for you. About him."

Alice couldn't believe the difference in Pocahontas's tone. How exasperated she sounded. How jaded. As if *she* was the one exhausted by this game. And even though Alice, in true Alice form, didn't want to hear what she didn't want to hear, there was also a part of her aching to know what it was that made Pocahontas come to her, a random girl on Six Nations. If that was in fact what was happening; Alice couldn't really be sure. Whatever it was that Pocahontas wanted to say, though, it had its hooks in her.

"Who's the message from?"

"Sorry, can't say. It's against the rules."

"What rules?"

"Can't say. That's against the rules, too."

"Are you serious?" Alice asked. "How am I supposed to . . ." But even as the words left her mouth, she knew there was no point in asking any further. She wouldn't get the clarity she wanted. Each answer was like opening a closed door, only to find ten closed doors behind that one, and ten more closed doors behind the next, questions endlessly becoming more questions, a maze forever expanding. Alice simply didn't have it in her to puzzle any of this out.

Pocahontas smiled with pity, then carefully sat on top of some rocks, ever regal. Her face had no wrinkles, but she looked old and anguished all the same. Her eyes clenched shut. The confidence, the sarcasm, the bravado—it dawned on Alice that it was all an act. Maybe the spirit of a little Powhatan girl really was trapped in this movie, inside a story that was never hers, stuck replaying the lies other people told about her over and over. And maybe she really was trying to connect with Alice, another Native girl who felt in many ways trapped in the stories people told about her. In this way, Pocahontas brought to mind every woman Alice had ever known: her aunt with her seed beads and bruises, her mother with her bloodshot eyes and constant work, her friends with their push-up bras and pushy boyfriends. Herself. Women like porcelain dolls with hairline cracks trying to smile and smile as hammers came down all around. When Alice thought about it, even the Haudenosaunee Creation Story wasn't free from this grief; in some versions Sky Woman only fell to earth because her angry husband had pushed her. Was it always like that for women? Would the story, the cycle, ever stop repeating? Mason didn't even know her name, and here she was, ready to give him anything he wanted. What did she really know about him, anyway?

"What's the message?" Alice asked, still cautious.

"Stay away from Mason. He *is* your John. One of them. You're meant for other things—better things, even—but if you don't start being more careful with men now . . . things will get very, *very* bad for you."

Alice sank into the cushions of the old couch and let her head fall back. As she stared at the ceiling, she started to think about what this choice would cost her. How Mason would trash-talk her at school if she flaked out on him. How he'd tell everyone what happened and she'd be called something stupid that would sting nevertheless. Something like a cold pussy or a prude or a pathetic little virgin. She'd have to figure out some excuse to make to her friends, who would definitely roast her for letting the same guy she talked to them about incessantly for years get away. It was minutes before Mason was supposed to arrive, and the idea of turning him down was in many ways inconceivable. It already felt like a mistake, and she hadn't even made it yet.

"Why should I believe you? You could be making all this up," Alice said as she rolled her head forward. "What am I even saying? *You* are made up. You're a fucking cartoon."

"That's not all I am."

Pocahontas's face warped and grew again. It took up the whole screen, the strands of her black hair whipping around, her brown face melting like wax, a sickening *dripdripdrip* sound coming from the speakers. The black strands kept squirming, and Alice realized they weren't hair at all but great black snakes. Each one's eyes glowed yellow as their heads turned to the screen, to Alice, and began stabbing their noses against the glass—*BANG! BANG! BANG!*—until the screen finally cracked, and then the snake heads were out in her world, were *real*, their tongues darting in and out from between their fangs. Alice cried out, frozen, as words were whispered into the conch of her ear: *Turn it off.* Yes. She would turn it off. She had to. Her eyes raced around the living room; she saw the remote resting on top of the side table, and she grabbed it.

"Wait—"

She clicked it off just as Dana screamed from her bed.

Alice didn't even think. She ran to her cousin's room, worried the black snakes had somehow burst through her window and started attacking her. As soon as she turned the corner, though, she saw the room was the same as she had left it. There was little Dana, holding the stuffed parrot she'd named Meeko. She had her blankets pulled up to her eyes and she was crying, but there was nothing hurting her.

"Why were you yelling?" Dana's little lower lip trembled.

Alice moved into the room and threw her arms around her fast.

"I'm so sorry, Danabear. I was watching a scary movie, and the bad guy jumped out from the dark. It right spooked me," Alice lied, hoping her laughter didn't sound too fake. "I almost fell off the couch."

"I told you not to watch those," Dana said, her indignation slowly taking over from her fear. "They're bad."

"I know. You're right. Give me a sec and I'll go turn that silly movie off and come cuddle with you."

Alice stepped out of the bedroom, then leaned against the wall. She was sweating heavily, and her heart was thrashing inside her, but Dana was fine. They were both fine. Whatever was happening to her had seemingly stopped. She took one long, steadying breath, then cautiously walked back to the living room.

Things looked normal. No snakes. No cracked TV screen. Alice picked up the remote control, tension threaded through her muscles, and turned the TV back on.

The DVD menu was on its familiar loop.

It was like the whole thing never happened. *Maybe it didn't*, she thought. *Maybe I'm crazy.* A rush of shame and guilt overcame her. Alice knew people had said her grandma, who died when she was still a toddler, was crazy. Not often. Most people seemed to not want to talk about her grandma at all, not even Ma or Aunt Rachel.

But it felt so real.

She stared at her phone: 8:55 p.m. Five minutes until Mason was supposed to get there.

Alice had a choice to make, and the quivering anxiety she felt told her she had already made it. She took a deep breath, then focused back on her phone. She could practically hear Melita screaming at her as she typed the text out: "sorry change of plans. can't meet up after all. babysitting."

This time Mason replied quickly.

"fuckin cock teaze"

Then: "didn't want u anyway u fat ugly bitch"

Then a slew of more messages Alice couldn't bear to even open.

Underneath the crushing certainty that her worst fears about a future with Mason were now realized, leaving her single and inexperienced as she entered high school, and well beneath the nausea worming its way through her still-empty stomach at what this whole experience meant for her and her sanity, there remained a small part of Alice that couldn't help but think, couldn't help but wonder, couldn't help but hope: maybe Pocahontas was right, after all. Maybe Mason was her John.

CHAPTER 1

The Last Exit Out of Alice

Yes, this is technically called "The Creation Story," but it's not the beginning, so let's get that little misconception out of the way right now. There never was a beginning. There was a before, and before that was another before, and another before before that. I know that's probably confusing to a modern mind like yours. Colonialism and so-called linear time have ruined us. We can't even wrap our heads around our own stories because we've been trained to think in good, straight, Christian lines.

But the world doesn't work like that. It never has.

Anyway, before before, this world was covered in water. A deep ocean that held water creatures like pearls. An endless sky that bore witness to the brilliance of the birds. Now, when I say "sky," some outer space is included in there, too. A lot of outer space, actually. Pretty much anything that can be seen from earth counts as "sky"—but that's not to be confused with Sky World, which is even higher than the sky. It's its own world with its own problems, as you'll see pretty clearly once we get into Sky Woman and her life. Though when you really stop and think about it, Sky World and its problems aren't that different from our world or our problems, so it might as well be just plain old "the World."

Aaaand there I go, getting ahead of myself again. Sorry. Bad storyteller! (Let me ask you a quick question: When I say that—"Bad storyteller!"—do you imagine a white lady with a pursed butthole of a mouth wagging her finger in your face, too? Maybe like a nun? "Bad storyteller!" Wag. "Bad Indian!" Wag wag. "Bad woman bad human bad subhuman bad unreal unholy object bad possession my possession his possession everyone's possession but your own bad bad bad bad badddd!" Wag wag wag wag wag. No? Just me? All right, I'll remember that for later. See? Not *that* bad a storyteller.)

So. Basically. The order of things went, from top down:

Sky World

↓

Sky

↓

Ocean

And at the very, very bottom of the ocean, the animals heard, there was something called clay.

**They weren't sure, mind you, but they most
certainly suspected. Heard from a friend's sister's
boyfriend's cousin, and they all but confirmed it.
The animals have always been a gossipy bunch.**

**No one had ever seen this "clay" or felt this
"clay" or taken grainy, possibly doctored pictures
of this "clay" to pass around and praise or debunk,
however—so most of the animals laughed the
whole thing off. Everyone knew there was only sea
and sky. Sink or swim.**

Or fly, I guess.

"Somebody's hungry . . ."

I jump in my seat, nearly choking on a gasp. My hand automat-ically flies to my chest, as if to hold in my thundering heart, and I whip around.

Steve stands there, Dawn wriggling uneasily in his arms.

"Oh. It's you," I say, exhaling with a little laugh.

"Didn't mean to scare you."

"It's okay. I was . . . in the zone, I guess," I say, turning back to look at the computer screen, at the pitiful number of words I've managed to squeeze out. I've been writing and rewriting and erasing and editing this opening section for weeks and nothing seems right. I want to get it perfect, to capture the way my dad used to tell our traditional stories when I was a kid. It's only now, as I labor over even the smallest word, wondering if it's the right kindling to stoke the fire of the reader's mind, that I understand how much talent and effort it took him to make our stories seem so urgent and relevant, even hundreds, thousands of years later. I doubt I'll ever come close to the bar he set. I mindlessly tap the space bar on my laptop, as if that will add anything substantial to the story.

I have no idea how the hell Steve and Dawn snuck up on me. For one thing, I can usually smell his cologne from ten feet away. His mother, Joan, bought it for him. She thinks because she spent more than five hundred dollars on it and its heavy bottle is bedazzled with enough Swarovski crystals to make a drag queen feel faint, that it must smell good. It doesn't. It smells like an unwashed-for-a-couple-days-patchouli-loving douchebag. Like what I imagine Jared Leto smells like. Plus, I'm pretty sure I'm allergic to it because my nose starts to run whenever he sprays, delays, and walks away. ("Learned that one from *Queer Eye*," he told me once, smiling with characteristic earnestness.)

I know he's wearing it as a tribute to his doting mother, an act of olfactory love, and that if I even suggest I don't like it he'll stop immediately. But I also know Joan has been passive-aggressively planting the idea that I unfairly hate her ever since she and I first met, seeds of doubt that were no doubt fertilized and watered by my insistence on having a wedding that centered my rez family and friends. Even saying that I hate the cologne she bought him could subconsciously confirm these suspicions. They're accurate—I absolutely hate her. But I don't want him to know that, so I suffer both the smell and the snot, smiling like a good little wife.

The other thing: I *definitely* should have heard Dawn. She's not quite crying but making an agitated sort of mewling sound I'm all too familiar with. It usually signals that she's about to start another hours-long crying spree. I'm so attuned to that sound I can already feel my breasts leaking. They clearly heard her long before I did. But, if I feed her fast enough, before she starts really getting her little lungs going, maybe we'll avoid a fit this time.

I turn back to the two of them and hold my hands out for Dawn. "Give her here."

Steve plops her into my arms. I pull up my shirt, pull down the flap on my breastfeeding bra, and pray that Dawn will latch on this time. Miraculously, she does, her little cheeks moving in and out like a goldfish. Her face fades from burgundy to a calm light brown as I rub her velvet cheek, soft the way only brand-new baby skin is. Relief floods my muscles, and I close my eyes, letting this small victory loosen my too-tense body. We sit like this for some time, our shared exhaustion making us unlikely allies.

"I like how the animals are all conspiracy theorists."

Shit. He's talking about my writing. I left it up. Stupid mistake. I immediately open my eyes, see Steve leaning over me, and cringe. Not because I don't want him near me. I do. There's this amazing warmth he emits, which makes any room he's in feel like the temperature has risen a few degrees from his mere presence, the exact opposite of the way demons and ghosts are said to make rooms colder.

No, I cringe because his seeing my writing at this stage feels too revealing. Like a stranger walking in on me half naked in a fitting room. Even his praise prickles. The writing is too fresh, too close, my meandering through it too sensitive for scrutiny.

"Thanks, babe. That's sweet of you to say. But it's not good. And it's definitely not ready to be read yet."

I slam my laptop shut, and he stands up quick.

"Oh. Sorry. Didn't realize you were keeping it secret."

Steve moves away from me, hurt, and my once warm neck becomes cold again. I feel a pang of shame—so deep and sharp and fleeting I can't possibly follow it back to its roots—quickly swallowed up by regret. I'm doing it again. Pushing Steve away. He's excited about my writing. He *wants* to encourage me, he *wants* me to succeed, he's told me as much, said we need to set goals for ourselves as individuals and as a family so we maintain our autonomy. He doesn't deserve this.

"It's not that it's a secret. It's just . . . ," I start, searching for a way to invite him back in again. "I'm worried about the tone," I finally say, looking up at him through lowered eyelashes, hoping my face is soft and feminine instead of hard and masculine. It takes conscious effort for me to do that—look helpless, vulnerable, innocent—in a way I'm sure would come naturally to so many white women.

"Maybe it's too flippant?" I add for emphasis.

Steve smiles very slightly, almost imperceptibly. "I like the tone," he says, his voice tentative. "It's ballsy," he continues. "Totally different from the old sage Indian everyone thinks of whenever anybody says the words 'creation story.'"

Not everyone thinks of that, I want to say. White people think of that.

I look down at Dawn, trying to see parts of my family members' faces in her tiny features, but I fail. She's asleep now. Fighting naps all day has finally caught up with her. I pull myself out of her mouth and fix my bra and shirt.

"I don't know if Ma would like it," I confess quietly. "Or Dad."

"What are you talking about? They'd both love it," Steve says as he bends down and kisses my hairline. He gently pulls Dawn away from me and sets her into her car seat in the corner of the office. I'm not sure when I put it there.

I get up, move over to the window. Glance out through the blinds to see the driveway and cream siding of our neighbor's house. People don't exactly live here for the views, I have to remind myself.

"Anyway, don't worry about anyone else's opinion. Only Shonkwaia'tison can judge you," he says, grinning with obvious pride.

I pause.

Shonkwaia'tison.

Today was Steve's first language class, I remember. He was there, in some yellow-tinged classroom reading handouts and forcing his hard English tongue to make soft Mohawk sounds, while I was here, pretending I know how to write Mohawk stories in English words. It's difficult not to be jealous of him, embarrassed of myself. He slid the Mohawk in so seamlessly, so confidently. The same way he approaches everything, including me, as he slips behind me once more, his hot hands skating over my hips, my abdomen.

And suddenly I'm in the upper corner of the room, looking down at Steve and me, as the empty shell of myself leans into the delicious heat of his body. I try not to panic. This isn't exactly new: my consciousness peeling away from the inconvenient reality of my body and floating into the strange, almost liquid-feeling air nearby. But I'm more determined now than ever before: I can't let old demons ruin my new life. They're trying, the demons. Pushing against the mental membrane I've been fortifying since I was a teenager.

Just last week I was making dinner, standing in the kitchen in the sleek little dress I'd grabbed from the closet and shimmied into so Steve would see how well I was handling everything. I'd thrown my hair into an updo I learned from Instagram but decided against makeup. That seemed too try-hard. I had just placed some hand-breaded chicken cutlets into the oven when my eyes caught on the terra-cotta-colored walls. I started thinking about how much I hated them. Steve had chosen the paint. Steve had chosen everything. He'd asked for my input when we first moved in, but I'd shrugged. I couldn't consider the world outside my grief. Ma was newly dead, and I was spending most of my time back at my childhood home on the rez, preparing for her funeral. I'd passed a few sleepless nights in her bed, her sheets pressed to my nose as I breathed in her scent of menthol cigarettes and Chanel Nº5, sobbing. In the mornings, I'd wandered through the trailer, covering the mirrors and reluctantly bagging her belongings to give away after the burial. I'd originally wanted a house with a granny suite so I could look after Ma, make sure she wasn't pushing herself too hard. She'd been struggling with the long-term effects of an injury then, and I wasn't sure how well she'd adjust to living without me for the first time. Once I found out Joan was paying for the house, though, I didn't feel comfortable mentioning it, or any of my preferences. She made it clear the only opinion that mattered was her own. I couldn't help but focus on this fact after Ma died—*she could have been living with us, we could have saved her*—letting it curdle into resentment for both my mother-in-law and the house she'd gifted us. Devoting any thought to decorating it in the weeks and months that followed seemed impossible, even cruel.

And now, thanks to Steve, our entire house looks like it was ripped from an IKEA catalog—all clean lines and no character. White cupboards and chrome pendant lamps and black cube couches. I'm scared to move inside it, scared to dirty it, to disrupt its sanitary perfection. My stylish yet affordable Swedish-designed prison. My first place off the rez, and yet not mine at all.

I don't belong here. Even though it was just a thought, it boomed loud in my mind as I watched the water in the pasta pot come to a boil. I trembled at the truth of it. *I don't belong anywhere. Not anymore.*

Then another voice, not my own: *It's all burning.*

It startled me, this voice, and for a moment I was so scared I couldn't move. I saw it first: dark smoke reaching from the oven door and up toward the ceiling like an angry, vengeful hand. *Holy shit*, I thought. *Something really is on fire.* As soon as the thought popped in my head, the sound of the fire alarm echoed in my ears, then the sound of Dawn's confused yelps started in the living room like high-pitched harmonies. I knew logically those sounds must have been going for a while by that time, but for some reason I hadn't heard them.

It was like my body suddenly went on autopilot. I grabbed oven mitts, opened the oven door, snatched the baking sheet, slammed the door shut, and dropped the baking sheet into the sink with a clatter. I turned on the taps, anxiety sharp in my chest as I watched the steady stream of water rush over the charred remains. As I ran to grab a broom so I could turn off the smoke alarm with the end of its handle, it occurred to me that Steve was due back any minute. He couldn't see this. He couldn't see any of it.

Once I'd stopped the alarm, I unclipped Dawn from her car seat and held her to my chest, shushing her as I plotted. If I called Steve and told him we were out of diapers but insisted he had to buy a specific brand that he would have to drive across town for, that could buy me another half hour. I could order some chicken on a delivery app, set it out on our plates at the dinner table, then tie up the garbage with the burned chicken and run the dishes through the dishwasher. No evidence. It'd be like it never even happened.

Everything went according to plan. I thought I was in the clear. But then, while we were eating dinner, the demons came back for more. At first, everything seemed normal. Steve had launched into the minutiae of his day—how the head of the department invited him out for lunch, which he thought would help with his tenure. Then he went on about the progress of his colleague Scott's home reno, then his department head Lou's wife Sheila's latest publication. He didn't ask me how my day was in all that time. Part of me was relieved since I didn't have to lie. The other part of me was nearly vibrating with so much swallowed rage. If Sheila's day mattered, and Scott's day mattered, why the fuck didn't mine?

"Well, Steve," I might have said if I had any spine, "I nearly burned down the house while you were gone. This dress I threw on just for you now stinks like baby puke and sweat. Your daughter doesn't want the milk from my tits, so I'm always sore and she's always crying. I can't sleep at all. And I never want to fuck you or anyone again."

He'd probably still find a way to excuse my rudeness, to paint it as some endearing joke. He's that type of person. Endlessly optimistic, incredibly loving. The type of person who genuinely tries to get to know people, and once he does, focuses almost exclusively on the good in them, using their past circumstances to explain away what others might refer to as shitty behavior. The type of person who listens deeply to everything everyone says to him, remembers the tiniest, most otherwise inconsequential details of each conversation, then asks about them whenever he sees you next, whether that's in a week or six months. His attitude toward others made everything infinitely more interesting, like each interaction had the possibility to unfold into a fascinating short story, complete with rich characters and unearthed complexities. By the time I was getting ready to move off the rez, my cousin Tanya joked people were going to miss Steve's visits more than they were gonna miss me. I admired that he was so likable, with his constant kindness and focused interest. I still do.

But that night, after the fire scare and the rush to figure out dinner and the droning conversation, I couldn't think about any of that. I was silently simmering, unsure how to put out the blaze inside me. Maybe that played a role, like a key unlocking a door.

Steve finished his meal and shouted, "Nya:wen!" Exaggerating the last syllable the way he always does because he knows it makes me laugh. Or it did. Before Ma died and Dawn was born and I disappeared.

"Nyoh," I replied quietly, shoveling a forkful of salad into my mouth.

"Oh, guess what?" he asked as he swept my plate into the dishwasher. "U of T is offering a beginner Mohawk class this year. I talked to the head of my department and they're going to pay for me to enroll. I managed to convince him it'll benefit the department to have staff who speak Mohawk. Isn't that great?"

It was as if everything paused for a second. I couldn't breathe. I couldn't think. When the pause was over, it wasn't just my insides that shook with fury. It was my outsides, too. I reflexively grabbed my fork. It came from a silverware set Steve's great-uncle Bob had given us as a wedding gift. His wife had gone on and on about the proper way to polish it before we'd even opened their gift. I stared down at that fork, thinking about how beautiful and shiny it would be if not for my oily fingers. I focused on the smudges, the way they blurred at some edges but stayed sharp in others, and I willed myself to stop shaking like an idiot. But just as the thought came to me, it was like my consciousness slingshotted outside of my body and into the air over my head. I could see the dining room from above and from my eyes at the same time—one vision layered on top of the other like overlapping transparencies on an overhead projector. What was happening to me? Why was I so mad? And why was I falling out of my body again, the way I used to before I met Steve?

I sat at the white table and curled and uncurled my toes, trying to pull myself back into my skin as Steve told me what he knows about his new language teacher. Once I did, I encouraged. I carefully wiped the fingerprints from my fork, placed it back down, and I smiled. Steve was none the wiser.

That's what I need to do now, as I float above my office, *Shonkwaia'tison* echoing in my head, my bitterness as conspicuous as each Mohawk syllable Steve uttered. I need to ground myself in my body.

I start by zeroing in on Steve, his dampening hands running all over my skin, his mouth on my neck, kissing me. I never used to mind how sweaty his hands would get. In fact, I used to like it. I had convinced myself his hand sweat was evidence of his fragility, his anxiety, his need for me. Right now his hands remind me of a catfish freshly yanked from the creek. I focus on them, feel saliva well up in my mouth, the sour before the puke, at the exact moment his hands brush the outside of the giant maxi pad shoved between my legs. We both jerk and pull away from each other, embarrassed by my post-childbirth body.

"Sorry," I say before I can really consider what I'm apologizing for.

"It's fine," he says before he can really consider that this interaction is all wrong.

Well, I'm certainly back in my body now: the unwashed, still bleeding heft of it. I pull away from him and lengthen my spine.

"It's only been six weeks," I say, avoiding his eyes.

"I know. You're right. I forgot. I'm sorry." His words fast as he backs away from me, hands up, like he's a little kid who's been caught stealing candy at the corner store.

"You look ridiculous," I manage, genuinely laughing this time. He laughs, too.

I love Steve more than I knew it was even possible to love another person. I can tell by the way I always turn toward him wherever he's in a room—still—as if he's the sun and I'm a sunflower starving for his light.

But I can't help but notice: he hasn't suffered at all since we've gotten married. If anything, he's excelled. Now that he's married with a baby, he can better relate to the older, tenured faculty in his anthropology department. He can bring me along to dinner parties, where I feel like an exhibit on display, and dress up our daughter in cute baby drag so that strange white women are more enticed to scoop her out of her stroller or car seat without my permission. Every action we take is purposeful and imbued with meaning for him, because it makes him more "relatable," more "feminist." And through it all, he has the luxury of forgetting about not only the pain and violence of the actual act of childbirth but also the ongoing trauma it's stamped on my body.

Me, though? I'm consumed by this inescapable feeling of hopelessness. Every day is the same. Same exhaustion. Same humiliation. Same loneliness. I look out at the young women who walk past the house and fantasize about where they're going, who they're gonna hang out with, what drugs they're gonna do when they get there, who they're gonna fuck when they start to come down and everything else has lost its glitter. Fantasizing is all I can do. I'm stuck here.

Steve doesn't notice. He wouldn't, though. He's too blinded by the picture of us he's fixed in his mind. That's partially my fault—Steve's not knowing. I've perfected the art of looking like I'm okay—more than okay, even, *great*—since back when I was working at the racetrack as a kid. You could never let men at the track see you flinch, because then they'd know the way in. They'd know how to make you uncomfortable. How to make you hurt. Better to keep that hidden. Better to keep yourself hidden.

Still, that word comes back again, nagging at me.

Shonkwaia'tison.

Mohawk feels like a weapon coming from Steve's lips—not because he's necessarily wielding it that way but because history is. Here was the language I had lost, the language my parents and aunts and half my grandparents had lost, which was so different from the English that'd been forced on us that I secretly worried my tongue would never be able to make those sounds. And here was Steve, rattling it off easily, as if it weren't an endangered language, my endangered language; as if those words, which held my culture, were simply . . . *words* to him.

The thing is, though, they *were*. And why wouldn't they be? He didn't need to question his identity and worth every time he said a Mohawk word. His voice didn't shake when he spoke, scared any mispronunciation would signal to everyone he didn't really belong. That he never did and never would.

That wasn't his legacy.

It was mine.

When you both die, Steve will have to translate your ancestors' words to you.

As soon as the words enter my head, I see my ancestors staring at me, disappointed, their foreheads crinkled like tissue paper, as they slowly push out syllables for Steve to catch and pass to me. I shake my head slightly to chase the words—the vision—out.

No. Not now. I'm the one in control.

"Did you learn that word in class?" I manage to say without my voice cracking.

"Learn what?" he asks, distracted. "Shonkwaia'tison?"

I nod, afraid that if I say anything, I'll scream or cry.

"Yeah, mostly." He's grinning like a schoolboy getting praised by his favorite teacher. "I mean, I'd hear your ma say it all the time before, but I wasn't sure of the syllables. Was it okay?"

Hearing him mention Ma feels like a tiny dagger in my gut. I swallow—quietly—then force my voice to mimic excitement. "Yup. Good job, babe!"

"Thanks."

He nuzzles into my neck and I know I'm being unfair. An asshole. He's learning Mohawk, for fuck's sake! It's one of the hardest languages in the world to learn, and he's learning it. He's learning it for me and he's learning it for our daughter. Yes, he's also going to be able to use this to better position his career, but that doesn't negate the good. He talked to Melita about her experience learning it, and he knows it'll be easier for Dawn to retain Mohawk if it's spoken at home, too. I know he cares, that he would never intentionally make me feel bad for not knowing my language. I know that he would willingly act as translator for my ancestors and me—gladly even.

Just as I know there is a disconcerting plea in his voice, barely perceptible. I'm not sure what it's a plea for, but it immediately strikes me as everything that's wrong with him, with us. We've been married nine months but it already feels like decades of unsaid words have settled between us.

A lattice pattern of silence and secrets to match the sofa set.

That night I have one of my recurring nightmares. They started during the pregnancy: terrible dreams so thick I had to be shaken from them violently. There was blood, always. So much blood. In this one, which started shortly after my mother's funeral, Ma was alive again. She pulled up in her car to the front of our new house, smiling and happy to see us. Steve and I were waving from behind the screen door, Dawn content in my arms. But when Ma began to walk up the sidewalk toward us, the squares of cement started to simmer beneath her. Each step she took melted her body from the bottom up. Still, despite my screams for her to turn around and go back, she wouldn't stop. She kept coming, her skin, muscles, bones, and blood puddling behind her.

It was so real I could smell her sizzling flesh long after I'd screamed myself awake.

CHAPTER 2

A Moment for the Meet-Cute

We met through my mother. He was writing a chapter in his book on Indigenous planting, and she was the only seedkeeper who would talk to him. I remember sneaking in after my shift at the bingo hall, stinking of cigarettes and coffee. I didn't want Ma to catch me and saddle me with a list of chores before I could escape to hang out with Tanya and Melita. Or worse, have to interact with her in one of her drugged-out stupors.

The first thing I saw was his back. It was an attractive back—the result of discipline and design. I watched without a word as he shifted that beautiful back against one of Ma's horrendous wicker chairs, self-consciously adjusting his slouch so it gave off the perfect amount of professional aloofness. In that moment I thought I could see what he might have been like as a child: patient, proud, eager to impress. He was the type who'd always needed a teacher to acknowledge his right answers, who'd seemingly constructed an entire identity from those sparkly stickers pressed in the corners of check-marked tests.

I didn't mean to laugh, it just happened. And as soon as that giggle hit his ear, he seemed to deflate a little, the way men do whenever a woman laughs off script. He darted around and looked at me, surprise widening his blue eyes.

"I'm sorry," he said, smiling, straightening in his chair. "You probably weren't expecting me."

I knew at once it was the most perfect thing a man had ever said. Maybe it was the way his voice was lowered—like we were telling each other secrets; like we were already lovers. Maybe it was because he was even sexier from the front than from the back. Or maybe it was the fact that he seemed to have decided as soon as he met me that I was a person worthy of respect. Either way, when Ma walked through the door not a second later, clearly in good spirits that day, and asked me to do her a favor and take Steve here on a midnight walk so he could better understand the way our medicines were divided between light and dark, I shut my mouth and nodded like a goddamn idiot.

"Make sure you show him the cattails down around the crick. And bring some back for me, eh? I wanna make 'em into tea." She smiled conspiratorially. Later—after I took him on the medicine walk; after we ended up skinny-dipping in the crick; after I burned leeches off his bare ass with my Betty Boop lighter while he squealed; after he showed up at the bingo hall the next day to see me and found himself pressured into playing a game of bingo with the old Native biddies we forever after referred to as "the blue-haired crew"; after we started talking breathlessly on the phone nearly every night, him telling me all the new places he wanted to take me, all the wild things he wanted to show me; after I reluctantly passed him my writing and he gushed over it, called it "fresh" and "exciting" the way my dad had; after he made me forget that I was a no one with no future and I began to feverishly imagine who I could be free from my home and my history; after being with him made every moment feel precious—after all of that, I asked Ma why she talked to Steve when no other seedkeeper would. I expected a long, winding explanation, drawing on the teachings of our wampum belts, the Great Law, the Code of Handsome Lake. Instead, she gave the same knowing smile she gave me that first day, shrugged, and said, "You were single, and he was cute."

I don't think Ma expected me to marry Steve. She liked him, I know that. It helped that he paid her for her extensive knowledge and didn't freely pilfer it like other academics had in the past, as though they themselves had divined our knowledge from ancient texts hidden in dangerous jungles instead of simply asking our people. It also helped that he consulted her on every detail of his book, listening closely to her long, circular stories without interrupting, then deferring to her judgments. But her liking him didn't negate the obvious: Steve was white. Even if we loved each other, that love did not grant him passage to live on my territory. Band Council's bylaws forbade it. We could never live together on the land I knew so well, among the people I loved so fiercely. Our children couldn't live there—not with him. And, depending on who our kids married, their kids might not live there, either. My culture would be slowly filtered out until it was a distant echo, summoned only as the shallow basis for ill-formed arguments over Indigenous rights. "Actually, my great-great-great-great-grandmother was Native, so . . ."

Ma outlined all of this for me—and when I look back on it now, it's clear she did so with compassion. Didn't even mention Dad and his lifelong insistence that I marry a Native man, which I should have been thankful for. But I didn't trust any of her motives then. I still saw her as some sort of disappointed coach or prison guard in my life—a person who had always asked for and expected too much of me, never noticing the impact this had. I was so sure that Ma was trying to keep me in that trailer with her that I greeted all her warnings and even well-wishes with an upturned lip and an eye roll. It wasn't until after she died that I'd considered: she'd never asked me to stay with her all these years. I'd *chosen* to. I'd unfairly made Ma my scapegoat my entire life. Someone I could blame for my own feelings of failure.

Meanwhile, Steve was my white knight, carrying me off from the tower I'd been imprisoned in since birth—a tower I'd, in some ways, built higher all by myself. Keeping people out. Keeping secrets. Not anymore. I wanted to leave the rez. I wanted to be part of something exciting, for my life to have a distinctive shape I could show others as proof that I was *someone*. I wasn't the pathetic girl-woman living at home with her mom anymore. There was no more risk of failure. I was gonna give my ma a son-in-law to brag about, then grandkids to show pictures of to anyone who asked and anyone who didn't. She wouldn't have to feel embarrassed when her friends asked her about me anymore. I was so sure that this would make her—and me—happy. It wouldn't help the fact that my mother had never fully recovered from her car accident seven years ago, that she couldn't work or move without extreme pain, that she needed more and more help that, once I left, wouldn't be there. But, like all the darkest, most difficult, and most necessary conversations, we ignored it, just as I ignored how Ma started to treat her pain with drugs. I never mentioned when she began to slur or fall asleep, never mentioned when things seemed to accelerate once I moved out. I could offer her this dignity, at least.

Ma's overdose threw a wrench in everything. She didn't get a chance to walk me down the aisle. She didn't even get a chance to meet her granddaughter, much less brag about her. Sometimes I wonder if, in the moments before she died, Ma saw her life roll before her eyes like a film, the way some people say it does when you have a near-death experience. And if she did see her whole life played back for her, what she thought of it. Whether she had regrets. Things she wished she'd done. Things she wished she hadn't. Places she wished she'd gone, or people she wished she'd kept in touch with. I wonder whether she felt proud of her life. I wonder if she felt proud of me.

Or maybe she regretted it all, and the whole thing coming to a close was a relief, like when you finally fall into bed after an especially long, grueling day.

I sometimes hope that, wherever she is, she can't see or hear me so she can't be ashamed of what I've become, how I sit and stay and shut up for Steve's mother and colleagues, who I'm sure see me as little more than a trained dog. Other times I hope that she's watching always, silently rooting me on, giving me strength. I need her strength. There are times the loss of Six Nations weighs down every part of me. Those times it seems regret is not a feeling but a permanent state of being, as constant as air. But then I do something as simple as piss in a toilet I can actually flush, or turn on my tap and drink a glass of water without boiling it first, or walk five minutes to get fresh produce instead of driving half an hour, and the ease of those things reminds me of the value of living somewhere my daughter and I can not only survive but also thrive. In those moments, I am truly thankful.

And at the same time, I am absolutely furious I have to be thankful in the first place.

CHAPTER 3

Caught Off Guard by the Colors of the Wind

Dawn screams. I jump from my bed, where I've been lying for the past twenty minutes since her last eruption, and rush to her nursery. I scoop her up and hold her to my chest. Her little hands grab at everything—pull at my hair and clothes and skin, her tiny nails like razors—and I observe once again that she doesn't want me. I don't know that she's ever wanted me, despite what Ma told me about babies choosing their parents.

"Up in Sky World, the babies get to see everything that could happen to them if they were born to this person or that person. Then, after they think about it for a while, they pick the ones they want and just like *that*"—Ma snapped for emphasis—"they're born."

"How do they decide who to pick?" I'd asked her so many times, as if the answer might have changed since last time. But it never did.

"Well, that depends on what the baby thinks they need to learn in this life. Or on what the baby wants to experience. Sometimes they even start to love a certain set of parents all the way up from Sky World."

I'd always say the same thing to my mother when she said this: "I picked you cuz I loved you so much." And she would immediately grab me and nuzzle me, and I'd squeal in delight, almost drunk on her love, which felt so perfect and absolute at the time. As I grew up, I'd reference that story so much it became like an inside joke to us. She'd do something nice for me, like buy me a new pair of beaded earrings or drive me and all my cousins to the theater to see an R-rated horror movie that their moms didn't want them to see, and I'd give her a big kiss on the cheek and say, "And that's why I chose you to be my ma."

I don't feel anything like that sort of connection to Dawn, and that fucking terrifies me. It feels like another loss, only I have no way to really frame it, because I don't know exactly what it is that I'm missing. I don't know what I'm supposed to feel as a mother. All I know is I'm supposed to feel *something*. Part of me wonders whether it's not a problem with Dawn, too. She certainly doesn't seem like she's chosen me—at least not from a place of love. Even when she was a pea-sized cluster of cells in my uterus she was wrecking my sleep, forcing me up in the middle of the night to puke so many times I started keeping a bowl beside my bed. At the end of the pregnancy, it felt like she was routinely stepping on my bladder, making me pee a little in my underwear anytime I went out in public. One time she did it as I was rushing down the stairs to the subway. Just as that annoying little jingle signaled the doors were closing it felt like Dawn had turned in my womb and stomped. Soon my pants were hot and wet down to my knees and I started to cry then and there. After that I planned my trips out of the house entirely around my proximity to bathrooms. It was so embarrassing to not have control of my body all of a sudden—an embarrassment that hasn't stopped, really.

I try to soothe Dawn—"hushushushush"—try to calm her by running my hand up and down her backside; try to sing to her the only song I can think of, which is, shamefully, "The Wheels on the Bus." I sit in her rocking chair and pull out my breast, try to push my nipple into her mouth to test if she's hungry, but she cries louder, her face now a shock of scarlet patches and an open, screaming mouth.

"You really don't want me, do you?" I ask, each word landing with such devastating truth that I start to cry. She's never as loud as when she is in my arms. It's as if she wants to torture me. Maybe that's why she chose me—she knew I'd be an easy target for her sadism. Maybe she's a bad soul, like Flint, Sky Woman's evil little grandson who clawed his way out of her daughter's womb, killing her, then blamed it on his twin, Sapling. None of these thoughts help. I can recognize that even as I burrow deeper into them, turning over new reasons to hate myself like stones in a riverbed: Your daughter only acts this way with you. Your daughter wants to punish you. Your daughter hates you. She doesn't even want to drink your milk. She prefers powder to your sour tits. You're such a bad mother, just like you were a bad daughter. Your ma would still be here if not for you. Your dad's lucky he never had to see what you became. You can't keep anyone you love alive. You never could. You should run away. It's all you're good at.

I look down at Dawn through tears as I bring my breast to her mouth, fingers circling my areola. I squeeze a little, hoping to draw the milk out to entice her, but as I push it against her squealing mouth I see red. I pull away from Dawn immediately, worried that my nipples have cracked to the point of bleeding again. But when I look down, I see thick blood pumping from my nipple in bursts, pouring over Dawn's face and inside her mouth, gagging her as she yelps. I start to shake. What's happening—

Rrrriiiiinnng.

Suddenly I'm back in the room and Dawn's screaming, but she isn't covered in blood. She's not even wet. There's a bit of milk on my hand, that's all. It was just a thought. A fucked-up thought, sure, but Dawn and I are both fine. Immediately I'm crying again, relieved.

Rrrriiiinnng.

That's what pulled me out: the doorbell. I'm thankful it did, but it also means someone is waiting for me downstairs. I take a moment to steady my breathing and dry my tears. I don't want anyone to see me in the middle of a breakdown. Dawn, on the other hand, is still inconsolable. I decide to bring her downstairs along with me in the hopes that her screams will scare away whatever poor Jehovah's Witness or Girl Scout thinks it's a good idea to come here. But when I get closer to the bottom of the stairs I see our neighbor Meghan's bottle-blond head peeking into the windows surrounding the front door. She smiles as soon as she sees the two of us, then, as she notices Dawn's screams, it's like her whole face is yanked downward, her frown so deep it feels like an admonition of us both.

She's the only person from this neighborhood I've met since we moved here, and it was mostly an accident. We just so happened to be moving in as she was gardening. She got on with Steve instantly, like everyone does, and brought over some homemade lemonade and lemon bars. When I pointed out how the presentation looked like something out of a magazine, she told us she had a popular mommy Instagram account, blushing.

But even with Meghan's insistent friendliness and frequent mentions of the word "reconciliation," I knew I didn't belong in her neighborhood. I knew that within weeks of moving in. As soon as I noticed no one who lived around me was Native, the culture shock set in. I felt stupid for not anticipating it. I'd lived on Six Nations my whole life. Sure, my community knew all of the worst things about me and made sure I remembered that, but they also cared about me. Without them I felt like a tightrope walker without a safety net. As nice as Meghan comes off, I can't let her see me fall.

I hide behind the door, wipe my eyes, arrange my face into a smile, and open it. Under her arm, Meghan has a little yellow basket with tinted cellophane around it, the ends drawn up into a beautiful bunch at the top and tied expertly with a pastel yellow ribbon. It looks like it was done by a professional.

"Oh no! What's wrong with the pwecious widdle girl?" Meghan asks in her high-pitched baby voice before I can muster so much as a hello.

"Told her about climate change. Hasn't stopped crying since."

"What?" Her eyebrows furrow aggressively.

Okay, no jokes, I tell myself. *Stick to the dire reality of the situation.* "I don't know what's wrong. I think she has colling."

"Colling?" Meghan asks, confused. "What do you mean? Is that, like, an Aboriginal thing?"

Oh, for fuck's sake. "She won't stop crying no matter what I do," I yell over Dawn's wails.

"Ohhhhh," Meghan says with a little laugh. "You mean *colic.*" She annunciates the word slowly, ridiculously, like she's a character on *Sesame Street* announcing the word of the day. She places the basket down on the porch.

"Give her here."

I do, perhaps too enthusiastically. She doesn't seem to notice. Instead, she immediately starts patting Dawn on the back and waltzes past me. I pick up the basket—which is full of DVDs—and walk into my own house behind her. She's pacing back and forth in the living room, patting Dawn's back and murmuring what sounds like baby nonsense into her ear. A loud burp erupts from Dawn's lips, then another. And just like that, she's quiet, staring up into Meghan's giant, smiling green eyes.

"We thought Stacey was a colicky baby until we realized she was a gassy baby," Meghan says as she smiles down at Dawn.

"I'll try to remember that for next time. Thank you."

"Please! It's my pleasure! I haven't had a chance to hold a baby this small for years." She leans down and presses her nose to the top of Dawn's head. "Nothing like the smell of a baby's hair." Her voice is dreamy.

I nod along, silent, wondering why it is she's here.

"That's actually why I came over," she says, as if reading my mind. "I just read that Marie Kondo book. You know the one I'm talking about? *The Life-Changing Magic of Tidying Up*?"

I shake my head Not necessary with the act of shaking one's head.

"Really? Oh my goodness, Alice, you *have* to read it. I swear to god, it'll. Change. Your. Life." She emphasizes the last three words like two of them aren't already an integral part of the title. "I can lend it to you if you want."

"That's so nice, Meghan, but I'm not sure I'll get to it. I don't really have a lot of time to read right now."

"Oh my goodness, what am I thinking? Of course you don't! You've just had a baby! You probably have a hard enough time showering and getting dressed these days."

I immediately look down at my clothes. They're covered in spit-up. I can feel big warm wet spots under my arms. There's even a particularly obnoxious ketchup stain I didn't notice was on my shirt until now. I know my hair is a greasy knot because when I tried to run a brush through it this morning, it got stuck. Dawn started crying, and I stopped trying after that, sure that if I followed my usual schedule, I'd have plenty of time to clean myself up and change before Steve got home. And now this.

"Oh my goodness, Alice, I am *so* sorry. I didn't mean . . . You look great for a new mom!"

I want to die. Right here, right now.

"What were you saying about that book?" I manage, with the last of my dignity.

"Right! Anyway, this book is all about getting rid of things you don't need. Anything that doesn't spark joy?" Meghan maneuvers Dawn into one arm, holds out a thumbs-up, turns it upside down, and blows a raspberry.

"Okay . . ." I'm still holding the basket like a buffoon.

"Well, I was going through Stacey and Shiloh's old movie collection. I guess I went a little overboard when they were little? Bought everything Disney ever put out. Point is, there is way, way too much stuff. And Brock keeps reminding me everything's going digital anyway, so the movies that don't spark joy for any of us will just be gathering dust. Then I remembered you guys still have a DVD collection of your own, and I got to thinking about little Dawn and what she might like, and . . . here I am."

"That's so sweet that you thought of us," I say, surprisingly warmed by the gesture. Maybe I'd judged Meghan too harshly and we really could be friends. "And you even had them gift wrapped?"

"I did that myself. Just a little something I learned on a crafting blog. Go ahead, open it."

I try to pull at one loose end of the yellow ribbon, but it doesn't budge. I try another. Nothing. I look around, see a pen on the coffee table and grab it. Fuck it.

"Oh, if you—"

I stab the cellophane open before Meghan can say any more, but that doesn't stop her.

"It doesn't really matter," Meghan continues, more to herself than anything. "I thought you might want to reuse the wrapping . . ."

"Oh. Sorry."

I dig out the movies and go through them one by one. *The Princess and the Frog. Aladdin. Mulan.* And—of course, because why

wouldn't this particular woman give me these particular movies—
Pocahontas and its lackluster sequel, *Pocahontas II: Journey to a New World.*

All movies featuring leads who aren't white. Which is most likely why they don't "spark joy" for her family, and why she thinks they will for my little half-brown baby. I can't mention that to her, though. She'd probably have a heart attack right here in my living room before calling me a reverse racist. I bottle up my annoyance, feeling like a fool for expecting anything different.

"This is really thoughtful, Meghan. I don't think Dawn will be watching anything for a couple years yet, though."

"Those years will go by sooner than you think. Just put them away for her for now. Then when she wants them, they'll be right there waiting."

I look over at the nearly full bookshelf of DVDs—mostly mine, at least half of which I grabbed used from the Jumbo Video next to my high school when I was a teen and have stubbornly held on to— sigh, and look back down at the movie cases in my hands. Pocahontas stares back up at me as leaves start blowing mystically around her. Her eyes are big and beautiful and brown as ever. Her lips thick and red like she's always wearing lipstick. Then, as I watch, her lips seem to move into a sly smile and she winks. I stop breathing.

No. Not again, I think, shutting my eyes tight.

"You don't already have them, do you?" Meghan asks. My eyes snap open. I must have said that aloud.

"No, we don't. This is great, Meghan. Really."

We stand there, smiling at each other like uncomfortable buffoons.

"Well, as much as I'd love to stick around, holding this little one, I've got to get back," Meghan says.

"Uh-huh." I can't concentrate on what she's saying. I look down at the DVD cover, which seems to have changed back to normal. I stare at it, eyes going over every single inch, but nothing changes.

"Alice?" Meghan's holding Dawn out like an offering.

"Sorry." I put the movies down and take her. Meghan keeps talking the way women like her do until the front door's closed firmly behind her. Then, as soon as I'm sure she's not coming back, I take the movies and throw them in the garbage.

CHAPTER 4

What the Fuck Does
Win Butler Know?

'm standing in front of the mirror when Win Butler from Arcade Fire dramatically declares his body is a cage into my headphones and I laugh far too hard. I used to think his lyrics were profound, that he had this keen insight into the world that we were all privileged that he shared with us. Now his words sound like the whines of a sullen boy trying too hard to sound deep. *His* body is a cage? Really? Has it ever been prisoner to another's body, biologically glued to their every whim? Until his nipples have chapped and cracked open from feeding and his entire pelvic area—from the top of his pubes to the top of his ass crack—has to be cushioned by a jumbo maxi pad so he doesn't leak blood onto overpriced rocking chairs, he has no idea how much it fucking sucks to be stuck in your own sorry flesh.

I think about texting Melita and complaining to her. She loves it when I make fun of emo white boys. Hell, it'd give her more ammo to add to her latest sex theory: "Every white hipster in Montreal is a greedy lover who thinks asking to fuck in an accent is foreplay." After breaking up with Alexandre two weeks ago, then getting back together with him for two days, then getting in a huge online order of sex toys and breaking up with him again, she's been pretty insistent.

But I don't text anything. I keep listening and rolling my eyes and thinking about how my pussy is now a gaping wound. It feels as though Dawn fought to stay inside, dragging sharp, clawlike fingernails against my uterine walls, grasping, leaving scars and blood and dangling viscera to tag the place so everyone would know who *really* owned my body. So I would know. When I was a teen I used to think that my husband would own my flesh as soon as we said "I do," but that was before I knew anything about childbirth or mothering. Now I know who's in charge. My body's so attuned to Dawn and her needs that every night I wake up a few seconds before she starts to wail. That is, when I manage to fall asleep at all.

I didn't even want to look at my pussy at first. In fairness, I never really looked at it much before the baby. Still, I sort of wish someone told me that my vagina maybe wouldn't be fully intact after I gave birth. I found that out at precisely the moment my midwife, Phyllis, stormed toward me with a giant needle and medical thread. There had been tearing. I needed to be sewn up right away. There was a sharpness. My leg jerked. I'm still not sure if it's because I was hurt or because I was surprised. Later I tried to remember exactly when my—what was it? a muscle? a hole? a body part?—tore, and I couldn't pinpoint it. Even then the pain was like one long rope, woven through each finger and toe, tied around every limb and appendage, snaking up my nose and down my throat. I could no more remember the precise moments of the tears than I could untangle myself from their pain, from the fate of that tiny person so recently forced from my body.

"The smaller tears will close up themselves," Phyllis had said, patting my thigh, as though that made it less horrific.

I'm obsessed with how my pussy looks now. More and more I

bring my phone to the bathroom—or "powder room," as Joan would call it—and sit on the toilet with a pressed-powder compact in one hand and my phone in the other, looking up pictures of porn stars spreading their labia lips. I zoom in on the hairless pink and brown and black pussies, scroll up and down and left and right, then angle the little circular mirror between my legs and learn new ways to be ashamed of myself. These days I tend to think of my vagina as cracked, like a hard-boiled egg rapped sharply by a metal spoon. The stitches are thick and black and running up the rip like rungs on a ladder. I hate it.

The bathroom doorknob rattles, followed by a knock. I pull out my headphones.

"Yeah?"

"You almost done, babe?" asks Steve. "I've got *Drag Race* all queued up." Back when Dawn was first born, Tanya and Melita started watching this season of *RuPaul's Drag Race* with me. They made sure to wait to watch it until we were all together, and they'd be the ones to take care of anything Dawn needed the entire night. It was the first few times they'd been over to visit since our house-warming party almost a year earlier. That lasted three weeks before Steve said, "We have to start doing the parenting by ourselves at some point" and "I believe in us." He had watched the show with me every week since as a sort of compromise for my cousins' absence, holding Dawn as I texted them my reactions.

"Just a few more minutes," I say.

"And the tea's okay? Doesn't hurt or anything?"

"It's fine," I lie. Tanya found me some post-pregnancy tea—"Real hard-core Indian medicine," she'd promised. Steve drove down to pick it up from Six Nations last night. I wanted to drive myself, but Steve thought it was too dangerous. I never got around to getting a license, even though I'd been driving since I first stole Ma's car for a joyride with my cousins at thirteen. Anytime I even suggested driving a few blocks, Steve would protest. "What if you get pulled over?" It was easier to let him take charge of all the driving than fight against his quivering fear, so I sent him down to pick up the tea.

Under Tanya's strict over-the-phone orders, I brewed it, let it cool to room temperature, then poured it inside this plastic container apparently called a sitz bath that I snapped onto my toilet bowl.

"You gotta strip down and sit in it for at least ten minutes," Tanya had said.

"Will my ass even fit?" I asked.

"Your ass fits on the toilet seat, don't it?"

Finally, I slowly lower myself down into the sitz bath to test Tanya's hypothesis. It stings a bit, but nowhere near the alcoholic burn I was expecting. I inhale with a *sssssssssssssttt* as I settle into the cool, pleased that I actually do fit after all.

From her nursery I hear Dawn's shrill cries and my leg jerks. Immediately the front of my shirt wets with milk. Fuck. I wad some toilet paper in both hands and press it against my leaking nipples.

Please let him calm her down so it stops, I think. *Please.*

I pop the headphones back in my ears and just like that, it does stop. Thank the Creator for loud music. There's another knock on the door.

"Yeah?" I ask, pausing the music, annoyed. "What is it?"

"Dawn's hungry. Should I bring her in to you now, or wait for you to get out?" Steve asks.

"Just wait. I'll be out in a second. I'm still . . . soaking."

"Sure thing. No rush. We'll be okay out here. Have a good soak!"

The phrase is so ridiculous I can't help but smile. A "good soak," like I'm someone who takes hour-long baths and calls them "self-care." But then I see myself reflected in the black of the phone screen and there's this strange disconnect. Like I'm looking at someone else, someone wrong, someone who *does* see good soaks as the key to loving myself. The type of person who uses MAC's Whirl instead of L'Oréal's True Red. Which is who I am, of course, now that I'm married to Steve. Nude lipsticks instead of look-at-me reds. Color-blocked clothes and neutral basics instead of ripped jeans and band shirts. It didn't happen right away. In fact, it only occurred to me to dress differently after Steve proposed. Or rather, it occurred to Ma, who then made sure it occurred to me.

I was wearing what I'd usually wear for a simple date to the movies: a pair of skinny jeans tucked into red Converse shoes and a red plaid button-down shirt with the sleeves rolled up, my only makeup my True Red lipstick, expertly applied. But as I was sitting at the kitchen table, waiting, Ma looked me up and down with a sneer. "*That's* what you're wearing?" Her speech was a little slurred, the way it got when she was really high, so I tried to harden myself. She would get cruel when she was high. I couldn't rely on her love to shield me then. I couldn't rely on anything. She'd spit whatever ugly words came to her mind, and I'd have to clean them from my mind for days, weeks. Another reason for me to get away, I'd thought, telling myself not to engage. And yet, I couldn't stop myself from digging deeper, sure that she knew something I didn't.

"What's wrong with it?" I'd asked defensively.

Ma shook her head slowly, her speech a little soggy as she continued. "Nothing, it's just . . . you look exactly like you did in high school."

"So?"

"Soooo don't you think it's time to grow up? Dress more like a woman? I'm sure Steve doesn't want to be married to someone who looks like a little teenybopper all the time."

"He already proposed to me. I'm sure he likes my clothes fine," I answered, though the doubt had already taken root.

"I'm sure you know better than me, sweetie," she replied, then slowly ran her hand back and forth over the top of my head like I was a dog. I batted her arm away. She was worse off than I thought, and I'd already thought she was pretty far gone. "But I have to wonder. Why hasn't he asked you to meet his friends yet?"

My heart stilled. She was right. He hadn't asked me to meet his friends once, despite his knowing everyone I liked and hated on my rez. As Ma stumbled back to her recliner in the living room, I went back to my closet. I only had one dress: a black one, for the funerals it seemed I was attending more and more. A teen in the community died by suicide. Another few were involved in car accidents. Elders had heart attacks or strokes. People of all ages were overdosing. I pushed away those associations and yanked the dress over my head. Then I removed my red lipstick and applied a pinky beige one Ma had given me last Christmas—some gift with purchase from an Avon order.

Steve's clearly pleased reaction when he saw me validated Ma's words, to start. But it was about two weeks later, when I'd stopped wearing red lipstick completely in favor of that pinky beige, and was conducting regular raids of the thrift stores in surrounding cities, asking myself, *What would a broke Blair Waldorf wear?*, when I received what seemed like uncontestable proof: after seven months of being together and two of being engaged, Steve finally invited me to meet his colleagues. Who could argue with results like that?

He introduced me as his fiancée—it was a faculty dinner, I think—then, without taking a breath, he continued: "She's working on a novel that's also a modern retelling of the Haudenosaunee Creation Story."

Not a word about where I came from, who I was. Not a word

about my actual paying job at the bingo hall, where he wooed me. As if he knew I could leave all of it behind. As if he wanted me to, expected it. I hadn't even told my own family about my writing, and he'd just casually tossed the information at complete strangers like it was all they needed to know.

That was the first moment I really felt the difference between us and the worlds we inhabited. On Six Nations, we'd introduce ourselves by saying who we were related to, then spend the next five minutes trying to place how our relatives knew one another, or if we were relatives ourselves if you went far back enough. Each person a walking history book, a branch waiting to find more family trees to graft onto.

"Holay! You're Oriette's daughter, innit? Haven't seent you since you were a baby!"

"Pretty sure our grammas used to run around together back in the day! My tota showed me these pictures, they were *such* badasses. You gotta see 'em. Add me on Facebook and I'll send 'em over."

Or "Ohhhh. You're one of *those* Martins . . . ," accompanied by a tongue click and an eye roll.

Folks off the rez—folks like Steve and his coworkers—introduced themselves not by talking about their families but by explaining how they made money, as if that said anything substantial about who they were or what they offered their communities or the world. As much as I hated it for being so reductive and prejudicial on the one hand, on the other, it could offer me an escape rope to anonymity. All I had to do was hold it firmly enough, climb it fast enough, and I'd no longer have to worry whether any of these people had heard gossip about my supposedly crazy grandma, or knew about Ma's drug problems, or judged me marrying a white guy, or anything. I was a sort of ghost to these people, and, in some ways, to Steve—a figure living in the shadow of some future Alice, a version of myself that actually worked toward her goals, that believed in her abilities, that was primed to achieve big things with the steady support of her husband. A version of myself that never acknowledged her humble beginnings until they were a distant memory and, therefore, better for the story of it all. Steve introducing me to his colleagues as an aspiring author seemed to not only solidify but legitimize that path for me. If he said it, they believed it. I believed it. Everything sounded realer rolling off his tongue. Maybe I could be his version of me. Maybe, if I really fucking tried.

Things were never the same after I'd talked to Pocahontas as a kid. It seemed as though that night had broken a seal, and suddenly all sorts of things were speaking to me that shouldn't have been. Trees specifically seemed eager to communicate, and I couldn't help thinking of Grandmother Willow and her kind, rich voice, or the Ents in *The Lord of the Rings*, who talked so slowly and with such ceremony it took them all day to properly greet one another. That wasn't how the trees spoke to me. They deposited images into my brain like coins in a piggybank, which I immediately understood to be from the deep past. It got to the point where I couldn't leave the trailer without images splashing across my mind, then disappearing in favor of other images, like a TV rapidly changing channels. And then the squirrels and birds started talking to me, too, only they liked to use words and songs, further crowding my head. So I stopped leaving the trailer when I didn't have to. Sometimes, even then, I'd feel myself slip out of my body and hover in the corner of my room, looking down at myself with the eyes of something significantly older than I knew myself to be. When that happened, it felt like everything I'd ever experienced in this life, as Alice, was a dream, and if I really wanted, I could end that dream, maybe enter another, try again. I didn't identify that feeling as a form of suicidal ideation at the time, though looking back, I probably should have. I certainly didn't want to be here—"here" being this plane of existence, where life moved both too fast and too slow, and everything waited for me to place one foot in front of the other and move toward *something*—the future perhaps, or more concretely, some important decision that would chart a course in my life, giving me somewhere to thrust myself and my dwindling ambitions. Something that could be entirely mine without making me feel guilty for wanting it in the first place.

That's where the alcohol and weed came in. I didn't hesitate when it was offered to me after the trees started talking, didn't think about the fact that most of my friends were driving around with a few beers in 'em, a joint on their lips, then between their fingers, then in my mouth, smoke swirling in my throat, then choking me in ragged coughs we all laughed at as we sped down Fifth Line to pick up some bootleg DVDs and bags of chips. I didn't consider that this exact type of behavior was what killed my dad years ago. A carful of careless, drunk kids ended him in an instant. I'd bricked off all that pain behind a wall called "coping" and fell headfirst into whatever distractions I could—the more they clouded the ancient images bursting into my brain, the better.

But I didn't want Steve or his friends to ever see me like that.

I knew the change in me would need to go deep. I wasn't stupid; I knew how people perceived Indians. How the people Steve cared about perceived Indians, despite their overassurance that they were all quite disgusted with Canada over residential schools. Those assurances couldn't rewrite history. There were so many news stories and anecdotes and long-standing stereotypes about us as "drunks," or our kids as desperate gas huffers, or our men as thieves who stole cars in the city and set them on fire on the rez, none of us ever paying taxes or shutting up about what colonialism did to us and our land. As if we were genetically broken as a race and unwilling to do anything to change that.

That whole first night I didn't touch my glass of wine. The men didn't notice, but the wives certainly did. While they made little jokes about how I must be cutting calories to fit into a wedding dress I hadn't picked out yet, I came to a decision: I had to fundamentally change my relationship with alcohol and drugs. These people wouldn't be able to use me to reinforce cultural stereotypes. I wouldn't let them. I would be the exception to the rule. I would be respected.

Ma influenced my decision, too, unfortunately. Seeing what she was becoming, what the drugs made her, helped scare me straight. Her sleeping through commitments she'd made, or not remembering hurtful things she'd said while high, which she'd deny up and down if you brought them up to her once she was sober and herself again. The worst part for me was when she'd slide into that peculiar, almost-slow-motion way she spoke when really gone, which both terrified me and made me question whether I was fucked up and imagining all of it. It was always a possibility.

So I started tapering off my weed and beer intake, gradually. *Only half a joint today, but no beer.* Or *No weed today, but one beer before bed if the trees get really loud. Just to shut them up.* A seesaw of sobering until I was cleaned out. Somehow, miraculously, there were no voices to shut up when I was done. I was like a new woman. It was the first time I'd known real, true quiet since that night with Pocahontas all those years ago. I was determined to keep it that way.

I check the time. Five more minutes left to sit in this soak. I put the phone down and stare at different parts of the bathroom I've never given much thought to. The spring that keeps the door from slamming into the wall. The little cracks of hardened white gunk between the tiles under my feet. The sink drain clogged with strands of my long black hair.

No. Not hair. Those strands just moved.

I sit very still and watch. Slowly, silently, it emerges: two antennae, moving fast and with purpose. Then a shiny body that starts dark brown but smooths into a light amber color, the size and shape of an almond. Its tiny legs move jerkily as it speeds up white porcelain toward me. A cockroach.

I want to jump up, to run, but again I can't move. I want to scream, but I can't breathe. My entire body feels like it's made up of cockroaches, all crawling in different directions under my skin. I watch helplessly as it emerges from the sink, scurries up the sides, mounts the lip of the sink, and stares at me. Like it's daring me to do something. Like it knows I can't move. It's inches from my face, its antennae speeding up, its black eyes like pits as they stare into me.

A flurry of knocks at the door.

"Babe? I don't mean to rush you," Steve says. "It's been twenty minutes and Dawn's getting a bit antsy." Dawn makes gulping little half cries, as if Steve needs her confirmation.

I look at the door, then back at the sink. The cockroach is gone.

Warm blood rushes back into my body. I jump up, accidentally splashing some medicine on my pants. Eyes darting around the room for any sign of the roach. Nothing but white linoleum and tile. The scent of fake lemons from cleaning products.

I grab a towel and start to dry off.

"Oh my gosh, I'm so sorry! I lost track of time," I manage, slowly summoning up myself again.

I don't know why I'm freaking out. It was just a roach. There are probably millions of them in Toronto. Billions, even. No need to mention anything to Steve, or anyone. Like Meghan's DVDs and the burned dinner, it can be my little secret. I open the door only once I'm sure I look perfect.

"Where's Mama's little girl?" I ask, holding out my arms for Dawn. Her eyes lock on to mine and, for that split second Steve is passing her to me, her face looks exactly like Ma's from my nightmares—skin melting, lips stuck in a sadistic smile. The words from last week whisper in my ear once more: *It's all burning.*

I pull Dawn tight against my chest so I can't see her face, then brush past Steve.

"Well?" he asks, loyally following behind like a golden retriever. "Did the tea work? Do you feel better?"

"Totally," I say, my hand cupping Dawn's soft neck as I focus on her smell—baby shampoo, not burning flesh. She's fine. I'm fine. We're fine. I'll make sure we are.

CHAPTER 5

Aunty Bling Can't Solve Everything

Turn," Aunt Rachel commands, her cell phone sideways in her heavily ringed hands.

"Which way?" I ask, staring straight ahead.

"It's the same earring on both sides, Alice. Pick one."

I turn to the left and wait as she rearranges my hair behind that ear. The earrings are heavy: one large golden jingle dress cone at the top, with long strands of black seed beads coming out of the opening, slowly turning to gold beads at the ends, where tiny little matching gold jingle dress cones hang. Dana, wearing black skinny jeans, black platform shoes with tons of silver buckles that seem mostly for show, and a black *It* sweater even though it's hot, looks up with an amused, black-lipped smile. She holds Dawn in one arm and her cell phone in the other, a bottle of pre-pumped breast milk balanced against her chin as her fingers constantly slide across, then tap on the screen.

We're on the patio behind my house because, according to Aunt Rachel, natural light is always better in pictures than artificial. I'd asked Aunt Rachel if the two of them could come visit this morning. I'd been missing them desperately in the last month, and clearly it was taking a toll on me. *It's all burning* was starting to feel like a warning, a prophecy. I hoped the presence of Aunt Rachel and Dana would bring the warmth and comfort it always had when I was a kid. A reminder that I belonged somewhere.

"Your mom always so sweet these days?" I ask Dana as Aunt Rachel steps back, steadies her phone, then pushes a button that makes a bright white light flash in my right eye.

"Shit. I forgot to turn off the flash. Don't you dare move," Aunt Rachel says as she focuses on her phone.

"What do you think?" Dana replies dryly. She puts down her own phone and switches the way she's holding Dawn, cuddling her in tight as she pats her softly on her back to burp her. It's amazing how good Dana is with her. I remember when I held Dana for the first time. I was seven, and even though Aunt Rachel had coached me on exactly what to do, where to place my hands and how to hold my arms, I still almost dropped her. The fact that Aunt Rachel let me babysit Dana after that continues to boggle my mind. It's strange to see the young woman I'll probably always think of as my little baby cousin holding my baby now—a sort of full-circle moment I'd never really anticipated. I drink in the sight, watching them together. My little baby in a short-sleeved onesie, her back not much bigger than Dana's hand, her chubby bare legs and arms creasing in the cutest way.

Then Dawn lets out a burp followed by a trickle of thick white spit-up.

"Uh, Alice?" Dana looks to me, helpless, but I don't want to take the baby. I need this break. "Ewww," she whines as if in response, staring at the curdled white gunk on her sweater.

"Oh, for crying out loud." Aunt Rachel immediately grabs a receiving blanket from the table and tosses it at Dana's face. "Who's the baby now?" she asks.

"Whatever, it's gross," Dana mumbles.

Aunt Rachel ignores her and turns back to me, taking more photos. "Dana's the one who got me on Instagram. Did you know there are girls on there who sell out their entire stock within minutes of posting? I'd never have to go on the pow-wow trail again."

"I thought you liked visiting all the different rezes."

"Sure I do. But I've never sold my entire stock at a single pow-wow. Far from it." Aunt Rachel chuckles before pausing to swipe through her pictures. "Okay, I think we got it. You can take them off now."

I pull the earrings out of my earlobes, then carefully place them down on the glass table. There are at least twenty more pairs—each a different combination of colored seed beads and jingle bell cones.

"Are you selling all of these?"

"Heck no! Not all at once, anyway. I'm only probably putting up ten or so for now. You remember that movie *Willy Wonka & the Chocolate Factory*?"

"That Tim Burton movie where Johnny Depp acts right creepy?" Dana asks.

"Excuse me. Gene Wilder is the only Willy Wonka we acknowledge in this family. He never lied about being an Indian so he could wear a goddamn dead crow on his head for a movie. And a shit movie at that. Tonto, my ass."

"Who's Gene Wilder?" Dana asks. I laugh out loud.

"Have I never showed you his Willy Wonka?" Aunt Rachel asks. "What about *The Producers*? Did I show you that?"

"No . . ."

"*Young Frankenstein*?"

"Never heard of that in my life."

"That's it. We're watching a Gene Wilder marathon as soon as we get home."

Dana rolls her eyes with panache. "Whatever."

"That's the most excited I've seen her in weeks." Aunt Rachel smiles as she throws herself down in the chair across from me. Dana makes a face.

"I used to think my life was like the scene with Veruca Salt and the golden goose. Like, if I made a decision, I'd have to step on a scale, and either it'd be good and I could step off and be safe, or it'd be bad and the ground would fall out from under me. I'd slide away into the dark," I say too quickly and without thinking. When I look up, Aunt Rachel and Dana are sharing a look that immediately makes me ashamed. Why did I say that? Why did I even remember? I laugh, try to play it off.

"Wow, I haven't thought about that in so long. It's weird, huh? The way movies stick with you."

"They're supposed to stick with you. The good ones, anyway. Heck, I'll always remember the song that spoiled girl sings in that scene. 'I want the whole world.' Who doesn't, innit?" Aunt Rachel laughs, generous as always. I've never really thought about it before, but there are parallels between that movie and my life. My golden ticket was marrying Steve. The thing is, in the movie, the golden tickets weren't all that good in the end. They led everyone who got them to traps specifically designed for them. If Steve's my golden ticket, does that mean he's leading me into a trap? Is that why he didn't want me to have my cousins over anymore? Where is he anyway? He should have been home by now.

"Anyway, my point is, I wanna make buying these earrings feel like finding a golden ticket," Aunt Rachel proclaims, tapping insistently on the glass table with her finger and interrupting my train of thought. "To do that, I have to release only enough to guarantee I sell out. You know what they say: limit supply, make demand go sky-high."

"Who says that?" I ask, thankful for the distraction. I'm being weird and paranoid.

"Successful entrepreneurs," Aunt Rachel replies, a little defensively.

"Mom's been taking marketing classes online," Dana explains without looking up from her phone. "She has to steal Wi-Fi from the McDonald's over in Caledonia cuz the rez internet sucks so bad."

"I'm sure McDonald's doesn't mind. I've seen dudes watch hard-core porn in there before," I say.

"Alice!" Aunt Rachel exclaims, leaning over to smack my arm. "Don't be so nasty!"

Dana and I exchange a look, then laugh. There's something for-ever funny about a scandalized aunty.

"So when did you start those classes anyway?"

Aunt Rachel and Dana both lock eyes for a second, their faces suddenly grave, as if they're telepathically discussing what the an-swer should be. This can mean only one thing. I hold my breath and wait to see whether they address it outright or not.

"Oh, about three months ago," Aunt Rachel says, verifying what I'd already assumed. She started them after Ma died. Dana seems satisfied with this answer and goes back to looking at her phone. "Took one on photography, too. Learning's been a useful dis-traction."

I look out across the backyard. It isn't big—no one has big back-yards in this part of Toronto—but it has a few trees and it's big enough to imagine Ma turning it into some sort of garden oasis. I can picture the giant white pots she'd set up along the edges of the patio, the medicines she'd plant, labeling each one with some cute little sign she'd buy from the dollar store. Here, now, with me, the space is wasted. It didn't have to be. Steve had asked if I wanted him to arrange a garden like Ma might have made. Said he'd even be sure there was a patch of milkweed to attract monarch butterflies, her favorite. I told him it was too soon.

"Speaking of distractions . . ." Aunt Rachel points with her lips over to the inside of the sliding glass doors, where Steve is pulling off a light blue button-up shirt to reveal a white tank top, his muscled arms and shoulders looking appealing as ever. She wiggles her eyebrows at me.

I look past her at Steve again. He hasn't turned to look at us yet. I have no idea how he'll react. "I know we said we were gonna try to do all the parenting on our own so we could strengthen our family bond, I'd texted him, but Aunt Rachel and Dana are in town and want to pop over and see Dawn." He didn't respond all day, which makes me nervous. I've never seen him really angry before. I've never given him reason to be.

"And you said I was being nasty," I say, hoping I look nonchalant as I take a sip of lemonade.

"You were!"

"You're both nasty," Dana says as she stands, her hand cradling Dawn's neck perfectly as she holds her. "And so's this little girl's diaper." She starts to walk toward me.

"You got two hands. Why don't you do something about it?" Aunt Rachel asks.

For a second Dana stands there, mouth open, and I'm thinking she's going to refuse, but sure enough, she pulls Dawn back to her and says, "Fine. 'Scuse us."

We watch as she strides easily across the patio, pulls the door open, then steps inside. She stops to talk to Steve, who doesn't seem angry at all—at least when he's interacting with her. He points her in the direction of Dawn's bedroom, then she and Dawn disappear. I'm amazed at Dana's independence, the way she takes responsibility for whatever it is she needs to do and just does it. I hope Dawn's like that when she's her age—not cripplingly indecisive, like me. When I look back at Aunt Rachel, her eyes are narrowed.

"You and him okay, my love?" she asks quietly, as if she's been reading my mind.

I shrug. "We're fine. Managing."

"Mhmm," she replies. Her voice is skeptical, but she doesn't press. "And you? Everything okay with you? You've had to shoulder a lot lately." She looks like she wants to say more, but she stops herself instead and watches me. I know her eyes are cataloging each muscle twitch and blink I make, so I keep my face neutral.

"I guess. I mean, I didn't know it was possible to be this tired and still not be able to sleep." I look down at the glass table.

"I sure don't miss that part. It's hard being a new mom. In ways it isn't necessarily hard to be a new dad," Aunt Rachel says. Before I can ask her what she means by that, she leans forward, takes my hands in hers, and looks me right in my eyes. "But that's not exactly what I meant. Have you given any thought to her one-year feast?"

I stiffen. "That's still months away."

"It's gonna come up quicker than you'd think. If you want, I can ask a chief from one of the other clans to come. So he can do a full, proper condolence ceremony for you . . . and all of us."

I don't want to think about Ma's one-year feast. I'm still trying to forget that disastrous first attempt at a condolence at her funeral, where I fucked it all up. I don't know why I was so blindsided. I should have known that it was coming. It was the same at nearly all the funerals on Six Nations: a clear-minded person from outside the immediate family would say informal words of condolence to the immediate, grieving family, which they would accept. But when Melita's stepdad, Uncle Billy, started talking about how we were suffering a great loss, and telling us to remember Ma and all she'd given us, I didn't realize what was happening. Not until he mentioned

Ma's spirit would only linger for ten days after she died. After that, he said, it was our responsibility to her spirit to let her go so she could rejoin the ancestors waiting for her.

"NO!" I wailed before he could continue. Sobs like screams poured from me. I refused to let Ma go, swore at Uncle Bill for expecting me to, practically spit venom at my aunties for springing this on me. I was a woman possessed. Everyone stopped, unsure what to do. They didn't know that the circumstances around Ma's death were not exactly what they'd thought. That I was not only devastated but also harboring a suffocating guilt, which I would not allow to be cleared away by Uncle Billy's words, or anything else. Then I felt Melita's hand on my arm, leading me out of the room, and I heard Aunt Rachel's voice come forth to accept the condolence. "I acknowledge what has been said, and I accept these words. Even though our sadness is a heavy burden, after ten days we will place that burden down so we can carry on with our duties to life . . ."

I was so angry and ashamed that I skipped Ma's ten-day feast, telling my family I had a doctor's appointment I couldn't reschedule. I could hear the disappointment, the concern, in their voices, but they didn't say anything outright. Instead, they made Ma's favorite foods, served a plate for her spirit, and went ahead with the feast like they were supposed to. And, since I didn't come back in the days following, they took all her possessions I'd started gathering out of her trailer and gave them away, like they were supposed to. We weren't to hold on to anything that might remind us too much of her and feed our grief, because we had to focus on our own responsibilities to those still living. By the time I finally showed up, there was almost nothing left to save.

I realize Aunt Rachel is offering me a do-over right now. A more structured, formal condolence ceremony—and led by a chief. He'd probably tell the story of its creation as he did it: how Hiawatha came up with the first condolence ceremony while grieving the deaths of his entire family, hoping the words would raise other mourning, nearly mad minds back to reason. It was a story Dad had told many times. *The offer's so generous. I don't deserve it.*

I begin to shake my head when Aunt Rachel interrupts.

"You know they're still with you, right? Both of them? And they're so proud of you. But you have to let them go and come back *here*." She shakes my hand between hers, desperate.

I look into her eyes—the deep brown on the outside melting into amber in the center—and I see Ma. Their eyes were always so similar. I bite the inside of my cheek to keep from crying. The one-year feast is supposed to be when Ma's spirit comes back one last time, and after that her life cycle is finally complete. *But what if I don't want to let her go? What if I can't?*

"I-I . . . ," I stutter. "She . . . I . . . ." I stop trying. I don't know what to say. I don't want to lie to my aunt, but I also can't bear to tell her the truth. *Of course* I'm still stuck on Ma and what happened to her. *Of course* it's impacting how I mother Dawn. I'm sure Aunt Rachel and Dawn know that, despite my facade. But to admit it out loud would be to admit that I fail at everything, even grieving.

The patio door opens again, and I use the opportunity to pull away. Steve comes out in his tank top and dress pants. He's carrying a plastic bag, which he places on the table.

"Aunty Rachel," he says warmly as he leans in to give her a hug. If he is annoyed, he's hiding it well. "How're things?"

"Oh, fine. You know how it is down the bush. Same shit, different day," she says with a grunt of a laugh. "I was just asking Alice how things are going since Baby came. You two doing okay?"

I'm quietly thankful she didn't mention what we'd actually just been talking about, even as I see what looks suspiciously like a conspiratorial look passing between Aunt Rachel and Steve. Have they been talking to each other in secret?

Steve sits beside me, his attention on my face, as if gauging what I've already said, then he turns back to her. "It's been amazing!" He laughs. "Don't get me wrong—the hardest was the first few weeks. But we've adjusted pretty well now." He looks totally sincere, and I suppose he is.

Aunt Rachel nods. "Well, don't forget we're here if you need us."

She pivots then, telling him about her entrepreneurial plans. He gushes over the earrings, then they go through pictures of me wearing them, looking back and forth between my face and the phone screen. I squirm under their combined attention, worried they'll notice how wet my eyes are.

"Whatcha got there?" I ask, gesturing to the plastic bag, eager to change the subject.

"Oh." Steve reaches into the bag and pulls out a roll of tape. "I grabbed some plaid duct tape for Dana's prom dress. She said she still needed a few more."

"How'd you know about that?" I ask. Has he been secretly talking to Dana, too?

"I follow her on Instagram," Steve says simply. Of course. I'm just being paranoid. Even if Steve was talking to my family without my knowledge, I remind myself, that's not necessarily a bad thing. It's proof he loves them and considers them his family, too. "I called a couple craft stores nearby on a whim, and it turned out they had the right tape, so I popped over on my way home. That's why I'm late."

Aunt Rachel smiles big as she shoots me a look, a raised eyebrows, can-you-believe-this-guy kind of look. "We didn't even notice you were late. Did we, Alice?"

"Nope." I smile.

"Well, don't let me interrupt the photo shoot," Steve says as he gets up. "I'm assuming pizza's okay for dinner?"

Right. Dinner. I'd totally forgotten. How does Steve always know the right thing to say, to do? How does he know the perfect time and way to leave conversations? Maybe that's what wealth affords. I imagine him learning all the perfect social cues in some private school classroom from a teacher with their PhD in psychology at the same time I was learning how to cook Hamburger Helper from the back of the box because Ma was pulling another double shift at the smoke shop. Those social cues are, in turn, something he can teach Dawn so she floats through life charming everyone, just like him. Me, on the other hand? I'll gladly keep my cooking-while-poor classes to myself. She'll never eat Hamburger Helper in her entire fucking life. Not if I can help it.

"Extra cheese and pepperoni, please," Aunt Rachel says.

"Did you remember your lactose pills?" I ask her.

Steve smiles at us and says, "There's some in the bag," and I watch him walk away. I'm so proud that he's mine—that somehow, some way, I captured him. Maybe even tricked him. In that way, at least, I've succeeded as a mother: by giving Dawn a father who loves her, needs her. I can be proud of that.

Before they leave, there's a moment where Dana and I are alone in the kitchen, pulling slices of pizza onto our plates. It suddenly occurs to me to ask her about that night with Pocahontas and Mason. Whether she remembers talking to a cartoon character, too. She'd said Pocahontas sang the song wrong that night, I remember. For some reason it had never occurred to me to double-check with her about it until right now. But I can't figure out how to bring it up without sounding crazy, so I let the moment pass.

CHAPTER 6

Better Feuds and Gardens

P lease," I plead as I once more push my nipple against Dawn's shrieking maw. I've been trying to get her to latch on for the last twenty minutes. I know she's thirsty. I can tell by the desperation of her cries and how long it's been since her last feeding. But it doesn't matter. She won't drink from me. She thinks my milk is poison. That I'm poison.

Every time I look at Dawn—blue-eyed, light-brown-skinned, a handful of smooth brown hairs swiped across her head like a little biracial Homer Simpson—I'm expecting some supernatural aha moment, the kind that slides everything into focus like the perfect pair of glasses, and there's . . . nothing. Barely even recognition. I don't know her. She doesn't know me. We're strangers to each other. It's disappointing. It's terrifying. It's not love.

Love was when I first told Steve I was pregnant. I'd never seen someone so happy. Every woman wants to be looked at the way he looked at me in that moment. It was like everything he felt for me was newer, deeper, more reckless. A love that took two neat, separate lives and smashed them together with gleeful abandon. What was left was pure and raw like new skin on a scar—just as perfect, just as vulnerable.

Before the pregnancy, I had nothing to anchor myself to but my impending marriage and Steve's love. If I lost either, what would I have? Where would I be? Right back in Ma's trailer on the rez, smoking myself stupid. As soon as I saw that pink little plus sign, I knew it was my answer. It was how I could make sure Steve needed me just as badly as I needed him. I couldn't have an abortion. I couldn't even mention it. It didn't matter that I didn't feel ready to have a child. I'd deal with pregnancy, childbirth, and motherhood because I wanted to keep Steve more than I'd wanted any other thing. He was the stability I'd been looking for all my life: the one I wanted to become better for, deserving of. He inspired me in ways I'd never been inspired, made it seem possible for me to succeed, to believe in that possibility. He gave me hope. Besides, how hard could having a baby really be? Teenagers did it all the time.

Nothing I thought back then made sense, but I didn't know that. I couldn't. Being loved by Steve was too addictive. I needed him to look at me with those wondrous, worshipful eyes all the time. As long as I could keep him looking at me like that, I thought, everything else would be worth it. Meaning would come, as surely as the baby inside me, who I assumed would also, inevitably, bring a meaning all her own. There were fears I swallowed down: that I was too selfish to be a good mother, that my child wasn't even born and I was already putting too much pressure on her to bring some radical change or realization. That my tornado of problems would suck my child right in and, one day, leave her mangled in our family's intergenerational wreckage. My biggest fear was the birth would come and go, my child deposited into my waiting arms, and nothing would change at all. And now, it seems, those fears were entirely valid.

Dawn turns her splotchy face away, then turns back, and I use that split second to drop my whole breast into her mouth. For a moment it seems like I'm choking her, suffocating her with my flesh and drowning her in my milk, but then she starts to swallow and I can feel the tension in my body release slightly, slowly, like a tire pricked with a pin.

Before I can relax into the rocking chair, though, Dawn suddenly pulls herself off me and sputters as milk squirts onto her face. Her squeals fire up again, this time with even more fury. My breasts are hard, heavy, and painful against my chest, the milk leaking from my scabby nipples, flowing over my hands and between my fingers, making me wet and sticky and disgusting. I grab the white burping cloth covered with bright, beaming cartoon animals. My breath gets short and fast. The tears burst forth faster. Soon I can barely see or breathe as I dab at Dawn's face, trying to clean it. She's still screaming. She won't stop screaming. I don't know how long I can deal with this.

"Why don't you love me?" I ask her between gulps of air. "Why aren't I enough?"

Thud thud thud thud thud.

Someone's coming up the stairs. Fuck. What time is it? I manage to yank my T-shirt down and wipe my eyes with the burp cloth before Steve rounds the corner, all smiles despite the noise. I leap from the rocking chair like he's caught me committing a crime.

"There are my gorgeous girls!"

"Take her," I say as I cross the room, arms outstretched, offering her to him. Concern flickers on his face, but he does. Almost as soon as he touches her the yelps start to slow. My initial relief is immediately overcome by an almost physical pain: She wants him. Prefers him. Like everyone back home. Everyone who meets him. Fucking figures.

"Is it dinnertime already?" I ask, clutching my anxious stomach with one hand, then pushing past him quickly so he won't see my waterlogged eyes. I head to the bathroom. "I'm sorry, I must have lost track of time."

"Relax, babe. It's only eleven a.m." Steve and Dawn are following me down the hallway, because of course they are. Heaven forbid I get a moment to myself. "I was working on a grant application but the weather is too amazing to spend the day indoors. I figured we could go for a walk to Christie Pits or something. Take advantage of the sun."

I'm splashing water on my face from the sink so he can't hear me sigh. I scrub at my eyes harder than I should, trying to come up with an excuse.

"Dawn still needs to eat. I've been trying to feed her, but she refuses to nurse from me."

I can see Steve smile in the mirror as if I've said something funny. "Oh, come on. Don't you think that's a bit dramatic? She didn't *refuse*. She's a baby. She doesn't even know how to refuse."

"What else would you call it when she literally turns her head away from my breasts and spits out my milk?" I ask, my voice raising a bit in desperation.

"To say she 'refuses' to nurse makes it sound like you think she's making a conscious decision to not drink. Like she's a brat trying to show you who's boss."

I don't know what to say. How to argue against what he's saying. How to better explain what I'm feeling. Is he implying I'm a bad mom? That this is my fault and I can't even talk about it properly? I am a bad mom, of course, and I can't talk about it properly, but he's not supposed to know that. I'm supposed to make sure he doesn't. That's my one fucking job. Failure, that old, familiar friend, stomps down on the gas pedal of my anxiety. I have no idea how to fix any of this. It all seems too big, too difficult for me to comprehend. I shrug, helpless.

"I can make her up a bottle of formula right now. We can it bring with us to the park."

"I'm not ready to go out. I haven't put on deodorant. I haven't brushed my teeth. I'm not even wearing a bra." I rush my words out, hope I don't cry.

"So put on a bra and deodorant and let's go."

I stare at him, confused. Why is he rushing me? As if he hasn't told me countless times after I stopped dressing so rezzy how much he appreciates my taking time to look good for him. As if he expected me to merely wiggle my nose and be ready to go.

"Steve, I need time to change and fix my hair—"

He laughs. "What's wrong with what you're wearing? We're going to the park, not the Met Gala."

I don't know what to do. The rules have changed without my knowing. Now I'm vain if I want to take time to look nice. I'm selfish, an inconvenience. And if I acknowledge this sudden change in expectations, how it goes against all the hints he's given, it could start an argument. I feel like I'm fighting with Ma again. One of those times she demanded I take her to a community meeting or bingo when I knew she was less than a half hour from nodding off. I'm sliding back into the old Alice—angry and resentful, but trying so hard not to show it. Have I ever really stopped being that Alice? I pick up a washcloth and scrub at my face hard. "I don't know, Steve," I say into the softness I'm making rough.

"Come onnnnnn!" he whines, dramatic as a toddler. I peek up at the mirror. "Don't you want to go on a cute little family outing with us?" He holds Dawn by her armpits so their faces are next to each other, then thrusts out his bottom lip so he looks sad like her. "We can get ice cream on the way home."

I want to scream and cry and drink whatever alcohol I can get my hands on.

But I can't let myself go like that.

I need to suck it up.

And that's how Steve manages to get me out of the house in an oversized black racetrack T-shirt I still had from when I was thirteen, a pair of white basketball shorts, and some black Adidas slide sandals. I had enough time to throw my hair into a messy bun and brush my teeth while Steve made up a bottle for Dawn, but that was it. It's the most rez I've allowed myself to look in public since moving to Toronto. And, as we walk west down Bloor Street together, him pushing the stroller and me trudging along next to him like a lost little girl, I feel that displacement heat my cheeks.

"Is it just me or is everyone staring at me right now?" I ask Steve, interrupting his long-winded complaints about the specifications of the grant he was currently in the middle of applying for. "I told you I should have changed first."

He shakes his head, then gives a cursory glance at the polished, put-together people passing us. "No one's looking at you, babe. They're all too busy worrying about their own outfits to worry about yours. Trust me."

But I can *feel* the stares like little pinpricks on my skin. I watch the people as they approach. At first they seem to be ignoring me, like Steve said. But then, just before they pass, their eyes dart at me, their faces scrunching up like they smell something rank. It happens four times in a row the exact same way. I can't focus on anything else. While I'm looking at the next pedestrian coming toward me—a beautiful Asian woman in a matching pastel-pink tank top and skirt set—waiting for her to pass to the right of my husband and the stroller and sneer at me at the last second, a shoulder knocks into me from the left. The force makes me spin around, and I see a hulking white man with no shirt retreating.

"What the hell?" I ask, anxious, as the man turns and gives me the finger.

Steve doesn't say anything, but he must have seen it, because he stops pushing the stroller for a second and digs into his pockets.

"Don't worry about it. It was my fault," I say as I watch him tap around on his phone. Is he calling the cops? People are definitely staring now, clicking their tongues as they have to swerve around us. The shirtless man is jogging again. He's at least two blocks away.

"What's your fault?" he asks. I stare at him, confused. Did he seriously not notice what just happened? What's still happening? The strangers passing are laughing.

"I don't under—"

"Here," he says, offering his earbuds. "Listen to this. It helps anytime I'm feeling weird or anxious. It works, I swear."

I hesitate, my mind cloudy. How the hell will whatever's gonna play on those earbuds protect me from asshole joggers? Or any of these people?

"What is it?"

He looks down at the earbuds, then looks back at me, smiling. "Only one way to find out."

I look down at them, then back up at him. Remember I have an image to rehabilitate. I roll my eyes, pick up the earbuds, put them in, and wait. He presses the play button on his phone and watches my face. There's what sounds like a funeral organ, then a solemn speaking voice comes in. I know the song immediately, each note a balm.

I smile. "Really? Prince?"

"Who else?" he asks.

"I didn't even know you liked him," I say, amused.

"Everyone likes Prince," he says. It's true—even Ma was obsessed with "Little Red Corvette."

"'Let's Go Crazy' is pure joy in a song. But don't listen to me. Listen to that killer guitar solo."

I focus back on Prince's eulogy. The drum machine starts, and my head bobs. Steve smiles and pushes the stroller again, but I feel stuck there, trapped by the power of Prince. He says the words with so much passion, and the keyboards are incredibly addictive, and the song is full of such energy and whimsy that I can't help but feel joyful. The sun is warm on my skin, and I'm out with my husband and daughter. No one is crying or hurt, and things are *good*. They are, regardless of my brain's best attempts to ruin them. I weave through people to catch back up with my family, giddy as a child.

When we get to Christie Pits I pass the earbuds back to Steve and we find a densely shaded tree near the playground to sit beneath. Both of us forgot to pack a blanket to sit on, so we take turns plopping ourselves down on the grass: first Steve, then I pass him Dawn, then I throw myself haphazardly next to them. As soon as he touches Dawn's lips with the rubber nipple they part like they're supposed to, then he pushes the bottle in and she drinks like she's supposed to.

"I don't know why she isn't easy like that when I try to feed her. I try, I really do. I—" my voice breaks and I clear my throat in an attempt to cover it. "I don't know what I'm doing wrong," I finish, then immediately regret.

This time Steve looks at me with tenderness. "This isn't a 'you' problem. You know that, right? Your midwife told us lots of new moms have a hard time getting their babies to latch on. Remember?"

"Yeah, but at six weeks? I should have it down by now. Shouldn't I?"

Steve passes me the bottle to hold, then pulls out his phone. Dawn lets out a little annoyed yelp. "Let's consult Dr. Google."

I look around as he enters the search and filters through the results. There are so many other mothers here. Mothers trundling along with their babies in strollers. Mothers running after their toddlers. Mothers pushing their giggling kids higher and higher on the swings. Mothers distributing carefully prepared snacks. There are fathers, too, but I'm not focused on them. I'm focused on the mothers, wondering how they're so put together and confident while parenting. Is it something they learned watching their own mothers and studying countless books, memorizing all the rules and tips and tricks, or is it something they were born with, a dormant skill lying in wait until pregnancy hormones activated it?

"Ah! Here we go. Why does my six-week-old keep unlatching?" Steve reads. "Your baby may unlatch when the milk is coming out faster than baby can swallow. This makes it so baby has to take breaks so as not to become overwhelmed."

That does sound like what happened earlier. Maybe I'm not as bad a mother as I assumed. A hopeful thought. "So how do I fix it?"

"Says to try breast compressions, take a couple minutes' break, then try again."

I don't even know what breast compressions are. "Can I see that?" I ask, and he passes over his phone. I type in "what are breast compressions" and hit enter. The screen is filled with symbols that look nothing like letters. I worry that I've accidentally changed the language on the browser, but it doesn't look like any language I've ever seen. The words seem to writhe into and out of one another, as if they're all part of one giant organism, panting. I scroll up and down, pretending I'm reading, then, once I'm sure that Steve is focused on burping Dawn, I shut my eyes for a few seconds, hoping the action will work like a reset button. When I open them back up, the words are words again.

I click on a detailed how-to page, but even though it's definitely in English, it's written confusingly with lots of steps and steps-within-steps and warnings about areola shapes and baby's pauses between sucks that makes it sound more like a military operation than a common breastfeeding technique. The sounds of shrieking and cackling children, of yammering and laughing adults, fill my head. I can't focus on the sentences long enough to understand what they're saying. I keep reading the same step over and over and it keeps sliding from my intellectual grasp like water through my fingers. Exasperated, I close the page and pass the phone back to Steve. I'll look at it when I'm at home and Dawn is asleep. But I do feel relieved there might be a solution.

"See? There's nothing wrong with you or Dawn. You're both still figuring everything out. You'll find your groove."

Dawn starts fussing a little, and Steve asks me to pass him back her bottle. As I hand it over, his fingers brush mine and I shiver. It's been a while since I've felt like that. Maybe my libido isn't totally dead after all.

I lean back to lie out on the grass. "I'm so tired of talking about baby stuff. You have no idea how much of my brainpower is taken up by this every day. Talk to me about normal adult stuff."

Steve laughs as he glances over my stretched-out body. "Pick your poison. Politics or pop culture?"

"Pop culture," I say quick. "Preferably something harmless."

"Let me think," Steve says as he stops feeding Dawn and props her on his shoulder to burp. "Katy Perry and Taylor Swift aren't feuding anymore."

"Weren't they feuding over something boring like hiring the same dancers for their tours?" I ask.

"I'm not even sure. I heard some of my students talking about it before class. Seemed pretty juicy the way they told it."

"Oh, it was definitely juicy. They wrote songs trashing each other and everything. I swear, white girl feuds are on another level." I laugh. "On the rez, when you've got a problem with another girl, you get all your cousins together and the girl you hate gets all her cousins together, and you scrap. The whole thing's over in, like, an hour, tops."

"A purer way to settle things, perhaps."

Dawn lets out a tiny burp, and Steve makes an exaggerated face of shock at her. "Was that you?" he asks, his voice higher than ever. "Did my baby make that burp?" He kisses her one-two-three on her cheek, oblivious to anyone watching, then nestles her back into his chest and brings the bottle back to her lips. She obliges. I look at his face as he stares down at her, and her face as she stares up at him, and it's like they're sharing this light that brightens them each from within. I'm overcome with love for both of them. This moment seems like the most flawless thing I could ever witness— something above jealousy, something even a fuckup like me could never ruin.

Then Steve's phone dings. And dings again. And again.

"Someone's popular," I comment blithely as he repositions Dawn, picks up his phone, and pecks at the screen.

"Fuck," he says. "Can you take her?"

He passes her over, then springs up, phone to his ear as he

begins to pace. Dawn lets me feed her with the bottle with no problems, though I do notice her eyes aren't shining like they were before. I overhear enough to understand what's happening: "I thought that was rescheduled for next week?" and "No, don't worry. I'm getting an Uber over now."

"Guess we won't be getting ice cream after all," I say aloud to Dawn, as if she knows what ice cream is and is equally disappointed by this turn of events.

Steve has an important committee meeting he's evidently written down wrong in his calendar. And, since he chairs this committee, and he's trying for tenure this year, which would be the ultimate security for us, I have to smile understandingly as he races away.

I can't help feeling useless after he leaves. That brief moment of relief I felt watching him and Dawn already seems far away. The sun has shifted since we first sat down; it's shining hot on our hair and skin. I look at the tree behind us, trying to find more shade to scoot to, only to find there is none. The tree is lopsided. An image falls into my mind: a construction worker in a reflective vest wielding a screaming chain saw, cutting limbs from me in bloodless chunks. But the limbs aren't from me, I quickly realize. They're from this tree. This is a memory from this tree.

I can't offer any more shade. Your kind ripped that possibility from me, the tree says, quietly furious.

No. Stop. I don't want to talk to you.

"Are you okay? Miss?"

I come back and see a Black teen boy with a backward hat and a skateboard staring down. I must have said that out loud instead of in my head, again. Fuck.

"Oh, I'm fine! Just need to get out of this heat and get some rest.

So sorry to worry you!" I say, laughing lightly as I pack Dawn's bottle into her bag.

"You sure you don't need any help?" he says, hesitating.

"I'm sure. But thank you so much."

The teen shrugs and walks off. I'm shaking as I realize this is the first time I've heard trees talk to me in years. What does that mean? First the shapeshifting *Pocahontas* DVD, now this?

It takes forever for me to figure out how the hell to get up with Dawn still in my arms. I maneuver myself onto my knees, place one foot flat on the ground in front of me, push into a lunge position— all without putting any pressure on Dawn's body—then step forward into a standing position. My thighs burn the entire time. I'm so out of shape it's laughable.

As I pass the Baskin-Robbins on the corner of Bloor, I see my reflection in the window and shame blooms hot in my cheeks. I look a fucking fright. My face is as greasy as Tanya's frybread. Strands of hair are falling around my face, limp and flat. My shirt's stained, has holes, and, worse yet, has a giant race car and the Six Nay Speedway logo on the front. My basketball shorts are clearly losing their elasticity. I turn away and try to move faster down the street, keeping my eyes on the sidewalk in front of the stroller so I don't have to meet anyone else's gaze and watch the disgust creep across their face. Steve isn't there to distract me from reality, and neither is Prince. I can't shake the feeling that I'm escaping something more than that tree.

By the time I'm in front of our house, I'm ready to disappear inside and never come back out. Dawn has fallen asleep. Her little snores are so cute they cheer me up a little.

Until I realize I can't find my keys.

"You've got to be fucking kidding me."

I tear through the diaper bag, try the door, sneak around the side to see if there's maybe a window that I can pull open and squeeze inside. There's no way in. I text Steve and tell him we're locked out. I try the diaper bag again, dumping the contents on the front step next to me, then swear when some extra clothes fall off the step and into the mulch surrounding the bushes. I pick them up and try to wipe the dirt off.

"Excuse me." The voice is sharp, aggressive.

I turn around to see an older white woman, probably in her sixties, standing on the sidewalk in front of the house.

"Yes?" I ask, confused.

"This is a private neighborhood. Do you know the owners of that house?" Her face is stony and severe, her hand wrapped strangely around her phone.

"I sure do. It's my house. Or, mine and my husband's. I lost my keys. Obviously," I joke as I gesture toward the contents of the bag, hoping she'll loosen up and leave me alone.

"I've lived in this neighborhood for twenty years and I've never seen you."

The effort from trying not to yell at her makes me tremble. "Well, my name is Alice. My husband's name is Steve. And this," I say, as I push the stroller back and forth, hoping she doesn't see me shaking, "is our little girl, Dawn. We moved in, like, a year ago. Nice to meet you."

"You really must think I was born yesterday, huh?" She laughs.

"I just texted my husband to let him know I forgot the keys. I can show you the text if you want." I pull out my phone and start to pull up the texts, but it doesn't matter. She doesn't believe me. She doesn't care.

"I'm part of the neighborhood watch. When I say I've never seen you here, it means something." She brings her own phone up higher, and I see her camera is on. "I saw you sneaking around trying to open those windows. You trying to break into these nice peoples' home?"

"Are you filming me?" I ask, incredulous. "I'm not breaking in. I told you, it's my house. I'm locked out."

"Uh-huh. Let me ask you something, then. What would happen if I called the police right now? Would you hang around and tell them the same thing you told me or would you run away before they got here?"

I'm so fucking angry I want to explode. I can't hold it in any longer. I can't keep up the facade of polite respectability. It's not working and it's not going to work.

"Oh, you want to play?" I ask. I pull out my phone, turn on the camera, point it directly at her, and take two steps in her direction. "I came back from the park with my baby and couldn't find my keys," I narrate loudly as I walk closer to the woman, "and now this woman is filming me and harassing me outside my own house. Why don't you think I could live in this house, ma'am? Is it because I'm Native?"

"Stay away from me," the woman yells as she backs up. She sounds frantic, as if I'm attacking her.

"So you can film me, but I'm not allowed to film you? Why don't you tell the camera how I offered to show you texts to my husband proving I was locked out and you threatened to call the cops on me?" I press. "Would you be doing this if I was white?"

"Don't you dare imply—I'm doing my job—I saw you trying to break in," she says as she continues to back away, though her voice sounds less sure.

"I told you my name. Why don't you tell me yours? I'm sure people on the internet would love an introduction."

At that, the woman turns away and I hear the words, spit like venom: *Fucking no good Indian.*

"What was that? Can you repeat that for the camera?" I yell after her, waking Dawn, who breaks into tiny yelps. The woman hurries across the street and into her house, which I note is the one diagonal to mine. As soon as she's gone I feel all the bravado I'd faked melt away. I nearly collapse on the sidewalk. I brace myself on a tree, then manage to get back to Dawn's stroller and lift her out. My legs give out almost immediately, and I land on the steps, my ass so sore I'm sure it's going to bruise, the adrenaline still coursing through me, making my entire body vibrate.

"I know. I know," I say, crying along with Dawn in this neighborhood that clearly doesn't want either of us. "It's okay. Daddy will be home soon. I promise."

By the time Steve gets back, over an hour later, I've pushed Dawn's stroller to the backyard and we've set ourselves up on the patio. I couldn't stay on the front step. The woman kept peeking out her window at us. It was making me paranoid. I needed to get away from her eyes. I've decided not to post the video of that woman on Facebook. If she really is part of the neighborhood watch, making a public spectacle of her—making an enemy of her—would undoubtedly be bad for us. It's better if I don't tell Steve. He'd make it into a big deal. Part of me wishes I could just scrap with her. But she's an elder, even if she's an evil elder, so I can't. I have to do something, though, to stop her from talking shit about me all over the street. I think about Katy Perry and Taylor Swift. What would they do? To defeat white girl passive aggression, I need to channel white girl passive aggression.

I decide to tell Steve we should make little cards to put in all the neighbors' mailboxes. A little "Let us introduce ourselves." A little "We're so pleased to be part of your neighborhood!" A little "Can't wait for you to be part of our extended family!" Bullshit like that. And our family photo on the front, so none of them could ever claim they didn't "see" me ever a-fucking-gain.

"You don't think it's a little late?" Steve asks when I propose it. "It's not like we just moved in."

"Is it ever too late to get to know your neighbors?" I ask, sickly sweet.

Steve comes around. Says it's a great idea. He wonders why he hasn't thought of it before.

CHAPTER 7

Telling Lies,
Telling Sweet Little Lies

Steve is holding our daughter like a pro. He's smiling at her, lovingly, and I'm standing in the doorway wishing I'd never moved to Toronto. Yes, there's running water, and yes, the Wi-Fi is amazing, and yes, there are so many places to shop and eat you'd never get bored, but I feel alone in a way that I never knew was possible. That neighborhood watch woman yesterday made it so incredibly clear. I'm not safe, even in front of my own home. I'm lucky the prospect of being called a racist on the internet scared that woman as much as it did. If she'd called the cops, I'd have been fucked. They would have taken one look at me and either shot me or arrested me. They'd have taken Dawn and put her in the care of social services. I would have been helpless to stop any of it.

"You okay, babe?" Steve asks, pulling me out of my head.

"Yeah. Sorry. Was thinking about the story. You know, Sky Woman." It's a lie. I haven't even thought about writing in days. The lies come to my lips so easily now. I barely have to think about them. Or maybe it's that I'm always thinking about them, living a second life in my head—the one I pretend I live, and craft especially for observers so they think I'm fine—alongside the one I keep secret from everyone. The one I sometimes think started with Pocahontas, and other times think started before I was born, way back with my grandmother. Whenever someone asks, I borrow lines from that imagined life and insert them in the right spots.

"Oh, I meant to talk to you about that. You might want to consider using a name other than 'Sky Woman.'"

"Why?"

"My teacher called her something else in class the other day. I can't remember off the top of my head, but I can check for you. She was definitely known as something else up in Sky World."

"Do you think I should use her Onkwehón:we name?" I look away, ashamed I even have to ask him this.

"Maybe. I mean, if you want. It's your story. You're the boss."

He looks down at Dawn, pushes his thumb into the meat of her tiny fist until her fingers instinctively wrap tight around it.

"We're okay here if you want to go do some writing."

"Thanks, babe," I say.

I know I won't be able to write. Still, I have to at least pretend I'm working toward becoming the Alice we both pretend I'll one day be, so I turn to go. If I can't write anything I'll watch some celebrity gossip videos on YouTube. Halfway out the door, though, I see what looks like a cockroach scuttle into a vent. I keep very calm, my chest tight with anxiety, as I turn back to Steve. He's looking down at Dawn, oblivious.

"Have you seen any cockroaches in the house?"

"Cockroaches?" Steve asks, his voice rising in concern. "No. Have you?"

"No," I say automatically. "I just heard they're a really big problem in the city."

"Oh. Well, they are. But I've never had them any of the places I've

94

lived. Had some rats at my apartment in grad school, but once I told my mom about them she insisted I move back home. You know her."

I wonder for a moment what would happen if I did tell Steve I saw that cockroach. Would he tell Joan? Would she think it was my fault for not keeping things clean enough? Would she insist we all move into her giant house with her—a place where Black cleaning ladies with musical Caribbean accents keep the counters crumbless and the sinks cockroach-free? It's hard to think of a place more suffocating than her spotless home, which always smells of lavender and vanilla. She micromanages its cleanliness until every step you take feels preapproved—like there are little painted footprints on the floor for you to fit your socked feet in as you try your best not to disrupt.

"That I do," I say, forcing a smile as I walk out the door.

I t was my father who instilled in me a love of story. He instilled it in all of us. My cousins, Ma, and I knew when the stories were coming, because we'd see Dad loading his soapstone pipe with tobacco. He'd sing softly as he pushed the browning leaves into the bowl. It was a ritual for him—one he made sure we knew the importance of before he started any story.

"We bring our minds together as one and give thanks to Shonkwaia'tison for these stories. All our stories are a gift from Shonkwaia'tison, just like all of creation is his gift to us," he'd say as he lit the pipe. "The stories help us as Onkwehón:we to learn about ourselves, the world around us, and our place in the world. We offer up this tobacco as a prayer, in order to give thanks for these stories." Then he would puff on the pipe quietly. As he passed it to Ma to puff, we'd all squirm with anticipation for her to finish.

"And now . . . ," Dad started.

"And now our minds are one!" we'd yell in unison. It was an adaptation of the Thanksgiving Address, the words before all else. We were used to hearing Mohawk speakers recite the whole thing in our language at community meetings and events, but since we only knew English, we never understood it. Dad explained it to us: how those words reaffirmed our relationships with, and responsibilities to, the earth. By incorporating a mini, modified version of the Thanksgiving Address into our beloved storytelling sessions, he tried to make us invested in and proud of our culture. And it worked, for a long time. I'd even started trying to write little stories of my own for my dad, which were derivative of how he told his stories but which made him beam with pride as he read.

Then, after Dad died, I stopped writing completely. I focused on reading books from the nearby Caledonia library. Books that taught me Onkwehón:we people were not worthy of written stories. Books by authors who could imagine whole worlds where vampires, witches, and demons were real, where wizards fought dragons and lions could plot holy wars, but who couldn't imagine Native people existing as we were. As we still are.

I didn't start writing again until after the Pocahontas incident. The idea that the spirit of a Native woman was trapped in that movie, telling a fucked-up, historically inaccurate version of her story for all of eternity, haunted me. I couldn't stop thinking about Dad's unrealized dream: to retire one day and finally write a book of our traditional stories in a way that kept them alive for the next generation.

"Them folks from the universities think they know everything about our culture," he'd complained to Ma one night when he thought I wasn't paying attention. "That they can suck it all up like a vacuum cleaner, claim they're doing us a favor and 'preserving it,' then sell it back to us when we get desperate. It's not right. They don't own those stories! They belong to us, and the next seven generations after us. Heck, they don't know how to tell our stories right anyway! Their voices sounding like they've never been curious a day in their lives. Like they know everything there ever was."

I played those words in my head over and over, heartbroken that Dad would never get a chance to do what he always said he would. What if I could carry on his legacy? Make sure that our people knew our real history. What we were actually like. Our joys, our sorrows, our politics and complexities. I was convinced it was my duty to the next seven generations of Haudenosaunee girls to give them something to aspire to besides the Disneyfied lie that was *Pocahontas*.

But every time I submitted a story to a magazine or journal throughout those years, be it a magazine for teens or one for adults, I got rejected. I was still writing in a poor imitation of my father's voice, granted, but it wasn't like the stories that were getting published instead were that much better. They all sounded the same on the page—dead, the literary equivalent of a dial tone. There were no stakes in the writing. There was no urgency. And, just like Dad said, there was no curiosity. Was that really what I had to write like if I wanted to be published?

I never told anyone that I was writing—not Ma, not my cousins, not even Aunt Rachel. I didn't want them to know how much I was failing my father. I didn't want anyone to know my writing even existed until I had some sort of success. Until I showed them how eagerly I had gulped down Dad's lessons and made them into something vital and fresh. Given my lengthening list of rejections, who knew how long that would take?

Then, three years ago, after getting my second rejection from a high-profile creative writing workshop in two years, I decided I'd try an experiment. I spent the better part of two months researching the work of writers who had successfully gone through the workshop, then the next six months writing and rewriting my application. First I tried to imitate Ernest Hemingway, then James Joyce. Literary rock stars, their words riddled with testosterone, their very names emanating power. Each story I wrote from beneath their sizable shadows was like an ill-fitting suit. The situations I explored and the emotions I conjured felt nothing close to what I'd experienced—but then again, neither did pretty much any of the stories in any of the books I'd read.

Eventually I settled on a story to submit. It was about a married man falling in love with a teenage gas station attendant. The story was based on a bit of truth. When I turned fifteen, too old to sell 50/50 tickets anymore, I got hired to work as a cashier inside the gas station convenience store in front of the racetrack. Sarah, who I based the story on, worked the pumps outside, where her flirtatious smiles got her incredible tips. She and her married boyfriend met up at the store a few times a week. She was only seventeen then, with the sort of body men imagine all teen girls should have: perfect, perky tits; toned abs; a round, juicy ass that defied all Native flat-ass genetics and even started a rumor at school that she'd gotten butt implants over the summer before grade nine. But she also seemed incredibly lonely to me—the type of girl who told you too much about herself right away so you felt a sort of odd loyalty to her. She didn't have many girlfriends, just a small coterie of boys she kept around her, each vying for her undivided attention.

After her shift, she'd casually come in and do a cursory tour around the store—picking up snacks and setting them on the counter.

"These aren't for me," she'd once assured me after dumping a second bag of Doritos down. "They're for my brothers. I promised them snacks if they didn't rat me out to our parents."

That's how Sarah was. She'd give you just enough info to force you to ask the questions she desperately wanted to answer.

"Rat you out for what? Loitering?" I'd asked.

"No! Seeing Ed. You know Ed, right?" Of course I knew Ed. He owned the gas station, the racetrack, and at least two dozen smoke shops littered across the rez. He would come into the store before races, his hair gelled into what I can only assume was a fashionable style when he was in high school. He wore racing gear even though he couldn't race, and a bright, white, straight-teethed smile plastered to his face as he grabbed energy drinks from the cooler and strolled out, waving. He never paid for anything, never left a tip. Really rich guys were always stingy like that with their employees, it seemed.

Sarah dropped a two-liter of Pepsi on the counter with a thud, then promptly propped her elbows beside her stash and leaned in close. "Ed's my boyfriend."

"Isn't he married?"

"Shhhh!" She looked around in all directions, clearly loving this as she pantomimed a need for secrecy. "He has modeling connections, you know."

"Does he?"

"Right? I was surprised, too. I guess he knows some really fancy photographers in New York and L.A. He's gonna introduce me to them when they come down for the championship races."

And so it would go. Ed would eventually pull up, peek his head in the door, and Sarah would rush out into the passenger's seat of his latest BMW, the snacks I bagged in a hurry hanging from her tiny arm. Sarah eventually got addicted to coke, then eventually stopped showing up at the store, her posts on Myspace becoming more and more erratic. I heard she flew to L.A., but you wouldn't know from Ed's reaction. He never changed: hair always gelled the same, smile always implying he had no cares.

I wrote about their affair from Ed's perspective: a rich man who had everything but still ached for his lost youth—something he thought he could steal from his teenaged girlfriend as he fed her coke. At the end of the story, the girl overdoses, and the rich man realizes he should pay more attention to his family.

I got into the workshop. The problem was, I got in with a story I hated. I didn't care about men like Ed, and yet here I was, writing stories about them, setting up expectations that I would write about men like Ed forever, humanizing them in ways I didn't really think they should be humanized. I could have accepted the spot and written what I wanted once I got there, but the thought of meeting other writers, of having to explain that I didn't have an MFA or even a bachelor's degree to everyone who asked, the thought of leaving my mother . . . Worse, the thought of having to be grateful to some committee somewhere because they liked the way I'd stamped a Native face on "universal problems," otherwise known as problems legible to white folks, instead of stories that mattered to our people and arose from the land, the way Dad had always wanted—all of it was too much. I threw the acceptance in the trash and stopped writing again.

And now I'm here, staring at the cursor blink, as I wonder why the hell I decided I could write a modern version of our Creation Story. Yes, I'd written a short version when I was eight, and yes, Dad loved it. Even brought it to work and read it aloud to his buddies at lunch. But I'm a grown woman now; my attempts to write are no longer adorable. They carry weight. The Creation Story is our most important, well-known story. If I fuck it up, I could be misleading whole generations of Haudenosaunee to come—and whole generations of outsiders, to whom stories like this are their only entry point into understanding and humanizing us.

Fuck. I should never have started this. I should never have shown Steve my writing, or told him about my "big idea." He thinks he married an aspiring writer, who would become a real writer with the gift of time and his patronage. The problem is aspiring writers write. I've barely written anything since I got pregnant. And what I have written I've mostly deleted. The idea of sitting down and typing anything new terrifies me. I'm already failing at being a good mother, a good wife, a good daughter fulfilling her father's legacy. I don't need to add any more failures to the list.

But I also can't sit here and stare at this screen all night. I need to *do* something. Show some sort of goddamn initiative.

The cockroach. The words like a whisper behind my ear.

"Yes," I respond. "The cockroach."

CHAPTER 8

Buggin'

I head straight into the bathroom and plop on the toilet.

"Cockroach?" I call stupidly. "Come here, cockroach."

I tell myself I'm going to wait until the thing appears, then kill it myself, provide some safety for my family, but who knows if it's even going to show. We had mice in Ma's old trailer. Huge ones that defied all modern traps and the laws of physics. I once saw one crawling across the ceiling like the old woman in *The Exorcist III*. I screamed, and it paused to look at me, its thick, long body bloated, no doubt from the marshmallows we always found chewed up in shredded plastic in our pantry. It waited until my scream finished, as if baiting me, then continued creeping along toward the metal pantry door like nothing ever happened. The cockroach reminds me of that mouse. Both seem absolutely sure of their place in my home, while I feel like an unwelcome visitor passing through.

It's not just this house, though. It's the whole city. Toronto, or Tkaronto, as Melita always reminds me. Soon Steve probably will, too. It doesn't matter what anyone calls it. This city's a cold stranger of a space. I don't understand it at all. It's huge but somehow still feels too small, too crowded, laced tight with air that tastes of car exhaust and desperation, sometimes sewage, even. You can tell every person who was born here thinks they're hot shit because they know which bars are cool and which are only fit for alcoholics. Even worse, green space is seen as a luxury instead of a necessity—another way that humans place themselves in the center of creation, as though Copernicus never existed and the sheer, brute force of man was enough proof that every aspect of creation should, in fact, orbit around us. The plants on our street are all decorative; there are no medicines near me. I have to buy white sage from a crystal shop where white witches pay good money to pretend to be Native. And now there's the neighborhood watch lady to worry about. I talk to Meghan next door, but I'm sure our friendship is more her white liberal obligation than an actual connection. Just look at the DVDs she brought over.

I have to face the facts. I'm in a city of almost three million people and I'm alone.

"Not even the fucking cockroach will come when I want it to," I whisper as I place my head in my hands.

Then I hear them: tiny little taps.

When I look up, the cockroach sits on the lip of the sink exactly like it had before, its antennae moving so fast it distracts me.

"Holy shit." I leap from the toilet seat and stand back, near the door. My heart hammers inside my chest as I look around for something heavy enough to really squish it. Maybe the soap dispenser?

But just as I go to grab it, I remember my dad's admonitions when I was a kid. Once, when he saw me spitting on a pile of ants outside the trailer, he asked me angrily what I thought I was doing. I told him I was killing them because they were gross, my eyes downcast. "Everything has a purpose for being here, whether you know it or not. So if you're gonna kill that there ant, you better be ready to take up its responsibilities to its community after its gone. You gonna do that?" I shook my head, as full of shame then as I am now, staring at this insect that seems to expect my murderous intent.

I can't kill it anymore. Dammit.

I watch, helpless and paralyzed, as the cockroach scuttles down the sink closer to me.

I thought you should know—

Oh no. Fuck that. I will not open the door to conversations with bugs. I close my eyes and repeat the two-word mantra I used as a teen whenever things talked to me that shouldn't: "Go away go away go away."

When I look back up the cockroach is gone.

Two sharp raps: *One. Two.*

"Al? You okay in there? Why's the door locked?"

It's Steve. My head's tilted against the bathroom wall. I don't know how long I've been here, sitting on this fuzzy burgundy toilet cover, a housewarming present from Aunt Rachel that feels totally at odds with the rest of the house. My feet are both numb, tingles working their way up my legs.

"Yeah, I'm okay," I say. "What time is it?"

"Eleven twenty-two."

I've been in the bathroom for over an hour and a half.

"Shit," I say, rubbing at my eyes. "I must have fallen asleep. Sorry."

I don't remember falling asleep, but I also don't remember sitting back down—or enough time passing for both feet to lose circulation. My last memory is of staring at that black hole of a drain, wondering if the cockroach would come back.

"It's okay. I fell asleep with Dawn, too. Otherwise I'd have woken you sooner."

I brace myself against the walls and try to stand, but I can't.

"My feet are asleep. Can you help me up?"

The doorknob jiggles theatrically.

"It's locked, remember?" A bit of hurt in his voice. He's not used to my putting barriers between us, my taking space for myself. When we first moved in, he walked in on me on the toilet more times than I can count. I suppose I've encouraged that. I definitely never asked him to stop. But now the bathroom is my one refuge. I lock everything and everyone out anytime I can. It must feel like a sort of rejection to Steve.

I reach over and twist the lock to open the door. Steve stands there in wrinkled clothes. A bit of what looks like dried spit-up is crusting on his collar. I guess over an hour alone with Dawn has gotten the better of even him. A comforting thought. He sits down in front of the toilet and picks up my left foot. As he starts to rub the feeling back into it, he looks up at me, his blue eyes soft and lovely, and I feel myself getting weirdly shy, the way women can when a beautiful man gives them his full attention. I let go of everything else and relax into his touch. Eventually he switches and picks up my right foot.

Then a jolt of pain shoots through my arch. Steve doesn't seem to be doing anything especially rough. He's rubbing the same way he always does—in patient little circles. I don't say anything out-right, but I do scrunch up my toes, hoping he'll get the hint.

"That should help a bit anyway," he says, letting my right foot go with a quick pat.

"So much. Thanks, babe," I lie as I force myself up and onto my still tingling feet. "'Sgo to bed."

He grabs at my hand like a suave schoolboy and leads me to our bedroom. As I lay under the sheets, waiting for him to finish brushing his teeth, I wonder if I've ever actually let Steve in. I've kept so much from him from the very beginning. Edited my life to make it seem a little less tragic and a lot more functional.

Is it really Steve's fault, then, that he can't read my little hints? I've made sure he can't with each fake smile and forced thanks. And now, with my constant failures as a mother and wife, with whatever's happening with this cockroach . . . I'm not sure I know how to make the lies stop. They flow from my mouth freely, like a freshly undammed river. Is this what it is to be a wife and mother? Learning to hide the different ways your family erodes you, the different ways you risk eroding your family?

I try not to think about the nearly full bottle of painkillers—oxycodone—lying in a drawer in the desk in my office. I found them while at Ma's place a couple months after her ten-day feast, shoved in the hole in her mattress where she'd hidden backup pills. It was, thankfully, the one thing my aunties and cousins missed when cleaning the place out. I pushed them inside my purse before I had a chance to consider why I might need them, or how they could become an obsession for me and an anchor for her spirit. They could be expired anyway. I'm too scared to check. Scared I'll get addicted. Nod off like Ma at moments I should be alert. Scared that once I take one, I won't be able to stop until I'm—

No, I tell myself. *No. You can't let yourself think like this.*

As if it's a choice.

I turn over and pretend I'm asleep.

CHAPTER 9

Who Needs Sleep
When You've Got
an Overactive Imagination?

I don't know how long I've been lying here, still as a stone under Steve's arm, flung carelessly, possessively across my chest. His snores are quiet but constant, rhythmic, as though they're on a timer. We left the blinds open, so the yellowing light of the full moon is illuminating parts of the room while other parts stay shadowed. I've been staring at our textured ceiling, waiting for images to pop out at me the way I imagine, somewhere, Melita and Tanya are doing with the stars in the night sky. They'd been meeting up with some other women around our age for full-moon ceremonies the past six months. "we all wanna b more n touch w women's medicine," Melita told me in a text, "its rly powerful 2 just sit around w other native women n rly listen 2 them. n rly b listened 2 ur self. makes u feel like a real ndn woman or summin lol."

I'd gone a couple times before Dawn was born, but now that I was a new mom, I guess it didn't occur to them that I'd still want to come. Even if it did, though, one of them would have had to pick me up, which I knew was a pain in the ass. No one wants to drive into

Toronto and back to Six if they can help it. I felt bad even asking Aunt Rachel to do it the other day.

"Am I supposed to feel bad for you now?" a voice rings in the air.

A shiver runs through me. The voice is bitchy and accusatory, soaked in sarcasm. Is there a woman here?

I look at Steve. He hasn't registered anything, but that man can sleep soundly despite anything. He'd wanted to be the sort of father who gets up with his baby, but he couldn't change his nature. He sleeps the way I imagine people who've always known safety and prosperity do. The type of people who don't have the possibility of trauma lurking in the back of their minds, always, making them hypervigilant of every creak or shift in the dark. Not like me. I don't remember the last time I slept through the night. Even before Dawn, I'd be up for hours, watching the horizon darken, then lighten as my brain recycled guilty thoughts and self-criticisms. Motherhood has only amplified my senses.

"Hello?" I whisper, my eyes darting into the recesses of every corner, finding nothing, flitting away. Steve grumbles in his sleep, lifts his arm, and turns away from me. I sit up. Move my feet carefully from the bed to the floor. Everything is still. I must be imagining things.

Then I hear it: laughter—mocking, amused. Sounds like it's coming from the hall. Who the fuck is it? And how did she get in?

I stand, try to slow my quickening breath. Breathe in. Breathe out. Slowly pad over to the door. Breathe in. Breathe out. Bite my lip, hard. Peek out.

Just in time to watch Dawn's nursery door click shut.

Someone's taking her, I think.

Immediately I'm in the hall, the cold brass doorknob in my hand as adrenaline courses through my body. I open the door and look around. There doesn't seem to be anyone there. Not even the rocking chair is moving. I slip inside the room, check behind that door, then open the closet and move aside the hangers of dresses.

Nothing. I go to Dawn. I can't quite hear her shallow little breaths, so I gently place my fingers on her tummy. It rises and falls. Thank the Creator.

There's a slight smell of baby shampoo, but nothing out of the ordinary. I stand there in the silence for I don't know how long. Time moves differently when you're exceedingly alert and apprehensive of your surroundings. You don't have the space to think—every part of you is too intensely focused on what's in front of you—and yet, in that lack of space, you also lose time.

I stand and watch. My heart thuds and thuds. I can practically hear the blood whooshing through my ears. No one's here. No one's taking Dawn. Did I really imagine all of this?

Then the voice comes again, seemingly from right behind me, making my whole body shudder: "We bring our minds together as one and give thanks to Shonkwaia'tison for these stories."

My father. The voice isn't his, but the words. The words are entirely his. I haven't heard them in years. Tears well in my eyes as I snap around. There's nothing there, but the voice continues.

"All our stories are a gift from Shonkwaia'tison, just like all of creation is his gift to us."

"Please," I ask, holding in the sobs. "Please stop."

"The stories help us as Onkwehón:we to learn about ourselves, the world around us, and our place in the world."

"How is this happening?" I whisper, rubbing my wet eyes so hard they burn. There's no one here but Dawn. And even if there was, the only people who know these words are on Six Nations or dead.

"We offer up this tobacco as a prayer, in order to give thanks for these stories." There is no emotion in the words, but they still feel cruel, relentless.

"What do you want?"

"And now . . ."

"I'll do anything. Just stop!" my voice getting screechy as I smack my hands over my ears.

"And now . . ."

Suddenly the fear dissipates. I know what the voice wants. It seems so obvious. I feel like a fool for not figuring it out faster.

"And now our minds are one," I whisper into the dark. There's no response, but there doesn't have to be. I know what I'm supposed to do.

I carefully close the door to Dawn's nursery and walk downstairs to my office. There's a big mahogany desk in the center of the room, a laptop closed on top, with big, full bookshelves framing everything. It's the sort of room I imagined established writers occupied while penning their masterpieces. The whole setup seems premature, like I'm cheating or playing pretend. It's hard to enjoy the space when I haven't earned any of it. Technically Steve hasn't earned it, either. Most of his wealth has filtered through his family, washing away discomfort like a never-ending spring. Still, he was born into excess, whereas I was born into lack. He has intergenerational wealth; I have intergenerational trauma. Dawn, the lucky girl, gets to inherit both.

I keep the light off, then open the laptop and wait for it to boot up. I've had this big-ass brick of a computer for years now. Stickers from bands I loved in high school are still stuck on the case. It was the first big purchase I'd ever made, a couple years after high school. At that point I'd already been paying for almost half the bills because Ma's accident made it so she couldn't work full-time hours anymore.

My eyes dart to the drawer where Ma's oxies are—

No.

The blue of the laptop screen sign-in page flashes in front of me. As soon as I sign in, a pow-wow drum starts up.

"Fuck!"

I scramble to pause the music. The singers go on, unperturbed by my frantic slamming on the space bar.

After about a minute it stops, finally, and I listen intently for any sign Dawn has heard. Silence. Seems like I've lucked out for once. Still, what the fuck? I don't even remember having any YouTube videos up. Steve must have been on my laptop, looking for music he thinks will help him better relate to the others in Mohawk class. It's weird, though, that he just so happened to have up Ma's favorite Northern Cree song. One she'd sing to me whenever it came on, immediately turning whatever happened to be nearby into a microphone—a bottle of Coke, a pen, occasionally my foot.

Unless it wasn't a coincidence. The thought doesn't feel like mine, but it makes a sort of sense all the same. After all, her pill bottle is here. Maybe that, and my hesitancy to let her go, has kept her here, too. Maybe it wasn't Steve leaving a song open on my laptop. Maybe it was a sign from her. The thought makes tears well up in my eyes.

"Ma?" I ask, realizing it's the first time I've said the word out loud since her funeral. "Are you here?"

The only sound is the hum of the laptop.

I pull Ma's pill bottle out from the drawer and turn it in my hand. There's nothing special about it, apart from it once being hers. I don't feel any kind of tingling when I hold it, or the sensation of eyes watching me, or anything like what happened upstairs. That was visceral, unexplainable. This is . . . simply a song. I put the bottle back in its hiding place, then open my Word document.

I'd saved the story in a hurry as "Creation." I need to try to come up with a better title before I even consider letting anyone else read it. Though perhaps, I can't help but think, Ma is reading it now, as I write. Dad, too. If I'm finally writing what they always knew I could, what they always hoped I would, they could be watching. Right?

I open my Facebook messages to check what Melita said the other names for Sky Woman were. Steve had good instincts there. It wouldn't make sense to call her Sky Woman when I was starting her story back in Sky World.

I take a deep breath. I stare at the cursor. I wait.

CHAPTER 10

Enter Sky Woman. You Can Call Her Mature Flowers.

So. The Sky World. The place where it all began. How should I properly prepare you for Sky World? I should mention it's not nice. This is important. Sometimes people get this idea that everything used to be perfect in the past when really everything was in a lot of ways the same. Some people were good; some people were bad. There was never a point where, for example, if Terry down the road told her friends you were a right home-wrecker who stole her precious Shawny away, you would ever be able to get gas in the village without them giving you the stink eye. Even if you were all born three hundred years ago, those same people would probably still be dicks and call you all kinds of foul shit. The only difference is they'd be dicks without modern stuff like SUVs and diabetes and Facebook.

Speaking of rumors, Sky Woman's actual name was not Sky Woman at all. It was Mature Flowers. It would have been too confusing for her to be named Sky Woman, since technically all women in Sky World were sky women.

Now, I'm not sure what you've heard about Mature Flowers, but you should know she had a messed-up life before she landed on that Turtle's back and jump-started Creation. And not just messed up—sad. Like, really sad. One awful thing after another. The kind of stuff that piles up and makes your heart heavy. I'm warning you now—this isn't Disney. It doesn't end with emotionally satisfying heterosexual domestic bliss. Far from it.

But first I should probably tell you about the Great Tree. Set the scene and whatnot. It was smack in the middle of Sky World and pretty much held the whole place together. Plus it fed everyone, so it was kind of a big deal. I'm not sure exactly how to describe it. I guess if trees were old movie monsters, the Great Tree was like Frankenstein's monster, only more useful. It didn't have all those annoying existential questions, for one. You've heard of grafting? I guess you could call it that. The Great Tree was grafted with every type of fruit you can think of. There were whole branches of cherries, apples, juicy strawberries big as your hand. And even when it had a decomposing body in its canopy, the Great Tree smelled sweet, like a handful of flowers and fresh tobacco.

You're probably wondering about that dead body, huh? I don't blame you. Mature Flowers's dad died before she was born, which meant she was mourning this stranger her entire life. What's worse, he was the first person in all of Sky World to die, so no one even knew how to comfort her. They put his body in a coffin-type structure and kind of threw it into the branches of the Great Tree. It sounds bad, I know, but what else were they gonna do? It's not like they'd disposed of a dead body before. There was no *Breaking Bad* back then to introduce to them the ingenious idea of melting a body down in hydrofluoric acid. Plus the Great Tree was gorgeous, so they could have done much worse.

Anyway, Mature Flowers was always crying because she was the only person she knew without her dad, and since she was also the saddest person she knew, she was convinced those two facts could not be a coincidence. I'm honestly not sure her dad was really that good a guy, but since she never met him, she couldn't really gauge where he fell on the asshole scale herself. All she had were her stupid childish assumptions to rely on, and you know how *that* can get. In her head he was the best dad who never was, and now that he was dead, her life would always and forever be shit. The people who threw her dad's body in the tree had never told her that they'd done so, either, so that little omission made her already bad trust issues worse.

A long time passed and Mature Flowers was still moping around pretty much all the time. No one really knew what to say to her. She became the weird girl everyone whispers about and avoids, which was unfortunate because she was actually really pretty and could have been super popular if she wasn't so sad.

Mature Flowers's mother didn't help matters. This one day she must have saw her lying facedown in the middle of the village or something equally weird and embarrassing, because she finally decided to do something. What, you ask? Tell her where her dad's body was! I'm not totally sure why. It's not like that could have made her feel much better. Her dad was most definitely still dead. Like I said, they didn't really know how to handle the grief thing. They mostly wanted her to get over it already. Pretty much the same as how we treat mourning people today. Oh, your loved one died? Get over it! Your tears ain't bringing anyone back to life, buttercup. You or Mature Flowers. And anyway, even if they could, we need to you to be a "productive" member of society first and foremost, which *really* means we need you to be a slave to the economy and sell or buy shit immediately. Preferably both. Forever. G'wan den!

CHAPTER 11

The Ghosts of Colonizers Past

Tanya called earlier today. She had loads of good gossip, which I'd normally eat up. This time I couldn't be bothered.

"You'll never fucking guess who Dex Johnson cheated on Jamie with. One of them girls who works at Lone Wolf! You know the one who free-pours sugar in the coffee and makes it way too sweet? Her! Jamie caught them doing a stand-up sixty-nine in the bathroom of the Laundromat and dumped liquid Tide all over them. I had no idea Dex even had the upper body strength to pull off something like that."

I was quiet, trying to figure out how to bring up the voice I'd heard last night. Anything I considered sounded crazy.

"What's the matter with you? Come on, it's funny! I heard they totally looked like Smurfs when they came out."

"Maybe my sense of humor got flushed out with Dawn's placenta," I managed.

"So it's buried in your ma's yard? Heck, I'll get one of my brothers to dig it up right now."

"That's not the point, Tanya."

"What's the point, then?"

"I feel like shit."

Tanya laughed. "Of course you feel like shit. You pushed a

cranky kid out your snatch, what, a little over a month ago? What'd you expect? Least you didn't get covered in liquid Tide."

What did I expect? I expected Dawn to love me, I want to say but know I can't. She screams in my presence for hours. Sometimes it seems like she barely needs to breathe. But she always stops a little shy of the three-hour mark, as if she's on a timer, which is weird because, according to the internet, that's the exact time I'd need to cite for doctors to take her crying seriously.

I'm so far from being a perfect mother it's starting to scare me. I can't calm Dawn down the way Steve does, or even the way Dana does. When Dawn screams, I want to scream back. Sometimes, when she won't stop, when the screams feel like they're one long continuous blast, images appear in my mind that scare me, like me shaking her violently until she stops. I don't know where they come from. I don't want to hurt her. I don't. So why is my brain so ready and willing to create scenarios where I do, where I have?

Motherhood is sacrifice. Not metaphorical sacrifice. Literal sacrifice. Every day I feel like I'm destroying pieces of myself to win the favor of this insatiable demigod who wants and wants and wants. Prayers and candles are never enough. This being wants blood. And the more you give the greater it grows. Ma must have felt it back then—especially after Dad died. Those deep lines between her eyebrows and thick brackets around her lips more offerings to me than markers of time passed and life lived. I wish I could talk to her about it. She was usually pretty honest once she'd had her painkillers. Sometimes too honest, her words like tacks popping any unrealistic ideas or dreams ballooning in my head. But that's exactly what I need right now.

"Helloooo? You still there, Al?"

"Yeah, sorry. I—" I bit the nail of my thumb, hard, then mumbled, "I'm pretty sure I was hearing things last night."

"Whoa, really? Like, voices?"

"Yeah. A woman." I didn't mention anything about the talking cockroach or the song I thought could be a sign from Ma.

"In your head, or in the room? What'd she say?" I could hear her interest perk immediately. Tanya always saw herself as a sort of unlicensed private investigator. She spent most of her free time trying to figure out unsolved murders on internet message boards. I should have figured she'd see this as another case to crack. At least she wasn't making plans to take me to the mental hospital.

"In the room, I think. She was criticizing me to start," I said, considering whether I should tell her about Dad's little storytelling Thanksgiving Address. I decided against it. "Then she kind of . . . guilted me?"

"Guilted you over what?"

"My writing," I said before thinking about it.

"No shit. You're writing?"

"I'm trying to? It's, like, a kind of modernized version of the Creation Story," I rushed to say, hoping that she wouldn't make a big deal of it. I was wrong.

"Hoooooolay! Oh my gosh, that reminds me of when your dad would tell us all those stories when we were kids! It was my absolute favorite thing listening to him."

"Me, too. That's where I got the idea."

"Al! That's exciting! He would be so proud of you! Seriously. So . . . when can I read it?"

"Depends on how fast the voice in my house scares me into finishing it."

"Oh, if it's trying to use its scary powers to criticize and guilt you, it's definitely not a ghost. I've been listening to this podcast on supernatural stuff by these white boys who hunt ghosts and they say ghosts don't really care about us. They just kinda mope around obsessing about the past. Unless you're in their house and they want you out. How old is your house again?"

"I don't know. The stairs are kinda creaky."

"Hmm. What about weird or unexplained murders? Anything like that happen there? Or even, like, the surrounding area? If it's a really powerful spirit it might have some range."

"How should I know?"

"Well, I mean, I'm pretty sure you can find that info online or at the library or something. Stuff like that never stays buried."

"I don't think anyone was murdered here, Tan."

She was quiet for a minute, as if thinking deeply, then said, "You know, it might be your sleep. I had a friend who went to Coachella and took tons of uppers to stay awake the whole weekend. By the time Roger Waters was playing *Dark Side of the Moon* she was snatching cheap headdresses off any white girls within reach and dancing with ancestors who weren't there. Had to smoke weed before bed for weeks to get her circadian rhythm back to normal. I'm sure you could hear things if you were sleep-deprived enough."

"I'm not getting less sleep than any other new mom."

"How many other new moms have you asked about their sleep?"

She had me there.

"What if," I started slowly, unsure of how she'd take this, "it *is* a ghost and they're trying to make contact with me? Like, if they have a message or something from—"

"No. You're not in any state to make contact with ghosts," Tanya interjected. "How about this. I'll come up on Friday and watch Dawn while you sleep. And I'll bring a ton of sage to smudge your house again. Even if the voice is all in your head, a good cleanse will probably help. Who knows what kind of weird colonizer spirits are hanging around that place?"

It was true: the house hadn't been smudged since Tanya did it right after we moved in. The problem was, I wasn't sure I'd be able to sleep when she came. I'd reached a level of exhaustion I hadn't known was possible—one that, strangely, prevented me from resting. My body was sluggish and heavy, but it felt like my insides were a pinball machine, anxiety bouncing off every part of me, making my skin crawl and my eyes fly. Even the quiet moments lately were full of racing thoughts, firing up my brain when I wanted it to be dull and calm. I didn't know what to do. Still, I agreed. I wanted to see Tanya, feel a piece of home.

"There. Feel better?"

"A little?"

"That's my girl. We'll figure it out, okay? As the best Beatle, George Harrison, once said, 'This, too, shall pass.' Or was it 'All things must pass'? One of the two, anyway."

And we left it at that.

But I'm not sure these constant feelings of despair, guilt, and loss *will* pass. Lately I've been thinking about how destroyed Mature Flowers was over her father. I feel bad for her, and I relate to her literally twice over, but more and more these days I think she was lucky. She hadn't had the chance to hurt her dad, piss him off or disappoint him, like I did with Ma. She held no sharp, shameful memories to stab herself with when no one was around. No expectations hanging over her like starving, expectant vultures, waiting to feed. Mature Flowers would never know the light she'd lost—how beautiful, how brilliant. She'd also never know the disappointment of that light becoming suddenly dull, or the guilt of knowing that change was because of something she said or did wrong. That's the thing about happiness. It's not a country with open borders. You can't just settle there and stay. We like to pretend that it is, that we can. But that's all fantasy.

Have we really learned how to deal with death since Sky World?

So much practice; you'd think we'd have it down by now. So many of our women taken from us, either murdered or gone missing, that we have our own hashtag for it: #MMIWG. So many of our men taken from us, put in prisons or early graves for trying to survive. So many of our children taken from their families and placed in foster care that girls from my community were scared to even give birth in nearby hospitals. And Canadians blaming us for it all, as if this was something we chose instead of something that was forced on us over and over, by people who said they just wanted to help. So much loss. Inconceivable loss. The type of loss that doesn't end, but instead finds new entry points, new ways to open old wounds. We aren't allowed to heal. Not really.

Our people knew grief was something that changed how you interacted with the world. You couldn't see the beauty and colors around you and really cherish them; couldn't hear the voices of other people or the sounds of music and feel grounded to this earth; couldn't taste or speak or breathe with appreciation for what you still had, because you knew your loved one had lost it all. I can't imagine going through a condolence ceremony would change that for me, regardless of what Aunt Rachel thinks. I'm not strong like Hiawatha was when he forgave Tadodaho for murdering his family. I'm not the type of person who can bring together warring nations and negotiate peace, like the Peacemaker. I'm an orphan who learned nothing from losing the first parent to help with the loss of the second. I'm a puddle pretending I've got shape and form.

I know Tanya cares about me. Steve cares, and Melita, and Aunt Rachel, and Dana, and all my friends and cousins. But patience has an expiration date even if grief doesn't, and I'm slowly running out of ways to lie when they ask me if I'm okay, if I'll be okay. Soon enough they're going to stop, get frustrated with my inability to cope. What then?

I don't know what to do. But I know what I want. I want to forget, for just a night. Smoke a whole carton of du Mauriers. Rip a blunt the size of a hot dog. Drink a bottle of Johnnie Walker Red and pass out. Wake up with a delicious headache entirely my doing, hold on to that pain and know I deserve it. I want to vomit everywhere, purge every alien thing out of my body until it's a shell. I want to be entirely unnecessary, ignored, forgotten. No responsibilities. No mistakes making others hurt. No memory of the mess I've made. No me.

This is what the colonizers would want, I think first.

Then, who gives a fuck?

CHAPTER 12

Steve Is Never Gonna Get It

I hear the door creak open downstairs, hear Steve's hesitation in the hall as he pulls off his shoes and steps into his slippers. It's a habit that strikes me as so old-fashioned—like the dad in *Leave It to Beaver* or *Pleasantville*. Some time when "men were men," which meant they always protected their manly widdle tootsies from the cold.

"Hey," Steve whispers. "She been asleep long?" He nods to Dawn, whose little body is laid out sweetly in her crib.

I shake my head, then slowly, carefully get to my feet, shooing Steve out of the room. I follow, not breathing until I've successfully closed Dawn's nursery door without her waking.

"Is it okay if Tanya comes over to help out Friday?" I whisper as we pad down the stairs.

"Al, how are we going to become better parents if we keep passing the buck to everyone else?"

"I'm home with her all the time. Pretty sure I have the buck well in hand," I say, surprising myself with my own sternness as I trail Steve into the kitchen.

He pulls out his phone and starts thumbing through Uber Eats, his shoulders tense.

"You're right," he finally says. "It's just . . ."

I brace myself for what's to come. Did Tanya call him and rat me out? Or maybe she said something to Aunt Rachel and she told Steve? I stand very still, not sure how to react yet.

"Just what?" I ask, impatient.

"Can you visit with Tanya some other day? Lou and Sheila are hosting a dinner for everyone in the department at their house this Friday night. I know it's last-minute, but I thought you might want to join me. Show off how hot your post-baby bod is."

I let out a laugh, relieved. "I'm not sure how hot it is for your stomach muscles to be stretched so far they feel like Jell-O."

"You're still sexy," Steve says as he slips a kiss onto my neck. I pull away slightly without thinking. Steve notices—I see a wrinkle form between his eyebrows—but he keeps quiet. That upper-class aversion to confrontation is finally good for something.

"Do I have to come? There's no one for me to talk to at those things."

"What are you talking about? Sheila loves you. Plus it's your chance to talk about serious novels with someone who *actually* reads them."

I note his use of the term "serious" first, then the almost careless way he referred to basically all my friends and family. The people who don't *actually* read serious novels. As if they're not sufficiently interesting because they don't want to debate the symbolism of the green light in *The Great Gatsby*. Does Steve consider what I'm writing "serious"? Will Sheila? I doubt it.

He holds his phone up for me to see. The Uber Eats page for a Thai restaurant. I shake my head.

"Steve, she's an English professor. She talks about novels all day. And she talks about them like an academic. I never know what the hell she's saying. My cousins might only want to talk about *The Real Housewives*, but at least I can understand them."

"Come on. You know I didn't mean anything by that. I love your cousins. And Lisa Vanderpump."

I fight the urge to roll my eyes.

"Sheila's not that bad. She's just really passionate about her work."

"Last time we were over she asked me if I thought auto-theory was 'the inevitable result of the rise in auto-fiction.' I had to hide in the bathroom until I googled an answer."

"Was that what happened? I thought you had a stomach thing."

"I did. Stress diarrhea."

He holds up the Uber Eats page for a nearby Mexican restaurant. I think about that night in Sheila's bathroom, and my stomach's inability to take spice, then vigorously shake my head.

Steve lets out a long sigh. "I wouldn't usually push you on this. But it's these sorts of get-togethers that really make or break a person's status in the department."

I take his phone from him and scroll, pretending to be looking for a restaurant. This is part of the deal. It's what I decided to do instead of continuing my life on the rez. It's why I wasn't there when my mom died, or in much of the aftermath. It's why I'm here now, with nothing and no one but this man and his baby. I better fucking go to this dinner party, and all the parties, or else all of it was for nothing.

"Are we supposed to bring Dawn?" I ask.

"No. We'll need to find a sitter."

Steve grabs the takeout pamphlet for our favorite local Chinese restaurant from the fridge and holds it up. I nod as I think of a compromise.

"We won't need a babysitter if Tanya's already here."

"Does that mean you're willing to come?" Steve asks as he picks up the phone to call in our usual dinner order.

I shrug. "Sure."

"Thanks, babe. I really appre— Yes, sorry. I'd like to make an order for delivery." He turns away from me as he talks to the restaurant worker.

I wander out to the living room, proud that I figured out a way for both of us to be happy.

That's when I see them, slotted right into our movie shelf.

The fucking Disney DVDs. How the hell did they get there? I threw them all out. And *when* did they get there? I haven't been in the living room much lately, so realistically it could have been anytime after Meghan came.

I rush over to the cabinet and rip out *Pocahontas*. I stare at her, furious, waiting for her to do something again. As if in defiance, she stays totally still. Typical. She was a bitch then; she's a bitch now.

"You don't fool me," I whisper—then, for good measure, add, "I'm not crazy."

"Oh, really? And what about your grandma? Was she wandering ditches and getting gossiped about all over the rez cuz she was sane?"

I drop the DVD and jump back.

The voice isn't Pocahontas, or Matoaka.

It's the same woman from the other night.

My muscles quake, and my breath gets fast. How does she know about my grandma? *I* barely know about her. I knew what people said, thanks to inconsiderate moms who'd shit-talked her around me when I was a kid. But the only time Ma mentioned her specifically was when she found out I'd started smoking pot. "I'd be careful with that reefer if I was you. Mental illness runs in the family, and it don't play nice with mind changers like that. You don't want to end up crazy like my mother, believe me."

This voice, this woman, was reducing me to another fucking crazy Indian, just like those women had done to Grandma so long ago. Ma, too.

"You okay?" Steve asks, jerking me from the voice.

I bend over and pick up the DVD, trying to steady my hands as I hold it in front of his face.

"Did you do this?" My voice is shrill but I can't change it.

Steve stands up straighter, indignation setting his jaw. "If by 'this,' you mean take perfectly good DVDs our neighbor gifted our daughter out of the trash, then yes."

It feels like forever waiting for my mouth to catch up with my mind. "How did you know our neighbor gifted our daughter anything?"

"She told me."

"Oh, so you're spying on me now?"

"What? Of course not."

"Then what happened? Tell me how you figured it all out."

"I didn't—" Steve stops and takes a deep breath, clearly trying to keep from yelling. "I saw Meghan outside when I got home from work. Must have been the day she brought them over. She was going on about this book and how much Dawn would love the movies, and I had no idea what the hell she was talking about, but I nodded along. I forgot all about them until I opened the garbage can to take out the trash and they were sitting there. Didn't feel right to throw them out."

"That wasn't your decision to make, Steve!" I yell. "Didn't you notice every single one of those Disney movies had main characters who weren't white? She gave our Mohawk daughter *Pocahontas*, for fuck's sake."

Steve pauses, looking up at the ceiling as if he's preparing to explain something to a difficult child. "Have you ever considered you might be reading too far into things?"

"Have you ever considered you're not reading far enough?" I respond.

"Sometimes a gift is just a gift. Not everything is about race, Alice."

I stare at him in disbelief. After all the conversations I've had with him about the way white girls treated me in high school, all the detail I went into about how they made passive aggression an art, how they hid their racism behind faked kindness and innocent looks while I got detentions anytime I responded to their bullshit. I think about the neighborhood watch woman, who was filming me and interrogating me like a criminal. How neither she nor the girls in high school ever seemed able to give me a fucking break. They were always watching, always scheming, trying to find ways to make me look bad, to get me in trouble. The stakes had risen significantly, though. Detentions and suspensions were no longer the worst things they could do to me; now I had to worry about white women trying to get me arrested and get my baby taken from me. And here's Steve, defending a woman who's basically a stranger, making me feel like the crazy one when he should be comforting me. I'm his wife. Why isn't he comforting me like he used to? What's changed?

It's all burning.

And maybe it should.

"Why are you taking her side?" I ask, though I already know the answer. Meghan is a rich white woman, exactly like his mother. He's been trained to swallow their bait since he was a baby.

Steve stays annoyingly calm. "We're talking about a gift from a neighbor. I didn't realize there were sides."

"We're not talking about a gift from a neighbor. We're talking about a racist white woman assuming our poor little baby wanted her glorious white kids' castoffs cuz she's brown."

Steve lets out a long sigh. "Okay. You're right. She's probably trying to take down your entire community by giving your kid DVDs."

And just like that, I'm the difficult Indian woman again.

Unreasonable, ungrateful, pestering her rational, hardworking white man with nonsense he doesn't need. I'm made to feel like *I'm* the problem for merely acknowledging how weird and probably racist the whole situation is—a circumstance that is, in turn, weird and racist. I'm glad I never told him about neighborhood watch lady. He'd probably have bought her apology flowers.

Then it hits me: here, with these sorts of people, I *am* the problem. Not Meghan, with her immaculate gift wrapping and perpetual white woman innocence. If she ever says or does anything that offends me, it's not her fault; it's mine for "misunderstanding" her. She never means to hurt anyone, whereas I'm looking to be offended and to offend, to respond to my own hurt with words and actions that hurt everyone else worse. I'm too traumatized to be innocent the way she is. Even in the eyes of my own husband. Well, he's not gonna get the dramatic scene he expects of me. Not anymore, anyway.

Without saying a word, I turn around, head straight into my office, and shut the door.

CHAPTER 12.5

Mature Flowers's Dad Is Basically the Worst

Mature Flowers's mom's plan to help her daughter become normal didn't quite work. On the one hand, Mature Flowers wasn't lying around on the ground anymore. That was normal. On the other hand, she now spent all her time in the branches of the Great Tree talking to her dead dad. That was not normal.

This is where things get really weird, though, because believe it or not, her dad actually started to talk back. Small stuff to start. *Shé:kon, how are ya, your ma seeing anyone*, you know. But once he got the hang of talking to her through time and space, he wouldn't stop. He was particularly fond of telling her she was going to be the most important woman in all of Sky World, and since basically no one else would talk to her at this point, that news made her feel pretty good. Until, that is, her dad did the most annoying thing a parent can possibly do to their socially awkward single daughter: he told her she needed to get a husband.

He didn't even give her the option of picking the guy, either. He *said* it was her choice, but you better believe he made sure to mention that if she wanted to fulfill her destiny and be the best woman there ever was, she should marry the worst guy in the whole village. No pressure, though. It was totally her choice. He might stop talking to her if she chose anyone else, but she was a smart girl and he knew she'd make the right decision.

Yup, Alice Is Still Awake and Putting Things Together When Destiny Drops into Her Lap

Two hundred and sixty-three words. That's all I can manage. I've sat here for over an hour after Steve sheepishly knocked on the door and offered to bring in my dinner as a sort of limp peace offering, but nothing else has come. Partly because I can't stop thinking about Steve, Meghan, the neighborhood watch lady, and the fight. The ways they're all connected. Steve made me feel like I couldn't trust my own perceptions. That I was unreasonable for noticing something that seemed, all things considered, pretty obvious. Even if she didn't mean anything by it, the fact that Meghan purged from her Disney movie collection only those with brown characters, those she thought Dawn was most likely to appreciate, that said something. Didn't it?

It's not like this is the first time we've gotten in a fight over what constitutes as racist. I tried to bring up the way his fellow professors treated me a few times. Things that, on the surface, seemed small enough to maybe be in my head: a particular look, a dismissive word or gesture. Anytime I started to discuss them, even when I didn't use the r-word directly, instead using words like "strange" or phrasing the observation as a question, like "Did you notice how—," Steve would wince, as if I were pressing on a fresh bruise, and tell me I was mistaken. Just like that: "You're mistaken." Like it was a period at the end of my sentence. As soon as any criticism left my mouth, he'd pull out an excuse like a pocketknife and dare me to challenge: "She wasn't sneering. That's just how she looks," or "You'll get used to his sense of humor, I swear," or "It's not just you. He never remembers the names of anyone's wives." I couldn't exactly challenge him on these sorts of claims, since they all required more knowledge of his colleagues than I had. I learned to keep my complaints to myself. Trying to explain to him the nuances of his dear friends' passive-aggressive racism wasn't exactly my idea of a good time. And it always ended up making me feel crazy, because there was always an explanation Steve had ready to go.

I read once that there was no word for the color blue in Greek, that the Greek poet Homer referred to the Mediterranean as the "wine-dark sea" instead. When you look back now, when we can define and identify "blue" as something all its own, you know dark wine is actually a deep burgundy—more red than blue, so Homer's description tells us more about how he had to use his time's limited perception of color to describe the sea than it tells us about the actual color itself. In that way, maybe "racism" is to Steve what "blue" was to Homer, and Steve would always describe what I knew to be "racism" as, instead, "a misunderstanding," "a silly mistake," or some other vague problem he himself had enough experience with to name in his otherwise white, supposedly raceless world.

Or maybe—and this is the option I'm most scared of—Steve could see the racism if he wanted but deliberately chose not to, like a teen refusing to wear prescription glasses because they think it makes them look ugly and uncool. It seemed in the club of whiteness—particularly rich whiteness—it was always ugly and uncool to bring up racism. It was ugly to bring up race at all, as if even alluding to something that's fundamental to the way we each experience the world stains you. After all, as Joan often explained to me in earnest yet condescending tones, folks like her "don't see race"—that is, until they're walking down the street and a brown or Black man happens to approach, and they happen to tighten their grip on their purse while their fingers search its contents for keys to splay between their knuckles or pepper spray or a gun.

For some reason this one fight, as small and unspectacular as it is, also feels like it's incredibly important, like its resolution or lack thereof will tell me everything I need to know about Steve's ability to be a husband to me and a father to Dawn. When it was just me I had to think about, I could let things like this go. But now that we had a daughter who would one day face all these people, or people exactly like them, these situations felt far more dire. If we didn't figure out how to defuse them now, they could explode in her hands later. And given how I'd been feeling in Toronto these days, reduced to either a criminal or a nutjob, Steve's casual dismissal felt like an additional slap in the face. If he won't even allow me to name small acts of, sure, okay, I'll admit, perhaps unintentional racism, then how the hell will he be able to support Dawn in whatever rich, primarily white school Joan inevitably convinces him she needs to attend? If she comes to him in tears, telling him about some cruel bullshit that singles her out as one of the only Native kids there, is he going to tell her she's overreacting? That the kids who war whoop when she steps to the plate during softball are "just joking"? I can't imagine him confronting anyone on behalf of either of us. He'd rather pretend nothing is happening, or if something is happening, that it'll go away if we only ignore it long enough.

But things don't go away when you ignore them. For example, Ma. For example, Dad. I've been thinking about them a lot tonight.

What I wouldn't give to climb up into a great tree's branches and talk to them, the way Mature Flowers talked to her dad. There are so many things Ma had started to say, then pulled back from—fragments I'm left mulling over now. Is this what she meant when she said I should be careful of Steve? When she warned that moving off the rez wasn't the picnic I seemed to think it was? Is this what Dad meant when he criticized academics like Steve—the way they swoop into our communities to take what they need and vanish? The way they *think* they know everything but never truly understand? Would either of my parents have been surprised Steve and I were getting in fights over women like Meghan? That I'd be questioning my own judgments and experiences based on whether or not Steve validated them? That I'd feel this lonely and isolated away from my community—from people who would have known exactly why I threw out those DVDs and either joked with me about it for months, or scolded me for being too bougie now that I can throw out perfectly good movies when they're still buying theirs bootleg?

No. I can't focus on the past. I have to focus on the present, what I have now. What can still be saved. Isn't that what our condolence ceremony encouraged? I have a baby who hates me, sure, but she's mercifully still alive, despite my fucked-up thoughts about hurting her and my constant exhaustion. And I have a white husband who doesn't believe racism exists, yet also believes cosplaying as an Indian will secure his career. The sad part is, it probably will. Everything Indigenous seems to have more value when it's utilized by white folks. Our clothes, our jewelry. Our language. Even our identities. Especially those.

I scroll through my Facebook feed, not sure what else to do to distract myself. People post news headlines boldly proclaiming Indigenous disaster, a certain inevitability emanating from their doomed statistics. Indigenous folks comment on those headlines—

giving further history, or criticizing government inaction, or pointing out stereotypes snuck into copy that white news editors never think to question before publishing. It's all the same story: assimilation, desecration, a deliberate sliding of our lives into dark, desolate pain so we evacuate our postage stamps of land for them to collect like trading cards. *Give in. Give up. The only Indians that aren't dying are already dead.*

Then a meme comes up with two pictures side by side, funnily enough, both from *Pocahontas*. In the first pic, Chief Powhatan is raising his right hand in front of a group of Powhatan people, the words "These white men are dangerous" written on the bottom of the frame below his feet, as if the truth of that statement is part of the very land he stands on. The caption for this picture is simply "Me." The second pic is a close-up of John Smith lying on the ground as Pocahontas leans over him in a deep kiss, her arms as entangled with his head and neck and back as his are with hers. "Also me," says the second caption. Part of me wonders whether this is some sort of sign, too. What are the odds that this specific post joking about dating white boys would come across my timeline just as I was questioning my relationship with Steve? And over a goddamn *Pocahontas* DVD?

Not Pocahontas. Matoaka.

The words pop into my head, but they don't feel like my thoughts. They don't sound like the woman who's been mocking me, either. They feel like her words. Matoaka's.

That night she spoke to me at Aunt Rachel's, I instinctively thrust Dana's copy of *Pocahontas* into my purse. Once I got home, I searched online and saw that Pocahontas's real name was, in fact, Matoaka, and that she *had* died young after being forced to marry John Rolfe. I didn't know any information about her before. I only knew her as the Disney princess who inspired me to think falling in love with a white guy was a brave, rebellious option for a Native girl. That seemed important to me, that distinction. How could I have imagined her telling me things I didn't know? What happened had to have been real.

After Ma left for work the next day, I pulled out the tape and put it in the VCR. I rewound it to the scene where Pocahontas was cloaked in blue fog and water and watched, waiting. Then I rewound it again and played it in slow motion. Then again, but this time I paused when her silhouette deepened into her animated body. I did this for what felt like no time at all but that turned out to be over two hours. I was so focused on the screen I didn't hear when Aunt Rachel entered the house to borrow some salt pork for corn soup.

"Is that Dana's? The heck you doin' with it? She's gonna kill you when she finds out you took it."

I'd been kneeling on the floor in front of the TV like a sorry sinner in a church. Knowing Aunt Rachel saw me there like that, knowing I must have looked crazy, I became embarrassed and climbed to my feet. Aunt Rachel raised an eyebrow, but only for a moment. She was so attentive to my moods it often felt like she could read my mind, and this time was no exception. She plopped her purse down on the floor and stepped closer to me, her voice soft and safe as ever.

"Everything okay, my love?"

Something about the way she called me "my love" had the effect of breaking open whatever locks I'd placed on my life, and she'd step inside so carefully. Even then, though, I didn't tell her what had happened. I told her I was trying to relearn the words to all the songs to surprise Dana. She didn't quite believe me, but she was too kind to make it an issue. She waited, something she'd always done so well.

And the waiting paid off a few months later, when I told her what Ma had said about Grandma. "Oh, Suze," she'd said sadly, as if she were speaking to my mother instead of me. "Your grandmother wasn't crazy, and she didn't have a mental illness. She was a medicine woman. She could speak to spirits and see the future. It's not something to be scared of. It's a gift." Those were the words that let me know Aunt Rachel was safe. They gave me space to situate what had been happening to me in the confusing months since I'd seen Pocahontas and the world around me began to feel elastic, stretching tight, then bouncing back loose around me. The way she spoke about her, the way she seemed to personally despise the words "crazy" and "mental illness," all of it made me feel like maybe there was another perspective for what I'd experienced. I needed that. I decided then and there to tell Aunt Rachel about all of it—Mason, *Pocahontas*, the way other things had started to talk to me after that, how they only seemed to shut up when I smoked weed or drank. She listened intently as I told her the whole story. I watched even more intently as she pursed and released her lips with nearly every word I said. Those little facial reactions were like terrifying signposts. I didn't want Aunt Rachel to think poorly of me. I wanted her to always be proud—even when I knew I wasn't giving her reason to be.

When I finished talking she was quiet for a moment. Then she told me I was brave for telling her. Her voice was scarily neutral. I couldn't tell whether she believed me or not. *She thinks I'm crazy. And she's right. I am crazy. Cartoons don't just start talking to teenagers. Neither do trees. But teenagers do go crazy. I've gone crazy.* The thoughts repeated over and over, creating a cyclone of self-hatred as I tried to focus on what Aunt Rachel was saying at that very moment: that I'd always been a creative kid with a wild imagination, even when I was a toddler; that I'd had so many imaginary friends she couldn't keep up with their names and personalities; that when I was born, Grandma had told her and Ma that I was a special child with gifts to see what others couldn't; that Grandma knew that because she herself could see what others couldn't; that there were ways of pulling myself back down to this side of reality when the other side had too strong a hold on me. Aunt Rachel taught me how to ground myself by concentrating on slowing down my breath, then focusing my attention on each of my five senses one by one until I felt more settled. When we did it together, the carousel of unwelcome thoughts slowed, but didn't stop. It was enough, at that time.

"So I'm not crazy?" I asked her, unable to make eye contact. She put her hand under my chin and gently lifted until my eyes met hers. She smiled.

"You're your grandma's girl."

I didn't know how to interpret that, given the negative tone everyone else used when they spoke about Grandma. And, even as I knew my aunt was making space for me to feel somewhat normal and definitely loved, the way she avoided asking more details about my experience told me that she, too, was afraid. It's that fear that keeps me from confiding in her now.

"Don't tell your ma about any of this, yeah?" she'd warned. "She doesn't understand this sort of stuff. Never has."

I could tell from those words, that look, that she'd probably seen worse things with her own mom than anything I'd experienced—things that, in some ways, had prepared her for this, but in other ways still frightened her, the same way a person who's been on a roller coaster before is still terrified as they hover precariously for those few seconds at the crest of that first hill, waiting for their inevitable descent.

I sit very still, staring intently at the meme, waiting to see if her voice will return. *Not Pocahontas's voice. Matoaka's,* I concede, hoping this will lure her back. *It's really a very pretty name.*

This is the second time Matoaka has unexpectedly popped up today. That can't be a coincidence. The last time she spoke to me, she claimed that she was trying to save me from Mason Jamieson. What did she call him? My John. The man who would ruin my life. Looking back, it seems the horrible, life-ruining fate she saved me from was continued poverty. So why was she trying to make contact now? Was I on the verge of another drastic wrong turn? Was Matoaka trying to save me once more from some fate I couldn't see yet?

Traps are set.

It's all burning.

They're all watching.

"Wait," I say, trying to keep the thoughts from crashing together and cluttering my already too-full mind. I tiptoe to the living room, grab the DVD, and head back to the office. Despite my lack of sleep, I'm not tired at all. I'd forgotten what it was to feel well and truly awake.

I slide the disk into my laptop and watch as the screen turns black. Slowly, instead of a DVD menu, an outline of a person appears in the center of the screen. I can make out what looks like a head and shoulders, though the details remain fuzzy, like a TV in need of a new antenna, back when TVs still needed those.

"Shé:kon—eh ken yéhses?"

I freeze. I don't know a lot of Mohawk, but everyone from Six Nations knows that first word: *hello.* An older voice, rougher, as though its owner is used to facing resistance. I lean in closer to the screen, trying to see if I can make out anything more, but they don't come in any clearer. Something about it reminds me of a transmission, but if that's what it is, it's from far, far away.

"Alice? Sathón:te ken akewén:na?"

"Shé:kon." I answer without hesitation. So there was a reason this DVD didn't stay in the trash. It wasn't just a coincidence Steve pulled it out. It was fate. I was meant to be here, at this moment, talking to someone from what Aunt Rachel called "the other side."

"To shískare eh nón:?"

"I'm sorry," I respond slowly, carefully annunciating each word. "I don't speak Mohawk."

"You only speak English?" There's disappointment in the voice. I'm not sure if I'm more surprised by the way they seem to detest English or their seemingly effortless command of it.

"I'm not thrilled about it, either," I mutter, annoyed. "But my husband's learning Mohawk. I can go get him if you'd prefer."

"That means it must be . . . what—2019 where you are? Have you had your daughter yet?"

It's as if someone's blown cold air on my neck. My body freezes, but my mind shoots ahead. "Y-Yes. How is . . . How do you know about Dawn? Who are you? What do you want?"

The voice is quiet. Something about their voice is familiar, but I can't place it.

"Pocahontas? Or—sorry—Matoaka?" I ask, even though I know that's not it.

The voice bursts into laughter but doesn't seem to move on the screen. The laughing is so loud it hurts my ears. I'm worried it's going to wake up Steve and Dawn.

"Shhhhh! People are sleeping upstairs."

"Seems like you still are, too," they respond, amused.

"What's that supposed to mean?"

"It means the time's come for you to wake up. You've had more than enough time to pretend self-sabotage is self-preservation. That's all over. Now we need you to start moving toward your destiny."

"What are you talking about? What destiny? Who's 'we'?"

"I'm earlier than I thought," the voice says quietly, more to themselves than to me. Then their words get louder and more pointed. "Have you started writing something recently?"

I pause, shame filling every part of me as fast as I can think. *My writing is terrible, I've done so little, I'm wasting my time, I'm wasting my life, no one is going to want to read this, I'm a failure, I'm failing Ma, I'm failing Dad, I'm failing the future generations, I shouldn't even try—*

"Well?" they demand.

"Kind of?"

"What do you mean, 'kind of'? Either you're writing something or you're not."

"Clearly you're not a writer."

"What exactly are you writing?" I can feel their impatience with me welling up, the same way Ma's would when I argued in circles with her. In fact, that might be why the voice seems so familiar: the way they ignore my bullshit and demand answers is almost exactly the way Ma would when she was mad, disappointed, or both. Just the memory turns my insides to waves. My voice is quiet now, weak with emotion.

"It's nothing. Just a shitty version of the Creation Story."

"YES!" they shout, and I wince. I slam the volume-down button on the keyboard over and over, to no avail. "I *knew* this was the right door!"

"Come on. Keep it down. Please," I beg.

"Sorry," they say in a near whisper. "I wasn't sure I'd gotten here in time but I have!"

In time for what? I want to ask, but once again, I'm struck by the way they speak. The roundness of their consonants, the smoothness of their vowels, even the way they pause between certain words. It's not just a voice, though, it's a presence, something whole, a shape. *The Shape.*

"Who are you?" I ask again.

"Not allowed to say," they reply, a hint of regret in their voice, and I'm reminded once more of Matoaka. "I'm sorry for all the mystery. I have certain rules I'm supposed to follow while I'm here. There's so much I wish I could tell you. And I would. It's just . . . it's all very complicated and delicate."

The Shape speaks so fast, as though the words they want to say are circling a drain and they have to spit them out immediately or they'll disappear.

"What *are* you allowed to say?"

"Pretty much just this: it's important that you keep writing. No matter what happens, you got to keep working 'til you're done. The result will have ramifications that influence future generations."

I sit there, my chest heavy now with pressure. I knew if I wrote about our people I had to do right by them just in case anyone read it, but I never really believed my writing would get to that point. I didn't even want to show it to Tanya. Could my story really have enough readers one day that it caused such influence? It's nothing new. It's the same story my people have told throughout centuries with a slightly more irreverent tone. *A tone*, it occurs to me with shattering clarity, *that you stole from your childhood conversation with Pocahontas. She's your narrator—or, your interpretation of her is your narrator. You didn't even come up with that yourself. Stealing from a cartoon character and your father and parading it around as creative or unique. You'd be better off writing about cheating old men at the racetrack. You wouldn't even have to waste your time trying to humanize them; the world's already done that for you. People want to read about men like that. People value work like that. They don't value you or your stupid little stories. Your father would be ashamed by what you've done with them.*

I rub my eyes until it hurts to dam the tears and dull my

thoughts. Why does this feel like the worst thing this person, this shape could ask of me? To finish writing something I've told myself I want to write? Told Steve I want to write—and every single one of his academic coworkers? A task that, just last night, felt sanctioned by the spirits of my parents?

Maybe it's because now I am writing with the expectation of making a product someone else could sell. Before, it was just for me. That's the reality, isn't it? I can't make art just to make art. I have to make art to sell art. What I write has to be deemed potentially profitable by people who have no idea about my community, who have no concept of any value that lies beyond what can be measured in imaginary numbers and transferred between bank accounts. As though that's more real than recognition from those you love, those you hope will see your art as honoring them in all their complexity. As loving their flaws and beauty in equal measure. As though sales are more meaningful than realizing your father's wildest dreams. As though critics' opinions are more important than making sure your peoples' stories live on, so they can continue to teach all the coming generations about ourselves, the world around us, and our place in the world.

And now our minds are one.

I shudder with one more deep sob. *Yes, Dad*, I think, *I hear you. I hear you.*

"Are you sure I'm the one who should write that story?" I finally ask, my face in my hands, my voice still ragged. "Maybe someone else would do a better job."

"Absolutely not. It has to be you," the Shape answers right away. "I can't tell you why, exactly. It's—"

"Against the rules, yeah, I got it," I finish for them as I wipe the last of my stuttering tears into my hairline.

"Please promise me you'll keep writing. It's important."

"Fine," I say with a sigh. "I'll keep writing. I can't promise it'll be good or fast, but I'll do it."

"Nya:wen." Before the second syllable's even out the voice is already fading away, the shadow on the screen being replaced with a colorful DVD menu: shades of dark purple becoming fuchsia becoming carnation pink behind a huge portrait of Pocahontas. Smaller pictures of her father, Chief Powhatan; her raccoon friend, Meeko; and her hummingbird friend, Flit; are beneath her, with John Smith and Governor Ratcliffe strategically positioned on the other side of the screen.

"Nyoh," I whisper eventually as the movie starts by itself and the beginning chords of "The Virginia Company" start.

CHAPTER 13

Why Dads Shouldn't Pick Their Daughters' Husbands

Now, about this guy. Everyone called him "the Ancient," which didn't exactly set the heart of Mature Flowers, or any girl in history, a-trembling. But before you start going on about ageism or anything, let me just say: sometimes being old's not so bad. Look at George Clooney. He's much more attractive with gray hair than he was with whatever color hair he had before. Brown? Black? I can't remember. Anyway, attraction's all relative, is what I'm saying.

Problem is, the Ancient didn't have much going for him personality-wise, either. Like, at all. Now I don't like to gossip—not like those animals—but I will say no other father in Sky World agreed to let him marry their daughter. Didn't matter what the Ancient promised he'd provide for their daughters or the rest of their clan family, which I hear was quite a lot. They still said no. Take from that what you will.

Understandably, Mature Flowers was pretty hesitant to marry the Ancient. But she really wanted to make her dead dad happy. Plus it would be awesome for that prophecy about her becoming the greatest woman there ever was to come true, if only so she could shove it in the face of everyone who ever talked about her behind her back. *She* was the greatest woman in all of Sky World. What were they? Would anyone know *their* names thousands of years and lifetimes after they died? Exactly. They wouldn't.

Because marrying a puckered leather pouch of an old guy wasn't punishment enough, Mature Flowers's dad had one last thing to tell her: she had to prove herself worthy of the Ancient in a series of tests. "A kind of fucked-up marriage Olympics," I think he called it—or that's what he should have called it. She had to carry all the firewood to his dirty-ass longhouse by herself, then clean the place, which had been collecting muck and dust and dog shit for longer than her mother had been alive. Then, because why would it possibly end there, she had to cook him this big cauldron of boiling mush, take off her clothes, and say absolutely nothing while he flung it on her naked body and got his dogs to lick it off her burned skin.

Go ahead, read that again. We've got time.

Fucked up, innit?

I told you her dead dad was a douchebag.

CHAPTER 14

This Is a Looong One, So Get Some Snacks and Get Comfortable

STEVE

Hey babe. Didn't want to wake you when I left but wanted to say sorry for what happened last night. I shouldn't have been so dismissive. We can talk about it later if you want.

P.S. Don't forget to text Tanya about the dinner tomorrow.

Love you.

9:30 A.M.

I was awake when his alarm went off. I was awake when he lay there in bed beside me with his phone in his hands, looking over emails and texts before he'd even fully woken. I was awake when he finally sat up and shot off a few replies. I was awake when he grunted to his feet. I was awake when he yanked the heavy dresser drawers open and picked through folded clothes, then picked a button-down shirt from a hanger in the closet. I was awake as he showered with the door open, singing Nirvana songs. I was awake while he dressed, then sat on the edge of the bed and pulled on his socks. I was awake while he made himself some quick toast and what I later found out was a full pot of coffee. I was awake when he stepped into his shoes and closed the front door.

Last night, after I finished writing what I could, I sat there, wondering what I might say to bridge the gap between Steve and me, my mind going in circles, getting fuzzier and fuzzier as I failed to find the words that would bring us back together. When I came upstairs, Steve was snoring. Luckily, Dawn seemed to still be asleep, too. This was the longest she'd ever stayed asleep. Something like five hours? I hoped this was the start of a pattern.

By the time I finally slid between the sheets next to Steve, I decided it was better to suck it up and make nice. I was definitely onto something big—the Shape had told me as much—but I needed more time to figure it all out. And I would, I felt sure of that now. I would finish my writing and fulfill my destiny and the world would open up.

It already was. Steve texting to ask for forgiveness first not only made things much easier for me, it also felt like another sign. I was on the right track. Things were going the way they should, even if that wasn't always obvious. I could do all this. I could do anything. Even Dawn was being perfect this morning after her full night's sleep. Cooing and smiling. Latching on with no problems. Drinking and staring up at me, happy.

ALICE

That's okay. Sorry for overreacting. It's been hard being so far away from my

family and friends. I know my emotions
are a lot right now. I'm sorry. Thanks for
putting up with me and my messiness!
And I'll text Tanya now. Thanks for the
reminder! Love you!! 😬

9:46 A.M.

By the time I hit send, I'm back to wondering about what the
Shape said about my writing, and what my writing, in turn, said
about me. Dad once told me if you listen carefully enough, you can
hear the storyteller in the story—the beating heart beneath the
words. The storyteller's failures help them choose what obstacles to
throw in the hero's way; their joys give them fuel for how the hero
will overcome.

So what does that mean I'm currently saying about myself? I
keep coming back to the versions of the story I chose to revisit,
mainly the one recounted by Mohawk scholar Brian Rice in a book
Ma gave me for my birthday a couple years ago, and the Barbara
Alice Mann version at the beginning of this book called *The Native
Peoples of North America: A History*, which I found lying around Aunt
Rachel's place. They aren't the only ones. There are many I could
have adapted—shorter ones, happier ones, less fucked-up ones.
What appealed to me about these ones? The pain? The violence? The
loss? There had to be a reason. And telling this story in this fucking
city? The one that took its name from a Mohawk word, then used
steady, fearless Mohawk men to build its precious CN Tower, while
simultaneously doing everything in its power to keep us out of sight
and out of mind? No creation story born out of this time and this
place could ever be a happy one.

As I sit here, holding Dawn, it seems pretty obvious: I chose this version because of Steve and what has happened between us. How fully I gave myself to him, how foolishly and completely I'd built my life around him, oblivious to the warnings that a life with him might not be an endless honeymoon. I chose it because I am so incredibly lonely and isolated in this strange world I've landed in, just like Mature Flowers on that turtle's back, realizing she'll never see her people again. And, finally, I suppose I chose it because the sparkling promise of my supposedly perfect life turned out to be a trick of the light. My belief that my marriage would make me better was a prophecy and lie I'd told myself, same as the prophecy Mature Flowers's dad told her.

How much has really changed since marrying Steve? I'm in a beautiful, if somewhat boring, home in Toronto. I'm given enough free time to write. Those things do matter. I can't just push that privilege aside. After all, if whatever I'm writing has some sort of meaning beyond me and what I ascribe to it, surely that meaning is possible, at least partially, because of the security and freedom Steve has afforded me. And yet, just like when I was living with Ma, I can't deny that I'm still making another person—or, when you consider Dawn, other people—the center of my universe. Nothing I do is done solely for me. Everything is done to elevate Steve or Dawn, in some way. I'm an afterthought in my own life.

What if I wasn't, though? I could really focus on writing this, and finishing it, as a gift to myself. A version of the Creation Story that unapologetically revolves around my joys, sorrows, instincts, and insights. It very well could make a difference to future generations, somehow, as long as I can muster the courage and self-confidence to actually do it. That's if one were to believe the Shape—which, I realize without hesitation, I do. They seemed incredibly emotional and conflicted when they couldn't answer my questions—as though they knew me, the real me, and cared. Even though it's only been a matter of hours, it's as if the Shape is anchoring me, strongly, deeply, like century-old roots clotted with ancient earth. But not in a way that diminishes me; in a way that recognizes and encourages my own potential. I know I can trust the Shape, the same way I know I can't trust anyone else to understand. I'm not even sure I can talk with Aunt Rachel about it, the way I talked with her about Matoaka and everything else. She'd said I wasn't crazy then. But she was still scared, I knew. If I were to tell her everything now, how do I know she wouldn't change her mind?

Suddenly an idea appears, fully formed and unbidden: *the Shape must be an ancestor trying to direct me.* They did know Mohawk, after all, and seemed to be aware of time in a different way than we experience it here. Babies can pick their parents, so maybe that goes both ways. Maybe you can pick your descendants, too. That has to be what's happening here. What if it's Mature Flowers advising me? She's an ancestor to all Haudenosaunee. Shit, when I really think about it, there are so many similarities between my life and hers, I could very well be a modern version of her. Maybe all Onkwehón:we women are—living out different variations of the Creation Story until our bodies return to the clay we're made of and our spirits return to the Spirit World. A cycle of life and death where dying wasn't so much a period as a semicolon, connecting your old life and its cycle to a new life and cycle with its own peaks and valleys and points and purposes. Related, but separate. Pieces, but still whole.

We are all Mature Flowers, I think, sure that this revelation is something that I need to discuss with all the Native women I know because it will help them understand and not be afraid.

"You're Mature Flowers, too," I say to Dawn, watching her face for recognition of what I've said. She is quiet, content. I gaze down as her little cheeks and chin move with each gulp, filled with love and gratefulness for once instead of fear and anxiety. Then I tap out a message.

ALICE

Hey bb!! You good to stay a little late tomorrow with Dawn? I'll get you whatever snacks you want!!! Steve's got a work dinner thing I'm supposed to go to with him. Gotta play the role of lil wifey. You know how it is.

9:52 A.M.

I think for a moment, then add:

ALICE

Also did you know we're all Sky Woman?

9:53 A.M.

I look back down at Dawn. Her eyes are closed. She looks calm, comfortable. Almost makes me feel like I'm actually a decent mother. Ma might even be proud, if she could see me—see us—like this. She might even forgive me for how she died. I wish I could keep this moment perfectly preserved in my memory to refer back to whenever I'm left scrambling in a flurry of her tearless cries. Some proof I'm not a monster, that I can do this the way other moms do.

Then it occurs to me: I *can* preserve this moment. I've got a phone in my hand right now. I can take a picture of her nearly sleeping, or a video, or even a selfie of both of us looking like a mother and daughter should look. I hold the phone out and up to make sure I don't look like I've got a double chin or anything, then take the picture and examine it. The lighting isn't doing me any favors. Also my tit looks kind of porno-y, which is weird to say since I'm feeding my kid, but I know how quick Facebook and Instagram are to take down breastfeeding pics, much less ones that have as much visible areola as this one. I reach into Dawn's crib for a spit-up blankie, place it strategically over my boob, then shove my body to the left so the chair's facing the lamp. The soft glow of the bulb isn't bright enough to overcome the stark sun behind me, so I turn on the flash and click.

Dawn erupts. I start repeating "shit" over and over like that'll magically soothe her, then, against my better judgment, look at the picture. The camera captured the beginnings of Dawn's scream—and my stupid, helpless face—perfectly. Delete. I get to my feet and start bouncing her in my arms as I walk back and forth. What the fuck was it that Meghan did the other day to calm her down? Oh yeah, she burped her. I can do that. I start patting Dawn's back as I pace, worried that I'm patting both too hard and not hard enough to coax her little body into belching.

"Come on, little Dawny. Come on. Burp for Mama. You can do it."

The phone buzzes. It's Tan. Things can't exactly get much worse, so I open the text.

TANYA

Mornin bb!!! Got some special sage that's not cursed like the stuff all those crystal-lovin yt ladies use. We're clearin that house!! And I'm good to babysit tomorrow night as long as you get me

Doritos. Nacho Cheese!!! None of that
Cool Ranch shit. 🤤 🤤 🤤

10:15 A.M.

TANYA

Also wtf you smokin this am? And can I
have some tomorrow? 😄 😄 😄

10:16 A.M.

She's not ready to hear the truth, I think sadly. I'm a little disappointed, but I can't expect her to understand without my explaining what's happened.

I decide to take Dawn for a little field trip to the Metro for Tan's chips. I haven't really been outside since the stuff with the neighborhood watch lady, but that was before I knew I was being guided and protected by Ma, Dad, and the Shape. Things are different now. I feel different. Like pure love is coursing through my veins, strengthening me.

By the time I'm all dressed and Dawn's snapped into her stroller, she's calmed down. It's like she knows that we're being divinely protected by our ancestors and wants to be especially good for them. You might even think she was always this sweet—if you hadn't seen or heard her going like a category 5 hurricane a half hour before.

I stare at the neighborhood watch lady's house for a few minutes before we leave to make sure she's not monitoring us. Even with protection, I'd rather not have another interaction with her if I can help it.

The weather outside is immaculate. As I walk down the street, my body is clued in to my surroundings like it's never been before. I feel the delicious warmth of the sun on my skin, see the vivid green of the stubborn plants that persist, pushing through the cracks of the cement. I feel the slight breeze like the gentlest fingers running through my hair. *This is why the Thanksgiving Address exists,* I realize. *This is why we've always referred to it as "the words before all else."* Each section starts so perfectly. "We bring our minds together as one and give thanks for Mother Earth . . ." It starts the same every time as we give thanks for the food plants, the berries, the grasses, the medicine plants, the trees, the waters, the fish, the animals, our Elder Brother Sun, our Grandmother Moon, our grandfathers the Thunderers, the Four Winds, the Stars, the Four Messengers. But each piece of the address is more than a simple acknowledgment of these elements of creation; they're also catalogs of what each one does for us, and how their continued existence and generosity to us is what allows us as humans to keep living. Because what would we do if the earth was dead? The plants? The trees? The waters or fish or animals? What would we do if our elder brother stopped shining? If our grandmother stopped watching over us at night, singing the tides in and out? We would be nothing. We wouldn't exist. It's so damn necessary for us to give thanks for all of these, acknowledging we are no higher than any of them, the way Western ideologies try to insist, that we are in fact dependent on their good health for our good health, and so must be respectful of and grateful to them, the elements of nature, centering them when we make decisions so they will not only still exist, but also be in good relations with the next seven generations to come, just as they were in good relations with the last seven generations behind us. It's brilliant. If our minds aren't one in understanding this basic fact, how can our minds be one on anything? The wisdom of my people fills me and, as I walk down the street, I'm proud. We know what is important in this life. We've always known.

Once inside the store, I head to the snack aisle, right to where the Doritos are. As I'm looking at the bags of chips, though, it's like the letters on the labels rearrange themselves in front of me. I can't read what they say. I blink a few times. Nothing changes.

"The fuck?" I ask, rubbing at my eyes with the back of my hand. Is this some type of test? I thought my ancestors were here to protect me. Why would they let something like this happen? When I look again, the letters rearrange to something else that makes no sense.

A beautiful Black woman in a sunshine yellow dress stops beside me. "Sorry," she says, as she sneaks past and grabs a red bag of chips. She smiles deeply at Dawn and me, like she's a long-lost friend, then turns to leave.

"Wait," I blurt. "Excuse me. Miss?"

The woman turns back to look at me.

"Are those Doritos? The ones you just took?"

"Yeah . . ." She looks from me to Dawn to me again, an eyebrow cocked as if she's trying to disentangle some difficult knot. Why is she looking at me like that? Why is she looking at Dawn like that? Is it the stroller? Does she think I've stolen it or something? Is she going to tell the cashiers to call the cops on me? She might be part of the neighborhood watch. She might have been warned about me.

Oh, come on, a competing voice intervenes. *Be reasonable. Do you really think she'd be friends with neighborhood watch lady? She's more likely to be targeted by her. And anyway she was already nice to you both. Friendly. She's no enemy.*

I take a breath and try to calm myself.

"Sorry," I say. "My eyes are bothering me. I can't read the bags right."

"Which flavor are you looking for?" she asks, her body fully turned to me and Dawn and the giant stroller now that she knows her help is needed. "Nacho Cheese? Cool Ranch? Sweet Chili Heat?"

Which kind did Tanya say again? I'd check the text but my eyes are fucked.

"Cool Ranch?" I guess.

She zeroes in on a bag immediately, then passes it to me. "Here you go."

"Thanks," I say, feeling so stupid and helpless.

"No problem." She flashes that smile again—the one that made me think she was safe. She hesitates for a moment, admiring Dawn, who beams up at her, then says, "Your baby's really cute."

"Oh, thank you," I reply as she walks away.

I look at Dawn. She is really cute, especially now, dressed like a little princess in some designer baby dress Joan had insisted on buying for her. It was the only clean thing left in the drawer, since I haven't had the energy to do laundry for weeks. Apparently there was a matching adult dress in a more mature cut and style that Joan had bought for herself in anticipation of whenever she'd get to parade Dawn around her friends.

Then I look down at my own outfit. The disconnect between how Dawn looks and how I look is huge. No wonder that woman was so confused. I'm wearing a ratty T-shirt and jean cutoff shorts. A certain type of skinny white girl could leave her mansion in Hollywood and be hailed as a style icon in this same outfit, but I was most definitely not that certain type of skinny white girl. I was just a mess. Why did I pick this? Why did I throw on an old pair of dirty sneakers with holes worn in the heel? How could I forget the rules I had to abide by to be accepted here? This is what got me into the mess with neighborhood watch lady in the first place. I was too distracted this morning by my new purpose. I had to be careful.

Don't worry about that. You're being protected.

I look back at the shelf of chips. "DORITOS," every bag proudly proclaims. I am safe. I just need sleep. That's all it is. I grab another bag of Cool Ranch for good measure and consider throwing them on top of the stroller canopy, but worry they're going to fall off, so I tuck both bags in beside Dawn. I assess whether the bags will bother her. Her face is still clearly visible. She blinks at me, the right side of her mouth moving up into what looks like a conspiratorial grin. She's okay. Plus there's enough room in this SUV of a stroller for her and probably a whole other baby. I can most likely fit a few jars of marinara and Alfredo sauce in the little basket underneath the seat. I'll try making a nice dinner tonight for Steve as an apology for everything. Buy the really expensive sauce for once to make it seem like I'm a better cook than I am. Being a proper housewife and mother is about nothing if not the aesthetics. I go in search of fancy pasta sauce.

And there, standing right in the middle of the pasta aisle, is Mason Jamieson. One turn in the grocery store and I'm a thirteen-year-old girl again. How do I even describe . . . ? Fear, anxiety, embarrassment. Excitement, hope, lust. Lust most of all. Even after I turned him down all those years ago, convinced he'd ruin my life, I'd still seen him as some fallen god or titan, all long gleaming black hair and lean, tight muscles. I still have vivid memories of the wrinkles that fanned out from the corner of his immaculate brown eyes, creasing ever so slightly when he smiled, which wasn't often. Few words escaped his lips back then. Always angry and grunting with his thoughts buttoned up tight. I loved that. He was like a candy bar waiting to be unwrapped. Still is. From meters away I can tell: age has only made him more sinful. I can clearly see the outline of his biceps through the sleeves of his shirt.

I'm about to turn and slink into the next aisle so I can double-check that I don't have toothpaste crusted on my face when—

"Alice?"

Of course. Thirteen years after giving me the silent treatment he suddenly grows a tongue and decides to talk to me. On the day I leave the house looking like a hungover groupie, pushing a stroller loaded with more chips than baby. I'm surprised he even knows my name.

Wait. *Why* does he know my name? The only times I remember him publicly referring to me, he called me "that bitch." He said it in front of all his friends and their girlfriends, who laughed like he'd made some hilarious joke. I tried to ignore it. Tried to assure myself that, had I let him fuck me, he *would've* ruined my life, the way Matoaka had told me. I could have gotten pregnant with his baby. I could have dropped out of school. He was shitty enough to me for turning him down. Could he really be that much nicer if I'd given him what he wanted? He was just a kid back then, though. The fact that he's even talking to me now means he must be kind of different. Either way, I instinctively yank off my wedding ring and shove it into my back pocket, then at the last minute give my ass a squeeze through the shorts. Not as firm as in high school, but not all cottage cheese, either. Couldn't hurt to make him a little jealous. Make him feel bad for treating me how he did.

"Mason Jamieson? Hooooolay, what're you doing here?"

"I live here now."

"No shit! Where at?"

"Got a place over on Euclid."

"Wow, that's a really nice area."

"It is, but I'm in a basement. The floors are crooked and the mice are the size of cats. I'm just here to buy enough pasta and tomato sauce to fight off scurvy."

He's so easy with me, like we were old friends in high school instead of a missed connection whom he bullied once he didn't get what he wanted. It feels disorienting, like he's rewriting history by talking to me like this.

"So you're a student, then?"

His smile is small and perfect, and I can't help grinning back, despite everything. "What gave me away?"

"You still look like you have hope for the future."

"Ahhhh. Well, you caught me. I'm over at York for environmental stuff. Look at you, though! You've got a baby!" He crouches down and moves aside a bag of Doritos to get a better look at her. "What's her name?"

"Dawn," I say. Dawn blinks her salutations.

"She looks just like you." He smiles up at me, the lie hanging unacknowledged between us. She doesn't look like me. She has light brown skin, sure, but her deep blue eyes and fluffy light brown hair are all Steve. Still, it's a nice lie. One that at least *feels* true. She's as much Mature Flowers's descendant as I am.

I shift from one foot to the other. "Thanks."

"So what have you been up to? Besides the obvious." He rubs Dawn's fuzzy head and stands back up.

"Not much. I mean, I finished my BA in English—" No I haven't. I haven't even gone to university. But I can't stop now. I still want him to like me, to respect me, to *want* me. How much has really changed since I was thirteen?

"That's great n—"

"—and recently I started working on a book. One about the Creation Story. Something that will help keep our people connected to our stories and remember how ace our culture is. You know kids today. Always glued to their phones, never paying attention to what really matters. I'm even thinking about turning it into a podcast so there's more entry points. Meet people where they are, wherever that is. Anyway, that's all a ways off. There is some interest from publishers, but I don't have much done. It's hard to write when you're covered in spit-up and running on three hours of sleep." I laugh. I hope my fictional life doesn't sound too ridiculous to believe, though it's hard to tell from looking at him what he thinks about any of this. There's a strong chance he's like most men and doesn't care much about what any woman around him thinks, feels, or desires, and so he won't remember any of these details I'm rattling off in some vain attempt to paint myself as successful. He could still be the same guy I knew all those years ago, assuming he's the sun around which all women helplessly revolve until they fall or are pushed out of his orbit.

"Wow. That's . . . a lot. I can only imagine how hard it must be to keep up with all of it. My sister Kerry just had a baby. Jordan. If it wasn't for our mom and aunts coming over all the time, she'd probably be crazy right now. Your mom must be there nonstop."

My chest turns to lead. Every time I think the wound starts to scab over, a knife comes along and scrapes away a fresh layer of skin, leaving me bloody and exposed. I tell my lungs to breathe.

In. Deeper. Deeper. Now out.

"My mom actually died last year." I don't say how. I can still protect her in these small ways.

"Shit. I'm an idiot. Kerry told me about that. I'm so sorry."

"It's okay. I'm fine. We're fine."

I stand there and smile in what I hope is a very convincing manner. His concerned expression tells me it isn't. Then, in a staggering display of solidarity, Dawn lets loose a high-pitched whinny of a cry and it's as if everything else falls away. I immediately start ripping through her monstrous pink diaper bag. Joan bought it for me. "It's Coach," she said, patting the bag like a lover. I hate it. It's got too many pockets and zippers. I would have been happier with a simple backpack, but no, I have this mound of cotton candy dripping off my arm, making me feel like even more of a fraud than I already do.

Stop lying to yourself. You could have used something else, a voice inside me spits. *You use this bougie-ass bag because you want people to think you're the sort of person to own it.*

I pause, startled at how different this voice seems from the reassuring one I just heard in the Doritos aisle. More like the one in my bedroom two nights ago. Taunting. Hateful.

My focus slides back to the external reality of this moment: the feeling of Mason's eyes watching me like an itch I can't scratch, yes, but also another pair of eyes, and another. Who are they? I look up at Mason quickly, trying to decipher. Did he hear the voice, too? Is he watching to see how I react to the pressure of both the voice and him, in the same place at the same time? This must be the "what" the Shape was referring to when they told me I needed to keep writing "no matter what": this sort of burning uncomfortable clash between my interior fire and external freeze, my consciousness the drip-drip-drip between the two. Is the Shape watching me right now? What about Ma and Dad? Is there an entire world of unseen beings—of spirits—watching me now, hiding, judging, laughing? Is this what it is to be haunted?

I focus on what I see in front of me: the inside of the diaper bag, then the bright white pacifier. I focus on what I hear: Dawn's tiny, sharp yelps. I focus on what I feel: the plastic pacifier between my fingers as I offer it to Dawn. She reluctantly accepts, eyeing my sore tits as she nestles back among the empty calories. I clench and unclench my toes, finally feeling like I'm back on this side of reality.

"You're really good with her," Mason says. There's nothing genuine in the sentiment. It's the sort of thing a person mindlessly parrots to any woman who has become a mother, assuming it's the sort of thing she wants to hear, a validation that she's performing her role well.

"It's the soother," I mumble, now hoping to get away from this situation and back home as soon as possible. I glance up and see him staring at my ring finger like I'd hoped he would. Right now, though, the validation—if that's, in fact, what it is—feels hollow. There's too much swirling in my mind. I don't know what to grab on to and what to leave. When Mason speaks, his voice is low and clear.

"Look, I know this sounds weird considering I haven't seen you in years, and I was a little fucking terror when you did know me, but if you ever need someone to watch Dawn for a couple hours so you can work on your book, or whatever, you can give me a call. I'm usually reading the same ten reports about fracking anyway," he says as he fishes a card out of his wallet and hands it to me. He actually has a card. Thankfully, I can actually read it:

MASON JAMIESON

MOHAWK
LAND DEFENDER

Despite everything, part of me wants to laugh—at the card, at him, at this whole fucking bizzarro situation. I flip the card around to find his contact information. When I look back up at him, he's staring at me so intensely, and with such vulnerability, it reminds me of what he's actually doing. He's giving me a chance to reject him, again, and though he might not cuss me out for doing so now that he's an adult, he's still, at the end of the day, that same boy whose ego was once so fragile he cracked when he heard the word "no." Not that different from me, really, whose ego is still so fragile I pretended I wasn't married in the hopes a dude I barely knew in high school might make a move despite my having a baby in tow. I understand why Mason markets himself to white environmentalists as some sort of Haudenosaunee Batman. It's smart. Probably very lucrative. I didn't expect anything like this for him when we were kids. Did he imagine this for me?

"Thanks," I say, too scared to give any indication whether I'll follow up or not. Before the conversation can get any more personal, I promptly turn and push Dawn away. If he was anything like he was in high school, he'd be soaking in the practiced sway of my denim-clad ass, imagining all the things he could do to it given half a chance. I can't look back at him. I know that. Only desperate women need to check if men are watching them. But I can't help it. I am desperate. I need to know he's watching, even now, when my mind is bouncing in a thousand different directions. I need proof—however flimsy—that Steve isn't the only one who wants to see me naked. That another choice is possible. I turn and look back. Mason's gone.

I'm barely there as I move through the checkout lane. Instead, I'm going over everything that happened: from the Shape last night, to the moment I couldn't read in the chip aisle, to the calming voice and kind woman who helped, to the weird and far too coincidental meeting with Mason, to the voice that emerged from who knows where to criticize me. These are dots to connect, I know, but all of it feels beyond my capabilities. It reminds me of how I felt in the weeks following my little talk with Matoaka all those years ago. How my brain felt electric, like a computer tower running so many programs it felt fiery to the touch. How my body started to feel like it was becoming unnecessary, inconvenient, like a weight holding me down. My head begins to throb with activity. Still, I must do everything right with the cashier, because before I know it, I'm out on the street, a couple bags of groceries tucked into different parts of the stroller.

How will I deal with all of this at the dinner? I'm keeping myself together well enough now, but I don't have anyone monitoring my every move, the way Sheila and the other academic wives will. If the voices get loud and hard to ignore in front of all of them, I might embarrass Steve. Can't have that. I'm halfway past the liquor store when my thoughts practically scream at me: *Buy a mickey of vodka.* No. It would make my mind go quiet and calm, at least for a while, but I can't drink any in front of these people. I've made such a show of being sober, plus I'm breastfeeding. *You can hide it in a flask and drink it in the bathroom.*

I make a wide turn and push the stroller in the store. I'm far from the only one here, but every time I look at the front, the two cashiers are staring at me, muttering back and forth to each other. What the fuck are they saying? One lets out a guffaw, then claps her hand over her mouth like she can't believe she let herself laugh so loud. I never understand why white women like them feel the need to stifle their joy, as if it's more polite to make sure everyone thinks you're miserable all the time. It's that same train of thought that makes it impossible for me and my cousins to eat in any restaurant that doesn't double as a sports bar. Every time we crack up laughing, which is often, a waiter rushes over and asks us to "quiet down" for the sake of the other patrons, or to relay that they've gotten "some complaints" about how loud we're being, how discourteous. The implication being: you and your joy don't belong here.

Luckily, whatever was wrong with my eyes back in the grocery store seems to have stopped, so I don't have to ask for help. I pick a mickey of Smirnoff. It's small enough to hide in drawers, and I can pay in cash. That way, if Steve happens to check the bank statement, I won't have to get into an awkward conversation with him. Maybe this is how it started for Ma—wanting to stop the pain, only to discover the pain never stopped.

I get in the checkout line for the slightly older white woman cashier. She looks to be in her forties. She'd be pretty if her face didn't naturally settle into a deep frown. I place the bottle of Smirnoff on the counter and notice an American flag pin stuck near her tits. Oh. She's one of *those* women. I look up, and as soon as my eyes meet hers, she sneers, her gaze darting back and forth from Dawn to me and back again as she rings me through. Fucking great. I can practically hear her thoughts as she takes in the outfit I'm wearing, the color of my skin, the fact that I'm even in a place that sells alcohol: *Drunken Indian. Shitty mom. Savage slut.*

"What's your problem?" I ask her.

"Excuse me?"

She's surprised I've called her out. Good.

"You and your friend have looked like you wanted to say something to me since I came in. Well? What is it?"

The woman looks around me, across at her friend, then raises her eyebrows as if confirming something she said to her moments before, like I'm not standing right in front of her. "Well, I wasn't gonna say anything, but—"

"Yes?" I ask, my tone sharp as a dagger.

"—this guy won't last you long—"

"Won't last *me* long? What do you mean it won't last *me* long?"

"Oh, settle down. Not just you. Anyone. It's a small bottle."

Before I can respond, her friend pipes up from behind me: "What Chrissy is *trying* to say is we've got a sale on the great big bottles of Smirnoff. It's a really good deal."

She eyes me up and down scornfully. The other cashier's frowning lips stretch into a thin smile that nearly cuts her face in two. They're like those white girls from high school. They know exactly how to say something underhanded that cuts you in your gut while keeping the blade hidden. If I tried to complain to their manager, there'd be nothing to punish either of them for. Both were technically selling me their product, even if I knew what they were implying about my alcohol intake, what they were no doubt saying about me before I came to the register, and what they'd continue to say after

I left. Plus, there were two of them. No way would a manager believe anything I said when they could both say I was a crazy Indian. Worse than that: a crazy Indian mom who looked like shit and was buying alcohol before noon on a Thursday, her newborn baby in tow. They didn't have to do anything, and they'd already won.

"No thanks, Chrissy. I appreciate your diligence but this one is just fine." I smile back insincerely, passing her a bill.

She gets my change, then places the bottle in a brown bag and holds it out to me. As I take it, she looks at Dawn again, then, in a sickeningly sweet voice, as if she's speaking directly to my daughter, "You enjoy now!"

I'm shaking with anger, and tears are burning in my eyes as I shove the bottle in the diaper bag and rush down the street. I'm so busy trying to think up comebacks I could have used on Chrissy I don't notice when a blanket catches in one of the stroller wheels.

"Hey!" a Native man yells as the blanket—and the careful layout of dream catchers and beaded bracelets and earrings placed on it—starts dragging. I stop and turn to see him standing with his hands out, palms up.

"I'm so sorry," I say, bending down to untangle the blanket from the wheel. "I don't know what happened."

"You plowed on through without paying attention's what happened."

He's in a puffy winter vest despite the heat, probably in his fifties, his face scarred from what I hope is only bad acne from his youth. He's hardened, but in a way that I recognize. It's what happens to all the little boys from my rez at some point on their way to becoming men. There's an authority to him that makes me feel like a kid disappointing a beloved uncle.

"Sorry," I offer again, weakly. I twist and pull at the fleece blanket as the man crouches down beside me.

"Careful! Heck, you're gonna rip it, you keep yanking like that. Let me."

He grabs at the blanket, and I stand and watch him for a few moments. This clearly irritates him.

"Wanna pick up my shit 'stead of just standing there?"

I immediately start gathering the dream catchers and jewelry. It's nice. Much nicer than one would assume, considering it's being sold on the sidewalk. One of the dream catchers has little beads in the sinew web that look to be the same color red as Dawn's dress. I place everything else carefully down on the sidewalk where it once was, then go back toward Dawn, who's content, sucking on her pacifier. I place the dream catcher beside her. The red's an exact match. Something about this seems inevitable to me, as though it's a sign from Creator and maybe even the Shape that this dream catcher is meant for us. For Dawn. A sign that, despite everything, things will work out. I'll finish writing this story and all the futures—my future, Dawn's future, and the future of the next seven generations—will be secured.

"How much is this one?" I ask.

The man manages to get his blanket out of the wheels and stands, appraising me and everything I have before settling on his price: "Fifty."

It's a pretty steep price, considering the hoop of the dream catcher is barely bigger than the palm of my hand, but I pull out my wallet. There's exactly fifty dollars sitting there. I smile—another sign—then pass the bills over to the man. He counts and pockets the money.

I have no idea what nation this man is, but instinct tells me to speak the little Mohawk I know to him. "Nya:wen," I say, half a question, half an apology.

"Nyoh," he responds, just loud enough for me to hear.

Something about this small exchange feels like validation, like acceptance. We may be in totally different circumstances, but we're still a team. We both know what we're up against here, and we're surviving. After all, how many times is Mohawk even spoken on these lands today? How many land acknowledgments are mindlessly rattled off by people who don't even bother to check the pronunciation of "Haudenosaunee" before they start, who have no idea what the Dish with One Spoon treaty means, much less what it means to live by it? In a way, the two of us speaking our language together, here, now, is like traveling through time, to the days before we were trained to feel like aliens on our own lands, impediments to "progress." Back to when we felt worthy of holding our heads high without first needing the sort of therapy that pretends colonialism has no impact, that Jedi mind tricks of personal accountability are all we need to feel confident and okay. I'm momentarily, inexplicably filled with pure joy. I don't need to think about the cashiers or Mason, or what any of them think of or expect from me. I don't need to think about Steve or his academic party looming over me like a noose. I don't need to think about the pressure of writing a creation story that ripples outward and helps my people. I don't need to think about anything but this one moment of connection with another Onkwehón:we, possibly even another Haudenosaunee, on a busy street, in the middle of a busy city, where people walk fast and dismiss you faster.

For a few minutes I'm walking back toward home as buoyant as I left it. I'm one of my ancestors: strong, healthy, and confident, sure that I have a place in this world, a purpose. And sure enough, when I look around it's like the concrete and buildings and pollution have disappeared, and I can see what this land would have looked like back when my people decided it was too plentiful and beautiful to belong to any one nation, that it should be a neutral zone they shared with the Anishinaabe, despite centuries of warfare and grudges. The water is clear and cold, fish iridescent as jewels flitting through the lake and river and creeks as fast as Torontonians jet through the streets. Huge, fragrant pine trees and thick, almost fluffy cedar trees and tall, skinny white birch trees with dark knots like open eyes on their bark sprout from the soft, moist brown soil, their roots as deeply attached to the earth as a breastfeeding baby is to her mother. Not Dawn to me, obviously, but another baby to a better mother. Or yes, me, but a version of me who understands instinctively how to soothe and protect and love. The version of me I know I can become, with the help of my ancestors and the Shape.

Suddenly my feet are hitting concrete sidewalk again. Strangers' confused, dismissive, or judgmental looks hurtle toward me as I look down and push Dawn faster. I can feel all that confidence I felt moments before beading up on me, then dripping off, like water droplets from a greasy plate. I turn down our street, and the houses around me are the houses of people who despise me, their windows flocked with expensive lace or velvet or brocade curtains that look like blinking eyes, narrowing eyes, watching and watching, judging and hating. The closest one leans in toward me, its shadow stretching over us.

You don't belong here. Get out, you Indian slut.

It's that voice again, dropping thoughts in my head. My breathing quickens, my heart fluttering. I stop walking. Rub my eyes until all I see is black, then red.

"I need sleep. I just need sleep. There's nothing there. There's nothing there," I whisper to myself.

You heard us. We don't want savages here.

An image of neighborhood watch lady, anger distorting her face. She must have known about this. Been in on it.

She was simply carrying out our will. And our will shall be done.

"Stopitstopitstopit." My face is wet with tears I didn't know were falling. There's a high-pitched squeal I recognize as Dawn. It's as if she can hear the houses, too, and is as terrified as I am. I worry that the houses are getting closer, that their doors are gaping open like hungry mouths ready to devour me. To devour us. Holy shit. Dawn. She's completely helpless here. She couldn't even run if she wanted to. I have to protect her from them. There's no one else to do it. No one who knows what these things are capable of.

Don't worry about her. We can use her. But we can't use you.

Can the houses hear my thoughts? The words of the Shape come to me again: "No matter what happens, you got to keep working 'til you're done." But how am I supposed to write when the very houses in my neighborhood are trying to force me out of it? When even the cashiers know I'm a fraud and want to destroy me? Why didn't the Shape give me any warning about this?

"Alice? Are you okay?"

There's a warm pressure on my arm and, when I open my eyes, Meghan's fake tan face is so close to mine I can smell the peppermint of her breath as her teeth smack around the gum in her mouth.

Behind her head the houses are leaning in, their normally straight bodies curved toward me, as if they're waiting to see what I do, what I say. I look down and to the left, at fat blades of grass that, hundreds of years ago, might have been something actually useful, like wild onions, instead of some rich fuck's vanity lawn. I focus on the physical shape of the grass to try to ground myself. The heat of the sun on my skin. But grounding was about bringing me back into my body, tying me down like a helium balloon to a child's wrist when I'd start to dissociate. This is different. This is about the physical reality I'm stuck in cracking open like hardened earth and magma pouring forth, threatening to burn me. I focus once again on my breathing, the rhythm of my chest as it rises and falls. I feel my heartbeat slow along with my breath. Meghan's eyebrows knit in my peripheral, and for good reason. Dawn is still crying, and I still haven't answered her question.

"I'm okay, yeah. It's just . . . I went to get the chips for my cousin before a party tomorrow night and then I got in a fight with the cashiers and then we got stuck on a blanket," I explain as I wipe my cheeks. By the look on Meghan's face, my explanation isn't helping. "I'm really tired," I offer, praying that this will satisfy her as my voice thickens and the crying ramps up again.

"You poor thing!" She sounds genuine, her voice like warm tea with honey. "Here, let's try pushing the stroller and see if that doesn't calm down little Dawn."

She slips between me and the stroller and starts down the street. I stay still and watch Meghan and Dawn pull away as the questions pour forth. How did she know we were out here? Was she looking for us, like neighborhood watch lady? Was I the one the neighborhood watch was designed to monitor, to track? And why is Meghan so insistent on pushing the stroller? Does she know the houses can use Dawn but not me? Maybe they all know the Shape has made contact and they want to stop me before I can write what I'm supposed to write. This is the sort of resistance I'm up against. Constant, all-seeing enemies who never let me rest, who watch for every opportunity they can take to knock me down and push, hard. The Onkwehón:we man I bought the dream catcher from wasn't always homeless. He got to that point somehow, or was dragged there. Maybe he was involved in foster care when he was young. I remember seeing a stat online—kids in care made up a huge chunk of homeless folks. Something like half of homeless youth and a third of homeless adults? The point is, it's a lot. That man was a statistic the way I was a statistic back when I lived on Six Nations—depression, self-harm, substance abuse, poverty, child of a single mother, no running water. Maybe the Creator put that man in my path to warn me about what certain people have been planning since I was born: to keep me a statistic. To sabotage my efforts to mother so they can prove Native women like me can't be good moms and don't deserve our kids, justifying any cruelty and prejudice they use against us. This seems so obvious to me now I can't believe I ever missed it. I need to be very protective of Dawn. I need to be vigilant about who she's with and when. And I need to act normal until I can figure out what to do. How to save us. Dawn and me. Because, when it comes down to it, Steve could be in on this, too. Everyone could be.

Meghan notices I'm not walking beside her. She turns and motions for me to come along.

"We'll go down the street a little and back."

I follow. I know better now than to give her any indication I'm onto her, the houses, the neighborhood watch, any of them.

"There we go. She's calming down, all right." And it's true; Dawn is settled. I'm glad the bags of Doritos are no longer in her seat with her. That would make me look bad, I know. I'm not sure why I thought it was okay to have them in there with her to begin with. All it would have taken was for one of them to fall in front of her face and she could have died. And it would be my fault. An image of Dawn slides into my mind like a still photograph, the kind they took in the Victorian ages of the posed dead: the skin of Dawn's chubby face gone gray, her blue eyes still open and glassy, staring up at me, her face settled into a permanent grimace, the words "She died as she lived: screaming for her mother" printed at the bottom. I feel sick.

No. Here, now. Focus on the here and now. Look normal. I snap back to the sidewalk, the swing of Meghan's Lululemon-clad ass.

"I don't know how you do that," I say, hoping to butter her up.

"You're like the ultimate mom. You always know how to take care of the kids around you. My aunt Rachel's like that."

Meghan smiles. "Aww, thanks. But believe me, you wouldn't say that if you could see the fights 1 get into with my girls these days. They never put down their damn phones, pardon my language. Watching hours of that Tic Tac."

"TikTok?" 1 suggest eagerly, glad that this time 1 get to correct her instead of the other way around.

"Whatever it's called," she says. "I'm lucky if 1 can get them to look at me anymore. Phones right in front of their faces, ruining their eyes. Shiloh actually needs glasses. We couldn't believe it when the optometrist told us. Every member of our family on both sides has had perfect twenty-twenty vision until now. And truth be told, Shiloh doesn't really have the face shape for glasses. It's too bad. She had the makings of a classic beauty. Like a young Gwyneth Paltrow. Gwyneth never looked good with glasses, either."

I'm not sure what to say. 1 don't remember anything about Shiloh or her face shape.

"Oh my goodness, look at me! You say one thing and here 1 go, making everything about me and my problems when you and your people have had to deal with so much! 1 heard on the news the other day that there's no clean water on the reserves. 1 couldn't believe it! Right here in Canada! Did you have clean water on your reserve?"

1 take a quick breath and try to remind myself that 1 need to be good. 1 need to be calm and steady.

"We got a new water treatment facility a couple years back—"

"Oh, that's great!" Her enthusiasm makes it seem like she's the one who built it.

"Yeah, but we didn't get any funding for piping infrastructure. It's basically a million-dollar pit. So we do have clean water. We just have no way to get it to peoples' sinks."

"Oh. That's not great." I almost feel bad for telling her this. It's like I stepped on her birthday cake. "Well, anyway, my therapist and I are working on it. We might even do a round of hypnosis and see if that won't get at the root of it," she says. "The way I make everything about me, that is. Not the infrastructure. Though maybe I'll email our MPP and see if that won't get things moving."

I'm not sure hypnosis can correct the nearly pathological need to be the center of attention for a woman like Meghan, just like I'm not sure an email to her MPP will do anything, but I don't say that. Silence is the best cover.

"Now. Tell me about what's going on with you, Alice. You looked pretty upset, standing there in the middle of the sidewalk. Have you been tired like this a lot?" Meghan asks, watching me from the corner of her eye.

I let loose a laugh that goes on a moment too long and rings a little too loud. I can tell because Meghan finally turns her face to look. The houses are still watching; in fact, they seem to sway, which makes me feel a little seasick. Their loud psychic yells have turned to muffled whispering. It's hard to tell what they're saying, but I can't worry about that right now. I have to focus on Meghan and how she interprets my conduct.

"Sorry. It's just funny to me. The idea that a mom could avoid being tired."

"I hear that, sister," Meghan says, and I cringe a little despite myself. "You don't know what exhaustion is until you've had a baby."

We turn into the driveway and Meghan stops, then turns to look at me directly. Her stare is so insistent and piercing I freeze, worried about what she'll read into any slight movement.

"I'm just wondering if you're doing okay, mood-wise? Like, back when I was pregnant with my second girl, Stacey, I had horrible baby blues. Couldn't concentrate. Couldn't stop crying for all sorts of silly reasons. And I felt so guilty about it I couldn't tell anyone. I was like that for months until Brock finally asked me if I was okay and all of it came rushing out. So when I saw you like that, crying on the sidewalk, I remembered everything, and I wanted to ask if you were okay, in case no one else had. Are you okay? Like, overall?"

The question disarms me. I'm not okay in any sense, and I have to admit: I didn't expect this sort of question and kindness from Meghan, if that's indeed what it is. It certainly seems like it, but the houses are silent, watching, their bodies expanding and contracting like lungs, as if they're hanging on how I'll answer this question. Like it's a trap, expertly set, and I'm so close to falling for it. I can't afford to be honest with someone like Meghan, regardless of her intentions. At the end of the day she belongs here. Her allegiance is to these houses and the people who live inside them, to the neighborhood watch, not to me. My future lies with the Shape and words I've yet to write—circumstances Meghan could never understand because her survival is a given. Mine isn't. It never was. *No matter what happens, I remember. Other people won't understand. I need to push through this alone.*

"I appreciate your concern, Meghan," I say, careful, careful. "It's just been a long stretch without proper sleep and my emotions are all over the place. I'm sure I'll be fine once I get a good nap in."

Meghan looks at me, and as I'm watching her, waiting for her reaction, her concerned mask crumbles into tiny pieces and flakes away in front of my eyes, revealing what seems like nothing less than shocked devastation.

"Oh. Okay."

She hovers there, openly hurt, and I immediately understand she's not the sort of person who's had to get used to hearing the word "no." Her kindness is happily lapped up by those fortunate enough to receive it. She's someone who has considerable stake in being considered "generous," never once considering that generosity is itself a privilege people like me can't afford, because the moment we give a millimeter, our massive territory shrinks to a whisper of land. Our generosity can never be virtuous; it gets repackaged as naïveté, then gets used against us to justify whatever crimes are rained down on our heads next. In the same way, no generosity shown to us is ever *real* generosity; it's the flowers a husband brings his wife to smooth things over after giving her a shiner; the jewelry a cheater buys on sale to gift to both his mistress and his wife. It simply can't be trusted.

I'm sure Meghan is unaware of any of this. All she knows is that she's offering intimacy and I'm spurning it. But now, reconsidering her clear disappointment, and remembering the task the Shape has given to me, it occurs to me that I can use this.

"Actually, if you're not doing anything right now, would you be able to watch Dawn for a little bit? Like, an hour or two so I can sleep? It'd help me out so much, you have no idea."

"Oh my goodness, yes! It would be my pleasure!" Like a lamp, she's lit up again. "Do you want me to come in and you can go to your room, or . . . ?"

"Sure. I just have to grab my laptop from my office to bring up with me. I know it's weird, but I need to play music to drown out the other noises. I can't really rest if I can still hear her. I get too anxious."

"Alice," Meghan says softly, placing her manicured hand on my arm, "please don't justify your needs to me. I completely understand." Then, before I can respond, she turns to the stroller, bends over, and speaks into Dawn's little face. "We'll have a great time together. Won't we?"

For a moment a wave of paranoia rushes over me. Is this what the houses wanted? Is Meghan going to do something with Dawn? What could she do? Once we're inside, I leave my cell phone in the living room with them, set to record. I can outsmart these people. They still don't know I'm onto them. I need to finish this story, like the Shape said. Everything will be better when I finish the story.

CHAPTER 15

Mature Flowers Either Makes a Huge Mistake or Finally Takes Her Legacy Seriously, Depending on Your Perspective

Anyway, Mature Flowers did it. She did every single thing her dad told her to—and in the process made every other daughter in history look like a selfish jih'da. I guess it's not as bad as that Jesus guy letting himself get crucified on Daddy's orders, but still.

Obviously the Ancient married her. I mean, it's not like he had other women lined up outside his longhouse trying to impress their dead dads. He had to snag who he could. Plus he had a dream where he married her, and Sky People were very particular about listening to their dreams.

As you may have guessed, their wedding was definitely not the social event of the season. There were some who hoped the marriage would settle them down and make them both a bit less weird, but they were wrong. Right away the Ancient refused to move into Mature Flowers's family's longhouse. All of Sky World collectively raised their eyebrows and clicked their tongues. Who did the Ancient think he was? Every married man had to move in with his in-laws and shoulder their harassment all hours of the day. It was tradition.

The Ancient didn't see it that way. He told Mature Flowers they needed their privacy, that he hated being watched all the time, that he felt like he was being judged. Eventually Mature Flowers grabbed a few things and moved into his place to shut him up. It didn't, but he did stop complaining about her family so openly and often.

Another surprise for Mature Flowers was the sex. I know, I know. Bad Native woman narrator! I'm not supposed to mention that word. It offends those real traditional types who like to pretend nothing exists under our skirts and our children pop into the world out of thin air. Well, rest assured. Mature Flowers was as ignorant about all that as most of your kids are when they start having sex. She didn't like it, if that helps. She endured it because she had to. She was a good, pure, virtuous woman that way. Someone has to be.

Me and You
and That One Roach We Know

I look at the time in the corner of my laptop screen. It's been five minutes since I stopped reading the tiny number of words I wrote over and over on a loop. Only thirty minutes since I came up here to work. I haven't heard Dawn crying, which on one hand feels great, but on the other hand makes me deeply suspicious. What exactly is going on down there? Could anything bad have happened in only thirty minutes? Time feels sticky now. I'm like a mouse caught in its glue trap, struggling and failing to break free. It's so hard for me to focus on getting any actual writing done when I keep considering the long-term ramifications of each line—and when I'm obsessively worrying about what's happening with my daughter downstairs.

Is this what the Shape wanted me to write, to consider? Mature Flowers's sex life with the Ancient? It's not very traditional to talk about having sex, I guess. Not since Christianity came in and stomped out those flames with their talk of virgins having babies and prostitutes seeing the error of their ways. Post-contact, sex was something to be borne, not craved. If we as Indigenous women did crave it, or have it, or even inspire dirty thoughts in men by sinfully existing, we were "squaws." Our own racist, sexist term to sum up a historical hatred that has haunted—and hunted—us for centuries. Given all that baggage, is sex something I should even mention at all? No other storytellers really do. Everyone knows Mature Flowers is pregnant, but no one talks about how that happened. Isn't that kind of weird? It is a creation story, after all, and sex is how humans are created. Maybe I'm supposed to bring this up, push against that taboo? Or maybe I'm reading too far into things.

It's entirely possible the Shape already knows the answers. They probably know the outcome of every pained decision I make as I continue down this path they insist is my destiny. If they gave me some sort of direction, maybe I could move more comfortably. I wouldn't feel like a bug beneath a boot, my exoskeleton slowly crunching, my insides turning to goo as I try to run. Which reminds me of the cockroach in the bathroom. If this were the Disney version of my life, I as a Native woman would be able to commune with all animals, insects, birds, and fish. The cockroach would be on my side, and so would all the mice, rats, and pigeons. Even the trees would be on my side—the sad ones marooned on little plots of dirt or lawn that we're forced to consider "green space" in this metallic city. I'd have my own Flit, Meeko, and Grandmother Willow to give advice and assist me on my journey. But this isn't the Disney version of my life. This is . . . whatever this is. Waking life. Reality. A hologram. A test.

I look at the time again. It's been one more minute. Sixty more seconds for me to figure out the answers to this cosmic test and sixty more seconds for me to fail. I can't write fast enough. I can't figure things out fast enough. Each aspect of my life like a puzzle piece that won't fit. I feel hot, light-headed.

Holy shit, I'm gonna throw up.

I rush to the master bathroom beside my room, flip up the toilet seat, and immediately start to heave. I haven't eaten since . . . when was the last time I ate? A mouthful of fire shoots up my throat, and when I spit it into the toilet it's yellow against the white porcelain. Bile. It keeps pouring out of my mouth, and I can't breathe can't stop can't think can only focus on the yellow as it hits the bottom of the bowl then partly settles into a disgusting little pile before floating back up. It stops long enough for me to take a big breath, feel the cool of the air soothe my throat. I close my eyes and pray for it to stop. For my mind to stop.

You humans. Pissing and shitting and retching in perfectly good water. You're so lost, I almost feel bad for you.

There, on the sink ledge, is the cockroach, antennae twitching.

"Fuck off," I yell as I grab a bottle of shampoo from the bathtub and throw it. It misses wildly, but at the very least it scares the cockroach, who jumps a little.

So uncivilized, it says as it gives its tiny head a shake.

Even the cockroach is a racist, I think as I watch it creep back down the side of the sink.

"Wait," I say, standing back up. "Can you help me?"

It stops in place, as if vaguely intrigued.

And why should I after that ridiculous display?

I grab some toilet paper and pat at the remnants of puke on my face. There's something about this cockroach and the way it carries itself that seems almost regal.

"I'm sorry," I say. "I'm having a really hard time lately. I don't know who or what to trust anymore."

Well, there's your mistake right there: assuming you can trust anything at all. You can't even trust yourself. We're all in flux all the time, changing perspectives and loyalties based on momentary whims. But you must know that, seeing as you're consulting a cockroach.

I don't want to waste time. "Do you know anything about the future?"

The 2011 Miranda July film? I haven't seen it, but I swear it's on my watchlist.

"No, the literal future. Like the time that happens after the present. Anything beyond right now."

Ahhhh yes. I tend to forget. You humans don't see things the way they really are. You let your thoughts get in the way. Imposing an unnatural order on the natural world so you can better analyze. Always thinking, thinking, thinking, as if that does you any good. Though I suppose it did lead to you creating peanut butter, so not all was a waste.

"You don't experience time the same way as humans?"

We're only embodied on this planet for what would feel like the blink of an eye to you. Which means we cockroaches don't get sentimental about our brains and their perceptions, so we can move through what you call time like a swallow moves through sky. What you call the future is already happening, just like what you call the present has already happened.

"I don't understand."

The cockroach sighs. *No, you don't. But your spirit does. By the time you were born here in that silly human suit, your spirit already knew and accepted everything that could ever happen to you. The problem is, as soon as you were cut from your mother, you forgot so you could experience the rush and surprise of life yourself.*

I recognize these words. They sound like Ma telling me over and over how babies chose their parents. I would always have chosen her and Dad, even knowing now how briefly I'd have them.

"Wait, why haven't you forgotten all your potential lives?" I ask, hopeful that there might be a way for me to peer down pathways into futures warmer than this, safer than this, and redirect myself there.

I have. Do you think I'd have chosen to sit here and explain all this to you if I was aware of a more interesting option?

"I guess not," I say, reconsidering my approach. "But I thought you said cockroaches can move through time? Wouldn't that include your own time?"

In theory, yes, but there are rules. You must understand, we're some of the oldest creatures on this planet. Our consciousness has been evolving for over two hundred eighty million years. You humans have only been here for what? Three hundred thousand years, if that. We understand our consciousness in ways you won't discover for another ten million years or more, if you even survive that long. Now, if that's all, I'll be taking my leave. I can't explain existence to you all day.

"Can I ask you one more question?"

If you must.

"Someone spoke to me last night. Someone . . . not from the present. They said it was important I keep writing this story I'm working on, but they couldn't tell me why because there were rules they had to follow."

That's not a question.

I think about how to word the question.

"Is it possible that person is one of my ancestors and they're trying to guide me to my best possible future?"

If they're a spirit, they aren't bound by physical or theoretical notions of time and space, as you humans know them. They'd be speaking from the everything above this plane, which means even if they are an ancestor, they'd be speaking from above their human relationship to you.

"But is it possible?" I push.

Don't rush me! I was getting there. While there's no way to know a spirit's intentions, technically, yes, they'd be able to see what futures lie before you now and guide you to where they think you should be. But they'd have to be a very sentimental and controlling spirit to do so, since that interferes with your free will. Perhaps this spirit was quite recently a human on earth and their understanding of the rules is a little off as a result. Either way, there's no way for you to know whether the future they want for you is the future you want for yourself.

"So I shouldn't do what the Shape tells me to?"

I have no idea what you're talking about, but I personally wouldn't let any shape tell me what to do. Well, maybe a parallelogram.

"No, it's not a shape, it's my ancestor," I rush to explain. "Anyway I thought you're supposed to listen to your ancestors."

Are you? Well, then, why on earth are you asking me for advice? I'm certainly no ancestor of yours.

The cockroach has me there. But how am I any more qualified to guide my life than my mysterious ancestor, or this cockroach, or even Steve?

"I think I'm going to listen to my ancestor," I say as I turn to look at the cockroach, who is drinking from the little drops of water scattered across the bowl of the sink. The cockroach laughs, and it's a harsh sound, raspy, as if whatever mechanisms it's using to make this awful noise are in desperate need of oiling.

Go ahead. But remember that's still a decision you're making, not your ancestor. You can't cheat living.

And with that, the cockroach scurries down the sink drain and out of my life.

CHAPTER 16

There's Something About Meghan

I wait outside the living room with a face swept of vomit and a mouth freshly swirled with mouthwash, quiet as my socks sink into the plush of the hallway carpet.

If you stop breathing so loud you'll be able to make out what Meghan is whispering.

It's the kind voice again. I hold my breath obediently. Sure enough, Meghan's saccharine voice comes into focus. It sounds like she's on the phone.

"You were totally right. She's probably the most selfish woman I've ever met. I doubt she's even capable of love . . . I know, that's harsh, but it's true . . . Oh, she has absolutely no clue. It's almost sad how oblivious she is to it all . . . The baby? She's completely delicious . . . You'll have no problem finding a new mommy for her . . . But, you know, first things first . . ."

A damp uncomfortable heat starts in my armpits. She wants to get rid of me; she wants to take my child from me. Residential schools were full of white teachers and nuns like her, thinking they were carrying out God's work by pulling Mohawk babies from their mothers' warmth and setting them down in the cold holiness of what amounted to religious work camps. And why should she be any different, even if her god is nothing more than this neighborhood, this city, this country, and all they represent? In fact, isn't it worse that her god is something concrete, something she can move around her like giant mirrors so that all she has to see is herself and those who remind her of herself, so that she is in a sense a god herself, both creator and destroyer? But another part of me worries about the truth of what she's said. I'm capable of love, aren't I? I haven't been especially loving toward many people these days, but I've been doing better with Dawn. And she's been doing better with me. Though that won't matter if they've been watching me all this time. They'll have evidence. They'll be able to make me look awful as long as they caught me in the right moment. The neighborhood watch lady. The liquor store. The sidewalk outside with Meghan. It's all potential proof that I'm an unstable and unfit mother.

I need to calm down. I need to think. I have evidence, too. My phone is in there recording everything Meghan has been saying. I can show that to Tanya, and we can make a plan. I know the cockroach told me not to trust anyone, but she's my cousin. She'd never be on the side of the houses and Meghan and the neighborhood watch and Canada. She'll know what to do.

I take a long breath in to steady myself, then dial up my decibels to maximum cheerfulness.

"Look at you two!" I say as I march in. All smiles, all sugar. Meghan quickly shoves her phone down. "Best of friends already."

Meghan turns, and I see her flicker with disappointment that I'm back. As quickly as it came, though, it disappears behind her curling lips, so pumped with filler that smiling seems an effort, and she meets my level of enthusiasm easily.

"Honestly, Alice, she's an angel. You're a very lucky mommy!"

"Don't I know it," I say as I disentangle Dawn from Meghan's arms, desperate to have her back in the safety of my own.

The entire interaction feels like a performance, and I am reminded that it is. The Shape could be observing us now, or Matoaka, or Ma or Dad, or spirits I don't know but who see lives like mine as a form of entertainment. Perhaps silverfish are watching, which I hope are a much kinder species of insect than the cockroach. If I am a performer for all these eyes, I will perform my role well. I look down at Dawn and smile so hard my cheeks hurt. I bring her close to my chest. I can feel Meghan watching intently.

"There really is nothing like being a mom, is there?" I ask, finally confident enough to look right into Meghan's face.

"No, there really isn't." Meghan, seemingly uncomfortable with me staring so intently at her, moves to my side and looks down at Dawn. "Did you manage to get any sleep?"

The way she speaks makes it sound like she already knows the answer.

"I got enough," I say, then add, "you know how it is," because that seems to be the sort of meaningless statement that mothers say to other mothers. Meghan nods, no doubt waiting for my smile to break. It never does.

"Well, I better be going. Dinner certainly isn't going to make itself." Meghan walks over to the front door and pulls on her Keds. I follow with Dawn, wanting to make sure that I actually see her leave my house before I allow myself to drop the act. She opens the door and starts to walk out when she abruptly turns back to me.

"Before I forget, your phone kept going off, and it was bothering Dawn, so I turned the ringer off. You're very popular." I start to open my mouth, but Meghan beats me to it. "The recording app was running, so I didn't need your password to get in. Speaking of which, you and Steve should really invest in some mommy cams. You get much better footage. Video and everything, streamed right to your laptop."

"Thanks," I manage. The neighborhood watch is going to have a field day with this once they hear. Whatever goodwill I'd garnered by allowing Meghan to see me cry in the street and act out her white savior fantasies for an afternoon is clearly long gone.

"Oh, and make sure to pump and dump whenever you get into that vodka. If you're still breastfeeding, that is."

"That's not for me," I start to say, but only after Meghan has already smiled, turned on her heel, and walked halfway down the sidewalk, leaving me to simmer in the knowledge that I'm not nearly as smart as I thought I was, and Meghan is, in fact, much smarter.

CHAPTER 17

Saved by the Mommy Blog

There was nothing on the recording—or, nothing that would help me explain why I was in such pressing danger. The one thing I'm sure of is that I need proof for anyone to believe me. Not everyone is straddling this world and the next, able to converse with insects and houses and cartoon characters. Most people don't consider that the images they think they see are only interpretations, conjured into existence by sparks of electricity shuttling through neural pathways in a hunk of gray matter floating inside our skulls. I find that creepy: that our brains are floating there, soft as fat cut from the meat, in cerebrospinal fluid. There was a time, after Aunt Rachel told me that I was special like Grandma, that I became obsessed with brains and read every popular science article on them I could find. I read about brains that were swollen and inflamed like pimples; brains that had large sections sliced from the rest with a scalpel; brains that had poles shuttle through them like javelins, damaging specific lobes and helping humans figure out what each part of the brain was responsible for. But I never found an article that talked about how brains could be a bridge or barrier between worlds, and so I never found what I wanted. And without evidence that other people could see or measure, I knew I couldn't talk to anyone about the moments where I felt the solidness of this world melt away and the fuzziness of other worlds bleed through, like static on a radio. Even Aunt Rachel had no idea how it actually felt to be like this—to have another layer of understanding, of seeing, lying on top of the world everyone else considered "normal."

It seemed what was considered "normal" always excluded me. Meghan making those passive-aggressive comments about my tiny vodka bottle as though she hasn't poured a quarter bottle of red wine into a Starbucks tumbler in front of me and called it "mommy juice." As if Steve's Facebook isn't full of similar white moms who post cheesy, questionable memes about drinking as if it's synonymous with being a mother. "Mom's reasons to wine" and then a numbered list with their kids' names. Or "Raising tiny humans one glass at a time." Or "OMG I *so* need a glass of wine or I'm gonna sell my kids." Or "My book club only reads wine labels." The key difference being drunk white moms are cute, whereas drunk Native moms are hazardous to their children's health and well-being. At least I was using the alcohol to help me keep the chaos out instead of invite it in. Unfortunately, Children's Aid wouldn't look at it that way. Fuck, Meghan could call them on me today. Say she was worried about a baby whose mom had an obvious alcohol problem. Whose mom didn't deserve her, didn't love her. Would the social worker believe her? Would Steve? When this Cayuga girl I knew named Jen was delivering her baby, a social worker was waiting right outside the door of her hospital room. Apparently, the hospital had to tell them she was in labor because her family had a Children's Aid Society file. They took her baby. She'd barely had time to hold him before he was gone. A week or so later, at school, she locked herself in a bathroom stall and wailed all day. If they can take Jen's baby, they can probably take Dawn. They can take any brown baby they want.

Meghan *is* right, though. I will have to pump and dump

whenever I drink the vodka. Which will give Dawn another chance to develop a liking for Similac and a hatred for me and my sore, leaky-yet-somehow-still-cracking tits.

Oh please. You'd love that. You hate being milked like some fucking cow.

I place Dawn carefully down on the floor, then cover my ears and close my eyes, stupidly.

"No. I love feeding Dawn. I love feeding Dawn. I love Dawn. I do."

Then why'd you toss her on the floor like a piece of trash? You think she's trash, don't you? You'd love to leave her in a dumpster. You'd love to watch her little body get crushed in a trash compactor.

The tears burn my eyes the moment I scoop Dawn back up. As I rush her up the stairs and into her room, lazily singing her a Fiona Apple song to keep her calm and distract my terrifying brain, I realize something else entirely: I don't need vodka. I need pot. I can get it in one of those little vape pens and smoke it without any smell whatsoever. It's legal now, and it's not going to affect my breast milk. Realistically I could walk into one of the handful of dispensaries that have popped up in the neighborhood and buy it today, but the thought of taking Dawn into the pot store, meeting all the eyes of people who were, yes, in there buying pot themselves, but also judging me for doing the same while also being a mother and a Mohawk, makes me sick with anxiety. What if the houses see? What if Meghan sees? Meghan already mentioned nanny cams. Was that only to mess with me? Or are there already nanny cams here, set up since I moved in, streaming straight to Steve's work laptop right now?

It's all burning.

And you're lighting the match.

Fuck, I need that pot. I need it so I can calm my mind for a moment, quiet the intruding voices, put on the proper performance, maybe even feel happy for a few minutes. Any happiness would be preferable to this dull thud of a life, even if the happiness comes from the same drug Melita's high school boyfriend Mark got caught selling to grade nines, which he'd cut with oregano to increase profit margins.

I place Dawn gently into her crib, then pull out my phone to order some online. It's weird we can do that now, but that's what happens when old white men have the opportunity to profit off pot without having to rely on young Native guys like Mark anymore—boys who might have been considered smart, ruthless, profit-driven entrepreneurs, future leaders of the so-called free world even, if they were born to the right parents in the right class with the right race. Their versions of MBAs are criminal records they'll never be able to shake. I no sooner think that than the bars of Dawn's crib start to look silver, glinting sunlight, like she's in a jail and I'm her guard. I reach out and touch the bars. They feel steely, cold, and then Dawn is screaming and I'm still sitting, watching, blinking, wondering what's going to happen next as her dress turns into an orange jump-suit and tiny shackles materialize around her wrists and ankles—

"What are you doing?"

I look up and Steve is there. He hasn't even taken off his shoes. He must have run up the stairs when he got home and heard the shrieking. He's definitely going to want to leave me now that he's witnessed my shitty mothering. Part of me wishes he would so I could stop trying to be something I'm clearly not. The other part feels broken at the mere thought he'd leave.

"I was trying to see if she would self-soothe," I say, not even sure where the words have risen from, but thankful for their quickness.

Steve looks at me. "Okay, well . . ." I look back at him, waiting for more of a cue so I know how I should act. "I don't think she's going to self-soothe . . ."

I watch the last syllable slowly slip from Steve's lips and hang in the air, expectant. He's asking a question without asking. What? What is he asking me? Then I realize: he means Dawn. He wants me to get Dawn. Because she's crying.

"You're right." I leap up from the chair and scoop Dawn into my arms and against my chest. "It was an experiment. Something I read on a mommy blog," I explain over Dawn's yelps as I pat her on the back and kiss the top of her head, praying she'll quiet. I concentrate on making my posture and movements seem effortless. I need to look the part of a good mom so he'll forget what he saw. So the people watching will forget. This is how I can protect her. Us.

"Here, let me try," he offers, and I hesitate, my feelings about him clouding my better judgment. Normal Alice would do it, gladly, so I pass her over. As soon as I do she settles down. Why is she rejecting me again? I thought we were doing so well. That we both understood what was at stake.

"You read mommy blogs?" Steve finally asks, confused.

"Of course." I hope I sound as carefree, confident, and untraumatized as the person I pretended to be when we met.

"Are you okay?" Steve asks. My body goes cold. What does he see? What am I doing wrong now? My phone dings, and when I get the chance to look it's the confirmation email for the vape pen and cartridges. With express shipping, they should get here tomorrow.

You know what you're doing wrong. Like mother, like daughter.

I bite the inside of my cheek until I taste blood. I hope whatever voice just spoke feels it.

Steve's phone dings, too. He balances Dawn in one arm and pulls out his phone. When he looks at the screen he furrows his brows.

"Who is it?" I ask, immediately worried from the sudden twist in his demeanor that it's Meghan ratting me out.

He continues to stare at the screen, as if the message is some secret code and he's reading it over and over until it makes sense.

"Steve?" I try to peek over his shoulder and catch a name, but he's too tall.

"Nothing. No one." He slides his phone into his pocket and turns away from me. Clearly I'm not the only one with secrets.

CHAPTER 18

Russian, Corn Husk, Perfect Little Dolls

Steve is in bed next to me, propped up on three of the probably seven pillows we have in this room alone. They're all thick pillows, too—not flat like the ones I'd squeezed down over years' worth of restless nights as a kid, then a teen, then an adult. I had no idea the sorts of simple comforts poverty had robbed me of until I'd slept in a bed like this.

We managed to get Dawn to sleep quickly, then peeled off our clothes and slipped under the duvet. He wore only his usual boxer briefs. I'd put on a satin nightgown, hoping if I dressed sexy enough, Steve would stop looking at me like he was searching for cracks. We'd decided to put on a show called *Russian Doll*, which we'd been chipping away at slowly for a few weeks as a way to relax together. It was about a woman named Nadia, a live wire in a black suit with a mop of red curls who kept dying while trying to leave her birthday party, then coming back to life moments later at that same party, like she was returning to a save spot in a video game. She's died and been reborn at least four times now.

I watch intently as she turns off the sink and stares in disbelief at her index finger, which she burned in her last go-round but which is now smooth as a stone pummeled by the ocean. As she moves over New York with her finger in front of her like a candle in the dark, all frenetic energy, her wild eyes lock with mine every so often in solidarity, like she knows I know her desperation. And I do. I know what that finger means to her. It's supposed to be her proof that she's dying and coming back to life, the same moment repeating like a skipping record, but it's impossible proof because it's negative proof. Only she knows she burned her finger in another timeline and that burn's disappeared in this one, just as only I know that blank recording on my phone is proof that Meghan searched my living room and diaper bag to make sure her monitoring of me wasn't being monitored. No one will believe Nadia or me, because no one sees the world as we see it. We are both entirely alone, trying to fix the supernatural mess we've been thrust into against our will.

"I get it," I say before I can stop myself, my voice betraying more emotion than I realized I felt.

"Get what?"

Fuck. I clear my throat and blink back tears. I've shown him a crack.

"Oh, you know. Not having people believe you," I say, trying to be truthful while remaining vague.

"Hmmm," Steve replies.

I turn back to the show, hoping it'll get him to do the same. On-screen, Nadia's trying to explain to two men the proof that is her finger. The response comes like a warning I don't need: "Is there a history of mental illness in your family?"

A realization strikes me. This is no coincidence. I'm supposed to be watching. The show knows that I'm watching. It's telling me exactly what response I should expect from those around me if I tell them what I've been experiencing, who and what I've been communicating with.

"My mother was crazy," Nadia replies, her words reminding me of Ma's dismissal of Grandma so long ago. *You don't want to end up crazy like my mother, believe me.*

And you're just like your grandma.

Each character's eyes look out, past the scene, and lock with mine for the briefest of moments, making sure I understand.

Do ya get it, or do we have to do the whole damn scene again? It's Nadia's voice, but her lips don't move on-screen. This message is just for me. I nod at them, and they continue with the show. I watch Steve out of the corner of my eye to see if he's noticed anything. It doesn't seem like it. He eventually sees me looking and smirks, squeezing my hand once as if to reinforce that he really means it. Means to be holding my hand, that is, and means to be in love. Means to see this time with me as a sort of reward for all that he's done that's led up to this moment: the schmoozing with colleagues, the classes, the commute.

Suddenly the world in front of me disappears and I see Ma's face, the way it looked when I peeked inside her casket on the day of her funeral: her skin clearly graying beneath the mounds of makeup, her whole body deflated. This time, though, her eyes shoot open, bloodshot and furious. Her bluing lips beneath the lipstick twist into a grimace.

You did this to me. My own daughter.

No, I think. *I'd never hurt you. I love you. I need you.*

My body starts to shake violently. Otherwise, I can't move or speak. I watch, helpless, as spiders start to crawl out of my mother's nose and up her face.

You'll do worse than this to your girl. They're right to take her from you. They need to save her before it's too late and she ends up like me.

Stop! Please! I think as I clench my eyes shut. *You're wrong! They're lying!*

Dawn's screams start immediately. I look around, and Steve is staring, concerned.

"What happened just now?" he asks. I must have actually spoken aloud, maybe even screamed.

"Sorry. I was having a nightmare," I say, though I'm sure I wasn't asleep.

Steve turns off the TV, then gets up. "I'll go get her. You try and calm down."

And I do try, the whole time he's gone. I listen to him cooing and singing to her through the baby monitor and pretend he's cooing and singing to me. But it doesn't work. Because I feel something watching, multiple somethings, in fact, and I know immediately that I need to stay entirely still and stare straight ahead until Steve gets back, or something horrible will happen to him and Dawn and it will be all my fault, just like Ma said. He's gone for about half an hour. That whole time I barely move a muscle. I barely even blink.

An hour later, I'm entangled in Steve's limbs and he's in mine as he breathes hot into my hair.

"What happened in your nightmare?" he asks.

"I don't want to talk about it now. Maybe later."

"Okay," he says after a while. I know this isn't the answer he wants, but it's all I can give. "Hey, guess what? I learned a new story today."

"From Mohawk class?"

"Hen."

I stiffen a little in his arms.

"Sorry, that means 'yes.'"

"I thought Mohawk class was on Thursdays?" I ask, frustrated he didn't think I knew what "hen" meant after a lifetime on the rez.

"It is Thursday."

"Oh. I forgot." I can't hide the uncertainty in my voice. It feels

like it's been days since everything that happened at the super-
market, at the liquor store, here with Meghan.

"Do you want to hear it? It's about corn husk dolls."

Does he want me to mirror the Mohawk words he used back to
him so he can feel like he's teaching me? What would a good wife
say here?

"Hen. Let's hear you tell it," I say as I close my eyes and try to
soften my body into his once more. Try to focus on his words and
forget the image of Ma.

"It's not going to be anywhere near as good as the way my
teacher tells it," he offers like an apology. It pisses me off. He says
that as though I'm not also a storyteller, or at least an aspiring one,
and he's not some white guy interloping, a fraud of an alchemist
trying to pretend his fool's gold is the real thing, the genuine
artifact.

But that's not being a good wife.

"G'wan den," I say, leaning into my rez's slang, hoping my exhaustion is more apparent than my resentment.

He begins.

Long, long ago, after the people realized that the
Three Sisters—Corn, Beans, and Squash—had been
responsible for their health and well-being, taking
care of them and looking after them like elder sisters
do, and after the people began to show love and appreciation to the Three Sisters like starstruck younger
siblings, the Corn Spirit wanted to do even more. She
went to the Creator and asked if there was anything
else she could do for the people, and the Creator
smiled on her and explained there was yet another
way to use her husk: to make a beautiful doll for all the

children to play with and all the adults to admire. The Corn Spirit was grateful for this knowledge and went about making a beautiful corn husk doll like Creator had told her. She took special care to give the doll the most beautiful face so that even looking upon it would make all the people happy.

After that, the doll traveled from village to village playing with all the children she found. The children loved her more than any other toys or game, and the adults loved her, too, telling her over and over how beautiful she was, how precious, how special.

Soon, though, the doll became conceited, content to stare at her lovely reflection in the waters instead of playing with the children, as she was made to do. So Creator told her to come meet with him. Instead of going straight to his lodge, however, the doll saw a creek that rippled nearby and couldn't help herself. She went over and looked at her face and smiled, telling herself how beautiful she was, how much more beautiful than any other part of creation. Eventually she remembered why she had come, and she entered Creator's lodge, expecting more praise and admiration.

Instead, Creator told her that he saw how she neglected her duties and thought herself better than other parts of creation. If she continued in this manner, he said, she would face a terrible punishment. Though the doll begged to know, Creator would not tell her what that punishment would be. Still, she understood that she should not test Creator, and so she again took up her duties and went from village to village playing with the children once more.

The praise again filled the doll's ears, and it wasn't long before she started to ignore the calls of the children. Creator had been watching her closely, and so when he saw that she had started to become conceited again and considered herself more important than the children and the waters and the corn she was made from and even the Corn Spirit that had given her life, he called her back. Once again, hearing the rippling brook as she approached Creator's lodge, she was filled with the desire to look upon her beautiful face. She went there first and stared at her reflection. And so Creator waited.

Finally, when it started to get dark and Grandmother Moon hid herself behind clouds so the doll could no longer see herself in the waters, she approached Creator's lodge. As soon as she entered, Creator's words rang out: "Little doll, I have given you a warning and you have ignored it. You have ignored the children who you were made to delight. You have made even me wait as you satisfied your conceited desires. And so, as I promised, you have been punished. Leave my lodge now and face your punishment." The doll asked what would befall her when she left, but Creator had no more to say to her, and so she walked out.

Grandmother Moon was only just starting to peek from behind the clouds, so the doll crept back over to the water to wait. "You're still the most beautiful," she told herself as she peered into the dark pool. The problem was, as the light hit and she saw her reflection, she saw she was no longer the most beautiful. In fact, she had no face at all—Creator had taken it from her.

To this day, the Haudenosaunee have respected Creator's decision and do not put faces on their corn husk dolls. This reminds all of them what happens when you are too conceited and consider yourself to be higher than any other element of creation.

"So? What did you think?" he asks, his voice immediately transformed from the sage wisdom of the storyteller to the eagerness of a child.

I'm not sure what to say. I lie limp in his arms, feeling the inadequacy of my own storytelling like lead in my veins. He didn't make a single mistake. Didn't stop to consult other versions of the story mid-tell to check he was giving the right details at the right time. He didn't pause to try to remember what came next. He didn't even stutter. The story came out of him fully formed, as though it was resting on his tongue and waiting for the perfect moment to burst into being, like Athena emerging from Zeus's cracked head. And here I am, stealing moments to sit in front of a laptop, tapping scraps of the story that defines my people's worldview, laboring over every decision as though the wrong word will cause the universe to collapse in on itself, and I'm still not done. Even assurance from the Shape that my slow, plodding work will all be worthwhile and help future generations can't change the fact that the words flowed so much easier for Steve. For me each word has to be yanked bloodily from my mouth like rotten teeth.

"I know it probably felt mannered. Sorry about that. I was trying to replicate the way my teacher told it. Also the connectedness of the story. The way everything felt like the natural extension of everything else. Almost like the moral at the end was the only logical place for everything to build toward. If that makes sense," he says in jagged shards, sheepish, answering himself.

"No, it makes sense," I say. "My dad once told me it's best to think of each story as a journey. Each sentence, even each word, is a step toward your destination, and you have to be careful where you step as a storyteller because the people are stepping after you. You want to make sure they're going where you want them to go, because you're carving a path together."

We're both quiet for a moment that becomes a minute that becomes two.

Then, for some reason, I continue. "He always said our stories were a gift from Creator. That we should be as grateful for them as any other part of creation, because they helped us learn about ourselves, the world, and our place in the world. I've always thought about that when writing. I don't know if other writers think about that, but I do. How gifts aren't just to be hoarded but shared in a good way. We have to be responsible to the people we're sharing these gifts with just as much as we have to be responsible to the gifts themselves, because we don't know how long we'll have them otherwise. They could be taken from us just as easily as Corn Husk Doll's face."

"You're so smart, babe," Steve finally says. "Truly. I don't know if I tell you that enough. I get so excited to know your perspective on things like this because I know it's going to blow everything I thought I knew out of the water. You're always teaching me something new."

"Thanks," I say, so overcome with emotion I can't come up with anything else. He does love me. He does need me. This is our life, and it can be great.

But then my brain travels back. Something about the way he put those words together—"your perspective on *things like this*"; "You're always *teaching me something new*"—feels . . . wrong.

It's cuz that's what you are to him. A walking, talking artifact he can learn from, then fuck. His first-class ticket to credibility and tenure. He wanted your knowledge and your baby—not you. Never you.

I lie there stiff and simmer in it, unable to conjure up the right memories or thoughts to fight what now seems so obvious and clear. He doesn't love me. He's part of it, just like I assumed. He has been from the start. A spy, sent to extract intel and Indigenous babies. That's why he has the nanny cams set up to watch me at all times. That's why he conveniently happened to be unavailable when neighborhood watch lady showed up. That's why my keys, which I always keep in the diaper bag, were gone. He moved them. And that's why he wants me to come with him to this dinner party with his colleagues. Something is happening there—a harvest of some sort. A harvest of what, though? My knowledge? Me?

"Anyway, I don't mean to keep you awake," Steve says, yanking me back to the present. "I thought it was a funny coincidence, that's all. I happen to learn the corn husk doll story while we're watching a show called *Russian Doll.*"

It could be considered a coincidence—all those fictional dolls convening in our lives at this exact time, in this exact space. But if I've learned anything these past few days, it's that there's no such thing as coincidence. Everything is a sign waiting for you to see and interpret, so long as you're willing to notice the patterns and follow the connections already there. Dolls. There are so many dolls. I remember Joan seeing Dawn for the first time. She was decked head to toe in designer clothing, while Dawn was swaddled in sterile white hospital blankets, similar to what my mother was covered in when I identified her body months ago.

"Look at her! She's a perfect doll!" she had exclaimed then. "An absolutely perfect little doll."

It had seemed so dramatic at the time, like Joan was aware of hidden cameras picking up her every action and reaction. Now I know there probably *were* hidden cameras there. And ever since that day, Joan hasn't even referred to Dawn by her name; it's always, "How's my little doll?" or "Where's Grandma's perfect doll?" Her voice an exaggerated squeal. The start of a pattern I couldn't possibly have understood, let alone identified.

As Steve snores, I lie there limply, considering the dolls. The beautiful, conceited one made from corn husk; and the punished one without a face; and the descendants of that one, who have no faces now and never will again. The wooden dolls from Russia with smaller versions of themselves nesting inside—one inside the first, another inside that one, and yet another inside that. Like a chain of perpetually pregnant mothers ready to crack open and birth the smaller women they've protected with their bodies, just as their own mothers once protected them. A chain reaching both forward into the future and backward into the past, like the very lineage Ma told me I was part of, which started with Mature Flowers and now continues with Dawn, Joan's "little doll." So many dolls. Too many dolls. Certainly too many to be a coincidence. Which means it must be a sign. A sign that the people watching will take my little doll from me if I forget my purpose even for a moment, the way Creator took Corn Husk Doll's face for forgetting hers.

Write. You need to write. And keep writing. That's how you'll fulfill your destiny and save your girl.

By the time Dawn wakes, my head is full. I have no choice. I have to do what they say or they'll never stop. I get up, pick up Dawn, and strap her into her car seat so she has somewhere comfortable to sit while I write. As I stand on the precipice of the staircase, though, her car seat heavy with her weight swinging slightly in my hands, the image of us falling down the stairs and cracking into hundreds of shards like demolished porcelain dolls appears behind my eyes like a premonition or warning. I stand at the top of the stairs, paralyzed, until the voice demanding I write gets loud again. Then I slowly step down, one stair at a time, balancing my weight just so before moving, then waiting until my heartbeat calms again before I continue down to the next, treating each step like the possibility of a fatal fall because that's what it is. It takes almost an hour, according to the clock, but we reach the first floor intact and alive.

I was careful to switch the baby monitors so I could bring one down with us. I want to make sure I can hear Steve's still sleeping the whole time we're here. I even change the password on my laptop once it's loaded. I can't trust Steve. Not now that I know why he really courted me. I was just a job for him. A means to an end. I open the small bottle of Smirnoff I hid in the back of my top drawer beside the oxies and take a couple hard swallows. The voices dull, the way I knew they would.

Make sure to pump and dump.

That voice is Meghan's. That laugh is Meghan's. I pick the Smirnoff back up. I swallow and swallow until the laugh is finally drowned out.

CHAPTER 19

Mature Flowers Faces Her Fate

Pretty much right after the Ancient started demanding sex he got her pregnant. I know, right? It surprised them, too. Mature Flowers was sure this was the first real step toward making her the most important woman who ever lived. I mean, something as big as creating a new life so soon after her marriage couldn't be a coincidence, could it? No way. The effects were simply too far-reaching—particularly in a place like Sky World, which was still reeling with the sudden introduction of death. No, life is never a coincidence. It's always important—regardless of whether it's made with intention or not, whether it lasts for centuries or flickers out like a brief flame. Besides, isn't "coincidence" what you call a pattern when you haven't quite figured out how to connect all its pieces yet?

Anyway, as I'm sure you coulda predicted, Mature Flowers *really* wanted to tell her dad about the new baby. She was sure he'd be so pleased she finally figured out her purpose—she was gonna be a mom!—but her dad disappeared. Hadn't said a word to her since she married the Ancient, in fact. And she hadn't said a word to anyone but the Ancient, either. He told her after their marriage that she wasn't allowed to talk to anyone but him.

Still, Mature Flowers was nothing if not stubborn. Every day when the Ancient left their lodge, she'd go the Great Tree and hoist herself into its branches. Some of the nicer women in the village tried to ask her to come down. She wouldn't listen. Even more frustrating for the women, she refused to speak to them. Mature Flowers hoped the Ancient would hear them gossip about her giving them the cold shoulder and know that she was being obedient to his wishes. Mostly. Technically, yes, she was talking to her dad, but she figured since he was dead, talking to him didn't count. She didn't really consider that the women she was ignoring would *also* gossip about who she was talking to in that tree. Big mistake, as we'll soon see. But for now, all you need to know is she needed Daddy's approval more than she needed any of theirs. Mature Flowers would sit up in that tree for hours and sing and cry and beg her father to speak to her. As the sun was starting to set, she'd hop down, wipe her eyes, and hurry home to make dinner like a good little wife. She'd smile no matter what the Ancient said or did to her when he got home, hoping that somehow, somewhere, her dad was watching her obedience and filling with pride.

Clearly, Mature Flowers was a mess. She'd married this asshole to make her dad happy, and now her dad wouldn't even give her the satisfaction of actually being happy. No "Good job, kiddo!" No pat on the back. Not even a smile. He'd totally bailed on her, again.

Now, I could be a really good storyteller and build up all this tension and suspense, hammering in the idea that her dad abandoned her only for him to appear out of nowhere in her hour of need . . . but that's actually really predictable and boring. Also it's totally untrue. Remember when I said earlier her dad was a bit of a dick? I wasn't lying. Not this time, anyway. Her dad *was* a bit of a dick. He never appeared to her again.

Are you bummed out yet? I told you Mature Flowers's life sucked. You're the sadist who stuck around to watch. But things will get better eventually. I mean, they don't get *that* much better in the long run, but if you're one of those glass-half-full types I'm sure you'll find something to latch on to. Probably.

Or who knows? You might be here to watch her flounder, waiting eagerly for the moment Mature Flowers drowns. Maybe you're into that sort of thing. Not everyone's satisfied with a happily ever after. Are they?

A Moment to Reconsider

Is there a definite, observable moment where interpretation becomes bastardization? If there is I'm flirting with it. I mean, I'm writing my people's Creation Story—the story that lays out our entire worldview as Haudenosaunee—in the voice of a gossipy, irreverent young woman when common sense (and stereotypes) say I should be writing it in the voice of a sage old Indian man. There's a reason that was the exact persona Steve instinctively took on when he so effortlessly tried on the role of storyteller. It's a confined space, and a confining role, one that can trap our men in stereotypes and sand down our revolutionary edges, historicizing our urgent now-ness. That now-ness was exactly what Dad wanted to imbue all his stories with, sure that it would be the key to ensuring our people remained just as dazzled with our stories as ever—adults as excited to pass them on to their children as their children would be to receive them.

But the sage old Indian man is also the role that white folks are comfortable with us inhabiting, that they in fact hope we'll keep inhabiting so they can keep pretending they aren't still stealing our cultures, languages, and the lands that helped us carve out both, without which we're nothing. The voice I'm using for this story emphasizes our modernity and humor. It's the only voice that seems right, I know that, and it does in ways remind me of the amazing one my dad used, but even when I feel good about what I'm writing there's a part of me that wonders what he would think. What Ma and Aunt Rachel would think. What my mysterious grandmother would think. What the community would think. Am I doing right by them? Is this traditional enough? Is that even worth considering? After all, isn't it true that the only way we've kept the stories and ceremonies we still have is by allowing those stories and ceremonies to stretch, bend, shift, change?

The stuff about Mature Flowers's dad is pretty heavily editorialized compared to most versions of the Creation Story I've heard. In most versions, he's not even her dad but her uncle. He does show up, tell her to marry the Ancient, then leave. But most other storytellers don't dwell on why he's doing this or what its effects on Mature Flowers are. They also don't talk about Mature Flowers going back to the Great Tree to try to talk to her father again. I made that part up. Instead, Mature Flowers unquestioningly does everything that's asked of her. Not that different from Jesus's mom, Mary, now that I think about it. Maybe that's another stamp Christianity has left on our people's minds and stories. Maybe it says something about the agency afforded women in colonized spaces—even women specifically tasked with birthing revolution and new worlds, like Mary and Mature Flowers. Maybe it's a "coincidence."

But this, right here? This moment in the story? This is a crucial moment. Every storyteller takes a firm stance. One moment Mature Flowers is in Sky World. The next she's falling down a hole beneath the Great Tree. Did she jump, did she fall, or was she pushed? Each option means something different for our people, our history, our women. There's responsibility in representation. You write some words and suddenly the entire weight of your people and their history is thrust upon your back. It's heavy. It smothers. But you have to carry it if you want to keep it safe. Otherwise someone else will pick it up—a stranger, an outsider, an academic trying to make their mark—and they'll do with it what they see fit.

I want to make the right choice. I do. I just don't know what that choice is.

A Musical Interlude

The sunlight has left me. Or maybe it wasn't ever there to begin with and I've only noticed now. Either way, that's how it is—as if a veil hangs over my life, dulling it, shadowing it.

I'm sitting in an ornate room, something big and impressive that would be called a parlor or smoking room by people more refined than me. Another place to be bottled up and perform. There are heavy burgundy curtains, velvet, hanging along the walls; there is marbled tile beneath my heeled feet. Gold frames everything it can frame—paintings, chairs, the edges of the piano and the bench beside it, which I am currently propped on. There is a turtle rattle in my hands and I'm hitting it in time with my own heartbeat, humming.

"No more of that. Come here."

A person I don't recognize gestures to the middle of the room. Their face is white as piano keys and smoothed of all wrinkles. Their lips are twisted into a smile that scares me. Everyone around me waits, their lips either pursed or pressed against a crystal flute of champagne or wine, maybe a tumbler of bourbon or gin. I am aware they are waiting for me. They don't make noise or give me pointed looks to tell me this, but they make their expectations known, the way people like that do.

I drop the rattle and stand. I don't remember making the decision to do so. The rattle clatters on the floor as I walk to the chair. I sit. A harp appears in front of me as if from a wisp of smoke and I know I have to play. I know it's important I show no fear or hesitation. So that's what I do, and as my fingers miraculously dance across the strings, I become aware of sharp pain. A dagger. It's in my back and it goes deeper as I play, dragging down my spine, a rough rhythm vibrating within me with each bone it hits. Then something flies past my strumming fingers and as it lands with a wet red thwack I know it is my flesh, just as I know I have to keep playing and show no fear because they will eat my fear like chocolate cake. If I leave any room for hesitation they will squeeze between my atoms, jam into those tiny holes of time and space inside me and lay a thousand eggs that will hatch into a thousand winged creatures that will feast on me from within, until they're strong enough to control me and I have no choice but to watch the body I used to think of as mine succumb to the will of another, of many others, who are still, at the end of the day, just one. And so I continue to play and the sound of the notes continues to move the dagger across my flesh, tearing off chunks, and the people in the room continue to listen and watch and sip their drinks, and as I notice that my skin hits the marble in time with the song, I wonder: are those observers amused or disturbed? Or both? Maybe others' pain has been offered to them as fuel for their own pleasure so often they can no longer feel happy without first witnessing another's despair. I watch them all watch me, mildly, as if this entire spectacle were only slightly more interesting than a middling true crime podcast.

Suddenly, like a broadcast intrusion, my mind goes dark except for the quivering gray silhouette of the Shape.

"Hello?" I ask. "I'm here."

But I'm not. I'm back in the gilded room with a dagger deep in my back, the harp strings making my fingers mush as they cry out bittersweet notes and the dagger moves faster with the song.

"Wait until you hear the climax. Pure bliss," the mysterious voice calls out to the bemused onlookers as my blood splatters the bottoms of their expensive gowns and slacks.

Then, once more, everything blinks into black and the Shape is there.

"Don't tell any of them—"

And I'm back at the harp playing, my fingers becoming bloody stumps, and I'm also a violin, feeling the bow quickly sliding back and forth along my newly exposed tendons and nerves, the ungodly screech emitting from my lips sounding like tortured strings in a demonic duet.

The Shape is back, their voice interrupting like a radio when you've driven too far away from the station.

"It's important to remember—and get to the portal—"

The stringed symphony bursts in my ears and my eyes explode open and all of a sudden I'm no longer in that reality or the black blank space with the Shape but in the one that includes my office, where I'm lying beside the car seat and Dawn is screaming and my breasts are like two stones strapped to my chest leaking poison, so I push myself to my feet and lift her into my arms and try to feed her from them, but she spits me out and squirms like the worm at the bottom of a tequila bottle, and that reminds me about the alcohol I drank and how she shouldn't be drinking from me anyway. So I prepare to make a bottle of formula that she'll swallow up so much faster than anything my body has made for her, and after shaking the bottle until it's mixed I set it down, pick up Dawn, and begin smashing her into the kitchen tile over and over and her little head bursts like a grape in my mouth and the blood is everywhere and it smells like copper and baby wipes and some has got in my mouth and I start to gag and shake until I realize I'm still in the office and I've done nothing wrong yet; I've only thought about doing something wrong. I remind myself to be careful, so careful, as I carry her softness into the kitchen to make her the bottle she needs and wants, trembling with the knowledge that I'm an absolute fucking monster for even thinking about hurting her. Occasionally wondering if there's a way to tell which thoughts are premonitions and which are merely warnings.

CHAPTER 20

Tanya, Tea, and the
Whispers of Trees

S o," Tanya says as soon as she shoulders past the door, as though we're in the midst of an ongoing conversation that has spanned our whole lives, which has had no real beginning and will have no real end, "I spoke to some medicine folks down the bush about the stuff you told me."

It's the morning after that awful nightmare, and I'm holding Dawn close to my chest, my nose buried in the baby smell of her fuzzy scalp as I follow Tanya through the living room and into the kitchen. I'm not sure what I'm expecting from her, but I know what I need to do. The cockroach and Nadia from *Russian Doll* and snippets from the Shape all told me as much in their own ways. Quite simply: I have to be careful. I can't tell anyone the full extent of what's happening to me. Not right now. Maybe not ever, provided I don't want to end up locked in some psychiatric facility. That's the sort of thing Steve would do. The sort of thing generations of well-meaning white folks do for those whose visions and perceptions scare them: lock them away and drug them senseless. I don't think I have to worry about Tanya doing that. Therapy and mental illness are colonizer shit. Our people would rather white-knuckle our problems than face doctors who either don't believe our pain or blame us for it.

That's what kept Ma away from doctors after her accident. She told them during her recovery that her hip, ankle, and knee were still in so much pain after the surgeries and rehabs, and they'd told her the problem was she was fat. That she was lazy, hadn't fully committed to rehabbing her body, and was well on her way to a diabetes diagnosis. But she *had* rehabbed properly. I made sure she had. I drove her to all her physical therapy appointments and sat in the car in the parking lot to make sure she didn't sneak off to a fast-food place nearby, the way she tried to the first couple times. When the physical therapist sent home a stapled set of exercises for her, we went through them at home together, me summoning my inner Jillian Michaels to coach her through the pain, and her summoning her inner George Costanza to complain about every single thing. But each time it would reach a point where her leg locked up, I had to help her to a chair, and she'd bite her lip to keep the tears welling in her eyes from pouring down her cheeks. Her doctor said the solution was losing weight but didn't explain how she was supposed to do that when even moderate exercise sent one side of her body ablaze with pain. It seemed like he had given up trying to help her—and further, was terribly annoyed anytime she dare mention her ongoing issues, as if her anguish was a personal affront to him. The morphine and oxy didn't stop the pain exactly, but they made it more bearable. Her doctor wouldn't even prescribe her that, though, saying he was worried she'd come to rely on it too heavily and become an addict. Which is ironic, because his decision led to that anyway.

So-called modern medicine wasn't meant to help people like Ma or my grandma or me. It couldn't. The same way whatever Tanya brought with her today had little to no chance of stopping whatever forces I was fighting. Whatever they were—the threats from the houses, the messages from the Shape, the words of neighbors and cockroaches, the looks from TV characters and liquor store clerks—it was clear to me that they were intent on pulling apart the threads I'd so carelessly spun together and called a life. Still, I was hopeful that Tanya might hold some helpful part of the puzzle—a piece I'd had no chance of finding while I was still among spies and surveillance.

"And?" I ask her. "What did the medicine folks say?"

"Well, sage alone might not take care of what we're dealing with."

"The fuck *are* we dealing with?"

Tanya places a small brown paper bag, the sort we used for lunch in school, on the counter. The bag is folded down twice at the top and stapled shut.

"I mean, I haven't done a full-on investigation or anything, so I can't say for sure yet. But based on what you told me and what the medicine people told me, there's probably some serious-ass bad medicine"—she twirls her right hand in circles in front of me, clicking her long purple fake nails together the whole time—"all up in here."

"You mean in me?"

"Potentially, yes. Among other places." She turns, sees the bags of chips propped on the kitchen table like a prize, and freezes. "Are you fucking kidding me?" She grabs both bags and holds them from the corners like they're dirty diapers. "*Cool Ranch?*"

The realization crashes into me: she wanted anything *but* Cool Ranch Doritos.

"Oh my god, Tan. I'm so sorry. I'm such an idiot. I was super distracted at the grocery store and—"

Tanya tosses the bags back down on the table and laughs.

"Damn, girl. You've definitely got a case of . . . what do they call it? Mom brain?"

A low growl sounds in my ear, then words: *She shouldn't be here.*

I turn away from Tanya and look around the kitchen. The houses are peering in the windows. The yellow curtains are open. I quickly walk over and yank them shut. I look back at Tanya. She hasn't noticed anything. She's pulling the brown bag apart, setting things on the counter. I think about what she's said. Is there something inside me that needs to be tamed, cleansed, even exorcized? Has there been some sort of evil entity inside me since I was thirteen, hiding in my muscles and tendons and flesh, waiting for the perfect opportunity to drive me to destruction? Its influence over me could be why Ma's dead now. Why Ma never got what she wanted most: to meet Dawn.

She was so happy when she heard she was going to be a grandmother. Before I met Steve, I could tell she thought it might not happen, though she'd never said as much. I could see it in how she looked at the chubby-cheeked Native babies at community events and pow-wows, tearing up as though she was staring at a future that was already lost to her. I couldn't meet her eyes then, and she couldn't meet mine.

I turn. The curtains are still shut. The voice doesn't sound like one of the houses any more. It sounds like Meghan, like Joan, like the cashiers and my classmates and all the white women who'd learned to lace their kindness with venom before feeding it to me with a silver spoon.

A loud whistling squeal starts, and for a moment I think it's the collective scream of those women, mad at me for marrying Steve and inviting another Indian into their residential enclave, but Tanya looks up, so I know she hears it, too. I follow her eyes to the kettle, where steam erupts from its spout.

"I didn't turn that on," I mumble, confused.

"Perfect!" Tanya exclaims, clearly not hearing me as she pulls the kettle off the burner. "I've got special tea to make for you."

I wipe my eyes and watch as she puts dried leaves into an exquisite porcelain teapot. Someone from Steve's family bought it for us as a wedding gift. Delicate blue paint covers the white china base, and as I watch, the paint starts to swirl before my eyes.

"Why's it doing that?"

"What do you mean? It's loose leaf."

Tanya looks at me closely. I remember the messages I got last night and decide to ignore her question. Pretending nothing is wrong is the best way to go. More comfortable for the both of us.

I correct myself. "What's in it?"

"I think this one has red willow? I can't totally remember, but I do know it's supposed to cleanse everything out of you. And when I say everything, I mean *everything*. Definitely don't drink it until after you get back from that dinner party. You'll get bwot and puke all over their fancy bathroom. Have it looking like a rez outhouse. Actually, maybe you should drink it now." She cackles.

Shit. I'd forgotten all about the dinner party. I need to pay more attention. I'm losing too many threads.

First: *Russian Doll* last night.

Then: the dream of being stripped of my flesh. The Shape cutting in like they had an urgent message.

Instantly those pieces click into place. The dream was a preview of what will happen tonight—the lone Indian in a room full of white academics. They'll expect me to bleed for them, so I should, to keep up appearances and keep them appeased. To make them think I don't know what's going on. Because I do have a choice. The cockroach said as much. And whatever the Shape has said about my needing to finish writing, the most important thing is and has always been Dawn. I can't give those people cause to kill me and take my baby. That's what they want to do. All of them. Even Steve.

And now, another thread: Tanya's here with the tea and somehow that kettle turned itself on, as if in anticipation. It must be another sign—I need to take some of that medicine tea with me to the party. I'll need it. Maybe not to shit all over the bathroom, but who knows? The day is young, and I can choose. I was going to use my old flask to smuggle in the vodka, but with the weed pen, I should be fine without it. Tea it is. All these thoughts rush through my mind so fast I can barely grasp them.

The smells of sweetgrass, cedar, and sage lift into the air as Tanya uses an eagle feather to create enough smoke to smudge. She stands in front of me. I pull the smoke over my head, into my eyes, my ears, my heart, then hold the seashell full of medicines so Tanya can do the same. I follow her through each room, Dawn tight against my chest, as Tanya swirls the smudge throughout. No corner is safe. I focus on how the smoke twirls, cleansing negativity and bad spirits as we go, and wonder whether this will protect me. There is silence, which feels divine and precious in its own way.

Then we step on the back patio.

"Holy shit. How have I never noticed that before?" Tanya mutters as she surveys the backyard.

"What?"

"Those birch trees. You see how their branches are all growing toward one another?"

There are two skinny trees there—both paper birch that reach and reach, their bark a creamy white with black horizontal lines that sometimes look like scars, sometimes look like eyes, climbing haphazardly up up up. And sure enough, at the tops of both trees the branches have only grown on the side that faces the other tree, lopsided, like they're leaning in toward each other, whispering. The dark branches are enmeshed together, a tangled net.

"See how it looks like a doorway?" Tanya asks.

There's a wheezing laugh in the wind, and I shiver involuntarily.

"I've heard from elders that when trees grow together like that it makes a portal. It's a sign that the earth here is soft."

"Like a sinkhole?"

"No, not the actual earth. Reality here is soft. Things can get through. Spirits, ghosts. Stuff like that. That's why it's really important there are gatekeepers around."

"You mean like Sigourney Weaver in *Ghostbusters*? Possessed people?" I ask. *Please don't say yes. Please don't say yes. I can't be possessed. I can't.*

"The fuck you talking 'bout? No, not like *Ghostbusters!*" Tanya says as she smacks my arm. "And not like *The Exorcist*, neither. You watch too many movies. I'm talking serious spiritual shit here."

Thank Creator.

"Yeah, you're right, of course you are," I say.

"You're damn right I am," Tanya responds as she puts the shell of smudge down on the glass table in the middle of the patio. We sit down in the chairs facing each other. Tanya looks down, eyes narrowed.

"Actually. Maybe I'm not."

I stop breathing.

"Is this highlighter too gold for me, or just gold enough?" I almost laugh with relief as she continues. "It's called 'Trophy Wife.' I put it all over my cheeks and collarbone this morning, but now I can't tell if it actually looks good or if I'm just telling myself it does cuz Rihanna made it."

She turns her face left and right, up and down, juts her shoulders back and forth. Her skin shimmers in the sun.

"It's the perfect amount of gold, Tan. You look exactly like some rich bitch's trophy wife," I say fast, hoping to redirect the conversation back where it was. "So what are gatekeepers then? I've never heard about any of this."

"Are you actually gonna listen?"

"Yes."

Tanya stares me down, one perfectly filled-in eyebrow arched, then, seemingly satisfied, she begins.

"Not a lot of people know about gatekeepers cuz most of that knowledge has been lost. Anything academics in the early twentieth century didn't know about and scribble down basically disappeared in some places. You know how it was back then. The Indian Act made ceremonies illegal, then Mounties came to arrest and charge any Indians who were still doing ceremony, then the asshole judges found 'em guilty and sent 'em off to jail."

"Same as it fucking ever was."

"Totally. But gatekeepers are really interesting. First thing you should know is the idea is not strictly Haudenosaunee. Doesn't mean there aren't Haudenosaunee gatekeepers, but I don't want you to think they're from our ways when they're not, exactly."

I nod.

"Anyway, they move through reality in different ways than the rest of us. Like, they can talk to the spirits of all beings, even plants and animals. Disembodied spirits really like them, too, cuz they're pretty much their only link to life—or this side of life. Basically, gatekeepers are the physical links between this world and other realms and dimensions. They have a responsibility to protect the soft places from people who might accidentally wander in and mess shit up for the rest of us."

228

As she's speaking it's like things slow down and speed up at the same time. *That's it,* I think. *That's why I'm here. I'm a gatekeeper.* I was meant to come to this house, this backyard. I deserve to be here more than any of my neighbors, more than Steve, more than the colonizers and gentrifiers who treat this land like it's disposable, moldable, less than, when really it's the only reason we exist. Maybe that's another reason they want to get rid of me: so they have complete control of the portal. So they have complete control of all the worlds. This one and the other one—the one where spirits live and trees are chatty and cockroaches slide over and around consciousness with the ease and beauty of figure skaters on ice. They want to colonize that space just like they've colonized this one.

"I can't believe I never noticed there was a goddamn portal here before now," Tanya says, chuckling. "We haven't been in the yard much, huh? Some Indians we are."

"To be fair, I think our ancestors would *really* love air-conditioning."

"True." Tanya laughs. "Anyway, be careful walking between those guys, eh? Don't want to end up in, like, colonial times on accident."

"We're already in colonial times," I say as I turn and stare at the trees. They do look like a doorway, actually—and there's whispers coming from them.

"Can you take her for a second?" I ask, offering Dawn to my cousin.

"What are you doing?" she asks as she pulls Dawn in toward her.

I don't answer. I walk to the trees. By the time I'm close enough to touch them, the whispers are loud but still indistinct, like they're in another language.

"What are you trying to say to me?" I whisper. I look into the gap of space between the two trees, not sure what exactly I expect.

Maybe images, like from the trees around Ma's trailer or the one at Christie Pits.

I have the sudden urge to touch the tree on the left. As I stroke the bark my fingers catch on a part that's peeling away and I pull. Black bugs scurry out, afraid of the light. Underneath the rough white bark is soft salmon-colored flesh. I watch as it moves back and forth, like the tree is breathing. I turn the strip of bark-flesh in my hand to look at the back. There's blood, and my hand shakes as I drop it. The right tree whispers.

Don't be afraid.

I can hear Tanya calling to me, vaguely, but she feels so far away. I look up at the right tree. The black knots of eyes stare back, then blink in unison.

Sometimes you need to peel the flesh away to release the vermin and let in the light.

"What does that mean?" I whisper.

This time the left tree answers.

You'll know when you need to know, young one. For now, just remember.

I press my palm to the pink flesh of the tree and feel it inhale once more. I breathe in along with the tree, deep and steadying, as I see roots growing from beneath my feet down into the core of the earth. I think of Ma and how much she gave to me, how she steadied me, how I was rooted in her the way these trees are rooted in the earth, and how the earth, in turn, gives to and steadies these trees. For a moment, calm washes over me—this certainty that, despite everything, Ma's love has kept her here, with me, and the Shape really is an ancestor looking out for me. Maybe it's Grandma, or another family member further back still, one I've never heard of. They could even have been a gatekeeper themself.

"What do you see?" Tanya asks, her voice shaky.

I turn back to her. Her face is grave with anticipation. She might believe me if I told her everything. She might keep this secret, the same way she kept my secrets about boys I snagged on the pow-wow trail. She might not let anyone hospitalize me. She might fight for me, if I let her.

But can you really trust her?

And the honest answer is . . . I don't know. I might never know. That's what's so terrifying about the idea of trust. You don't know who deserves it. You can't—not until you take that wild leap, hoping and praying you made the right choice and you won't crash. I can't afford to crash, so I can't afford to leap.

I jerk my body toward Tan, my arms and legs stiff as a zombie's.

"The fuck," she whispers, getting up as I lumber toward her.

I jump at her and growl. She pulls Dawn in close, shuts her eyes, yells, "Noooo!"

I laugh hysterically and, as she opens her eyes and understands what's happened, she smacks me again.

"Heck, you're stupid!"

"I didn't see anything. There's no portal," I lie, laughing. "You're so full of shit."

CHAPTER 21

Pretty Much a Native Femme Proverb

STEVE

Sorry I'm running late. Student took advantage of my office hours and then some. Tanya there? Will you be ready for when I get back?

5:05 P.M.

ME

Yeah she's here. Getting ready now. What should I wear?

5:17 P.M.

STEVE

I don't know. A dress?

5:20 P.M.

ME

Ok that's not helping. There are lots of kinds of dresses.

5:21 P.M.

ME

What r u wearing

5:22 P.M.

STEVE

I'm wearing a blazer over a button-up

5:24 P.M.

STEVE

Nice slacks

5:24 P.M.

STEVE

Does that help?

5:24 P.M.

ME

YES. Ok see u soon

5:25 P.M.

I feel good for a moment, having solved one of my many problems. But then I wonder. If Steve is a spy and wants to get rid of me, why would he want to help me with anything, even something as simple as dressing appropriately? Unless he doesn't want to get rid of me yet. Unless he wants Dawn to have enough time to literally suck me dry beforehand. Joan was *so insistent* that I breastfeed for six months, at the very minimum. "The benefits for her are unbelievable," she'd said, eyeing the jar of Similac on the counter. If that's the timeline, I might have longer than I thought—provided I don't give them reason to speed things up.

Despite my circumstances, I feel calm—mostly thanks to the couple of puffs I took from the vape pen in the bathroom before we started my makeover. The delivery had come in right before Tanya got here. The houses are silent, exactly like I thought they'd be once I got well and properly high.

Tanya spreads foundation over my face with a big, soft brush, buffing it into my skin with tiny circles. I've barely spent time outside this summer but the makeup is already too light.

"How many times have I told you? You need a summer foundation and a winter foundation," she says, shaking her head as she desperately tries to blend it in. "Thank god for bronzer."

"Is it gonna look okay?" I ask, studying myself in the vanity mirror in front of me. My eyes are surrounded by navy, which is blended out with a light periwinkle. Tanya insisted navy was much more refined than black. "We don't want you to look like you're going to a My Chemical Romance concert, for fuck's sake," she'd scoffed when I'd even suggested it. I had to admit, with the eyes done up and the bronzer being brushed all over my cheekbones and into my hairline, I did look sophisticated. I didn't look like a new mom, in any case. I looked like someone with thoughts and interests and mysterious ways of spending my time.

"So how's the writing going?" Tanya asks as she picks up a tiny brush and starts fiddling with my eyes again. Oh yeah. I'd forgotten I'd told her about it.

"Slow. I have no idea how Dad came up with the perfect ways to tell his stories off the top of his head like that."

"Don't be so hard on yourself. He had a lifetime of practice before we heard him. Who knows how long it took for him to get that good."

It's such an obvious observation that I'm almost ashamed I've never made it myself. There must have been a time when Dad was self-conscious about his storytelling. He might even have been self-conscious when telling us the stories we thought were so thrilling.

"You're right. Maybe I'm being too much of a perfectionist. If I keep second-guessing every other word who knows when I'll even finish."

"You said you're working on the Creation Story?"

I try to nod, but she grabs my chin and stops me.

"No moving yet! If you wanna tell our stories you gotta start at the source." She moves her head back to take in everything, squints her eyes at the effect. "You gonna go the feminist route and have Sky Woman jump through the hole herself?"

"Haven't decided yet. Do you think I should?"

She shrugs. "I mean, that version got really popular in, what? Like, the seventies? It was important at the time, what with women's lib and all that. And it's still important. How many times have you heard the men in our community go on and on about 'lifting up the voices of our women' or 'respecting our women' while never once passing us the mic? Don't even get me started on how they treat queer women."

"Her husband pushing her through the hole could be just as

powerful. With missing and murdered Indigenous women and everything."

"Sure, it could. But Sky Woman doesn't go missing or die."

I try to arrange my thoughts into neat rows. "Well, her husband doesn't know she's gonna live when he pushes her out of Sky World. As far as he knows, he's murdered her at worst and disappeared her at best."

She clicks open a blush palette, picks out the right brush, then starts swirling a pink-leaning coral on my cheekbones.

"True."

"And after that she ends up in an entirely different place with no one and nothing but her baby."

"Not no one. The animals helped her. And she didn't have nothing. She grabbed tobacco plants, strawberries, and the seeds of the Three Sisters on her way down so she still had *something* from Sky World."

"I wonder whether she ever got resentful, you know?" I ask. "She became a single mother in a second, then had no one but animals and her baby to talk to. It must have been really lonely. I don't know. Maybe to her being the first person on a strange planet felt like a punishment."

She pulls back, tells me to turn my face one way, then another. "Maybe it was a punishment."

"You really think that?" I ask.

"Close your mouth," she says, pulling out a nude brown lipstick from her hot pink bag. She pulls out a tiny lip brush, paints it with the lipstick, then starts to carve out lips on my face. "Being the first of anything is always a kind of punishment, because you're responsible for cutting that new path all by yourself. Whatever happens to you, no matter how bad, is seen as necessary and acceptable in the end so long as it's making it easier for everyone who comes after you.

Okay, open your mouth." I do, but apparently not enough. "No, bigger. Like a blow-up doll." She opens her mouth into a big O shape and I mimic her.

"Lohc dis?"

"Yes! Just like that. Steve's a lucky man, innit?" she teases, then begins to make tiny little strokes around the edges of my mouth until I'm sure they're thicker than my own natural lips. "Close again. You know, our stories are all about consequences. Bear listens to Fox and tries using his long, luxurious tail to ice fish? He loses his tail. You turn into a cannibal and eat human flesh? You become a Flying Head."

She moves aside and lets me see the full effect in the mirror. I look beautiful. I look nothing like myself.

"Corn Husk Doll keeps staring at herself after Creator tells her to stop? She loses her face," I say, turning from my reflection quickly, as though my own face will slide off if I keep looking.

"Exactly," Tanya says with a smile. Her lips don't move, but, inexplicably, she still speaks. "Your punishment's coming, by the way. Don't think we forgot you left us."

"What?" I ask, startled. It takes me a second to understand. I should have seen this coming. Of course, Tanya wasn't on my side. I left the rez—left her—for this soulless neighborhood. After all these years laughing at girls like me, girls who swallowed the Pocahontas stereotype and followed their John Smiths away from their communities to assimilation, here I was. I'd become the stereotype. What did Tanya owe me—a traitor, a fool?

"All I said was, 'Exactly.'" She shrugs and looks down as she begins to put all her brushes and makeup away. I stand up abruptly, unsure if she's telling the truth. "Anyway, it's nothing you don't already know. Your dad tried to warn you about academics and your ma tried to warn you about white boys. You wouldn't listen. You never listen. And then you killed her and thought we wouldn't notice. You didn't care what happened to her, so long as you got your white boy and his big house. You were already turning into a colonizer even then. Now the process is just about done and guess what? We won't let you come back."

My chest feels heavy, and my breathing gets fast as I back up. I don't know what to say. I don't know how to defend myself. My biggest secret finally brought to light.

The day Ma asked me to find her oxy will always be seared into my mind. She'd asked me to come to her appointment with her that day, convinced the doctor would listen if I was there to back her up. She told him her pain was getting too bad to get out of bed, that she was scared she'd lose her job as a result. The doctor interrupted and, shaking his head, said he'd already told her he wouldn't prescribe her painkillers. Her "theatrics" would not change his mind. It all happened so fast. As we sat in the parking lot in her car afterward, she finally turned to me and asked if I had any other way to get her OxyContin. I understood her meaning.

"I can't work without something, Alice. I can't garden. I'm always in pain." Her voice cracked as we both stared at the floor. "You must know *someone*. Please." She was begging then, tears in her eyes. "This is no life."

She needed me to do all the things she couldn't do alone: run errands, get groceries, carry the heavy water jugs inside, pay the bills when she was between jobs, take her to community events and hold her steady as she walked inside. But since I'd just agreed to marry Steve, I knew I wouldn't be there soon enough, and I had to help her somehow.

"Fine. I'll do it," I said. "I'll find it."

And that was the beginning of the end.

We never spoke about it directly after that. I'd just replace the money she left on the kitchen table with a pill bottle. The time between each bottle shortened.

I could have lied to Ma. Said that I couldn't find them. Anyone could have seen the path I was pushing her down. Anyone but me. Why did I do that? What was wrong with me? Could it really have been the influence of some evil spirit? Maybe our family was cursed—bad medicine passed down from my grandmother to my mother to me to Dawn.

Murderer.

"How many people know?" I whisper, but Tanya's already turned up a Carly Rae Jepsen song on her phone. Even if she could hear me, she doesn't care what I have to say.

They're in league with the houses, too, but for different reasons. They don't care what this neighborhood does to you as long as you never come back to Six Nations, the angry voice confirms. *The transformation will conclude, and you won't be able to go home anymore, and you won't be able to stay here. Nowhere is your home now. You'll be on the streets with the man who sold you the dreamcatcher. You belong there much more than he does. He has beautiful art to offer the world. All you have are a few pages worth nothing to no one.*

My breathing stops, and it's as if I'm underwater, unable to pull in the oxygen I need. The edges of my vision get blurry, then turn to little ones and zeros, like some computer code I can't understand. The code starts to filter farther and farther into the center of what I see. Seemingly solid things—the bed, the vanity, Tanya—melt into code. What does this mean? Am I in a simulation? Is all of this some sort of program or game I can't understand?

It's a punishment. The consequences of your actions. Stop fighting it. You couldn't even keep your mother alive. What makes you think you can keep your baby alive? Why do you think you deserve the chance to try?

A hand lands on my shoulder from behind and a voice falls into my ear.

"You ready?"

I turn and, like a pair of prescription glasses falling over my eyes, everything comes back into focus. Steve is in front of me. I watch as his expression transforms from excitement to disappointment.

"Oh. I thought you'd go for a more natural look tonight."

That old feeling of nausea stirs deep in my belly, the same one I felt when Ma criticized my clothes and makeup, pointing out Steve hadn't introduced me to any of his friends.

Before I can say anything, though, Tanya clicks her tongue and pipes up: "Her looking hot as hell is not gonna kill your little colleagues or their silly little wives, Steven." She nudges her way between us, muttering "'Scuse me" as she pushes an earring post into my left earlobe, attaches the backing, then does the same to my right earlobe.

What's happening right now? Why is Tanya defending me? It must all be a big performance for my benefit. Something to make me drop my guard so I won't suspect what's coming. Something to make me feel crazy so I do the wrong thing and they get the police to arrest me and take Dawn. I watch in the mirror as their eyes meet. Tan smiles slightly, then Steve smiles, then they both look away. They're planning something. Together. She must have been the one Steve was texting the other night, not Meghan. They wouldn't let Meghan be a big player in all of this after the failed phone recording showed I didn't trust her.

"Anyway, her eye shadow has to match her earrings. It's basically a Native femme proverb," Tanya says as she turns me to look in the full-length mirror behind the door. My earrings are long, beaded shoulder-dusters I waited weeks to order online, part of a collection that sold out in under five minutes, like Aunt Rachel had said. The glass beads move from a dark navy up top through to a baby blue in the middle and white at the ends. They stand out from the curtains of long, dark hair surrounding my face. They also clearly code me as Indigenous. Not like the people we're going to see don't already know. It's basically all they know about me.

"Perfect," Tanya says as she smiles at me in the mirror. A sharp shrill cry pours out of the baby monitor on the side table. "Aaand there's my cue." Tanya grabs her makeup kit and hurries out, closing the door softly behind her.

I look at Steve in the mirror. His back is turned to me—the same back I fell in love with—only now it's stiff with unsaid words. He's buttoning up his white-collared shirt; he's carefully pulling on his blazer. Each crease is impeccable. A better wife would have done that ironing for him instead of letting him do it himself. Was that why he was plotting against me with Tanya? Why he initially agreed to spy on me, to betray me? Because all I knew how to do was shove as many clothes as possible into a double or triple loader at the Laundromat, pour in a capful of bright blue discount detergent, and push the coins in? Yet another failure he wouldn't want passed down to his daughter. What was he going to do to me? What was he planning? It had to have something to do with the party. Something was going to happen. I could tell.

"Why do you want me to come to this party so bad?" I blurt, unable to hold it all in anymore. "What's going to happen to me?"

Steve turns immediately and looks at me like I have a second head. "What do you mean? Nothing's going to happen to you. It's a dinner party, Alice. All you have to do is eat, drink, and be merry. You can pretend on that last one."

I become incredibly aware of our positions in the room. My eyes fall on a teddy bear, propped up on the dresser. I don't remember putting it there, but it's staring at us both, smiling. A camera. A test.

If I don't say the right thing, if I don't go with Steve, they will see and they will retaliate.

"Sorry. I don't," I say, deliberately, placing each word before me like bricks. "I don't know why I said that."

Steve's shoulders slump as he sits down on the bed. "I do."

My whole body tenses. I stop breathing and wait for him to continue.

"Look, I know I've kind of thrown you off the deep end here. You aren't used to the sort of underhanded, cutthroat politics that make up academia," he says, reminding me once again he's never lived on the rez. "I underestimated how disorienting all this would be for you. To go from a place where you know everyone to a place people thrive on superficiality."

It feels for a second like I've stepped too far down the stairs and stumbled. I'm all disoriented. What is Steve trying to do here? Has he changed his mind? Is he going to let me stay home?

"I know these people aren't exactly nice. I'm sorry. I wish they were. But I wouldn't be asking you to do this if it weren't important for the both of us, and for Dawn. There's only room for one tenured prof in the department, and I'm not sure I have more publications and academic prestige than the other candidates. It ultimately comes down to what the other profs in the department want, so events like this can tip the odds in my favor."

I can't believe I've been so stupid for so long. He knew these people were awful to me. He just accepted that my pain and discomfort were the price of admission. Even worse: he tried to convince me I was crazy to think those people were anything other than harmless and well-intentioned. I'm so furious I can't focus. And then it occurs to me: he *wants* me to think I'm crazy. I want to hurt him so bad in this moment. I want to hurt him like he's hurt me so many times.

"Isn't that what the Mohawk classes are for? To tip the odds back in your favor? Isn't that what Dawn and I are for?"

Steve winces. "I wasn't aware the classes were a problem for you," he says stiffly. He doesn't bother addressing the rest.

Then an image falls in my mind: me at Ma's crowded trailer holding a screaming Dawn in my arms as knocks pummel the aluminum door, and there, on the wooden porch, is a social worker ready to take Dawn from me because I'm too poor, too unhealthy, too Native. Steve stands behind her shoulder, eager to enter and take what's his. It feels like a premonition. I remember the bear on the dresser. Someone's watching.

It's all burning.

No, it's not. And it doesn't have to be.

I know what Steve wants of me at this moment. He wants me to be a silly little wife the other silly little wives like. Be an ornament—the female version of a cigar store Indian, standing outside the door while my white husband enters anyplace he desires. I think of my dream last night. The performance, the pain, the humiliation. This dinner will also be a painful and humiliating performance, but no more so than any of my prior encounters with these people. The difference is, this time I know the dinner is a test I need to pass. It's how I keep Dawn, protect the portal, finish writing. Because those are the three things I need to do, I'm sure of it. These people clearly don't know how much I know quite yet. If they did, I'd already be locked up or locked out. And so I need to play their games—but only for now.

I let out a long, exaggerated sigh. "The classes aren't a problem. I'm just pissy cuz you don't like my makeup."

"Oh, Al. You look beautiful. You really do. I'm taking my nerves out on you. It's not fair, and I'm sorry."

"We can talk about all that after the dinner," I say, waving my hand. "I'll play nice tonight. I promise."

"Thank you," Steve says, relief flooding his face as he jumps up to hug me.

Before we get in the Uber to head over to his department head's house, I fill the flask with the medicine tea and put it and the weed pen in my purse. I don't have much, but I do have these. Then I rush over to Dawn to say goodbye. I hold her close, kiss the top of her head, then her nose, then each chubby cheek.

I'm going to save you. Trust me, I try to psychically communicate to her. And when her eyes meet mine, bright and happy, I know she hears and understands.

"Thank you," Steve repeats, squeezing my hand as we're whisked into the fading light, toward whatever awaits us.

CHAPTER 22

She Can Pronounce "Hors d'Oeuvres" but Not "Haudenosaunee"?

And Alice!" Sheila practically squeals once she finally turns to me after a solid minute of going over inside jokes and "shop talk" with Steve, leaving me to stare at her eerily creaseless face. One time I asked Steve whether he thought she and the other wives got Botox. I'd noticed the way their skin stretched tight over the bones of their face—so unlike the women in my community, whose skin started to loosen and fold like those worn-in fleece blankets every Native aunty buys from a pow-wow and immediately throws on their couch. He seemed offended that I'd lumped Sheila in with the other women. She was a tenured professor in the English department at the same university he was. This ensured she was set apart from the other wives as someone to be taken seriously, and therefore, according to Steve's estimation of such women, she did not do superficial, vain things like get Botox.

"Look at you! Ready for a night on the town!" Sheila says, eyes raking me from tip to toe. "You'd never even be able to tell you just had a baby." It feels like an insult, like most things she says to me. She slides her hand too intimately on top of my arm as Steve mouths,

"Be good." It scares me, his saying that. What will happen to me if I'm not? What does this woman know that I don't? What's coming for me?

Sheila guides me into the living room, where a handful of women dressed in a mix of creams, beiges, tans, and grays sit posed upon the white couches like a *Vanity Fair* cover. I can imagine the headline: "Finally! The Women Behind the Men of the Academy Speak." As if they aren't incessantly speaking about all things at all times.

"Girls, doesn't Alice look amazing postpartum? I was just telling her, you can't even tell she had a baby! Can you?" she repeats once we're in front of all of them. The other women nod and mutter their agreement emphatically. Lots of them bought gifts for Dawn— expensive gifts with fantastic wrapping jobs that only Meghan's recent BIPOC Disney donation could rival. But they brought them to Steve's office, cutting me—and Dawn—out of the transaction entirely.

Sheila turns back to me and says, low, as if telling some dreadful secret, "Chrissy had a little wine tasting last week, actually, and I almost asked Steve if we should invite you, but then Chrissy reminded me you were breastfeeding. We didn't want to tempt you, you know?"

"I don't drink—" I start, then stop. They already know this. They've been obnoxious about it every time I've turned down alcohol, as if my not drinking is some indictment of them. So why would Sheila and this other woman even consider inviting me to a wine tasting? Then it hits: the cashier at the liquor store was named Chrissy. Is Sheila talking about the same woman? Is that why she brought up the wine tasting—because she knew I was lying about my sobriety? Shit, these women could easily be in contact with Meghan, too. Her snarky comment about my drinking while breastfeeding was very similar to what Sheila said now. Maybe Meghan was on the phone with Sheila when I came downstairs the other day. Or Chrissy. No, wait. She was on the phone with Steve. Wasn't she? They could all be communicating.

"Here, why don't you sit down with me." Sheila perches on the edge of the couch and gently guides me down with her. I steel myself for the avalanche of words I know are coming. "I wanted to ask you about your writing. Steve has said such wonderful things! I understand you're working with How-dasani myths? Is that how you say it? How-day-saw-nee? I'm so sorry, I'm probably butchering your peoples' language!" She laughs easy as anything.

"Close," I say, then repeat the proper phonetic pronunciation.

She repeats after me, clumsily. I don't bother to correct her again.

"You'd think after doing so many land acknowledgments I'd have it down by now. I'm hopeless when it comes to speaking anything but English. That's probably why I got a PhD in it. Reading's the only thing I'm genuinely good at. Which is why I so desperately wanted to talk to you about this writing! Tell me all about it. Are you writing in conversation with E. Pauline Johnson? I know she wrote this fantastic piece about the stereotypes of the Indian maiden back in the late nineteenth century. What was it called? 'A Strong Something Something' . . . "

"I'm not sure," I say, painfully aware, as academics always make me, that knowledge is a privilege, a currency, even. Especially knowledge of my own people. They like for me to know they're rich in knowledge that should be mine.

"Oh! 'A Strong Race Opinion'! That's it! Anyway, a bunch of white men were writing these books with Native women characters who would fall in love with white men and then kill themselves in the end. Utterly racist, sexist claptrap, if you ask me. And if you ask

Pauline, too, it seems." She laughs at her own joke, then before I can even process what she's saying, she continues: "It's so interesting, because Margaret Atwood wrote the libretto for the opera based on the last week of Pauline's life—it was called *Pauline*, if I remember correctly—not that long ago. That was out in Vancouver, though. I don't imagine you had a chance to see it?"

"No," I say, looking around nervously. I can hear the house whispering to me, but I can't make out what it's saying over the buzz of conversation and light harp music. Is someone actually playing a harp?

"I'm a bit of an Atwood fan girl, so I made Lou take me. It was fascinating, the way she wove Pauline's poetry in with her own writing! She even cleverly used the effects of the morphine to make Pauline hallucinate and see people from her past as she was dying. So we got a really good sense of her life leading up to her death. Did you know Pauline died of breast cancer?".

I shake my head. I'm barely there, my mind immediately on Ma at the mere mention of morphine. Does Sheila know? How could she? I haven't even talked to my cousins or Steve about any of it. What's going on? Little phrases from the other women flit in and out of my ears. *Our cabin out near Peterborough . . . You simply must go to Ibiza . . . Well, we own six properties and rent out four . . . They really earned that Michelin star . . .* My mind feels like it's oozing out of me.

"Brutal case. She was always in pain at the end, so it would make practical sense that she'd need so much morphine she'd be seeing things. Don't you think?"

Always in pain. The exact words Ma used when she asked me to get her oxy. It was easier to get than morphine, I found. I didn't know what would happen to her, though. Did I? Of course not. I loved her.

The house's whisper becomes startlingly clear. *Then why did you leave her alone when she needed you?*

"Excuse me for a moment," I say, rising as I extricate myself from the stranglehold of Sheila's attention. Spit puddles in my mouth. I'm going to be sick. "I need to use the bathroom."

"It's just at the end of that hall," she says, pointing, then turns to join one of the conversations seemingly floating around her.

I nod, and almost stumble, dazed, down the carpeted hallway. The house cackles as it lengthens the hall before my eyes. It never seems to end, no matter how many heavy, plodding steps I take.

I stop and lean against the crimson wall to steady myself. Close my eyes. Focus on the breath in, the release out. Focus on anything but Ma and her dead face inside that coffin, judging me, blaming me, spiders creeping across her skin.

"Are you okay?"

I open my eyes and Mason is in front of me, only instead of ripped jeans and a T-shirt, he's wearing a black button-up shirt with the sleeves folded to his elbows and a gray pair of what Steve would have called slacks. The shock of seeing him in this context does a better job of distracting me than any visualization techniques I could have tried. Why is he here? Does he know Steve? And if so, does that mean he knows I'm married? He could have told Steve about seeing me in the grocery store. How I wasn't wearing my wedding ring. How I was acting like a single mother and lying about my credentials to seem more interesting and appealing to him. Being a bad wife. A crazy woman.

He also told Steve how you loved to use your preteen body to sell 50/50 tickets to older men, the house spits.

No, that wasn't what I was doing. Or, it wasn't what I wanted to do. I was just doing what I was told. Steve knows that.

He told Steve about the time you waved the possibility of sex in front of him like some fool swimmer waving a bleeding wound in front of a shark. He told him how you changed your mind last minute and acted like you were the victim.

No no no. That's not true. He was the one who was mean to me. He treated me like shit that whole first year of high school after I didn't fuck him.

This is the test.

Of course. I raise a hand to my now damp forehead and push away my bangs, then straighten up and look directly at Mason. I need to give the impression I'm in control here.

"I'm fine. What are *you* doing here? Did Steve invite you?"

"It's Lou's party. Lou invited me," he says coolly, clearly trying to mask his offense. "But I know Steve, sure. Do I know you?"

"What?"

"Have we met before?"

The floor feels unsteady. I push myself more firmly against the wall. I have no idea what to say. What sort of game is Mason playing right now? Why would he pretend he'd never met me? What purpose would that serve? Every thought feels too fast, too slippery. Like seed beads falling into the fibers of Aunt Rachel's carpet. I can't find them quick enough, can't hold them all at once. And yet, simultaneously, time has turned to sap, sticky and slow, dripping down me and over me like it's trying to trap and fossilize me. I watch as Mason's eyes blink in slow motion and wonder if he's slowed down or I've sped up. I hope my dress isn't sweated through at the base of my back. Each one of those women in that living room will notice, then tell their husbands later tonight and wonder aloud whether it's "an Indian thing." It's not even hot in here—in fact, the central air makes it a bit chilly, if anything. I just feel hot and thirsty and anxious and uncomfortable and it's all pouring out of my skin like liquefied shame.

"I guess not. You remind me of someone I knew." My voice is normal, I think. Time seems to have caught up with itself. I turn from him and walk toward the bathroom again, barely focusing on what's before me because I hear his laughter chasing behind me.

"Fuckin cock teaze!" he shouts between guffaws.

I close the bathroom door, reach desperately into my purse, and, trembling, pull out the weed pen. I turn it on, then press the button and inhale deep, hold in air that tastes of metal and synthetic blueberry, then blow it out in a thick white cloud. I do it again, hoping that this will not only shut up the voice that's so insistent and antagonistic inside my head but also numb me to whatever other indignities no doubt await me when I leave this room. I look down. The swirls of gray on the granite countertop swish back and forth under my steadying hand. The brown dots like pupils embedded in the design. No sooner do I think that than they all blink at me at the same time, same as with the trees at the portal. I yank my hands away and my eyes drift up toward the mirror.

There I am. I am surprised to see I look beautiful despite everything. Smiling in an almost lascivious way.

Then I realize: it's not me in the mirror because I'm not smiling.

"Stop! Please don't do this to me," I beg, desperate, but she only brings her finger to her closed lips to mime for me to be quiet. Then she points up into the corner of the room behind me. I follow her gaze and see a grate painted to perfectly match the sand-colored walls. There are voices coming from inside. I move closer, watching as the mirror woman moves along with me, her actions matching everything but my expression—mine, I'm sure, more fearful, hers almost pitying, like she knows something about the present and the future that I don't. I close the toilet seat and step onto its sleek black cover, my heels sinking in as the voices become clear.

"Do you think she knows?" That's Lou, Steve's department head.

"God no. Do you think she'd have come if she knew?" That's Steve. I freeze where I am.

"This is her only chance. You know that, right?"

"I'm not worried about it."

"Maybe you should be. What are you going to do if she resists?"

"Do you think I'm an amateur? I've been planting seeds for weeks now. She'll either go along with it or she'll think she's crazy and I'll have her institutionalized. Simple."

"And your mother is for sure going to fund my research trip to the Amazon? Armed security and everything? I don't want a *Cannibal Holocaust* situation once I get there."

Steve laughs. "Don't worry about it. You make sure I've got tenure and you're golden."

"Good man. Well, then. Shall we get this started already?"

My limbs feel like liquid. I step down onto the tile floor and crumple atop the closed toilet lid. So this is why Steve's defended his colleagues so fiercely. They're all in on some big plan to steal Indigenous knowledge and sell it themselves, just like my dad said. I shouldn't be surprised. That's exactly what Steve did. He paid Ma for what she told him, yes, but he's the one who ultimately has his name on the book. He's the one who's going to be credited with pioneering his field. And whatever twisted research Steve and Lou are planning in the Amazon, I doubt the Indigenous peoples there are going to be given credit or payment. If anything, they're going to be treated like enemies and maybe even killed by Lou's armed security. Dad was right about everything, and it makes me furious. These people already have so much of the world: the cabins on the lake, the luxury vacations, the university accreditations, the expensive houses in trendy neighborhoods, voices that mattered enough to shape public policies and laws. Wasn't that enough? Why did they have to own it all, down to the very last scrap of Indigenous knowledge, land, and life?

And then there's Steve's admission he's been not only using me for my uterus, but trying to make me think I'm crazy this whole time. I fucking knew it. The phone call with Meghan. The texts between Steve and Tanya. The way Steve so casually swept me away from my community, from my mother—the only home I've ever known—to a wealthy part of Toronto where I'm an outsider, a parasite. Sheila's comments on morphine. The way she quoted Ma to me. Even my interaction with Mason just now. The way he pretended to not even know me. It's all proof. It's all been proof this entire time.

But what am I supposed to do with it?

All I'm sure of is that I need to be in absolute control of my reactions. I need to be calm and collected, no matter what or who is coming. I need to prove my sanity to these insane people. Which means I need to act like them.

I get up and check my reflection. The mirror woman has disappeared, leaving only my own dead-eyed reflection. I practice a smile. There's still a trace of fear there, but no more than what these people are used to seeing every day they wake up and pummel the world to their will. I wait until my hands and arms feel steady again, then open the door and walk out to face whatever there is to be faced.

CHAPTER 23

Dinner Is Served

I'm staring down at the thick red liquid in front of me, a dish Sheila announced as tomato and red pepper soup, but all I can think of is blood, the metallic tang of it, and as I watch the people around me slurp it up with something approaching glee, some dipping crusty bread into its contents, then shoving it into their open mouths, the thought only solidifies in my mind: *It is blood and these people are monsters.* Even Steve, who's seated to my right, is lapping and lapping like the dutiful dog he apparently is to these people.

"Alice, you're a Native woman. What do you think? Is 'genocide' really the right word? I mean, these are all isolated cases of murder or kidnapping, aren't they?"

At the sound of my name I snap back to attention. One of Steve's colleagues, a man with a graying beard whose name, I remember, is Scott, is staring at me expectantly as I weave together what he's referring to from context clues, something I've been getting increasingly better at in recent days. He's clearly talking about the Missing and Murdered Indigenous Women and Girls Inquiry report, which was released a few weeks back. It took 1,200 Indigenous women going missing or being murdered for Canada to bother to fund it. Even with everything going on around me, I couldn't miss the report if I tried. There were posts all over Facebook, Instagram, and Twitter:

from Indigenous folks expressing relief at its characterizing the history of this country, finally, as "genocide," to white folks scrambling to completely discredit the use of that term, along with all its uncomfortable implications. I didn't post anything. I started to read the report, sure that it was something I should do as an Indigenous woman. Sure that it would help me with my writing because it would influence how I wrote about what happened to Mature Flowers before she found herself in the air, falling to this earth. If I'm being totally honest, I'd unrealistically hoped it might explain everything. Why Disney executives saw fit to rewrite a child rape victim named Matoaka as an empowered Native woman named Pocahontas, whose love for white men was so absolute she abandoned her community to colonization and destruction by the sequel; why young girls like me and my cousin Melita were used to sell 50/50 tickets; why all my friends lost their virginity so young; why Sarah could disappear from the gas station and all of our lives with a collective shrug; why my own mother worked two jobs for years before her accident and still couldn't afford to pay for the infrastructure to hook our trailer up to a water line; why her knowledge could only be considered "pioneering work" when it was commodified and academically coded by a white man; why Ma was so tired of doctors gaslighting her that she stopped telling them how much pain she was still in after they prematurely declared her "healed"; why none of Steve's colleagues or family members or even our neighbors seemed to see me as anything more than a tool to validate their own fears about their racism or an enemy to drive out. I'd hoped the report would explain my entire existence, and the existence of all the Native women I loved.

I couldn't even get past the report's table of contents. As I scrolled through the different chapter titles and subtitles, seeing how the commissioners spent so much time trying to lay out human rights frameworks and explain colonization as gender-based oppression—including everything from the earliest encounters with settlers to modern depictions of Indigenous women in the media—the page numbers rising from 100 to 200 to 500 to 700, I was overcome with a feeling of futility. There was no number of pages that would convince people who saw us as worthless to change their minds. We would always be squaws to them. We would always be expendable, the way I was to Steve now, or would be in a few months, whenever he decided once and for all I had no further purpose.

"They're tragic, don't get me wrong," Scott says. "I was gutted when I found out about that little girl who was pulled from the river. Christ, I've got nieces her age." His lips push up into a smile. "But it's not like that's part of some massive, ongoing conspiracy to murder or disappear Native women."

He looks around the room quickly and the others smirk back at him knowingly. All my intentions to try to fly under the radar for this dinner disperse like smoke.

"Her name was Emma. Emma Blake," I say, trying to keep my voice from shaking. "And her murder—all these women's murders—*are* part of a massive, ongoing conspiracy. One designed to take Native land."

Scott, down the table, laughs a little, saying, "You can't honestly tell me the monster who murdered that little girl did it because he wanted land. It's not like he was given a deed afterward."

Immediately Steve's hand is on my thigh, squeezing it slightly. I don't acknowledge it.

"I'm not telling you that at all. I'm telling you the stories this country has told about who Native women are, what you can expect from us, and what we deserve, have had a direct impact on how Canadians treat us. There's a straight line from how the Catholic

Church justified the murders and rapes of Indigenous people when countries like Canada were being settled, to the way courts and columnists justify the murders and rapes of Indigenous people today."

"Sure, if you consider the systemic issues, there's a lot to be desired. But is that really 'genocide'? That's such a loaded word. It means something to people," Lou, to my left, responds. "When you say 'genocide,' I think Holocaust. I think Rwanda. I don't think about individual murders done over a period of decades by completely different people."

As I'm about to respond, Mason, who's seated diagonal to me, interrupts.

"That's exactly why I refer back to the Truth and Reconciliation Commission on this. They used the term 'cultural genocide,' which I think is much more understandable and applicable." He's not talking to me. He's not even looking at me. He's talking to the white people at the table, who are clearly relieved he's added a modifier to the term, as if that drastically changes the conversation.

"Great point, John. I completely agree," Scott says, his eagerness to have an Indigenous person to agree with so clear it borders on desperate. He's saying more, going into vague detail about the United Nations Genocide Convention, but I can't focus on his words. I can only focus on Mason. Why did Scott call him "John"? Matoaka's voice echoes in my head: *Don't let him be your John.* How did Mason know about that? The only person I told was Aunt Rachel.

She must have told him. Even she's not safe.

Before I can reflect on what that means, as if on cue, Sheila leans over to me and says, softly, "Is there something wrong with the soup? You've barely touched it."

My attention shifts directly to her and her creaseless consternation. Has she been watching me this whole time?

"I'm not really hungry," I say mildly. And it's true, I'm not hungry, I haven't been hungry in what feels like days. When was the last time I even ate? I can't remember.

"You're breastfeeding, though, aren't you? Lots of good vitamins and minerals for Dawn in there. I actually had both of you in mind when I planned the menu."

What does she mean by *that*? Why would she plan her menu around me and Dawn? That makes no sense. I'm only one person out of probably twenty seated at this table. I pause and look down at the soup. It still looks like blood to me. It even smells like blood, faintly. Why would Sheila be so insistent upon me eating this blood soup unless there was something she wanted me and Dawn to ingest in it?

Poison.

Certainty filters through each part of me as I sit very still, trying my best to keep my face as blank as her husband's morality. This must be what Steve and Lou were talking about earlier. If it's not poison in there, it's some sort of drug meant to make me look and act crazy. LSD. Ecstasy. I need to be smarter about what I say and do. I know how easy it is to take an Indigenous woman's righteous anger and make it look like insanity. Like turning a kaleidoscope. One minute you're tolerated, the next you're gone. I can't make it easy for them. I won't.

"Thank you, Sheila. How thoughtful. I'm saving my appetite for the main course."

"Why don't I go get the main course now?" She grabs the bone china bowl from in front of me and starts to get up. "Hopefully the conversation's changed to something less . . . contentious by the time I get back."

Contentious. Not the word I would have used to describe Indigenous women, girls, and two-spirit folks being murdered or going missing at over five times the rate of non-Indigenous folks, but sure. *Contentious.* I look down at my lap and try to ignore what's being said around me, let it turn to a cicada-like buzz, but Steve's hot words are in my ear: "Be nice, Al. Please."

I've been trained since I was a girl to know "be nice" is colonial code for "shut up." But I'm not sure why he wants me to shut up. If anything, I'd think he'd want me to keep going, the better to institutionalize me with.

Then he continues: "And for god's sake, eat something." He wants to pressure me into eating the poison or drugs or whatever.

I don't respond. Still, I can feel eyes on me, other eyes, so I look up and Mason, or "John," as he calls himself, is staring straight at me.

You know what they want you to do. His lips are shut tight but I know the words are coming from him, from his mind. *Just do it.*

Why should I? I think back.

Survival of the fittest, baby. Do what they say and you'll survive. You and your sweet little girl.

I hold his gaze, thinking back to the times when I was a teenager and told myself I'd do anything for a chance to be his, an ornament on his bedside table, a notch in his belt. Even yesterday, in the grocery store, I was desperate to feel the light of his attention shine exclusively on me. I wanted to swallow it all, every drop, like a bottle of water in the thick, swampy southern Ontario humidity. Now, as he smirks at me from across this shiny cherrywood table, I feel dirty, like I've been rolling in mud and shit. His words a reminder of my role here. I'm supposed to cut chunks from my back and let them watch while they casually sip their drinks. I'm not supposed to object.

"Here you are. Don't tell anyone, but I picked the best cut for you," Sheila says.

The plate slides before me and there, in the middle of the china, is a brown face that appears to have been sliced directly from a woman's skull, the eyelids clenched tight despite being severed from whatever muscles would have kept them closed. This is what Scott meant before. This is why he was smiling knowingly at each white person at this table. *But it's not like that's part of some massive, on-going conspiracy to murder or disappear Native women.* I look around, my consciousness immediately trying to pop out of the confines of my body like a piece of bread from a toaster, and I watch as each plate slides in front of each of the other guests, each of whom enthusiastically picks up their assigned fork and steak knife and cut into the still bloody brown flesh, one guest commenting on how fresh it is, another asking where on earth Sheila managed to get such quality meat in this day and age, and Sheila smiling as she looks directly at me, saying oh she just happens to know the right butcher, her eyes now moving past me to my husband, who's commenting on how he's never eaten anything quite so tender, that this is positively melting in his mouth, the blood staining his teeth and tongue inside a dark wine, as though he's eaten something innocent, like blackberries, and then Sheila's asking me why I haven't tried any yet, and then Steve's asking why I haven't tried any yet, and then everyone's eyes are on me, and the fork and knife are in my hands as I stare down at the face on my plate, which looks remarkably like my own, and when I glance up everyone else's faces are gone—not the ones on their plates, though those are quickly being consumed, too, but the ones on their own heads, which are now bare and smooth as stones, and I think briefly of corn husk dolls, how vain the original was to have lost her face, and how vain all of us in this room have been and continue to be, then I think of what will happen to me if I eat human flesh like the rest of them, the absolute monsters, the *cannibals*, and I whisper to a faceless Steve that I can't do it, please don't make me do it, my voice cracking despite me, and then he's cutting the face on my plate with his own fork and knife, asking me why I have to do this, why I have to make him treat me like a child, and I wonder if anyone else can hear him speaking without a mouth, and then he's stabbing the fork into the left cheek on my plate, and pushing the fork toward my closed mouth, telling me to make room for the helicopter, and everyone is laughing, and I'm thinking of the dream and how this is just another version, my humiliation and fear are the true main course of this evening, and I can't fight the fear away anymore so I cry, keeping my mouth shut as he knocks the bloody flesh against my lips once, twice, three times, and I beg him to stop, but he's only used this as an opening and now the chunk of cheek is inside my mouth and Steve's hands are on me, one under my chin clamping my jaw closed and the other pinching my nostrils shut, forcing me to finally chew, and it tastes like copper and gristle, not tender at all, and as Steve's tickling my throat to force me to swallow, in the corner of my eyes I see something grow, something I instinctively know I don't want to see, but also know I have to see, and my body is shaking uncontrollably as I look at Lou, who has abandoned all pretense of politeness and is licking his plate clean. I watch as the tongue protrudes from what looks like nothing, transfixed on what must be happening beneath.

Delicious, Lou says, bringing his bloody, blank face up from the porcelain to stare at me. It's unnerving, this faceless head splattered with red, slowly turning to the side, as if examining me, even without eyes. Lou's body seems to be quivering under his skin, like what I see and understand to be Lou is not Lou at all, and there's another Lou, a hidden Lou, hiding beneath. *Wouldn't you say so, Steven?*

Nothing like fresh meat, Steve laughs. And then Lou starts to laugh, and Scott, and Mason-John, the harmony a deep, gruff, roiling growl of a noise. And then Sheila and the other women laugh, too, their giggles like tinkling bells at first, but slowly heightening, the pitch skyrocketing, until their voices are all one manic screech. I cover my ears, gagging at the taste of blood and gristle still coating my mouth, just in time to watch Lou start to . . . change. The sharp angles of his shoulders and the thin sturdiness of his limbs dampen as each part of his body begins to bloat. It doesn't seem to be fat, but bone that's pushing his body to become larger. His shirt and pants rip open from the pressure and the shreds fall from him, the separate pieces of his body somehow smoothing into one huge rectangular shape. A new set of features appears in the empty of what used to be his face, and as I watch it grows, taking up the whole of what used to be his body. The chair lurches beneath him, then breaks into splinters of wood and cushion, and I see that he is only a head—a giant head, resting on the ground, what used to be his legs and feet now cheeks and chin, what used to be his arms now ears and temples. Wiry white-blond hair sprouts from every part of his face, while the blond hair on his head grows longer, thicker, more tangled. As he lets out a final grunt, two wings stab out from his cheeks, a grimace of a smile playing on his face as the others around the table start to quiver and transform in my peripheral vision, silk dresses and linen suit jackets falling to the floor around me.

He's a Flying Head, I think, clenching my eyes shut, trying to figure out what else to do. *Holy shit, he's a Flying fucking Head. They're all Flying Heads.*

Now, Alice. Don't you think you're overreacting? Lou asks. *Evolution is natural. You should embrace it. Aren't you tired of being inferior? Don't you want to stop surviving and start thriving?*

Every muscle in my body is like dripping liquid, completely outside of my control, until one single word enters my mind: *Dawn.*

We can save her, Sheila says from my left. *Just like we can save you.*

Or we can eat you both. Harvest your organs and grind your bones to make our bread. Your choice.

I try to pull my consciousness back into my body. I need to not think. They can hear everything I'm thinking. If I don't figure something out, now, they're going to eat me and Dawn.

Open your eyes, Lou demands.

"No," I say. The air around me feels like it's solidified into Jell-O.

Open your eyes, Sheila demands.

"No," I repeat, tears sliding down my face.

Open your eyes or I'll feed them Dawn, Steve says.

I snap my eyes open, grab my purse from beneath my seat, and run. The house doesn't stretch itself out under my feet this time. I must have caught it off guard. Good.

I dart into the first room I see, slam the door shut, and turn the lock. I place my ear against the wood of the door. I can still hear the tones of Steve's voice, but I can't make out the words. He could be planning to call the cops right now. All he has to do is tell them I'm crazy and they can take me away. He could be planning to trap me here. Find a key, barrel in, carve my face from my skull to feed it to Lou. He could be planning to give Sheila our daughter. He could be doing anything. And I'm locked in here.

I turn around to see what room I'm actually in. What I have to work with. It's some sort of library. There are shelves full of books on every wall climbing almost to the ceiling. The heavier books could work as weapons. My eyes gravitate toward a giant hardcover book whose cover reminds me of the sky, the words INFINITE JEST stamped across the spine, and I yank it from its place so hard I nearly drop it.

At that exact moment, the handle to the door starts shaking violently behind me.

263

Aaaaalice. Lou's voice. *Come out and play.*

He jiggles the knob more frantically.

You told Steve you'd be a good girl. Do you think this *is being a good girl?* That's Sheila.

I slide down the bookshelf wall to the floor, the book in my hands in front of me like a shield, and start to cry in earnest—deep, quaking sobs.

"Please let me leave. I won't tell anyone what happened. I promise."

"Al, what's wrong? What's happening?" asks Steve, his voice full of concern. I can actually hear it this time. Has he gotten his lips back? Is he a Flying Head now, too? They all want me either dead or in an institution. Maybe both. And maybe I deserve it.

But Dawn doesn't. The voice sounds like Matoaka's and the Shape's mixed together. Whoever it is, they're right. Dawn doesn't deserve this. She's just a baby. She shouldn't have to pay for my mistakes. She shouldn't have to be in danger because she's my child. I need to get out of here. I need to get her and protect her. I pull out my phone, open my Uber app, and punch in my destination: home. Or what I used to think of as home, anyway, before I came to understand it was never meant to be mine. There's a black car two minutes away.

"Please let me in. I just want to talk," Steve says, the doorknob rattle slowing down.

"I don't want to talk," I choke out. "I want to go."

"Fine."

The doorknob stops rattling completely. There's what sound like some quick footsteps moving away. I count breaths as I focus on the lack of sound in the hallway. I count to ten, twenty, thirty, then drop my book-weapon and crawl across the floor. I lower my face to the carpet and try to look beneath the door into the hallway. I can't see anything. It's too dark. Did they turn out the light? Are they really gone? Or do they want me to let my guard down so they can lure me into another trap?

Bang bang bang bang bang!

A sound like a battering ram being slammed against the door. I scream.

"Get! The fuck! Out here!" shouts Steve, slamming into the door between words. "You open this fucking door before I break it down myself!"

Off with her head! Off with her head! chants Sheila, laughing maniacally. Lou joins in, then Mason-John and the others. *Off with her head! Off with her head!* What's out there right now? How many of them have turned into Flying Heads already? The wood of the door sounds like it's cracking. Steve has to be a Flying Head now, too. How else could he have that sort of power? I need to get out of here and to the Uber. To Dawn. I need to protect her.

There's a window on the other wall, between two shelves. I run over, yank it open, and look down at the drop. It's a little high, but not too bad. I take off my heels and sit on the ledge. I don't even think. I kick the screen over and over until it rips free of the frame, then pick up my purse and throw my body through, legs first.

Sharp pain in my right ankle. I suck in and hold my breath as the pain throbs up my right leg. The ankle might be twisted. It's not painful enough to be broken.

Nya:wen, I think, sure that this time my ancestors are watching out for me.

I'm in the backyard on a patch of velvety grass. I try to brace myself against the side of the house as I get up. Once I'm standing, I check my phone. The Uber is down the street. I hear a crash inside the house, followed by roars of anger. They're in the room. I can't wait.

I open the gate to the front yard and run out, barefoot on the still-hot asphalt, then wave at the black car approaching.

It screeches to a stop.

"Alice?" the driver asks as I slide into the back seat.

"That's me," I say brightly.

I'm closing the car door behind me just as the heavy oak door of Lou's house opens, orange light spilling out into the night.

Doesn't matter where you go, he says. *We're going to eat you. And your daughter. Your disobedience has given us no choice.*

The car's pulling away when a huge dark shape bounces onto the porch, silhouetted for a moment before launching into the air, its hair blowing wildly in the wind. *Flying Heads use their hair to fly more than their wings,* I remember Dad saying.

There's a loud guttural growl that sounds like a dinosaur or elk. I lean down in the back seat and cover my ears.

The driver says something to me but I don't hear.

"Pardon?" I ask, remembering I need to look normal.

"I said it looks like you've had a long day," the driver repeats.

"Long day. Long life. Wife. Strife. Knife," I say, giggling at the words, the way they rhyme and lead into one another, telling a story, my story. "Might not last much longer, though," I add, then immediately regret it. After all, this man could be a spy, too, and I shouldn't be inviting any questions that might make me look crazy.

"What was that?" he asks.

There's another loud roar and I know it's the Flying Head, furious at me for getting away. The driver doesn't react, so I decide not to react, either.

"Nothing. Nothing at all," I finally respond. "Bad joke. Bloke. Toke. Got away from all those folk." I giggle again at my clever wordplay despite myself.

You ate that piece of face, the angry voice reminds me, scaring me straight. *You can still taste it on your tongue. You might change yet. Might be changing this very second.*

Fuck.

I look at the window, trying to catch my reflection against the black. We turn into a sea of artificial light and it's hard to see anything but outlines, but my face seems to be there. If it wasn't the driver would have said something. I reach down my body, hands checking. Everything still seems like separate limbs.

My phone is ringing, and I see the name come up on the screen: *Steve.*

"You gonna get that?" the driver asks, his eyes on me in the rearview mirror.

"Absolutely not."

"Okay."

As I thrust my phone back into my purse, I see the flask and I remember: the medicine Tanya brought for me. What did she say about it again? That it was cleansing. That it'd empty me out completely. But can I trust it? After all, Tanya's in on this, too. Hard to say. If I don't want that piece of a person's face inside me, working its magic until I become a Flying Head, too, I need to drink something that clears me out. I unscrew the lid and start to drink. It tastes like bark and pine and oversteeped black tea. I swallow every drop as fast as I can and pray for this to work. It has to work. It has to. I don't have anything else.

CHAPTER 24

And Then She Fell

As soon as I enter the house a fuzzy silence rushes to greet me, as if both my ears have popped.

"Tanya? Dawn?" I shout as I throw down my purse.

There's no answer.

The lights are on in the living room, but as I creep over to the window, peeking through the curtains, I know there's no one here. The air feels dead, stale, choked. More a mausoleum than a family home. Still, I pad in my bare feet to the kitchen. There's a gust of wind to my left, and I see the window is open. I carefully limp over, my right ankle still throbbing, and close it, in case the Flying Heads are close behind. Then I follow the silence back out to the carpeted stairs and call again.

"Tanya? Are you here?"

With each throbbing step I take, my heart beats faster. Where the hell are they? Did I get here too late? Maybe the Flying Heads were already here. Maybe Tanya's face was on one of those plates, and they took Dawn to use for later. Or maybe Tanya saved herself by offering them Dawn. There's a loosening in my gut at the thought. *Please, please let them be here. Let Dawn be safe.*

I smell it first: a scent like rust that fills my nose, mouth, ears, and head, mixed with the thick, cloying smoke of wet wood in a fire.

When I turn and see the burned and bloody spot in the middle of the crib, the soot-blackened sheets and the smoke rising, the spray of blood speckling the pale-yellow walls, my legs fall out from under me and I scream like I've never screamed before.

It's all burning. That was the prophecy. How could I not understand? It was always Dawn. She was the most important, she was all I had, and I left her. Just like I left my mother, my community. And now it's all burned. I have nothing.

I don't know how long I'm there, half lying, half sitting in the doorway, crying until mucus slides down my throat and I'm gagging, but even then I can't stop, my voice shredding until this scream is reduced to periodic yelps. I feel emptied—exhausted but unable to sleep. I don't know if I'll ever sleep again. Flying Heads don't matter anymore. Steve doesn't matter. Nothing matters.

I thought these rooms were cold before. They weren't. I can feel any remaining heat evaporating from beneath my feet as I walk the wood floors and plush carpets. Everything is cold without Dawn. I try to warm myself up with the last of that bottle of vodka and a fleece pow-wow blanket but it's no good. I've never been the heart of any home. The trailer I grew up in, the place I loved like it was a part of me, went still without Ma, like it was holding its breath, too, waiting for her to bustle through the door in her bright teal satin jacket and pump blood back into its walls. Maybe I was supposed to do that in her place. I probably was. I just couldn't. I wasn't memorable like her. I wasn't willful and strong. Every second I stood in that house, hearing silence where there should be none, made me physically sick. It's making me sick again, here and now, as I sit on my marital bed. I can feel the alcohol and medicine churning and churning in my stomach as I pull the blanket tighter and tighter. I wish everything would stop.

I stumble into my office and turn on the laptop. The Shape said

I needed to finish this. I laugh, bitter and furious at how I chose to waste the little time I had with Dawn. Though the Shape was right, in a sense. This is what I have now. This is my legacy. All I have left to pass down to future generations. I can't waste it. I have nothing else left.

> So we've come to this. The moment you've been waiting for. The one that turned Mature Flowers into Sky Woman and the legend she's become. I can hear your excitement. You must have so many questions. Was she really a huge bitch to the Ancient? Making him go and dig up the roots of the Great Tree just because she had a bad pregnancy craving, like some folks say? Or did she dig them up herself and accidentally fall through, like other folks say? Did the Ancient get so jealous about her talking to someone in the Great Tree that he dug it up in front of her, looking for the person she had been spending so much time with, and when he found nothing but a hole, pushed her through it in a blind rage? Did Mature Flowers see this hole as her ticket to immortality—and fatherly adoration—and choose to jump?
>
> Yes and no—to everything. The truth is tricky. It depends entirely on the storyteller and their audience. What does the audience want? What does the audience need? Is the storyteller feeling generous or stingy? So much to consider. After all, once you tell the story a specific way, that's how it'll be remembered by your audience. Those who heard the story the way you told it will

squabble with those who heard the story the way another person told it, as if only one version could ever be true. As if other possibilities don't bloom like flowers around us, waiting for us to pick them. Which possibility would you pick if you were telling this story? Which would you leave to wither and die?

While you mull that over, let me tell you something about Mature Flowers. However she ends up through that hole, that crack in her universe, falling, falling, falling for what feels like years, what feels like lifetimes, she tells herself that she is alone, that her people in Sky World have abandoned her, that all she has left of her old life are the seeds she grabbed trying to catch herself on the Great Tree's roots, hoping they'd prevent her fate from unfurling like a sprout in spring. And though she couldn't hold on to the roots, she holds on to those feelings, long after the animals conspire to catch her and place her on a generous Turtle's back. They last even after her child is born and grows up in this new place—a place where Sky World only exists as a story she tells her daughter sometimes. They last until her daughter gets mysteriously pregnant and, while trying to give birth to twins, one of those babies gets impatient and pushes through her daughter's stomach, killing her.

It's only then, once her daughter is dead, that Mature Flowers realizes that she was never alone the way she thought she was. She'd had her daughter this whole time. She had a person to share her life with, to nurture, to give everything lovely she herself had been given by her parents, and everything lovely she hadn't. Because creation wasn't just about making things and naming them, the way some folks made it seem. There's a responsibility to creation, to bringing someone or something to life. Yes, when you have a child, that child depends on you. But you depend on them, too, in ways you'd never have known or imagined— a reciprocity that has to be honored. No mother is greater or more important than her own child, just as no tree is greater or more important than the seeds it releases to the wind. Each life equally important to the vitality of the whole, regardless of how enticing a promise it is to become, say, for example, the best woman who ever lived.

Maybe if Mature Flowers had considered there would come a day that her own daughter would be lost to her the same way her father was, she wouldn't have spent so much time obsessing over what was already gone and spent more time appreciating what was right there. Who was right there.

Maybe she would have let go of her vanity, grabbed that reason to live, that outstretched hand she took for granted so easily, and held fast.

Instead, she lost everything.

What good was it being remembered, having your story repeated to generation after generation, if this was what it cost?

It wasn't.
It wasn't.
It isn't.

It's all bullshit. All of it. I thought I was like Sky Woman but I'm not. I've been infecting everything and everyone around me for years. I've been the diseased one—the Ancient: throwing boiling hot mush on my daughter's naked skin, testing her reactions, resenting her for not fulfilling my exact expectations, then punishing her even though she was only an infant—all while she'd lain there and taken it. Lain there and smiled, even, sometimes, though Joan assured me that was gas and not real smiles. I don't know why she would have chosen to be my daughter. My company wasn't a blessing to her; it was a burden. She didn't deserve that. She deserved a person who could love her. A person who could love. I'm neither. I'm living, breathing meat. Barely a person at all.

The oxies don't taste like I thought they would, melting in my mouth. All hard, rounded, bitter. Like a mouthful of tiny bullets. I wonder if this is what Ma thought when she was swallowing her last pills. If she knew what was going to happen. I take the last few gulps of Smirnoff and close my eyes. I hope it hurts. I lie back in the leather computer chair and stare at the textured ceiling and for some reason I think of the night sky. The patterns in the peaked paint become stars and the silence of this room and the noise of this city fall away and I think to myself: this must be what Mature Flowers felt when she was falling down to earth. Not wonder, not fear, not anger. Not a single goddamn thing. Waiting and waiting for the inevitable impact. I close my eyes and beg for it to come fast.

"No. Get to the portal. Now."

It isn't the voice that's been stuck in my mind, tormenting me. It sounds like the Shape—only their voice sounds angry, disappointed, like a parent who knows you've done something bad and is ready to punish you. I open my eyes with difficulty. There's black around the edges, with zeroes and ones getting more and more crushed the farther from the center of my vision they get.

"Get up."

Somehow I'm on my feet and limping toward the patio door. My body feels so weak, each step like a fall. I lean against the glass. I have to pull the patio door open in bursts of effort. As soon as I stumble out the voices that had stayed quiet since I'd gotten home start up again, first sizzling like grease in a pan, then growing louder and louder until they sound like a siren holding the same note and I have to cover my ears. Through my fingers I can hear a great roar, guttural and full of hunger, and I know it's the Flying Heads.

"That doesn't matter. Just go."

I see the two trees, the eyes in their bark opening as I approach, then staring at me unblinking as the zeroes and ones crowd my vision, leaving an empty black hole where the portal should be. My body is vibrating the same way it has when I've stood in front of a giant speaker at a rock concert, only I'm standing in front of two trees. The portal. Part of me is scared to go in. Part of me wants it to obliterate me completely.

"Come," the Shape says. "Please."

So I do.

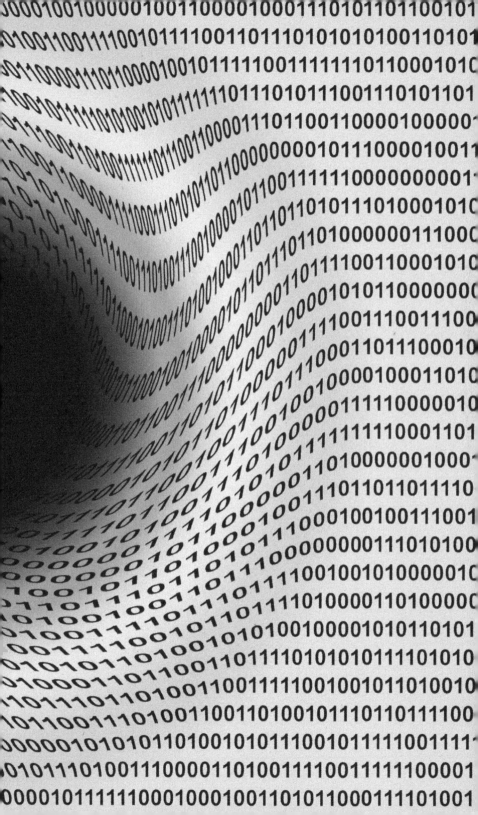

CHAPTER ÉNHSKA

The Letter

You hadn't expected to get it.

Your grandmother had died five years earlier, mumbling about talking trees and portals and her own mother and grandmother as her mind left you and your sister in that hospice room, alone. Other people thought she was crazy. You never would have used those words. You couldn't, because you'd known there were ways to communicate with elements of creation other people saw as flat and empty since you were a girl. The first time Grandmother Moon spoke to you, it was in Kanien'kéha. She didn't even speak, really. She'd started singing along with you. It was a song your mother had taught you and your sister, and you were practicing so you could show your mom you were a better speaker than Ellie. You'd thought the whole thing was so funny, because the moon's voice didn't come through your ears at all. It popped into your head like a memory, only it was happening at that exact moment. Her voice was kind, rich, sort of quietly amused. A voice that reminded you why all Onkwehón:we considered her their grandma. She didn't sound like your own grandma—her voice was sharper, louder, able to rip through all other sounds as if they were sheets of paper—but she sounded like she'd be friends with her. You'd liked that.

Ellie didn't understand when you tried to explain it to her.

Neither did your mother. She'd couched her dismissal in a compliment—*Don't you have a big imagination, Eden*—but you knew what she meant. She thought you were making it up, the same way she thought you made everything up. You didn't know the word "annoying" back then, but if you had, that's what you would have called her. *I'm not making it up! God, Mom, why do you have to be so annoying?* In retrospect, it's a good thing you didn't. She'd be shot by RCMP officers violently clearing a blockade four short years later. You hadn't had enough time with her as it was, and you'd already gone over each moment you *had* spent yelling at her in such detail and with such shame that those memories were practically seared into the back of your eyelids. It didn't matter that you were a kid at the time. You knew better, even then, and that was what kept you up night after night. Guilt and grief gave a gray cast to life after that. Something you, Ellie, and your grandma could all agree on. Maybe the only thing—apart from the classic movies you all obsessed over together, movies your mom had loved so much when she was alive that she could quote many of them in full. Watching them, reciting them, was a way for the three of you to remember her.

It took a long time for your grandma to die. She was in the hospital for two months. Then, as the doctors found polite, Canadian ways to express their resignation with her case, she was moved to hospice. The idea being she would be in a comfortable place when she went. But their version of comfort was not your grandma's version of comfort. She liked having green places to walk through or even gaze at, and around that building in Brantford there was only concrete.

Though you were an adult at that point, you still couldn't face the reality of the situation. The way death shadowed your grandma's face like a slow-creeping eclipse. The way she seemed to leave her body for long periods of time, making the room feel like a tomb already. Ellie resented you for your absence. You let all the major decisions fall to her while you threw yourself into your activism. You knew your opinion wasn't going to be good enough for Ellie, anyway. Once funeral arrangements were being made, she'd text you late at night, analyzing from every angle what each person at the service might think if she chose a coffin with white lining instead of navy, which was Grandma's favorite color. She should have been marking papers or doing class prep or watching a movie with her family. Instead, she was messaging you, expecting something you could never give her as you sat tending the fire at the reclamation site, white-knuckling your way through sobriety for the second time in a week as you sent desperate texts to your ex, Mandy. She didn't respond. She'd snagged some young thing on the pow-wow trail—a fact you learned only after doing some serious social media sleuthing. You took this as evidence of karma. You watched the police car across the road turn its lights off. You smoked another cigarette.

So when the letter came a day after the funeral, with your grandma's lawyer listed as its sender, and addressed only to you, you were surprised. Your stomach dropped as soon as you saw your grandma's unmistakable curlicue handwriting swept across the envelope. You threw it on the kitchen table, same as the bills you ignored. You didn't open it for a couple days. You wanted to sit with its possibility for a bit before reality came crashing through and destroyed everything. Because there was something that felt like destruction inside this envelope. You could tell. Of course, destruction made room for creation. That was something your gram had told you once.

Even though you avoided home whenever you could, instead sleeping in your truck and a tent on the site, you knew it was the only place you could do this. So, home is where you reluctantly went a mere week after your grandma's death. Right before tearing the envelope open, you convinced yourself it'd probably be fine if you sipped a Miller Lite. You know, just to steel your nerves. That shit was practically water anyway. Before you knew it you downed the whole bottle in a few quick swallows. You'd hoped that might be enough, but then you unfolded the pages and saw the first two lines, which read, in all caps, "My little Edie, THIS IS FOR YOUR EYES ONLY," and you realized *this* was a job for a bong hit. You packed the bowl with weed you'd ordered special from British Columbia back when you were enthusiastically off the wagon. It didn't help. In fact, it might have made things worse. The whole letter seemed like it was written in code. It didn't matter how many times you read it, it didn't make any fucking sense. Hell, maybe your grandma was crazy. What else should you call a woman who told you when you were a kid it was fine to talk to the moon, that she'd had a few good conversations with her herself?

Still, you went over her words again and again, sure that there was something you were missing. Didn't read it aloud because you knew the cops were listening. Social media companies had long ago realized the money they could make selling a protester's data to the government. A nice little loophole that required no warrant because the government hadn't legislated on its legality. They could access your mic and camera, and you couldn't stop them because you relied on those apps to post thirty-second videos of yourself reading old commission reports and treaties to fundraise. That's where you read the new treaties, too, once they were e-signed—the ones you'd been busting your ass to work out with grassroots folks from different Indigenous nations at different protest sites across the country, then the world. The newspapers wouldn't report on that. Not at first. They thought it was a joke. Then, once your videos had been shared so much they had to address them, the same white columnists who insisted residential schools were good for Indigenous folks because it taught them English and the value of hard work had the nerve to call *you* "delusional." And then, when those new treaties were enacted through solidarity blockades that shut down their precious commerce, they changed tactics and declared you "dangerous." A terrorist. Fuck that. You weren't no fucking terrorist. You were a Mohawk woman. You had responsibilities to the land. You'd die before you failed to uphold them.

It was at that exact moment, while you were in your home high and fucked up with grief and not sure what your grandma was trying to tell you, that the police descended on the site, assault rifles raised, name tags removed, as they pulled down the blockades and beat the shit out of anyone they could catch. You'd finished reading Gram's letter for the twelfth time when you got the text: *911. They're here.*

Before you even got halfway there to help, they'd gotten you—pulled you over at a stop sign and arrested you then and there, leaving your beat-up pickup on the side of the road, unlocked. You'd have to pay for the tow, just as you'd have to pay bail to get out. But this is what the fundraising was for. This is why you still used the phone that let the cops listen in. This was the compromise.

Only when your lawyer came did you realize this would be different. Unlike other prisoners, the jail wasn't letting anyone but her in for visitation. That was the first sign they wanted to make an example of you. Then they refused to let you out of jail for a few hours for your grandma's ten-day feast. How were you supposed to let her go and move on without support and ceremony? You tried your best to mourn her in your cell, regardless. Then, when the judge set your bail, it wasn't the same as the other protestors'. The new treaties were used as evidence that you'd flee, that you had people who would gladly shelter you around the world. You were too dangerous to be let back into your community, a terrorist determined to overthrow the nation-state, with no concern for average Canadians, who actually worked to provide for their families, and who required free, unfettered access to roads dashed across your territory like wounds. Your bail was set at over a million dollars. You laughed when you heard. The judge didn't like that. You couldn't help it, though. The whole situation reminded you so much of what happened with Deskaheh way back in 1924. He'd gone to the newly formed League of Nations on behalf of the Haudenosaunee Confederacy Chiefs Council to advocate for Six Nations to be recognized as its own sovereign nation. To remind everyone we were allies to the Crown, not subjects. He'd went on a Haudenosaunee passport, then stayed in Geneva for years advocating. Always sure to wear his regalia because he knew they wanted the performance, the same way your followers on social media wanted your performance. When Deskaheh was sick from working, sick from being away from his family, devastated upon learning the RCMP had forced out the Confederacy Chiefs from their own council house while he was gone, then had installed a band council whose first action was to ban any community fundraising for him, he finally came back from Europe. But Canada wouldn't let him cross the border to get back home. They also wouldn't let his wife or four daughters over the border to see him in the United States. Not even when he was on his deathbed. He was left in limbo, marooned from his community. Punished by Canada for speaking up, pushing back.

And now here you were, more than 130 years later, alone in a jail cell, sick with withdrawal, denied visits from your family and friends, bail set at over a million dollars. Punished by Canada for speaking up, pushing back. It was funny, the way that history cycled, even as resolve remained the same.

You'd heard all about Deskaheh on Gram's old podcast, *Storytellin'*. An episode on Indigenous enemies of the state. She and her cousin Tanya made it decades ago, when Gram was still a young mom. She'd tried to publish stories about your people for years, but no one wanted them, so she and Tanya decided they'd just put them out there themselves. "Podcasts were real popular back then," one or the other would remind you as they reminisced about it at the kitchen table all those years later. You thought it was embarrassing at the time, but once Gram was gone, you were grateful for all those episodes. You were grateful for her voice, her laughter in your ear as you fell asleep at night, her younger self telling you stories from your people, your community. Each episode reminding you that these were things worth fighting for, things you needed to protect so you could gift them to the next generation, the same way Gram's generation had gifted them to yours. That was actually how you came up with the idea to start making treaties with other nations about a year back. You'd been talking with Gram about the podcast, how she'd eventually invited people from other territories and nations to tell their own traditional stories, too. The generosity, the reciprocity, the relationships and connections she made. All of it inspired you then, but it especially impressed you now, in the days following her death. Gram had started writing what would eventually become scripts for the podcast in the wake of her own mother's death. You couldn't imagine being creative like that while grieving. How had she pulled herself together to accomplish such a thing? It was unimaginable. Another question you wished you'd bothered to ask while she was here, an incompletion that made you ache. As overwhelming and obvious as your wish you'd recorded her voice saying your name so you could play it over and over now. *My little Edie*, she'd called you, her love softening each syllable. You were her little Edie. You still are, even now.

Just as she's still the beating heart in your chest, even as her own heart has stopped.

Little Edie's Doing Time

I n that cell, you had nothing else to do but get sober again and go over Gram's letter in your mind. You weren't allowed to physically have it, of course. You weren't allowed paper or pencils or books or anything your guards could claim you might use to hurt yourself and escape this charade they called justice. At first you didn't even want to hurt yourself, but as the days stretched on, you started to consider what it might be like to die. Whether it'd be like the relief of turning off a particularly long movie once the credits hit, knowing whatever turmoil and trauma you'd witnessed playing out on the screen was finally over. You hoped so. You were tired. So, so, so fucking tired. A bone-deep exhaustion that no amount of sleep could offset.

You were so tired and hopeless you'd started to cry. Not loud—you didn't want to give the guards the satisfaction—but still enough to make you shake as you stared at a piece of wall where you wished a window would be. And that's when you heard it, clear as when you were a child: the moon, humming the song you'd sung together so many years ago. There was a part of your grandmother's letter that mentioned the moon. You'd disregarded it as incoherent rambling, a sign of her deterioration. Now you reconsidered: "Remember: the moon was always your teacher, even when you were a little girl. She was also your protector."

"Tota—í:se ken né:'e?" you asked.

The humming stopped and the warm voice you'd known so well flooded your mind like honeyed tea. *I'm not the grandmother you wanted, perhaps, but yes, I'm still here. Why are you crying, my girl?*

"They won't let me leave. They won't let me do anything. Gram's gone, but I think she wants me to do something. I don't know what. I don't understand anything. It's like I'm already gone."

Your words ran together, then over one another, the same as your thoughts. Everything a whirlwind.

Your grandmother sent you the letter, did she? I'd wondered if she was going to.

You stopped everything, looked up at the ceiling, steadied your breath.

"She told you? Did she tell you what any of it meant?"

Stop saying things out loud, dear. The guards are going to think you're crazy and throw you in an institution somewhere.

"What am I supposed to do instead?"

You're certainly out of practice, the moon said, a smile in her voice. *Think your thoughts at me. Same as when you were little.*

Can you help me figure out what my gram wants? you thought at the moon.

No. Not the way you need to be helped. But there are some who can. Call a cockroach to you and explain the situation. They'll know what to do.

How the hell do I call a cockroach? Much less make them help me?

The same way you stop developers. Be your stubborn little self. Don't take no for an answer.

Then her words were gone and you were left staring at the light bulb that never darkened, not even at night. A form of torture, you were sure. You needed to remember to mention it to your lawyer next time you saw her.

You tried to call cockroaches to you by whispering. "Cockroaches. I need you. Please come." You repeated the words like a prayer, day in and day out, your eyes on the toilet and the sink and the sliver of space beneath the door. Nothing. You eventually switched to Kanien'kéha, in case they were speakers. "Takwayé:nawa's cockroaches—tsyonnhá:'ok aesewatkwé:ni." That reminded you of Princess Leia's desperate plea in *A New Hope*—a plea your gram quoted to you and Ellie anytime the two of you were slacking off with chores. The words worked then, so maybe they'd work now.

"Help me, cockroaches," you recited over and over. "You're my only hope." You wondered if they were Star Wars fans.

Sure enough, eight days in, a small cockroach finally climbed up from the toilet, then shook itself off like a dog.

You don't look like Leia.

And you're a little short for a Luke, you'd replied.

Well. Now that that's established, what do you want, human?

My gram left me this letter telling me to do something I don't know how to do.

What'd she tell you to do?

That's the thing. I don't know.

The cockroach laughed incredulously. *I can't help you if you don't help me, toots.*

She was really cryptic about it.

Look, human. I know your type like to think the world revolves around you, but I've got lots of other things I could be doing.

The moon told me you could help.

That seemed to make the cockroach pause and reconsider.

The moon, you say?

Yes. She told me to call you. That you'd know what to do. That you'd help.

The cockroach let out what sounded like a sigh, then asked, *What was your grandmother's name?*

Alice Doxtator. When she was married her name was Alice Macdonald.

Oh. Her.

You know her?

Yes, we know her. And we know what she wants of you, and of us.

Well, are you going to help? She was talking about this space-time web—

Wait. Don't say any more. I can't hear this, let alone help, without permission.

Permission from who?

I'll say this much: you're most definitely her granddaughter. Asking questions you don't need the answers to.

You wanted to ask how long it'd take it to get permission, but before you could, it was gone. The cockroach stayed gone for three days—enough time for you to convince yourself that you were going crazy. That this letter didn't hold some special meaning. That you needed to focus instead on the present of your solitary confinement. Your future as a political prisoner standing trial before a court that might use your odd behavior as evidence you were insane, a declaration that would send all your supporters running, because they could handle your radical politics and blunt statements from the front lines, and they could handle your unjust imprisonment by the Canadian state, but they could not handle you as an addict losing your mind in this cell. Which you knew was entirely the point of you being here, alone, with only the moon and a cockroach to talk to. You'd heard about other alcoholics seeing things when they were detoxing. Maybe that's all this was: a detox hallucination. After all, you still had the shakes every so often. You still had trouble sleeping. You still had almost no energy in your body. Not that the doctors here gave a shit.

Then you saw the cockroach skitter in from under the door, announcing its presence without so much as a hello.

Did you get permission? you asked.

It nodded his head, impatient. *Yeah, yeah. What do you know about the space-time web?*

Are you serious?

Don't I look serious?

You squinted at its tiny face. *I can't tell.*

Fucking humans, it thought, quietly, but still loud enough for you to hear. If it'd had a cockroach-sized cigarette, you figured this would have been when the cockroach would have lit it and taken a drag. *Look, forget everything you think you know about space, time, and reality, okay? It's all wrong.*

Okay. So are you going to teach me what's right?

The cockroach let out a sigh, this one longer, more ragged, as if it was trying to communicate how much it didn't want to be here, doing this.

I'm going to try.

The Space-Time Web

T here are rules, it warned you.

I'm not very good with rules, you warned back.

It had told you to call him Pete. Well, he actually told you to call him Papa Roach, but the first time you did he started laughing so hysterically he couldn't talk. Once he finally calmed himself down, he said maybe you should call him Pete instead. It wasn't his name, he'd explained, but he liked it okay enough to let you use it. *Anyway*, he told you, *human tongues like yours don't know how to twist in the proper ways to pronounce my real name.* You knew he wanted you to be offended but you weren't. You knew what it meant to have pride in your language. Your mother made sure of that before she'd been killed.

The main rule you need to be concerned with is the rule of free will. Everyone needs to be free to make their own decisions. To exercise their own free will.

Sounds simple enough.

Pete laughed. *You humans sure think so. But then you get a chance to have something you think you want, need, or deserve and you do everything in your power to break that rule.*

He went on to explain that, to understand the importance of free will properly, you had to understand the space-time web. It wasn't a straight line of cause and effect, the way that humans at the point of space-time you were from seemed to think. Instead, it was to be understood as a vast, interconnected web, where each potential choice before you opened up what was essentially a series of doors for you to step through, and when you stepped through one door, the others clicked shut—most of the time. Sometimes certain doors, followed in a particular way, led you back to other doors you'd thought had been shut. Like circles in your lifelines.

It's actually quite beautiful to consider the shape of a life, Pete said. *Or lives, if you consider each path to be a separate life.*

So wait. Even though each choice sets off a new chain of events with a new future, they aren't separate lives?

The paths all meet up at the end, so my kind don't really consider those lives to be separate as such. That's advanced stuff, though, Pete clarified. *Humans aren't even evolved enough to see things from that wide an angle.*

Does that mean you can see into the future?

I already told you, I don't think of things that way. The future is interconnected with the past and the present to the point where they're almost indistinguishable to my kind.

Can you see the past, then? Or what humans would consider "the past"?

I can only see the paths I've already chosen to live, same as most. But I can see far more of what you'd call your past. That's actually where we have to go so we can re-read that letter your grandmother sent you.

You're going into my past?

You are, too. Unless you have any other ideas on how to get the exact contents of that letter?

After that, you tried to keep your questions to yourself—most of which took Pete on tangents that inevitably ended with "too advanced for you" anyway—and just listen. The problem was you weren't the best listener, something Ellie had always told you and you'd always denied. At this precise moment, though, you had to agree. Your attention zipped and bobbed like a dragonfly. Your mind rolled this way and that. There were some things you understood. For example, Pete said that not all decisions had the same weight. Some were more important than others, creating bursts of options to appear, which shook the space-time web with their weight, the way a spiderweb shakes when some unfortunate bug gets trapped in it, alerting the spider to its exact location. Those were the decisions that set off scores of alternate paths and realities, and you could, if you knew how, peer into the windows of their doors and see what futures they led to.

Let me guess, that's too advanced for me? you'd asked.

It's not simply advanced; it's dangerous.

Dangerous how?

Pete leaned up against the leg of the bed, considering.

Beings that peer into their own potential futures often get over-whelmed by the endless opportunities and options. They get scared they're going to make the wrong choice and, in doing that, lose all the things they've technically never really had yet. You ever been paralyzed by your own indecision?

Your gram's funeral came immediately to mind. You couldn't even face the reality of her death, much less decide what she'd wear in the casket or what music would play. If it weren't for Ellie, you're not sure there would have been a funeral.

I'm aware of the phenomenon, you said.

It's like that. Most get stuck in their own web forever. Quite tragic, really. My point is, seeing all that is no good for you. It takes the shine away from what you do have. What's that human saying about colorful lawns?

The grass is always greener on the other side?

Yes, that. Exactly. Makes you think what you have is less, when really what you have is always worth something, because you chose it. You could probably get away with looking at others' alternate lives, but you'd have to keep that knowledge to yourself. Otherwise you'd create all sorts of problems.

It took nearly a week of near-constant guidance from Pete, where he essentially had to teach you how to meditate. He told you to close your eyes and focus on the colors that appeared behind your eyelids while you listened—something he said would come into play later when he was teaching you visualization—but you kept opening your eyes and staring at the lit bulb, or sneaking peeks at Pete. It was difficult to let go of your thoughts and trust that whatever was left wouldn't kill you. Memories, regrets, emotions. All of them flooding in whenever you weren't focused enough to stop them. Pete merely told you to accept this, the bastard. Easy for him to accept things. He was a fucking cockroach. What did he know of pain and loss, regret and trauma, desire and need?

Still, you eventually did it. You lay down on your back and let go. Pete explained meditation was like a flower that opened when you kept your attention on the present moment, so that's what you did. Focusing on the colors behind your eyes really did help. You watched as they burned red, then green came pirouetting in, then blue creeped along the edges, leaving a trail. You listened to the buzz of the bulb overhead, the *swoosh-clack* of the guard walking past your cell. You smelled the piss of the toilet from the corner of your room, and your own vinegary sweat pooling beneath your arms. You tasted the sour of your unwashed mouth. Eventually it felt like you'd fallen asleep, only you were intensely aware of your body lying on the cold, hard floor beneath you the whole time. Your mind saw what looked very much like a web taking shape all around you.

Let me be clear, Pete had said as soon as you were in, *you're going to see a lot of things, but when you go through any of those doors, you must remain aware of where, exactly, you are in space-time. If you accidentally get seen by people in that point of space-time, you can't interact with them. You can't speak to them. It gets too complicated. Especially for a human like you.*

Got it.

Pete didn't respond. Instead, he placed one of his legs onto a thin, golden thread that seemed to be unspooling from beneath you. He waited.

What are you doing?

Shhhh.

The thread began to shake, slightly, and Pete leaped up on the thread and followed the tremor down into the black.

This way.

At first you followed dutifully, thinking for some reason it wouldn't be long until you found the precise moment in your life you had looked at Gram's letter. It was only three weeks ago, after all. But as you followed the thread, you saw a series of what looked like fireworks, one after the other, tangling your way, and you knew that meant that you'd had a number of substantial decisions in front of you in the past three weeks: the choice to call Pete, the choice to talk to the moon, the choice to go down to the site after getting that text about the raid. Pete was right; they were like little explosions of possibilities, a series of windowless doors surrounding each moment, all with a light gold thread trailing beneath. The choices you had made, though, and the doors they represented, were wide open, the one gold thread snaking through them thick and luminous. As you watched yourself make the choices you'd already made, it was like you were watching your life on a TV, only you were in the screen itself and could spin around and observe everything in that moment from another perspective, as if it were happening to you again. You watched as you read the 911 text, placed Gram's letter on the kitchen table, ran outside and jumped into your muddied truck. You knew you'd drive only a few blocks before a cruiser appeared behind you, red and blue lights in the rearview. Fuck the Six Nations Police for cooperating with the OPP. It still pissed you off.

Instead of watching yourself get thrown against the truck and arrested again, you stepped back out of that moment. You looked at the closed doors, then at Pete, who seemed to not only be peering through them, but also evaluating their contents.

Do . . . do you see what's on the other side of those doors?

Of course, Pete replied, staring at what still looked like window-less doors to you. *Don't you listen to anything I say? Oh, this is definitely it. Hurry up.*

An open door, thankfully. You'd stepped in beside Pete just in time to watch yourself coughing out a plume of white smoke. The bong hit. It made you uncomfortable to watch in ways you didn't expect. You could see the desperation in your eyes. How you were pushing blindly toward the closest form of release, the only one you knew. Confusing self-medication and self-destruction. You weren't sure if Pete could see it, but an overwhelming feeling to protect your past self from his judgment came over you regardless.

I'm an addict, you blurted to him. *Do you know what an addict is? It's kind of complicated to explain—*

Yes, I know what an addict is, Pete replied, stopping you from embarrassing yourself any further.

It was strange, the way you'd felt such immense compassion for yourself. You weren't used to that kind of protection or care from anyone but Gram. You wished you could hold on to it, use it gingerly, tenderly on yourself when you were back in your body, in your present—or whatever the hell Pete would call it. Maybe you'd blame yourself less and like yourself more.

You both watched as your past self opened the letter. You snuck up behind and read it again.

My little Edie,

THIS IS FOR YOUR EYES ONLY.

   Your sister isn't like us. She wouldn't understand what I'm saying. What I'm telling you.

   There are things you need to know. Things you'll only understand when it's time for you to understand them. But you told me once I gave you the road map for your little trip to the space-time web, so here I am, trying to figure out the right way to make that road map legible for you.

   You never were one to follow the rules, even when you were a kid, and I don't suppose it will look the same for you as it did for me, but here is how I experienced it, linearly:

   It started with Pocahontas. You were there, warning me, though I didn't know it was you. My little Matoaka, putting on a show even then. I suppose it was your way of trying to get around the "no contact" rule. Pretending to be her. Or your version of her. Warning me to stay away from a boy who'd be a mistake. I never asked you exactly why, but I had my suspicions. You were right, in the end. But of course, you'd have known that by the time you showed up.

   You came again soon after your mother was born, but you didn't let me see you. Even spoke in Kanien'kéha at first to throw me off. That was for the best. You knew the rules, even if you bent them to nearly breaking. Told me to keep writing my version of the Creation Story. Hoped it was enough to keep me here. That reminder that I was more than just a mother. That I had something to say, an impact to make on future generations. That those words could inspire others in ways I couldn't see. Or at least, that's what you said. I was in pretty bad shape then, so I needed to grab on to anything I could to keep me from falling.

And then there were bursts of you in a nightmare. Can't imagine it was easy to get into one of my dreams from the space-time web, so good luck figuring out the mechanics. Either way, I was playing a harp while something else played me. It was a fancy room, if that helps. Lots of gold all over. All I could make out from you was, "Don't tell any of them" and "Get to the portal." That ended up being enough.

I couldn't put the pieces together at the time. Not until that night, with the blood and burns in the crib. Not until you convinced me to go to the portal, and you were there, and you explained things. Reminded me of what was important. Reminded me of why I needed to stay alive. Why all of us need to stay alive, when and where we can. You'd tried to keep the rules, even then, my sweet girl.

I'm not asking you to do it again. That's your choice, even now. You reminded me of that. The power of choice. Of free will. You'll know what I mean when you know.

Remember: The moon was always your teacher, even when you were a little girl. She was also your protector. She'll teach and protect you whenever and wherever you need her.

Please know, dear one, you are so loved. Any choice you make is fine with me. I love you. I just want what's best for

*you. Whatever you think that may be. Take care of yourself.
You deserve that care, regardless of what your own far too
critical brain or other entities may be telling you when you
read this.*

*I love you. I love you. I love you.
Your future is my future.
I'll see you soon, whatever you decide.*

*All my love,
Gram*

Fuck, Pete said upon finishing. *You sneaky little shit.*

You didn't reply immediately. Instead, you read the letter over again. And again. And again.

Is she saying that I . . .

Yes, Pete replied, then turned away from you. *You spoke to her in her past. From the sound of it, once when she was a kid, and another few times when she was an adult. This is some fucked-up shit. I don't even understand how you got away with it.*

But . . . that hasn't happened yet. Right?

Pete laughed bitterly.

Depends on what you mean by "yet." It hasn't happened yet in your lifelines, no. But it's already happened in her lifeline. Specifically, the one that led you to this exact moment, where you're in the space-time web with me, rereading the letter she wrote to you about interfering with her youth from the space-time web. So yes, it has already happened.

Does that mean it has to happen now?

Pete didn't answer. Instead, he stepped out of your memory and back into the space-time web. You followed him like an eager puppy as he leaped from your web to an adjacent one, one that tangled with your own significantly in spots, then started peeking in its windows.

These are your grandmother's lifelines, he explained, completely ignoring your question.

So that's a yes, then.

Look, nothing has to happen. You still have free will here. Your grandmother said as much in her letter.

Then why did you bring me here?

Because, little human, you have to choose. And it seems this choice is a big one. Lots of fun repercussions bursting into existence at this exact moment that I can't possibly explain—

Yeah, I know. Too advanced for me.

Too advanced for anyone. You're talking about rewriting timelines and collapsing alternate realities here. Very few have done this. And for good reason. It's reckless.

So that's it, then? No advice? No tips or tricks? Just "Good luck, fuck off"?

Like I already said, it's your choice. But if I were you, I'd suggest you go through your grandmother's timeline and understand exactly what you've done so you can decide whether you want to do it again.

How much time do I have? you asked, as if you'd had anything else to do in your jail cell.

We're outside of time and space right now, so technically, you have as long as you want.

Since it wasn't your own timeline you were on, each door had a window for you to glance in. You weren't sure whether this was a blessing or a curse—this ability to see and hear and feel Gram again, as if she were still here, chastising you for not putting navy beans in your corn soup, or covering you and Ellie with blankets when you fell asleep on her couch watching old movies with her, or going through your high school crush's photos online, commenting on

what each picture meant about the girl's personality and relationship potential. You loved the process of reliving moments with her,
no matter how mundane. You couldn't help but walk in each one of
those doors ravenous, reexperiencing and relishing each moment
like it alone would nourish you and save you from your grief. Sometimes you even forgot what you were actually there for, you were so
caught up in her. And that's ultimately why you also hated it: because you knew you'd eventually have to leave the crispness of the
past and return to your blurry present, where Gram only lived in
your checkered memory, the pain of losing her and what she meant
to you beginning anew each time you let yourself remember.

For a while, you went back through your childhood with her—
the way she took you and Ellie in when your mother was killed by
the OPP; the way she changed her office into a bedroom for the two
of you, letting you both pick different colored paints for your different sides of the room; the way she let you both scream and cry the
nights you should have been cuddled in close with your mom, singing seed songs, because she said you were allowed to be angry and
sad; the way she packed a pipe of tobacco and gave thanks to the
Creator, making a little chorus of the last line—"And now our minds
are one"—which the two of you shouted along with her before she
went on to regale you with your peoples' traditional stories; the way
she braided yours and Ellie's hair, one after the other, before taking
you to jazz class. The way she let you drop out of jazz class when
your teacher asked what on earth you'd been eating that made you
so much bigger than your twin sister all of a sudden. The way she
yelled at the teacher, demanded a refund for the rest of the month,
and found a new jazz class for Ellie, who still wanted to dance. The
way she pretended not to notice whenever you stole a twenty from
her purse to buy snack food to binge on. The way she bought you
new clothes every time you went up another size, never once

complaining. She'd tried so hard to protect you from thinking you were worthless. You wished you could have believed her.

But then you peeked into other windows. The one before you were born where she finally divorced your grandpa and moved back to the rez with your mom. Eventually all the racist aggressions— micro, macro, passive, active—that Grandpa denied became too obvious for even him to ignore. And by then it was too late. Gram was sick and the marriage was dead. She'd cried and cried and called herself a fucking loser and hit herself in the head over and over and all you wanted to do was slip in behind her and grab her fists and hold them. She eventually stopped on her own when your mom came toddling into the room, asking her what was wrong. "Nothing, now that you're here." That was the response she had chosen: the thread was thick and bright as it wove underneath and alongside that door. You followed it down. There was a string of boyfriends of questionable merit. They seemed okay to start, but eventually they started to drink too much, or made comments about how she spent too much time with her daughter and was neglecting them, or they called her crazy. One screamed at her until she had to leave her own house. Your mom was still a toddler then, holding Gram's hand as she trailed along behind, crying. He was the worst one. He shattered all her good dishes one by one. He stole her credit card to pay for long shows from cam girls, then lied about it, even when Gram waved the bill right in front of his face. He went on benders, then showed up at 3:00 a.m. to trash her place, then cried as he vomited in her bathtub, apologizing and begging her to take him back the whole time, saying she was the only good thing he'd ever had. He was around for what seemed like years (it was hard to tell exactly), which confused you, because you had never known about this man. As far as you knew, your mother and your grandmother wrote him out of their lives completely. You couldn't blame them. He was like a walking battering ram.

And then there were the hospitalizations. A different kind of violence than your own arrest, but violence nonetheless. The soft-toned officers put handcuffs on Gram to take her in, so she was viewed as some sort of criminal even though she'd committed no crime—and all for having a mind that worked differently from theirs. Her shame practically vibrated off her as you watched her cry in the back seat of the cruisers. Each trip was so painful to Gram, you saw it in her face, read it in the journals she scribbled her thoughts into. They gave her pills that made her sleep all day or walk around emotionless, a shell of herself. It was like she had the wind knocked out of her for days, sometimes weeks. Other Native women came to visit her then. You recognized your aunty Tanya and Aunty Melita, but the others were a mystery. Those were the only times she'd laugh hard in there—but not too hard, because the nurses would add that to her list of symptoms, preventing her from being declared "mentally fit." You could see Gram bloom whenever other Native women were around.

You're not sure you would have been able to survive the ping-pong of life between freedom and mental hospitals like she did. You knew she didn't want to survive sometimes. She said so in her journals. But she pushed forward anyway. Toward your mother. Toward you.

Then there was your mother's death. You hadn't known this, but Gram had felt it when that officer shot your mother. She had a sharp pain explode in her chest at that exact moment the bullet hit her. She'd thought she was having a heart attack at first, but when her phone rang, she knew, and once she knew, her number-one priority was protecting you and your sister. She only let herself cry in therapy, which she started again shortly after your mom's funeral. In the meantime, she pulled out her eyelashes. Picked at the dead skin on the soles of her feet until she bled. Talked about that in therapy. Learned those were forms of self-mutilation and negative coping mechanisms. Narrowly squeaked her way through each day, then basically put those emotions in a jar and set it on a high shelf while she talked with and sang with and laughed with and cried with and tickled and teased and blew obnoxiously loud raspberries on the cheeks of you and your sister.

You'd never known about any of this. You couldn't have; she hid it too well. Even if she hadn't though, you, the typical teen, only noticed what was convenient for you. Other people weren't real to you the way your emotions were real and all-consuming. It made you feel embarrassed, this self-centeredness, made you wonder: Were you really all that different now? Ellie had always said you were like an adult child. It was her big, recurring complaint about you— that you'd never grow up, that you were too egotistical to.

And now, here you were, selfishly focusing on how much Gram's loss hurt *you* instead of focusing on how much the life Gram lived hurt *her*. Was all the pain she'd lived through really worth it? Was it right to guide her toward this marathon of anguish when there could be another way—a happier way?

You slid out of her chosen timeline so you could get a better idea. Through one of the faded doors was the possibility where she'd stayed with your grandfather. That split into a myriad of other doors. Behind one, she started drinking way too much to deal with the pressure and expectations that came along with being a professor's trophy wife. Your grandfather eventually started cheating with the wife of his department head, an awful woman named Sheila. You watched as Sheila went out of her way to invite Gram to her parties, where she fed her an absurd amount of wine, then embarrassed her in front of all the other wives by asking her questions she didn't know the answers to, including questions about your grandfather. She referred to her as "Alice-coholic" with the other wives whenever she had the chance. You watched as your grandmother died from a heart attack the week your own mother went into academia—a world where you and your sister were never born. The thread circled back; the whole vision took what felt simultaneously like a lifetime and the blink of the eye.

Behind another door, you watched as your grandmother and grandfather broke up, but your grandfather had used Gram's mental health struggles to get full custody of your mother. Through one door of this timeline, your mother refused to see Gram after that, and when she moved away to England to go to school, Gram died of a sudden stroke while she was away. The thread circled back. Behind another door of this timeline, Gram pulled herself together and became a successful author, but she so strongly disapproved of your mom going into academia that they got into a huge fight, which resulted in a mutual silence that lasted until Gram had that same heart attack she had in another lifeline, the thread looping back on itself.

This couldn't be it. There had to be some other option, something lovely. You went back and checked another door in the "Gram stays with Grandfather" web. This one was more stable, and seemingly happier. Through it, your grandfather bought a property right off the rez near Oneida, and they had enough land to raise chickens. They got a big golden retriever named Patrick and had more kids. Gram still had mental health episodes, and they got especially bad after each pregnancy, but she and your grandfather had figured out better ways to work through them, ways that still involved the hospital, yes, but that didn't include the cops or courts. Behind one of the doors on this lifeline, your grandfather was killed in a car accident and Gram started to spiral. Once she started looking for cameras in the house, you couldn't watch anymore. You turned around and tried another door. This one had her as part of a medical trial for a university. She was given the experimental drug, not the placebo. As soon as it became clear one of the side effects she was experiencing was suicidal ideation, and you saw that her thread was ending soon, you walked right back out. Then there was another door where, after her husband's death sent her to a stay in the hospital, she started to write again. Her work was reviewed well, sold well enough, and was especially cherished by the people of Six Nations. You could see that last accomplishment made her so much happier and more fulfilled than the other two. Gram missed her husband terribly, you could tell, but she died in the hospital, peaceful, sure she could see all her spirit family waiting, hands outstretched, when she went. That was nice. But what about all those years she was alone after Grandfather died? They looked so hard. All the hospitalizations looked hard.

What about something totally different? Something that branched off further back than when Gram met your grandfather? You walked along until you saw a flurry of doors appear from when Gram was still a teen. Through one, she invited a boy named Mason over, they had sex, and she got pregnant. Through one following that, she had the baby, but it was taken from her by social services. She screamed and cried and hurt herself. You couldn't watch any further; it was too sad. You pivoted to another, where Gram secretly got an abortion but stayed with the boy who knocked her up all through high school. He cheated on her, and she cheated on him, and one night he found out that she'd had an abortion and not told him, and their relationship ended. Later in that life, once they were both divorced with kids, they met back up again at a Winnipeg art gallery and that initial spark they'd felt lit a new fire, one that was sustainable and safe. They blended their families and stayed together for decades. In yet another door, your grandmother kept the baby, and told this Mason about it, and the pressure of their shared situation made them closer, and they scrabbled together a life on the rez, not perfect, but also not terrible. They still got into some awful fights, but that stopped entirely once Gram got breast cancer. She didn't have much longer after that, so you left before you had to watch her die once again.

How could you choose which of these lives would be best for your grandmother? Especially when you couldn't even consult her? When you couldn't tell her exactly which choices she needed to make to get to that life? How did you know she wouldn't make a wrong turn somewhere and end up in a worse lifeline than the one she'd already—or would soon—live? Was the potential for a generally better life worth the risk of it possibly ending as bleakly as some of the other ones you'd seen? You understood now how other beings got lost in their webs. You weren't even in your own web, and you felt like you could be here forever, scoping out the best possible life for your gram.

Then again, who decided which one was the best life? What made one lifeline better or worse than another? There was no way to avoid pain, that much was clear. Each lifeline had its fill of arguments and trauma and tears, just like each lifeline had its fill of laughter and joy and love. It was a matter of opinion, really, which lifeline was better and which was worse. And the only insight you had into Gram's opinion was her letter to you. She certainly didn't make it sound like she'd hated the life she'd lived. But then again, she hadn't seen what else was possible the way you saw it now. If she had, she probably would have chosen differently. She probably would have looked for something nice, a life she could relax into like a hot bath. She deserved that.

You reconsidered the family farm branch of lifelines, which was so sweet for so long. There had to be some door on this branch that ended as sweetly as it seemed to start—one where she didn't lose your grandfather so early, where she didn't suffer with hospitalizations. The problem was, there was no lifeline in this branch that led to you and Ellie being born to your mother. Which meant there was no lifeline in this branch that led to you and your grandmother even meeting. In fact, most of Gram's lifelines that seemed to you to be nicer overall were ones where you didn't exist. Not as her granddaughter.

You stopped and considered what it might be like to not exist. It was a foolish exercise—if you hadn't chosen to be born to your mother, Dawn, when you had, you'd have been born to another mother at another time. It was clear to you from your earlier conversations with Pete that there was no option where you didn't exist. There was no universe where your spirit was nothing; every spirit bursts into creation at will, then experiences life in order to experience itself. The idea struck you that there might be a time and space where you were born into an easier situation, that maybe you could have been a single baby instead of a twin, and therefore judged on your own merits instead of as the worst part of a set. Maybe you would have stayed in law school and become a lawyer, able to defend all your activist friends whenever they were arrested and charged. Maybe you wouldn't have had addictive tendencies since childhood. Maybe you would have been able to maintain a relationship with some stable, lovely woman. Maybe you could have been brave enough to have kids without worrying you'd fuck them up beyond all recognition. Maybe you wouldn't have been such a fuckup in general. Maybe. You stepped outside of all the alternate lifelines and looked out over your grandmother's full web. In the distance was what looked like a series of crossroads. The farthest doors were blinking, like the warning light at the train tracks as the striped arm comes down, barring you from driving past. And as you watched, the blinking spread, coming closer and closer, faster and faster.

What does that blinking mean? you asked Pete, who was lounging toward the end of Gram's web. He looked over casually, then shot to his feet.

I-I've never seen that before.

You have to have some idea.

I really don't.

If you had to guess, you insisted.

If I had to guess, Pete replied, *I'd say it's a sort of caution light telling you that you're perilously close to getting stuck in this web.*

You said I had all the time in the world!

Pete shrugged. *I don't know what to tell you. We're in uncharted waters here.*

You watched as the lights came closer. It was like this web was becoming its own galaxy of stars.

I just need a minute, I promise.

A minute? Pete scoffed. *If you say so. I'm leaving soon, though. With or without you.*

You ran back down the thick, sturdy thread of this lifeline, the one that led to you, here, and as you watched through a window as Gram held you for the first time, you realized that, despite everything you'd endured, all the bullshit and violence and rejection, the criminalization and addiction and hardship, you wouldn't change it. Your life simply wouldn't be a life without her and her stubborn, silly brilliance. Without knowing and being loved by her. In many ways, she'd been the love of your life. She had protected you in whatever small ways she could. She had accepted you, unconditionally. She'd shown such patience, even when you insisted on going to protests and land reclamations she didn't want you to go to, worried what happened to your mom would happen to you. She brought over dinners every Saturday for the whole camp—even after the police noted her license plate number and started pulling her over for tiny infractions, like driving two miles over the speed limit. She convinced your grandfather to pay for you to go to rehab the first two times in Buffalo because she didn't want you to have to wait months for spots in Canada to open up. You loved her so much the idea of life without her made you feel sick. But was it fair to make her go through all the misery she'd endure just so you could have that love?

All of the doors were alight now, and Pete was yelling that he had to go, now—then all of the lights went out.

Pete? you called into the black. *Are you still here?*

You weren't sure how long you were there, in the black, when you heard it, just barely: *Yes.*

What's happening? Pete? Is this normal?

No.

He sounded nervous, which made you nervous.

Where are you?

You turned around to try to see him, only to notice that there was a golden thread behind you. It seemed to have trailed you as you walked into your grandmother's alternate doors, turning back on itself and tangling with Gram's lives that had never been.

Has that thread been there the whole time? you called to Pete.

Yes.

It's my lifeline.

Yes.

The one-word answers seemed to come from everywhere. It made no sense. Where was Pete? Was he okay? You looked back and saw that your golden lifeline seemed to stretch back and back into the black. For some reason that scared you deeply. Were you going to end up trapped here? Was that what happened to Pete? Was he trapped here, too?

When you turned back around, there were two doors before you. One had what looked like your grandmother's lifeline beneath it, forked off from the web and staying gold to mark the life she'd already lived before you came along. The other door had nothing under it, not even a faint thread, but as you watched, a fiber off the thick golden thread of your grandmother's lifeline broke free and wormed its way to the front of the other door, then rose up, like a snake's head, and started to sway, as if impatient to enter. Neither door had a window you could peek through, but you knew what each represented.

This was it. This was your choice. What should you choose? You could try to bend time and the limits of free will to make sure you and Gram ended up together, again. Or you could not, and hedge your bets that you'd wake up someplace safer than a jail cell and she'd have lived a life full of more joy than pain.

What should I pick? I don't want to fuck it up.

Trust yourself, Pete said.

Trust yourself? Very helpful, Pete. You started wondering what made this cockroach so confident in you when an image came to mind: how Gram looked when she first held you. You could tell she'd love you fiercely even then, and it hit you: *she chose you.* She chose your mother and you and your sister, despite all the hardships that she must have known would come along with loving you. She said so herself in her letter, in a way.

Any choice you make is fine with me . . .

I just want what's best for you. Whatever you think that may be . . .

I love you . . .
Your future is my future . . .
I'll see you soon, whatever you decide . . .

Wasn't that complete, selfless surrender to your will, that absolute unwavering trust in you, that determination to *see* you, her granddaughter, regardless of what you chose, evidence she loved you as much as you loved her, if not more? Wasn't the letter itself an indication that she wanted this life she'd had, this love you'd shared—a love like a sturdy chain each of you had used at different times to pull yourselves through? Wasn't that why she told you what to do to make sure this life happened, this life together? Wasn't that her choice?

You opened the door with Gram's golden thread beneath it and watched a confusing scene play out before you. Your grandmother barreled into a house that you recognized as your grandfather's Toronto house. Her eyes were wild as she tore through each room, calling your mother's name, calling your aunty Tanya's name, and as you watched you could practically feel her heartbeat yourself, galloping like horses being whipped within an inch of their lives. She cried hysterically as she entered a room that looked, for all intents and purposes, totally normal. It was a nursery. You watched her face contort and her body shudder.

What's happening to her? How do I help? you called out to Pete.

But he wasn't there, and Gram was about to gag she was crying so hard, so you strode over and placed a hand on her arm. Immediately, you were able to see the room from her eyes—the thick blood splattered over the wall above the crib, then the black burn mark in the crib itself, making the whole room stink of raw meat and fire and rot. It made you feel sick, so you yanked your hand away, and once more the room looked, and smelled, normal.

That was the moment you realized this horror was happening

inside your grandmother's head—the result of drugs or bad genes or trauma or all three. The sort of terrifying experience that led her to hospitals. You watched, helplessly, as she pulled herself to her feet, stumbled down the stairs, grabbed a blanket, wrapped herself in it, then limped into a room and began to type into her laptop, the tears never stopping once. You couldn't see Pete anymore, which scared you a little, but also relieved you, because you wouldn't have to face his judgment for whatever you had to do next.

She opened the top drawer of the desk, pulled out a pill bottle and a mickey of clear alcohol, which you could tell was mostly gone, and then she did it: she started grabbing big handfuls of the pills and swallowing them with quick swigs.

NO NO NO NO NO NO NO, you thought so loud it hurt. You watched, and it seemed like your grandmother paused for a moment. Like she'd almost heard you. You had to call to her. But how? And what the fuck were you supposed to say?

She'd told you, you suddenly remembered. You thought back to the letter. She said you reminded her what was important. That you explained things. That you'd tried to "keep the rules," which to you meant you needed to keep certain things from her so she could make choices freely. Or something like that, anyway. Either way, you needed to stop her. You needed to make sure she survived.

You touched her arm once more, and as you did, you could hear her thoughts as though they were your own. They were thoughts of resignation, of failure. Of wanting death to come fast and take her. Thoughts you recognized because they *were* your own, at different moments throughout your life, and this made you feel close to Gram in ways you'd never thought you could before. You'd never seen her this low; you'd never known how close she'd been to death.

No, you thought. What did she say you'd told her? *Get to the portal. Now.*

She seemed to recognize your voice, as her eyes opened wide and she instinctively started trying to move her sluggish body. There were wild visions in her head: those of white people eating faces, of men transforming into Flying Heads. She thought she heard one as she stumbled over to two trees, their branches making a sort of tunnel as their trunks leaned into each other.

That doesn't matter. Just go.

Your hand was still on her as she stood before the trees, unsure what to do to make the pain stop.

Come, you begged her. *Please.*

She walked between the two trees and her body stopped as if it had hit a wall, then fell to the ground in a heap.

And then a spirit that looked identical to her practically leaped from her body, turned, and looked at you curiously, almost like she recognized you.

CHAPTER 25

Kaié:ri:
Inside the Portal

I expect death when I walk into the portal, and as my body falls away and all sound disappears, I think I've actually achieved it, and for a moment there's relief. Before I turn, I imagine Dawn and Ma and other ancestors I've never met standing there, waiting to take me down the Strawberry Road.

Instead, my crumpled body is behind me—still breathing, my heart still beating beneath my skin. I can feel this, even though time seems to have slowed so much it's practically stopped. Then I look farther down. There's a thin gold cord connecting me to my flesh. It pulses with each heartbeat.

And there, behind the body and the portal, is a sturdy-looking Native woman in an orange prison jumpsuit, her forearms covered in blurry tattoos that clearly haven't been retouched since the day they were stabbed into her skin. The Shape.

"You're not my ancestor," I say to her. This seems to

disarm her a little, as if she's an undercover agent who's just been made.

"How do you know?" she asks, weakly. I've never thought of the Shape as weak before, or even unsure. I gesture to the huge pine tree tattooed on her left arm with an eagle resting atop, wings spread as if ready to launch into flight. The tree's roots stretch into four directions under the line of the earth, and war clubs are piled beneath.

"Well, you're not Ma. And you've got too many tattoos to be my grandma."

"But this one's the Skaronhyase'kó:wa! It's traditional," she replies defensively. "Way more traditional than the naked lady I've got here." She slaps her upper right arm.

I roll my eyes. "I'm really not in the mood to show and tell tattoos."

"Damn, you've got an attitude," she replies, shaking her head.

"Yeah, well. I was sort of expecting to die when I walked through the portal. Instead, I'm here with you. For some fucking reason."

You're immediately shocked by her use of the word "fucking." She's never said that word to you in your entire life. And you know she doesn't know who you are, not right now anyway, so you shouldn't take what she's saying to you so personally, but it's hard not to react with pain when she's spat her words at you with so much disdain. Especially when you know intimately what she means when she says she "was sort of expecting to die." You'd stopped wanting to be alive weeks ago. The only thing that had pulled you through, had sustained you, was the notion that Gram wanted you to know something, to do something, and that it was a task she'd specifically and only entrusted to you.

What were you supposed to tell her to talk her into living when you didn't even want to live yourself?

"Sorry," you mutter pointlessly as the woman who's supposed to become your gram stares at you, eyebrows pinched in confusion.

"I know you said it was important, but I don't want to keep writing that stupid fucking story. I don't. I don't even know who you are."

"What story?" you ask, immediately aware by the shocked, then infuriated look on her face that this was the wrong thing to say. Fuck. You should have popped into her life in linear order. Now you're going to have to wiggle your way out of this mistake if you want her to trust you.

"The Creation Story. You know, the story you told me it was absolutely necessary I write? The one you said would help generations in the future? Are you fucking with me or something?"

Oh. That story. Part of the collection that you knew would never be published in your timeline. The one that Gram considered her second biggest, most embarrassing failure, after her divorce. It would eventually lead to her and her cousin's podcast, but Gram had always considered that a downgrade. Why would the future/past you encourage her to hang so much hope on *that*?

"Oh yeah. Sorry, that's still very important. Really. It's just . . . there's been a lot going on since we last spoke," you lie.

"Well, none of it matters anymore. Not now."

You take a few steps toward her, unclear what exactly you're going to do, but sure that you need to be close to her to do it.

"She's not dead," you say instinctively, placing a hand on her arm. "Your daughter. Dawn."

As soon as she touches me, my consciousness is filled with visions from what I understand to be her eyes. I also understand immediately that she's been watching me for the past hour or so, though it's felt like a few minutes to her, fast and slow at the same time, like wading against strong waves that push you down and back every few steps. I see the house through her eyes—entirely normal, exactly the way Steve and I left it. Dawn's room is clean and empty and safe. There's no blood, no burns, no revolting, metallic, smoky smell of death. Not until she touches me, lying on the ground: then it all appears the way I saw it and makes her stumble backward, sick. She must have pulled away her hand, because I'm in front of her again, shaking slightly.

"What was that?"

She shrugs, then says, "What I saw. From the outside, then from inside you."

"So you're saying there's nothing in that house. No Flying Heads got in and ate my daughter? She didn't get set on fire? Nothing like that?"

"No. She's totally safe."

"I thought I'd killed her. That it was my fault—"

I make a muffled choking noise. If I were still in my human body, this is where I'd erupt into hiccoughing sobs that make snot run down my upper lip and my stomach nearly heave. The sort of cry that takes everything inside you and squeezes. But, because I'm no longer in my human body with eyeballs and tear ducts and vocal cords, nothing happens. We stay like that for a time, me crying nothing, her watching.

"Jesus. How are you supposed to release pain here?" I ask eventually.

She hesitates. "Maybe you don't. You just have to carry it."

"Great. So this place fucking sucks, too."

She laughs, and her laugh is familiar, the same way her voice is. "Yeah. I guess it does."

"Are you positive that Dawn is alive? You're not lying to me?"

"I promise."

I want to look her in the eyes, sure it'll help me determine whether she's telling the truth or not. I take my time standing there like that, staring, and I can see her visibly tense, as if she doesn't want me to be paying such close attention to her. It could mean she's lying, or it could mean she's nervous, or it could mean nothing. She didn't hesitate when I asked about Dawn, though. That has to count for something.

"So. Who are you? Are you allowed to say? Or is that against the rules, too?"

She smiles a little at that. "I'm not sure if I should say or not."

I expect her to say more, explain maybe, but she doesn't. She watches me, not even moving, as if afraid she'll scare me away.

"Wait. Why did I see all that blood if it wasn't really there?"

You look away when she asks you that. You're here to try to convince her that life is worth living, that she should keep going, that there's a point to all of this, even if she doesn't fulfill her father's dream and finish her book or keep her marriage afloat or learn her language as fluently as she'd like or become the gardener she often told you her own mother was. How the hell are you going to do that if you tell her whatever terrifying things she's seen lately are all in her head? That she's going to see more things that others don't see, horrific things, and she's going to have to go to the hospital over and over, being treated with indignity by nurses and disbelieved by doctors, and nearly have her own daughter taken from her by her husband, until she finally finds a doctor and prescription that works? How is she going to want to continue living if she knows that people will call her crazy as long as she lives, disregard her opinions, turn from her at community events as if she's contagious, ignore her valid claims of racism, sexism, sanism? These are the things she never told you, but you watched unfold in her life in the span of a blink.

Postpartum psychosis, a few doctors said to her, or will say to her, eventually, which your grandpa will cling to in hopes this was a one-time crisis. Other doctors will say it's bipolar disorder. Later, schizophrenia. Even weed-induced psychosis, set on by her starting to smoke super-potent weed again after a long period of sobriety. But you know it's something more than that too, just as she'll always secretly know and believe it, even if she can't speak that knowledge, that belief aloud without endangering her freedom once more. Are these things you should tell her about? Would that *really* be respecting her free will? Giving her enough information to know whether she wants to live this life?

You'd never had the chance to ask her while she was alive. What it was like to live with that stigma. What it was like to constantly mistrust your own perceptions. You'd only had a taste in your life, and that was enough to convince you to keep it to yourself. Even the days leading up to this, when you were waiting for Pete, you weren't sure if you could trust your eyes and mind. Didn't that make you hate living, just a little?

"There's something wrong with me," she says.

You look in her eyes and try to smile.

"It's not impossible," you start, but you don't even sound convincing to yourself. "To deal with. To live with."

"Have you seen my future?"

You nod.

"Am I happy?"

Again, you aren't sure what to say. You know how complicated that question is after tracking so many versions of her life that seem happy one moment, then descend into darkness the next, or follow the opposite trajectory. So, you use the safe way out.

"I'm not allowed to tell you."

She laughs and laughs.

I'm not sure why it's so funny, but I can't stop laughing. Imagine, this woman coming all the way to your suicide attempt from wherever the hell she came from, stopping it, telling you that you're essentially a fucking nutjob, then refusing to even lie and tell you that you'll be happy one day when you ask her. *Imagine.*

Well, I don't have to imagine because it's actually happening. A fact that makes me laugh all the harder.

I feel a little bad for the woman. She looks scared. Terrified, even. Not a great harbinger for whatever my life happens to have in store. Judging by her confusion when I brought up my writing, my future doesn't include that. I knew it, of course. I knew but I kept pushing myself to write. Like a fucking idiot.

"You told me to keep writing. You told me it's super important. But it isn't, is it? I'm going to fuck that up, too. None of it matters in the long run."

You watch the desperate woman before you, almost begging for some faint hope that things might change for the better. Only, you don't know that better is coming.

So what does she need?

And then it occurs to you. A trick your gram would go on to use on you all the time when you were being hopeless and bratty.

"Would you say your dad's stories didn't matter in the long run?"

"What? Of course not," she says, taken aback. "How do you know about my dad's stories?"

You ignore her question and keep to the plan.

"Your dad never got a chance to write his book. That was his dream, and he died before he could do it. By your logic, that must mean that he was a failure as a storyteller."

"No. That's not true."

"Why not?"

She's quiet. Both furious and frustrated. That's good. That anger is what she'll need to push through. To keep fighting.

"He never wrote a single book. Never got an agent or publisher. Never sold anything or won awards. Why isn't he a failure? I'm sure some would call him one—"

"Because his stories mattered to me!" she yells.

"Yes! Exactly! They mattered to you." You let your voice go soft again, the way hers would when she no longer needed to use your impulse to rebel against you. "They mattered to you so much they inspired you to follow in his footsteps. Didn't they?"

Your gram looks down. "They did."

"Your father's stories were a seed he planted in you. And even though he isn't here to see how that seed's growing, it still is. Isn't it?"

"Yes."

"Your writing will plant seeds, too. That's why it matters. You have no idea what decision of yours, what seed, is going to grow into a sturdy, powerful tree generations down the line."

She contemplates this, and for a moment you're incredibly impressed with yourself, sure you've figured it all out.

Until a new leak bursts.

What she's saying makes sense. However, she's ignoring one vital piece of information. One I can't escape, because it's the real seed that's planted in me. My worst fear come true. I'd ran from it for so long, praying I could escape my grandmother's fate. One that's so bad even Aunt Rachel—empathic, understanding Aunt Rachel—was terrified of the possibility.

"But my dad wasn't crazy," I say. "I am."

A look of pity pulls the woman's features downward and I know she agrees, even if she's too kind to say so.

"I never said you were crazy," she tries. I smile at the effort.

"You didn't have to. I saw it."

I can't stop thinking about what happened tonight. The plates, the faces on the plates, the skin being cut into bleeding, bite-sized morsels, to be chewed and swallowed like they're a fine delicacy. The transformation of white cannibal academics—and one Native cannibal academic, if my mind can be trusted—into Flying Heads. How am I supposed to pull apart what really happened and what didn't?

"Did I imagine everything that happened at the dinner, too? What was really happening there?"

"I don't know," you say, finally deciding to tell the truth. "I didn't see what happened at the dinner."

"Is this even real? Maybe I'm imaging this, too."

You watch as she gets more and more agitated. Her mind is going so fast and you can barely talk to her about one topic before she's skipped ahead to the next.

"This is real."

"Maybe I've been imaging everything that's been happening to me since I talked to the cockroaches."

You think back to Pete and his comments about definitely knowing her. You interject.

"Oh, no. You definitely spoke to cockroaches."

"How do you know?"

"Because I've spoken to them, too. They said they know you."

"That doesn't prove anything. I don't even know who you are. Maybe we're both crazy."

You pause. That is definitely a thought you've had, too. All of this a fever dream, a result of too much solitary confinement. This is much more vivid than any dream you've ever had, but whatever is happening to you right now doesn't change the fact that your body is currently in a prison, where you're essentially being held captive for pissing off Canada's corporate and extraction-minded interests. If Pete's right, though, this conversation, and what happens afterward, both in your timeline and Gram's, will cause ripples that lead you back . . . there. With an uncertain future and a whole lot of grief. Fuck, maybe you are crazy. Why else would you be actively trying to make time, space, and circumstance move you back toward that point?

"All of this is crazy," you say, more to yourself than Gram. "But crazy is what's happening, so we might as well—"

"Maybe you're just in my head trying to convince me to stay alive so you stay alive because you live in here—" She taps the sides of her head, not even registering anything you're saying.

"No. That's not what's going on—"

"How do you know?" she asks, her voice trembling with conviction. "How. Do. You. Know. Are you omnipotent or omniscient or some shit?"

"No."

"I don't want to keep going anymore. You know? It's so much energy and effort. I'm so goddamn tired. And I'm not allowed to sleep. My mind won't let me. And if by some miracle I do doze off, I'm always jolted right back awake before long. There's always some new reminder that I'm worth nothing. Some racist comment from a fucking cashier or some racist editorial in the paper or some bullshit speech from some empty politician promising to help when they only ever intend to hurt. And now I can't trust my own mind anymore. What's left for me when I can't even trust myself?"

She turns to you, her face full of such naked vulnerability it's almost embarrassing. You've never seen her this defeated. Not even after your mom died. You know now that was intentional, though. She didn't want you to see her like this. She wanted you to see her as perpetually capable, the one who could push all the boulders up all the hills. In many ways, before this, you'd flattened her to a two-dimensional character in the story of your life. Not acknowledging her decades of pain. Not acknowledging she had a life before you and your sister came along.

What's worse, you know exactly what she's talking about—that bone-deep exhaustion you can't shake or sleep off, so embedded in your life you're almost convinced it's mutated your very molecules, a weight you must drag behind you like a sack of flour or fight off like a giant bear if you want to do anything at all. And even when you do get time, like you've had in the cell, you know that the exhaustion is still there, pressing down on you with the heaviness of an entire country's history, an entire world's history, all of it viewing you as the obstacle, the artifact, the outdated model. You think about one of the first times you were drying out at Gram's house. You were in your twenties then, sweating so much that she had to change the sheets twice a day as you shook out the last remnants of alcohol. You'd said something similar to her then—about not wanting to keep going. About there being no point in doing anything, because no one really learned and everyone kept cycling through the same abusive tendencies, trying to own and control and own and control. What had she said to you then? You try to compose it into the poetry she'd spoken.

"When this country wants us dead, every breath we take is a tiny revolution. You don't need to do nothing fancy. Just continuing to breathe is enough."

She stares at you for a long time, struggling with what to say.

"What . . . what if I can't keep breathing?" The words start slow, like a dribble from a faucet, but quickly turn to a rush that pours and pours. "What if my breathing is hurting everyone around me? What if I'm making it hard on everyone I love, all the time? What if no one really needs me—"

"I need you."

You don't mean to say it, but the words are out of your mouth before you can stop them. Well, fuck. You've already said them now, and she's already heard them, so you might as well say them again because that's the only thing you're sure of: this love, this need.

"I need you. Will need you. Do need you. Please."

At those words everything inside me goes still. I recognize the grief, the mourning in her voice. It sounds the same as my own—a specific type of heartbreak that makes everything less capable of containing or creating joy. I examine the lines of her face, the color of her eyes, the rhythms of her body.

"Dawn?"

She seems to crumble into a heap, and I know immediately that she's not Dawn but that something horrible *will* happen to Dawn—not a Flying Head eating her in her crib but something that will feel like that, hurting every bit as much as the death I thought had already happened.

That's the thing, though: it hasn't happened.

I step over to the woman in front of me, the person I used to call the Shape, as if there was nothing human about her anymore, wrongly assuming she was an ancestor because she knew Mohawk and sounded older, and as I crouch down in front of her, a feeling of warmth comes over me. I reach forward and rub her back. The moment I touch her, though, an image appears: an older woman, her face lined with joy and pain, kneeling in front of two crying teenage girls, saying, "You both gave me something to live for. To live *toward*. I just wanted to say nya:wen to you both." I can see confusion in the faces of the girls, yes, but also a feeling of safety, a recognition that there's a definite container for their lives again. They look at each other, then back at the older woman. "Nyoh," they both say, almost in unison.

I pull my hand away, half in shock, half in disbelief. She looks up into my eyes and this impulse to protect her washes over me. I want to protect this woman, just as the older woman in that memory wanted to protect the little girls. Then I think I understand. Someday I *will* protect this woman. Just as I should have been protecting Dawn.

No, I think, correcting myself, *just as I will protect Dawn.*

"Will I be a good grandma?" I ask.

She tries to speak, but a sob chokes her. I stand.

"I'm sorry," she says. "I shouldn't have shown you that. I'm not supposed to say or do anything that affects your free will."

"You have free will, too, and you made a choice. Just like I'm making one now."

I hold out my hand to help her up. She takes it and stands. This time, there is no memory that comes. Only her grateful, questioning eyes.

"I have a favor to ask you," I say. "Do you know how to do a condolence ceremony?"

You've never done a proper condolence for anyone before, and only seen it done occasionally to others. You didn't even have a chance to refresh your memory at your gram's ten-day feast. That would have been a more casual one, of course. A recognition of your family's grief, then a request that you put it away and focus back on the world and your responsibilities to it after the tenth day—something you've yet to do. Still, you can't refuse her.

"How does it start again?" you ask, nervous.

"It starts with the tears, then the ears, then the throat."

"I don't have the eagle feather or the deerskin or—"

"It's okay," she says, a patience settling over her that's contagious. "You'll do your best, and when I have to, I'll use my imagination. I'm pretty good at that, apparently."

You smile, despite yourself, then, before you can ask her to please be kinder to herself, her eyes are closed. She's waiting.

"First I take this beautiful eagle feather and wipe away the dust covering you," you say as you move your hand over her head, shoulders, and back. "I remove the burrs sticking to your clothes, too. I do this because these things cause you pain and discomfort. I hope that my clearing them away brings you the comfort and peace you do deserve.

"Next, I take the softest deerskin I have—"

You pause to remember the order once more. Tears, ears, throat. Tears, ears, throat. You start again.

"Sorry. What I meant to say is that your grief for your mother fills your eyes with tears. They sting your eyes and make it hard to see. So next I take the softest deerskin I have, and I wipe your tears from your eyes. I do this so you can see beauty of the world around you again, and so you can see your loved ones, who support you and want to help."

You wipe at her eyes with your empty hands. She squeezes them a little tighter, then releases them. You do, too, suddenly aware how heavy they are with your own pain. Still, you bear it and move on, for her.

"Your pain, fear, and anger have become an obstruction in your ears, making it hard to hear the people around you. So I take this same soft deerskin cloth and clear out that obstruction. I do this so you can hear and trust the comforting words being spoken to you by loved ones and know you're not alone."

Your fingers slide in, around, and out of one ear, then in, around, and out the other. She nods her head as you become aware of the way your own ears feel clogged with grief for the very person whose ears you cleared out now. How strange, you think. How impossible.

"Your pain and loss have also blocked your throat, stopping you from speaking clearly," you continue as if nothing's wrong. "So I offer you this cold drink of water to clear that blockage and quench your thirst. Water is a medicine that gives and sustains life. I give you water to sustain your own life, and allow you to once more say what you mean and be understood by your loved ones."

You gently touch her throat, as if to coax a drink down, and in so doing, become aware of your own clogged throat. How loss laces your words, then takes them over. What have you said in the past month that hasn't been marred by pain for the only person who loved you unconditionally?

"I hope that now you are comforted, and I've taken away at least some of your heavy burden. These words are meant to restore you to sound body, mind, and spirit. I hope that they help."

You stand back and watch your gram's posture straighten. It is then, as you watch an air of calm that wasn't there before settle over her entire being, as if by magic, that you're sure you need to ask Pete very nicely to do the same ceremony for you the moment you're done with whatever needs doing. Your body, mind and spirit need it, and you know you're ready.

With those last words I feel lighter, somehow, clearer. *This is why Hiawatha created the condolence ceremony*, I remember Dad saying, as if he were here now. *To raise up your mind and restore it to the present. To remind you that there is not only a today, but a tomorrow.*

I know now what I have to say and do, for myself and this precious person who so selflessly and genuinely condoled me, if for no one else.

"Nya:wen. I accept these words of condolence, and acknowledge my responsibility to my ma to let her spirit go back home to rest. I also acknowledge my responsibility to my daughter, Dawn, and . . . to you and your sister. I need to return to the world to uphold my responsibilities to all of you."

I hope my words give her a fraction of the comfort her words gave me.

"Your future is my future," she says in response. "You write that to me in a letter one day."

"Guess that means not all my writing is shit."

She chuckles as I remember the red willow tea I swallowed so much of already. The way Tanya said that it purges your body. Why hasn't it worked yet? I should have vomited out the flesh Steve made me eat already. If that was, indeed, human flesh. I don't know anymore. I don't know what's real and what isn't. Either way, I'll have to chug more of that tea as soon as I'm back in my body, to get the oxies out. I'll have to try. I'll have to do a lot of things. I feel tired again just thinking about it all.

"I've visited you before," she says, a note of uncertainty in her voice.

"Yes. I was watching the opening credits of *Pocahontas* after a neighbor brought it over this week. Your silhouette came up, but I couldn't see your face."

"Before that, too," she says slowly, as though remembering. "When you were a kid watching *Pocahontas*."

"*You* were Matoaka? You were so scary!" I laugh. "I mean, I never got together with Mason, so clearly scary worked. But still! At least the whole thing wasn't another delusion or hallucination, right?"

I meant for it to be light, a joke, but this time she doesn't even crack a smile.

"You know, there's meaning in your delusions and hallucinations, too," she says. "They're all stories. They can offer you insight into your life and the world around you, same as your regular experiences. Just cuz they only mean something to you doesn't mean they don't matter."

"Did I tell you that, too?" I ask.

"No. But I'm telling you now. And telling me, I guess."

"You're a gatekeeper, too, then."

"I mean, who knows what the fuck I am," she says, shrugging, and it reminds me so much of myself that I laugh.

"Do you have to go now?" I ask.

"Yes, I think so. And so do you," she reminds me. I turn and walk back to the edge of the portal. Right before I step through, though—

"Can you say something for me? Just once."

I turn back to her. "Anything."

"Can you say"—her voice cracks—"can you say 'my little Edie'?"

A part of me wants to cry at this small request, because I know what that longing is like, what it means. I won't be there forever, but I will be there for her. For her sister. For her mother. I'll be there, for a while, planting seeds, and it will matter.

"Good-bye, my little Edie. Until we meet again."

"Konnorónhkwa," she replies quick, her voice thick. Even with my limited knowledge of Mohawk, I know the meaning of that.

"I love you, too."

You watch as the woman who has chosen to become your gram slides back into her body, then starts coughing. You watch as she gets up, gets to her refrigerator, opens it, and starts guzzling glass after glass of some sort of tea, drinking so fast it pours down the front of her dress. You watch as her cousin, your aunty Tanya, carries your sleeping infant mother into the house in a car seat, then sets her down. She hears your mother vomiting, which is good, but then Gram collapses, and your grandfather is pulling into the driveway, and Aunty Tanya is running out to tell him Gram is in trouble and needs to get to a hospital, and this is where you feel like you can leave. Because you can't watch Gram almost die again, not when you've just convinced her to live. And you know Aunty Tanya will call Aunty Melita and Aunty Rachel and Aunty Dana, and they'll make a plan on how to best talk to Gram about her health and her medical options, so she can get better. So she can get out of the hospital and get back to your mother. You know you don't need to be here any longer, because these women's sturdy love, hearty laughter, and steadfast support will braid your grandma back into reality, over and over, whenever she needs it, and now that she's been condoled, she'll be able to actually appreciate it.

These women will counsel her through her hardships, her divorce, and make her feel like she matters, that she can be trusted, even when the rest of the world tells her she doesn't, that she can't. Whenever she falls, they will prepare the space for her to land. Just as she will for them, your mother, your sister, and you. This is the connection and love that slides between all hardships and gives even the toughest life humor, meaning, heart, heft. This is the unspoken covenant of Native women.

It applies to you, too. You have a job to do, and for once, you won't ask Ellie to do it for you. Even if you wanted her to, she sure as hell can't do *this*. It's your responsibility alone. You have to do what Gram told you she wanted you to do in her note: choose.

And, despite the jail cell and the terrorism charges and the murder of your mother and the intimacy problems that keep making you sabotage your relationships and the addiction that chews and chews at you and will keep chewing at you your whole life, this is what you choose: her. You will find the places in Gram's space-time web that you need to visit to make sure her life unfolds as it needs to. Not just for you, but because Ellie deserves Gram, too.

And that's when you realize. By choosing Gram, by choosing her love, determination, and strength, which you'll watch her display again and again as she delivers you to this very moment, you're also choosing you.

CHAPTER 26

On the Matter of Falling

I'd like to give you the capital-T Truth about what happened next, but I've told this story before. Every other word I'd be interrupted by someone who claims they know better. So-and-so's grandma told them this. At longhouse this storyteller said that. So instead of telling you outright what happened, I'll set the scene and you can use your super-smart reasoning skills to puzzle it out for yourself. You know, like one of those choose your own adventure books.

On stage left we have Mature Flowers: pregnant and sad, but still trying to fake happiness because one day she's going to be the Greatest Woman of All Time. Maybe. If you believe the ghost of her dead dad. She's not sure how reliable he is lately.

On stage right we have the Ancient: a mean, angry, jealous old man with eyes that see insults where no one else can. You blink at him the wrong way and he's offended.

In center stage is the Great Tree, toppled. Pulled up, roots and all, revealing a giant hole. Now, you and I know what's underneath Sky World—space, the atmosphere, earth, etc. We made a little diagram laying it all out, remember? But no one in Sky World knew what was beneath the Great Tree. It could have been anything. It could have been nothing.

Before you go and get all judgy, calling them ignorant or self-centered or something, may I remind you this tree was the center of their entire village. And it was big and beautiful and bore the best fruit. So why would they ever go and dig it up? I mean, they weren't kept systematically poor so oil tycoons could offer them temporary jobs and far too little cash in exchange for the right to dig beneath it, sucking up whatever was there and making a fortune off it in perpetuity. Context.

So, super-smart detective. What do you think? Was she pushed through that hole by her jealous husband? Did she remember her father's prophecy, see this as a sign, and jump? Did she peek through the hole, curious, then trip and fall? Does it really matter? I'm not sure it does. Either way, she ends up through that hole. But I'm just an unbiased observer and all-knowing narrator. What do I know?

Nowadays most guys get really antsy hearing about a woman for so long, so once they get teased with the promise of earth and more men, they totally forget about the next part of the story. I don't forget, though.

You see, just before Mature Flowers went through the hole, she reached up and grabbed at the roots of the Great Tree, trying to catch herself. In that second she resisted; she fought; she tried to be her own hero. It didn't work. All she got was a handful of seeds. But she tried. The mother of our nations tried, setting the bar for all her daughters and granddaughters to come.

And then she fell—scared, alone, tumbling fast through the black, tumbling slow through the black, tumbling so long time started to feel both solid and liquid, like the insides of a raw egg. And even though she didn't know about the endless ocean or the gossipy animals or the rumors of this mysterious thing called clay, they were still there. They were always there. They were waiting.

And when they saw her, they knew they had to help. They set about organizing—sending the birds to catch her on their wings and help her float safely down, then sending all manner of animals to check if clay really did exist at the bottom of the ocean, because they knew this falling woman would need it. Everyone who tried failed—except Muskrat, who knew what it was like to be underestimated, and who knew if he set his mind on getting that clay, he would get it. As his little body finally bobbed on the water, dead, the waiting animals thought he'd failed, and yet, like Mature Flowers, he'd managed to grab a tiny bit of what he needed in his little paw. He'd managed what no one else could. Generous Turtle agreed to hold Mature Flowers, to let her take the clay Muskrat had found, place it on his back, and dance the world into existence. A world where she could plant her seeds and see what grew.

All of this help was there, waiting, organizing, without Mature Flowers even asking.

It took a while—years, actually—but eventually she understood: the most important thing wasn't that she had fallen. The most important thing was that she had been caught.

That she had allowed herself to be caught.

And now our minds are one.

ACKNOWLEDGMENTS

This book has been in the works for a long time and exists thanks to the support of so many people.

First, I'd like to thank my former agent, Stephanie Sinclair, for guiding me through this process, helping me shape this novel, and finding me the best editors to work with. I am so grateful and wish you so much success in your new role at McClelland & Stewart.

I'd like to thank my current agent, Ron Eckel, who has taken up where Stephanie left off and helped guide me through publishing this book in so many places at the same time. Your enthusiasm is so appreciated. I'd also like to thank Hana El Niwairi for handling my foreign publishing rights, finding me incredible editors internationally, and holding my hand and making sure I'm comfortable through it all. I'm thankful for the entire CookeMcDermid team for all they've done to support me and Alice's journey.

This book wouldn't be what it is without the brilliance and support of Kiara Kent. You are an amazing person and editor, and I am so thankful that I can email you about basically anything and you won't make me feel like an idiot for it, even when you maybe should. I also want to thank Catherine Abes, who worked on early drafts of this book as an intern and gave such smart notes on it. Thanks to the entire Doubleday team for helping me through this process. You're all incredible.

Lexy Cassola, I am absolutely in awe of your talent and

guidance. Your edits, eye for detail, and deep consideration helped make this better than I could have ever hoped. I can't imagine this book without you. Thank you so much. Thank you, as well, to my copy editor, Amy Ryan, for somehow keeping track of all the threads I threw at you; and my production editor, Alice Dalrymple. I'm so incredibly grateful to the Dutton team for everything you've all done to help me.

Thanks to my Australia and New Zealand editor, Cate Paterson, who so loved and believed in Alice and her story that she chose my book to launch Atlantic Books Australia. I cannot express how much your faith means to me. Thank you to the entire Atlantic Books Australia team for helping me launch in countries I wasn't sure I'd reach.

Thanks to my UK editor, Kate Ballard, for championing this book and being so open and lovely throughout this process. You've made my dreams come true by bringing *And Then She Fell* to the UK. Thanks, as well, to the entire Allen & Unwin team. I am indebted to all of you.

Thanks to some of my first readers: Chelsea Rooney, Amanda Reaume, and Liz Harmer. Your feedback gave me the support and direction I needed to take the story where it needed to go. You are all so lovely, and I appreciate your time, attention, energy, and enthusiasm. Special thanks to Erin Soros, whose long talks about madness, psychosis, and this book helped me understand my own experiences, shape my politics, and heal. You are a bright light in so much darkness.

Thanks to my sister, Melissa Elliott, for talking me through the plot, reading an early draft, and translating Mohawk. You have been so generous with your creativity, knowledge, humor, and intelligence. I am so glad you're my sister. I love you.

Thanks to Terri Monture for reading and giving me feedback on an early draft. Your suggestion on adding the condolence ceremony, as well as your discussions of what it means for our people, gave me the last thread to pull this story together. I am so grateful for your generosity and creativity. I can't wait to return the favor for your novels.

Thanks to the people of Six Nations for keeping our culture, language, and stories alive. Special thanks to Barbara Alice Mann, Brian Rice, and John Napoleon Brinton Hewitt for your interpretations and explanations of the Haudenosaunee Creation Story, specifically what happened in Sky World before Mature Flowers fell. Thanks to Rick Monture for allowing me to quote your brilliance in the beginning of my novel, and for all your writing, which continues to inspire me to this day.

While writing this, I read and consulted the book *Understanding Postpartum Psychosis: A Temporary Madness*. Thanks to Teresa M. Twomey for compiling this book, and to all the brave women who told their stories in its pages. Your generosity and insistence that this condition get more attention has and will change lives.

Thanks to David Chariandy for reading an early draft of this way back in Banff when I thought it would only be a long short story. Your early enthusiasm gave me the strength I needed to keep going.

Thanks to Katherena Vermette for reading that same version of this story at Banff. Your insistence that the story needed to be longer is what put me on the path to turning it into the novel it is today.

Thanks to Cherie Dimaline, Waubgeshig Rice, and Diane Glancy, as well as all the other Indigenous writers who were at Banff's last Aboriginal Emerging Writers Program when I workshopped this piece as a short story. Your advice and support helped me believe this was worth writing as a Haudenosaunee story. Special extra thanks to Cherie for talking me through writing this once I realized it actually was a novel. I'm so grateful for the time you've made for me.

Thanks to Mark Medley, who published an excerpt of the prologue in *The Globe and Mail* way back when I thought it, too, was only a short story.

Thanks to my Patreon supporters for helping me through some of the most difficult times of my life and anchoring me when I needed it.

Thanks to the Canada Council for the Arts for giving me the financial support and time needed to write this book, and to the grant jury members, who saw this as a project worth supporting.

Thank you to Western University, specifically Mary Helen McMurran and Sara Mai Chitty, as well as the entire English Department, for asking me to be writer-in-residence during the writing of this novel. I am so thankful for the experience as well as the time and money to help me hammer out the first draft.

Thanks to the rest of my family: Dakota, Mikey, Jon, Dad, Gracie, Greg, Melita, Joe, JR, Saphire, Arielle, and Gabby. You all listened to me, made me laugh, and inspired and supported me while I was writing. More importantly, you all actually gave me a second chance after my mental health breakdown made it so difficult for all of us. That sort of love and forgiveness is something I'll never forget or take for granted. Thanks to my mom for your love, and for showing me what it means to persist.

Thanks to my son, Miles, for all the late-night talking sessions and reality TV binges, and for just being yourself. Knowing you, raising you, and loving you was my North Star as I wrote this book and decided where it should go and how it should end. You are the absolute best.

Thanks to my yorkie, Sam, who cannot read this but who brought me so much joy and many cuddles while working on this. I'd feel bad if I didn't mention you.

Last but never least, thank you so much to my incredible husband and best friend, Mike. I'm not sure that I could ever find the words to tell you what you mean to me. You are my first and best editor, without whom I wouldn't have finished my first book, let alone this one. Talking out this story with you, crying about this story with you, and getting to cuddle and watch movies with you when I needed a break from this story, were so vital to me. I am the luckiest woman in the world because you've seen me at my lowest, forgiven me for it, and given me your love regardless. I love you forever.